Harmony Eva

love stories. Sl

the Romance S

a double fina

Reviewers' Cl

City. For more

www.harmonyevans.com or follow @harmonyannevans

Writing romance for Mills & Boon is truly a dream come true for **Soraya Lane**. An avid book reader and writer since her childhood, Soraya describes becoming a published author as 'the best job in the world'. Soraya lives with her own real-life hero and son on a small farm in New Zealand, surrounded by animals and with an office overlooking a field where their horses graze. Visit Soraya at www.sorayalane.com

Debra Webb is the award winning, *USA Today* bestselling author of more than 150 novels, including reader favourites the *Faces of Evil*, the *Colby Agency*, and the *Shades of Death* series. With more than four million books sold in numerous languages and countries, Debra's love of storytelling goes back to her childhood on a farm in Alabama. Visit Debra at www.DebraWebb.com or write to her at PO Box 176, Madison, AL 35758.

After Hours

March 2021
Power and Passion

April 2021
Boardroom Temptation

May 2021
Falling for the Nanny

June 2021
Her Rebel Doc

July 2021
Royal Duty

August 2021
Under Cover of Night

After Hours: Under Cover of Night

HARMONY EVANS

SORAYA LANE

DEBRA WEBB

MILLS & BOON

First Published in Great Britain 2021
By Mills & Boon, an imprint of HarperCollins*Publishers* Ltd
1 London Bridge Street, London, SE1 9GF

www.harpercollins.co.uk

HarperCollins*Publishers*
1st Floor, Watermarque Building,
Ringsend Road, Dublin 4, Ireland

ISBN: 978-0-263-30242-4

MIX
Paper from responsible sources
FSC™ C007454

This book is produced from independently certified FSC™ paper to ensure responsible forest management.

For more information visit: www.harpercollins.co.uk/green

Printed and bound in Spain
by CPI, Barcelona

WHEN MORNING COMES

HARMONY EVANS

This book is dedicated to my daughter,
who has made me richer than I ever thought
I could be with her enduring love.

Chapter 1

"I will not tolerate anyone destroying what I've worked so hard to build. Paxton Investment Securities must prevail unscathed. Is that clear, Ms. Hilliard?"

Sterling Paxton, the firm's owner and CEO, stood at the boardroom window with his back to Autumn, his pale white hands clasped loosely behind him. His stance was relaxed, yet every terse word sounded as if it were uttered through gritted teeth.

A chill threaded through Autumn's spine, warning her to keep her guard up even as she sat frozen in place.

So this was what a bug must feel like, she thought, right before it's about to get squashed.

Sterling turned abruptly on his heel and smacked his hands together.

"I said, is that clear, Ms. Hilliard?"

Autumn winced and drew in a sharp breath before smiling sweetly. "Of course, Mr. Paxton. I'll do everything in my power to prevent that from happening. If Isaac Mason is committing securities fraud, rest assured, I will find out."

Sterling's lips thinned. "How long do you think that will take?"

Autumn resisted the urge to shrug, knowing he would be offended. Every client expected immediate results and it was her job to manage expectations. She was a damn good investigator, but she wasn't a miracle worker.

"A few weeks. Maybe a month. Undercover work is never an exact science," she cautioned.

Sterling slid his hands into his pockets, and she heard the tinny jingle of coins.

"Isaac must never know he's under surveillance."

"And he won't," Autumn affirmed with a nod. "Having Isaac mentor me as a new employee will enable me to build trust without arising suspicion."

Sterling's gaze narrowed. "For your sake, he better not."

Autumn bristled at his veiled threat, but she said nothing. It was obvious Sterling didn't trust Isaac. What she didn't know was why, but she'd surely find out, on her own terms and in her own way.

"You have full access to all his files, reports and records," Sterling continued. "I sent you the log-in information to our internal file system via email last night."

He crossed the room and sat at the head of the table.

The leather chair squeaked under the weight of his large frame.

"You and I are the only ones with knowledge of why I hired you," he said, folding his hands slowly. "Not even my daughter, whom you'll be meeting shortly, knows about this."

Autumn sensed extreme urgency in his tone. "I understand the need for confidentiality," she reassured him. "As soon as I have something of interest, I'll report back."

The conference room door opened and a tall, slender blonde entered into the room with a thick sheaf of papers in her hand. She closed the door behind her and glared at Sterling. But when she saw he wasn't alone, she took a step back and Autumn watched as her face quickly morphed into a smile that was as fake as the handbags sold on a New York City street corner.

The woman moved toward her and extended her hand. "I'm Felicia Paxton, director of human resources. You must be Autumn Hilliard."

Autumn stood. "It's a pleasure to meet you."

She shook Felicia's clammy hand and silently wished for a tissue. She was five feet eight, and Felicia towered over her in an oppressive way that was probably intimidating to a lot of people. But not to Autumn. She wasn't afraid of anything, except failing to solve a case.

"Please have a seat," Felicia instructed. She turned to Sterling and glanced at her watch. "It's 8:55 a.m. now. The meeting was supposed to start at 9:00 a.m., correct?"

"Yes," Sterling answered in a bored tone, not bothering to look up. He seemed engrossed in scrolling through his smartphone. “We were just chatting while we were waiting for you.”

A blush washed over Felicia’s taut cheekbones. She walked around the table, pulled out a chair and settled down directly across from Autumn.

“In addition to being CEO, my father seems to love to do my job.”

Autumn took Felicia’s contentious tone as a subtle warning that anyone who dared trifle with her had just better think twice.

Sterling eyed the stack of papers Felicia had on the table. “Not that part,” he barked. “With the level of technology that’s available today, why is it that our employees still have to fill out all these forms?”

Felicia uncapped a pen and held it out to Autumn. “Two words, Father. Paper trail.”

Autumn produced one from her notepad, not from her ear, where it normally hid in a mass of natural curls.

She held it up. “I have one, thanks.”

Felicia frowned, as if she took it personally that Autumn had her own ink. “The government still loves killing trees,” she continued. “And I for one have to agree with them. Paper is more permanent. Electronic records can be hacked or deleted.”

Sterling’s eyes narrowed and caught Autumn’s. “My daughter seems to have forgotten that paper can be shredded,” he said dryly.

Felicia ignored him, but Autumn could almost feel how much she wanted to roll her baby blues at her father.

With one finger, she pushed the stack of papers toward Autumn. "I prefer you complete these now, but if you must, you can bring them back tomorrow. I'm here by 7:00 a.m. sharp every day."

Autumn nodded and dutifully began to fill out the ream of paperwork, starting with her social security number. It was as fake as the new identity the government had bestowed upon her a few years ago. Just one of the so-called perks of settling out of court in one of the most high profile cases of corporate fraud in the United States.

She was just starting to fill out her name when the door suddenly opened. Her head snapped up, curls brushing against the side of her jaw, as Isaac Mason walked into the room, his stride purposeful.

It only took one look and Autumn knew this was one man she wouldn't mind sticking close to all night long.

Isaac wore a tailored gray suit cut to perfection, a crisp white shirt, maroon silk tie and black leather shoes shined to a gloss. It was standard corporate attire and likely designer, based upon his wealth and prominent position in the company, but she couldn't tell and didn't care. It wasn't his clothes that attracted her.

It was his face. Isaac was boyishly handsome with clean-shaven, mocha skin, a long straight nose that flared out just enough to be interesting, and full lips that invited lust.

Autumn found it especially difficult not to openly stare at his lean, muscular body. There was something irreverent about the way it seemed almost caged beneath the fabric of his suit.

So as discreetly as possible, she sized him up. From the top of his close-cropped black hair to the tips of his Brooks Brothers shoes. Because that's what private investigators were supposed to do. No one could blame her for trying to do her job even in the midst of extreme male temptation.

And in her professional opinion, one fact was clear: Isaac Mason was her hottest suspect yet.

Isaac shut the door and held up his smartphone. "Sterling, sorry I'm late. I just got your meeting request."

He stopped midstride, his eyes zeroing in on hers. From a distance, she couldn't see what color they were, but they mesmerized her just the same. Luckily, she was able to maintain a mildly curious look on her face, although on the inside she felt her professional resolve begin to disintegrate.

"Am I interrupting something?"

Only the normal rhythm of my heartbeat, Autumn thought.

"Not at all." Sterling waved him over. "I have someone I'd like you to meet. This is Autumn Hilliard, our newest analyst on the Paxton team."

Autumn swiveled in her chair and stuck out her hand. Before she could stand up, Isaac's skin warmed her palm and his smile instantly carved its way into her heart. It seemed that he held her hand a beat longer than necessary, but that could have only been her imagination. She was pretty but not gorgeous, and Autumn had a feeling that Isaac was used to the latter in his ladies.

He gave a little bow. "Welcome to the madness."

Isaac's voice had just enough depth to rumble in her ears, his tone pleasant and slightly mocking. He seemed distracted by something, and she wasn't vain enough to think it was her.

Sterling openly scowled. "Isaac, I realize the market is slightly down this morning, but you're going to be spending a lot of time with Autumn, so let's keep things positive, okay?"

Autumn's face tingled. The negative vibe in the room was getting more uncomfortable by the moment.

Isaac slipped his phone into his pants pocket. "You know me, Sterling." He shrugged calmly. "I was just playing."

He dropped into a chair next to Autumn and leaned back. She smiled and held his gaze, a tactic she used to build rapport with a client, a potential suspect or a man who was really, really cute.

An unbidden spark pulsed between them, like the feeling one gets when suddenly remembering a long-forgotten dream, and Autumn knew that she'd have to be careful not to succumb to temptation.

Suddenly Isaac shot up in his chair. "What do you mean we're going to be spending a lot time together?" It was as if he'd just now grasped the full extent of what his boss had said moments earlier.

Felicia's eyes narrowed at Autumn and Isaac before turning her attention to Sterling. "Yes, Father. Explain."

"That's why I called the meeting," Sterling bellowed, ignoring Felicia's glare. "For the next few weeks, Isaac, you're going to be Autumn's mentor. Getting her acclimated to the way we do things around here."

Out of the corner of her eye, Autumn saw Felicia's hands tense.

"M-mentoring!" Felicia sputtered. "What are you talking about, Daddy? My new employee onboarding process doesn't begin until next month."

Sterling pressed his index finger on the table and shook his head. "It starts now, Felicia."

"But the process hasn't been fully vetted," she protested.

Sterling shrugged and leaned back in his chair, as if the matter was settled. "What better use case than a real scenario?"

Felicia smoothed her blond-in-a-bottle hair. She was probably very pretty when she smiled, but that wasn't the case now.

"Legal won't like it," she warned.

He gave a disgusted sigh. "Have you forgotten that our in-house attorneys report to me?"

Felicia threw up her hands in exasperation. "I haven't even completed all the required documentation."

Sterling looked up from his cell phone and rolled his eyes. "Great, just what we need. More paperwork."

Autumn cast a glance at Felicia and stifled a laugh. If she had a pencil, paper and an artistic bone in her body, she would sketch two plumes of steam erupting from each of her ears and fire blazing in her eyes. The woman looked that angry.

Sterling's phone beeped loudly and he stood. "You'll have to excuse me. I'm due at another meeting in a few minutes." He handed Isaac a manila folder. "I'll leave you two alone to get acquainted."

Autumn smiled at Felicia and she could almost see the wheels turning in her head. Her gaze lingered on Isaac for a moment, as if that would lure him away. She seemed to sense something that neither Autumn nor Isaac could have imagined.

Sterling opened the door and exhaled impatiently. "Felicia, are you coming?"

Autumn tapped the stack of papers with her pen, breaking the tense moment.

"I'll have these back to you this afternoon."

Felicia rewarded her with a nod and a thin-lipped smile.

"Right behind you, Father."

She waited until Sterling was gone, and then rose from her chair slowly, as if she were still reluctant to leave.

Autumn felt Isaac's gaze upon her cheek. She dug the toes of her shoes into the carpet in a vain attempt to hold on to the twinge of pleasure that zoomed through her body.

"Isaac," Felicia said sharply. "Be sure to show her my office, won't you?" Her voice suddenly dropped to almost a whisper, like dark silk hiding a double-edged sword. "You know the way."

Without saying another word, Felicia quickly walked out of the room, closing the door behind her, leaving an empty vacuum of silence and longing.

The statement was an invitation for Isaac, backed up by veiled warning meant for any woman who might interfere.

Namely, Autumn.

But what Felicia didn't know was that Autumn wasn't a threat to whatever hold—real or imagined—she had on Isaac. Sterling hadn't hired her to bed the man, although at first glance the thought did cross her mind. No, she was here to conduct an investigation into a possible case of corporate securities fraud.

Autumn didn't know what, if anything, was going on between the two of them, but if it affected the outcome of this case, she would damn sure find out.

Chapter 2

Isaac leaned back in his chair and almost smiled at the irony. He hadn't been expecting a beautiful woman on the agenda for Monday morning. Then again, he'd never expected to be cooking breakfast every day for two children, either.

Or trying to cook. His kids were not pleased with having to settle for Pop-Tarts. Again.

He sniffed lightly wondering if the stench of burned bacon was still on him and what Autumn would think if it was.

Isaac mentally slapped himself upside the head. If he cared even a little bit about the opinions of this perfect stranger, this gorgeous stranger, the stress must be really getting to him. He had two children to think about now, not impressing a woman.

He was a father.

"Anything wrong?"

The concern in Autumn's voice sounded so genuine, he nearly blurted out, *Everything.*

And it was true. His life was in a state of total upheaval right now. Sure, the chaos was the result of choices he wanted to make, but that didn't make things any easier.

Instead Isaac opted for the answer likely echoed in countless offices across the country on any given morning. Men and women just like him who wished someone would care, but who also realized that most people were too busy just trying to make it in this crazy world to bother.

He faked a yawn. "I was running late and missed my morning coffee."

Isaac kept his gaze trained on the boardroom window. The mid-January sky was a bleak and dirty gray, the kind that makes you wonder if the sun will ever shine again. For reasons he didn't understand, he didn't want to look too deeply into Autumn's eyes. It wasn't that he was afraid of what he would see in them, but of what he wouldn't.

"I don't drink coffee."

Her voice wove through his ears, piercing the fog of his thoughts. It was throaty, insistent and knotted with just enough innate sexiness to make his groin twitch in a way that made him glad he was sitting down.

Just to be on the safe side, he rolled closer to the table and turned his head toward her.

"What mortal doesn't drink coffee?" he said in an

incredulous tone. "What gets you up in the morning? Your extremely good looks?"

No sooner were the words out of his mouth that he realized he'd overstepped the boundaries between simple curiosity and workplace etiquette. Rule number one: never acknowledge the physical attractiveness of your coworkers.

He hated the fact that his stomach clenched as he waited for her reaction, but Autumn just sat there with a blank expression on her face.

If Felicia was still in the room, she'd probably write him up. Ever since she tried to seduce him and he'd turned her down, he'd been paying for it. She watched him like a hawk circling prey.

Did she really think he was stupid enough to bed Sterling's daughter? His working relationship with his boss was strained enough without any additional help from Felicia's shenanigans. Although Isaac doubted Sterling knew anything about Felicia's unwanted advances, he couldn't be sure without actually asking him.

Still, Isaac had a nagging feeling that the partnership he'd busted his butt working for his entire career was now out of reach, and he didn't know why.

Autumn's voice broke in on his reverie. "No. What gets me up in the morning is," she replied, leaning forward, as if in secret. "Pure. Adrenaline."

Her plump lips, coated with just a hint of pale pink gloss, turned up into a very kissable half smile. She seemed amused rather than offended at his statement, which made her even more attractive.

Her perfume, the scent of a flower he recalled but

at the moment couldn't name, teased his nose. At that moment, he knew he would drive himself crazy trying to remember and wishing he could smell more of her.

Isaac whooshed out a breath of relief. "Ah, yes. I remember those days."

The times he couldn't wait to get to the office. He was always the first to arrive, the last to leave and the chump who didn't mind coming in on weekends and holidays. All B.K.

Before kids.

Thank God, they'd saved him.

Autumn settled back in her chair. "So what happened?"

Isaac's heart squeezed again at the caring in her voice and he drummed his fingers on the table under her intense gaze. Although the question was a legitimate one, he wasn't about to tell her—or anyone else—the truth.

"The world's financial markets collapsed one by one. Making our jobs a whole lot tougher. You need more than adrenaline to survive in this business now. You need a magic wand and the ability to predict the future."

Autumn's warm laugh resonated throughout the room and sank into his bones, and for a moment he felt carefree and relaxed.

Her expression quickly sobered. "That's part of the reason why I'm here."

He frowned, sorry to see her smile disappear but suddenly knowing why. "Another victim of downsizing?"

Autumn nodded. "We'd lost so many clients that it didn't make sense to keep all our analysts around. Or at least that's what they told me."

He couldn't imagine being jobless. In the past, it was something he'd never had to worry about. But with the way Felicia was acting toward him lately, he wasn't so confident. Since she was Sterling's daughter, nobody at Paxton really knew how much influence she had over him. To be ensnared in her web was one place no employee ever wanted to be.

"Their loss is our gain," Isaac replied with what he hoped was a reassuring smile.

Her exuberant grin was infectious. "Thank you. I'm really excited to be here and to be working with you."

Autumn tilted her head and he watched her curls skim the edge of her jawline. He wondered what that hair would feel like in his fingers. Her white, long-sleeved silk blouse did not detract his eyes from coveting what was beneath. In his mind, he saw his hands around her trim waist as she hitched up her navy blue skirt.

Isaac's groin tightened painfully and he shifted slightly in his seat as his body involuntarily reacted to a sudden desire for Autumn that he didn't understand. But he did know this: furtive glances at her across the cafeteria or in a meeting room would never satisfy him.

He bet that, beneath the stark corporate garb, she was as soft and fleeting as the snowflakes that were beginning to swirl outside. Yet he sensed she was tough to catch and even tougher to hold on to. That's why he had to stay as far away from her as he could manage.

He picked up her résumé to distract himself. There was no current home address listed, but he assumed she lived in the area. As was his custom, he flipped to the last page so he could review her work experience in reverse chronological order.

Reading quickly, he learned that Autumn had a bachelor's degree in Economics and Mathematics, and a master's degree in Statistics. All from Yale University. She was an Ivy girl, she was smart and she loved numbers. Plus, she had a killer body. It added up to some serious trouble for a man who was trying not to be attracted to her and failing badly.

"I hope you won't let our respective universities affect our working relationship," she said in a teasing voice.

He glanced up from the paper in front of him. "You're referring to the long-standing rivalry between Yale and Harvard."

She nodded and crossed her legs, sheathed in sheer hose he yearned to rip away.

He smiled. "A little bit of competition always makes things more interesting, no?"

"Most definitely," she responded. "But I'm glad I'm on your team, rather than fighting against it."

Isaac raised a brow. "Because you know you would lose?" he said matter-of-factly, hoping he didn't sound arrogant.

She shook her head. "Not at all. But winning isn't everything."

Isaac glanced over at the door. "Don't let Sterling ever hear you say that."

Autumn didn't ask why and Isaac was glad he didn't have to explain. If she wanted a career at Paxton, she would learn for herself soon enough.

He returned his attention to her résumé and noticed something that puzzled him.

Like Autumn, Isaac had also made the decision to pursue an advanced degree directly after college. But the difference was that when he finished graduate school, he'd gone straight to work for Paxton, which was one of the leading investment firms in the country.

On the contrary, Autumn had worked at some mid-level investment banks all around the country. Los Angeles. Phoenix. Miami. Companies whose names he'd never even heard of.

He considered pressing the issue but decided against it.

Multiple job hops might make some people nervous, but not him. Autumn was young, intelligent, and she obviously knew when a situation wasn't working to her advantage. Ambitiousness was a quality he admired, especially in a woman.

Besides, if Sterling trusted her enough to hire her, why shouldn't he?

Still, he couldn't let her off the hook completely. "Your résumé is impressive," he began slowly. "But you've moved around a lot. Surely that's not because of the economy every time, is it?"

"I always leave myself open to the possibilities of a greater challenge or something new."

He flipped back to the first page again. "Your previous place of employment was in Cleveland?"

Autumn's lips curved into a mischievous grin. "What can I say? I love to rock and roll!"

Isaac laughed aloud, pleased by the free-spirited tone

in her voice. He found her playful attitude refreshing and very appealing. Even in the overbearing atmosphere of the boardroom, not to mention the pressure of the first day in a new job, she had no problem being herself.

Most women tried everything they could to impress him. The girls in the office knew he was single, available and one of the wealthiest men in New York City. Out on the street, the women knew him as a regular guy who was hotter than the asphalt on a July afternoon. In the winter, they worshipped the ground he melted ice on.

He'd be the first to admit that sometimes he took the bodies they willingly offered and he enjoyed them. The one-night stands most of these women hoped would turn into a lifetime of ardor and passion meant absolutely nothing to him.

While the opportunity to bed a beautiful woman and run the other way the next morning was still there, now he had two good reasons to refuse their advances. His children.

Consequently, he hadn't slept with a woman in a very long time. Whether becoming a father caused him to feel a sense a guilt or greater moral virtue, he didn't know.

The more likely reason was that he was tired of being a pawn in a two-player game that never went anywhere. Of pretending he didn't want a woman to love him for more than his face, his body or his money.

Isaac checked the time on his phone and stifled a yawn.

He'd been up late again helping his son, Devon, with

his math homework. He couldn't remember the last time he'd had a good night's sleep. And tonight, he expected that thoughts of what Autumn looked like without the corporate jail suit would impede his rest even further.

"What do you say we rock and roll and get a jump on that tour?"

"Sounds great," Autumn replied. "You can show me the cafeteria and we can finally get that cup of coffee you missed out on this morning."

Isaac tried to swallow back another yawn. When it escaped, they both laughed.

"Yeah, you can tell I really need it, can't you?"

His eyes caught hers again. God, she was even prettier when she laughed. Thank goodness, the analysts occupied a space on another floor in the building.

His phone beeped, bringing his attention back to business. He pulled it out of his pocket, looked at it and groaned.

"Unfortunately, the tour is going to have to be a quick one. I've got another meeting in ten minutes and I think I've used up all my Get to a Meeting Late cards for the day."

"How do I snag one of those?" Autumn joked.

"Trust me, you do not want to be in Late Club," he said, in all seriousness.

"Why not?"

"Because I'm the one and only member." His gut did a little flip when she pursed her lips at him. "I didn't used to be," he backtracked. "I mean, it was only when I—"

He stopped abruptly at the winsome look on her face

and realized he was rambling. Something that was completely out of character for him. Worst of all, he'd almost told her about his kids. No one at Paxton knew about them and he wanted to keep it that way for now.

"Just do your best to never be late to a meeting, especially one with Felicia or Sterling," he said curtly.

"I appreciate the heads-up," Autumn affirmed. "By the way, is there always that much tension between them? My neck was beginning to hurt watching their verbal ping-pong match."

"Yeah," Isaac snorted. "But you'll get used to it. We all have. Felicia plays the Daddy's-girl role around here to the hilt, but she's very capable."

And lately very dangerous.

Isaac had heard rumors of people getting terminated, supposedly because Felicia didn't like them, but those were typically lower-level employees. They were the unfortunate ones she liked to trample on the most.

Hopefully, Felicia knew better than to mess with him. Isaac had too much stake and longevity in the company to throw it all away just because of her passive-aggressive antics.

If only he could figure out why Sterling was giving him the cold shoulder all of a sudden, then he'd be able to come clean about his kids. They meant more to him than anything in the world, and being made a partner at Paxton would secure his new family's financial future.

He wouldn't let anything or anyone stand in his way.

Not a bitch like Felicia.

Nor a beauty like Autumn.

Isaac felt her eyes examining his face, as if it would

reveal all his secrets, so he got up and walked over to the floor-to-ceiling window.

The snarl of people far below seemed to belong to another world. He always liked to remind himself that he was one of them, especially during those times he was afraid of losing everything.

"Can I ask you a question?"

Isaac turned away and faced her. "Sure, anything."

"What do you like best about working here?"

Isaac took a few steps and leaned against an empty console.

"That's easy," he replied. "I get to play with other people's money, and make a bundle of my own. What about you? What attracted to you Paxton Investment Securities?"

She folded her arms. "The reputation of the company in the industry. Plus, the fact that I love to analyze every investment to insure we are maximizing profits and shareholder value while maintaining the highest ethical standards in every transaction."

He was surprised that her bold confidence excited him, making him stir in all the wrong places. When a woman's strong work ethic was a major turn-on, that's a sign that one was severely undersexed.

"You sound like Sterling," he said with hidden admiration. "No wonder he hired you."

Although he truly meant it as a compliment, she brushed his comment aside.

"I just try to do the right thing, in any and all situations."

"That's wonderful. That's the way it should be," he asserted. "You are reporting to Sterling, right?"

Something flashed in her eyes. "Wh-what do you mean?"

He gave her a strange look. "He's your boss. You're his direct report, not mine, right?"

Autumn nodded. "Yes. Sorry, I blanked out for a bit."

Isaac was relieved. At the moment, he worked solo and that's the way he liked it. Having to manage Autumn would be a major distraction, one he couldn't afford to risk right now.

"It's kind of an odd arrangement, isn't it? That analysts report directly to the president of a firm. Especially one of this size."

Isaac shook his head. "Not at Paxton. Sterling wants there to be a clear division between the investment bankers and the analysts. He feels it's easier for the analysts to remain objective and impartial, in order to avoid any conflict of interest.

"Have there ever been any issues?"

Isaac clenched his jaw. While he appreciated her curiosity, she needed to know that there were some questions that were off-limits at Paxton. But it wasn't his place to tell her that. All he was supposed to do was give her a tour of the building and that was it.

Ignoring the question, he eyed the stack of paperwork on the table. "We'd better get a move on it. You'll want to get those forms filled out and turned in quickly. Paxton has one of the best employee benefits package in the industry, especially if you have—" He choked back his secret. "I mean, if you're married or have a significant other."

Not reporting a life change, namely the adoption of his children, was another rung Felicia could hang him by. But if he reported it to her, she'd run to Sterling and tell him right away, and that would be the beginning of the end of his career at Paxton.

Even though Sterling had a daughter of his own, he was well-known for being antifamily. His priorities began and ended with Paxton, and he expected his employees to have the same love and dedication for his company that he did.

Isaac was certain that if Sterling found out about his children, he could pretty much kiss the partnership goodbye.

Needless to say, he was praying his children wouldn't get seriously ill. Although he was already very wealthy and had private insurance coverage, depending on the injury or severity of illness, he could end up in a financial bind. After growing up poor, that was something he never wanted to experience again.

Isaac pushed himself away from the table and rose. "Let's get this show on the road."

He strode to the door and leaned against the wall, waiting while Autumn gathered the rest of her things. Everything she did—straightening the papers, stowing her pen in her purse and then hitching it over her thin shoulder—seemed larger than normal in his eyes.

But of course it wasn't.

It was only him, without understanding his need, trying to soak in as much detail about her as he could, as mundane as it might be. Before he had to turn her loose and go on about his business.

Although he knew he shouldn't, he couldn't stop his eyes from wandering all over her slender body, from tip to toe, as she walked over to him, clasping the thick wad of paperwork in her arms like an innocent schoolgirl. Her curly mane beckoned him unknowingly, her body forcing him to bite the inside of his mouth as he stiffened once again.

"Ready to go?" she asked.

Thank God she was standing an arm's length away, because if he could have it his way that stupid paperwork would be littering the floor and she'd be wrapped in his embrace.

At just over six feet, he was taller than her, yet he knew instinctively she'd be a perfect fit.

"Yeah," he muttered thickly, hoping she couldn't see or hear his desire for her.

He opened the door, bowing slightly. "After you."

She murmured her thanks, giving him a strange smile as she walked out of the room. The sultry way Autumn's skirt clung to her backside was almost too much for one man to bear, especially on a Monday morning.

He'd just turned off the lights in the conference room when his phone rang.

"Hi, Sterling, what can I do for you?"

As he listened to his boss and the man that was almost a father figure to him, his heart raced with excitement and dread.

He ended the call and glanced quickly at Autumn.

"I'm going to need to postpone the tour. Are you going to be okay?"

Her brows knit together in confusion. "What was that about?"

"I'll explain at lunch," he replied, shoving the phone in his pocket. "Meet me in my office at noon."

Without waiting for Autumn's response, he turned and jogged down the hall, feeling her eyes on his back and her smile settling in his heart.

Chapter 3

"And we're off," Autumn whispered under her breath as she watched Isaac round the corner.

Way to go, Sterling.

Her plan was falling together nicely. Though she was curious what her new boss had said on the phone to make Isaac invite her to lunch, it hardly mattered. She routinely left the initial minor details of a surveillance case up to the client. Experience taught her that doing so put her on the fast track to gaining her client's trust. In the end, she did what she wanted, when she wanted to do it, whether the client liked it or not. All was forgiven when she solved a case and got the answers they wanted.

Autumn shifted the stack of papers in her hand, wishing she could toss them into the nearest trash can.

She had no need for any of the Paxton benefits, the government took care of her quite nicely. Whether she had a nosebleed or a gunshot wound, she could walk, run or crawl to any hospital and get medical help. No questions asked and no payment required. Being a friend of Uncle Sam was the best insurance policy in the nation.

Hopefully neither of those injuries would occur on this case. But Autumn wasn't so sure about what would happen to her heart. Over the past few years, she'd been in some pretty scary situations, but none of them made her heart beat as hard as it did when she looked at Isaac, or when he looked at her.

The raw power that he exuded, even when he was relaxed, made her unabashedly wet between the legs.

She smiled with pleasure. It wasn't until the end of the meeting, when she had stood before him and his hot gaze sent a jolt of fire down her body, that she'd realized his hunger was for her.

Sadly, she'd almost laughed. The man had no idea that she was there to potentially destroy him.

It had been a while since she'd seen that look in a man's eyes, and even longer since she'd welcomed it.

But Isaac? He was different. If she were to be truly honest with herself, there was something about Isaac that made her want to run into his arms. Yet, for the good of the case, she knew she would do well to remind herself on a daily basis that she was there to learn the truth, not hop into bed with the most gorgeous man she'd seen since—well…ever.

What she needed right now was a distraction. A nice

cup of tea would make her forget about Isaac's tawny-brown eyes and help her refocus on the investigation.

She was just about to try to find the Paxton cafeteria herself when she heard a voice calling her name. She turned to see Felicia walking toward her. How she didn't manage to trip in those stiletto heels was an unfortunate miracle in itself.

"There you are. I've been looking all over for you, and here you are exactly where I left you."

Felicia's voice was so syrupy sweet that it made Autumn want to gag.

She opened the door to the conference room, peered inside and quickly shut it. "Where's Isaac?" she demanded.

Autumn pasted a smile on her face. "He had to run to a meeting."

"You mean he left you here without giving you a tour?"

"No. He gave me the tour," she lied. "We stopped back at the conference room because I accidentally left my paperwork on the table."

Autumn grasped the wad and waved it in Felicia's face so hard her eyes blinked. "See?"

Felicia pushed the paper away with annoyance. "All I see is that it's not filled out. You'd better get to your desk and get started."

"Sure. I would be happy to do so if I knew where my desk was located."

Felicia touched the back of her hair. "All analysts are housed in the cubicles on the second floor. Didn't Isaac show you?" she said impatiently.

Autumn shook her head. "No, that was our last stop but then he was suddenly called into a meeting."

Felicia let out an exasperated breath. "Come on, I'll show you." She started down the hall, muttering under her breath. "I guess if you want something done right around here, you've got to do it yourself."

"Wait," Autumn called out. "Sterling wrote down the location of my work space. He said it was somewhere on this floor."

Felicia swiveled on her heels, her eyes narrowing. "Are you sure? This floor is for members of the Paxton executive team only."

Autumn accidentally dropped the scrap of paper Sterling had given her earlier. She bent to retrieve it and when she stood, Felicia rudely snatched it away.

"Let me see that." Felicia's cheeks reddened and she crumpled the paper into a ball.

Autumn bit back a smile. She had no idea where her work space was located, but it was obvious the woman didn't like it.

They walked down the carpeted hallway, in the opposite direction from where Isaac had run, and through a small corridor. A few minutes later, they stopped in front of a door with no nameplate. It was constructed of heavy wood and there was a thin plane of glass running vertically down one side of the door, the view through which was obstructed by cardboard.

"I think my father has made a mistake. We use this room for file storage."

Felicia's hand shook a little as she placed it on the knob and turned. "I don't understand this," she shrieked.

Autumn stepped into the small but clean room. Two rusty gray file cabinets lined one wall, one of which was graced with a plastic houseplant that had lost most of its leaves. The old-fashioned metal desk had a couple of beat-up chairs in front of it. On the desk was one of those spotlight lamps, the kind with the lightbulb that burned so hot it could singe anything that got to close to it.

Clearly, the room had been hastily furnished with some vintage finds from somebody's attic or basement. A laptop was the only modern thing in the whole place.

Autumn walked around the desk and set down the stack of papers she was lugging around, as well as her purse. Then she sat in the vintage wooden chair and spun around to face Felicia, who was still by the door.

"It's perfect!" she exclaimed with a broad smile. "What's wrong with it?"

"It's…it's…*ugly,*" Felicia sputtered. "The furnishings are horrendous, not at all what we have in the other offices. Not to mention the fact that this is a file room and no one but me is supposed to be in here."

Felicia looked out into the hallway before she moved deeper inside the room and looked around. "But where are all the *files?*" she wailed, her eyes wide to the whites. "This room was nearly filled with boxes and now there are only about half left."

Hopefully, only the ones I need for the investigation, Autumn thought, snickering inwardly.

Sterling may be a grump, but he was turning out to be very, very handy.

Felicia walked up to the desk and planted her hands

on her hips. "I'm sure this is only a temporary office," she said with a note of derision. "There must be some issue with getting your cubicle ready on the second floor. I'll speak to my father and we'll get this matter straightened out right away."

Autumn nodded and tugged on the middle drawer of her desk. "Sounds good." The drawer stuck, so she tugged even harder and when she finally managed to pull it open, the metal on metal scraped together so loudly that Felicia covered her ears.

The drawer was well stocked with office supplies. Another plus for Sterling. She grabbed the first pen she saw and quickly uncapped it. "I'll get started on that paperwork now and will have it to you by lunch, okay?"

"Fine," Felicia snapped, looking over her shoulder again, as if she was expecting someone. "I should have this work space issue corrected by then."

Autumn rose and went to the door, feigning eagerness to finally start her first day on the job, in the hopes that Felicia would leave. "Thanks for all your help. I'll drop by your office in a couple of hours."

She leaned against the jamb and watched as Felicia suddenly hurried down the hall as fast as her stiletto heels could take her. The woman seemed genuinely distraught and confused about the whole situation. She was about to shut the door when she looked up and suddenly realized why.

Isaac Mason's office was directly opposite hers.

Isaac smoothed one hand over his close-cropped hair and then got to work reknotting his tie. It was almost noon and he'd made it through his morning meetings, his clients were happy, and there were no frantic phone calls from his children.

Like one of his favorite rappers once said, "It's been a good day." But Isaac knew it was long from over.

He wasn't happy about what Sterling had asked him to do, but if he wanted to make partner, he had no choice.

With his tie neatened to his satisfaction, he took one last glance in the mirror, ignoring the rumble in his belly and hammering of his heart.

It's just lunch, he told himself, and Autumn's just another coworker. But he knew she was more than that, or at least he wished she could be.

Isaac walked over to his desk and password-protected his computer. After glancing out his office window, he opened the door and was shrugging into his coat when Autumn stepped out of the opposite office.

"Well, hello!" she greeted him.

Isaac pulled on the lapels of his coat. "What are you doing in there?" he asked, pointing his finger at the closed door. "That's the file room."

She gave him a cheery smile. "It's my office now."

Before he could ask any more questions, she started to walk away.

"Where are we going to lunch? The cafeteria? Because I'm starved."

The thought of food was distracting enough without having to watch her sumptuous bottom sway down the hall and not be able to cradle it in his hands. During his morning meetings, his mind had wandered into random thoughts of her—a kind of subtle curiosity that would only be satisfied by seeing and feeling this woman who could never be his, except in his dreams.

"Um. N-no," he stuttered, feeling a little like Clark Kent chasing Lois as he quickly moved beside her. "I thought we'd go somewhere a little quieter. I have something I need to talk to you about."

"Sounds serious. Is everything all right?"

"No, but it will be."

It has to be, Isaac thought. He had to find a way to get back into Sterling's good graces again. If he could pull this off, he'd make partner for sure.

He leaned against the wall as they waited for the elevator and admired the clean lines of the soft gray coat she wore. Tailored at the waist, it accentuated her trim figure and ended midthigh, which suited him just fine. The more leg she revealed the better, and from where he stood, Lord knows she had two mighty fine ones.

Damn.

There were thousands of women in New York, and the only one that had piqued his interest was off-limits and off-the-chain gorgeous.

Isaac cleared his throat and turned away before his lower body gave away his thoughts.

"It was snowing earlier. Better button up."

Autumn nodded. "Good idea."

Except for the occasional screech from the elevator cables, they rode down in silence until Autumn started to giggle.

He shifted his feet. "What's so funny?"

Autumn pressed her lips together and finished buttoning her coat. "I was just remembering the look on Felicia's face when she saw I had the office opposite yours. She was so pissed. I wonder why?"

Isaac knew why, but he wasn't about to say anything. It was embarrassing enough how Felicia had thrown herself at him, luring him into that very room, where she was hidden among the boxes, stark naked.

He shuddered at the memory. Although he didn't have a type, per se, Felicia definitely wasn't it.

Now Autumn, on the other hand, was a different story. He'd only met her a few hours ago and already he was entertaining fantasies of a hot and heavy office romance. Whether this sudden lust was the result of a lack of coffee, fumes of sleep or zero sex, he couldn't pinpoint. But if it involved two hearts possibly getting broken, one of them being his, he wasn't about to take the risk.

The cold January air was like a rude slap in the face as they walked out of the Paxton Building. The winds didn't help, either. The weatherman that morning had said they were blowing out of the northeast, but they felt like they were from Antarctica and their new home was in the bones of everyone who had ventured outside.

"Wh-where are we headed? I—I'm freezing already!" Autumn ground out through chattering teeth.

Isaac pulled up the collar of his black wool coat. "Not far, just a few blocks."

They joined the throng of people huddled against the chill and walked south, passing a variety of street vendors braving the cold and selling gloves, hats and scarves plastered with "NYC."

"Toasties! Toasties! Two for a dollar," cried one enterprising man. His West African lilt was as welcome as the little hand warmers he was selling.

Isaac stopped and bought four of them. He gave the guy a fifty-dollar bill and told him to keep the change.

"For the way back," he said, giving a pair to Autumn.

He wished he could warm up her hands in his own way, but these would have to do.

Her grateful smile was all the warmth he needed. He'd almost forgotten how nice it felt to give to someone other than his children.

"Thanks. This wind is a killer. I forgot my gloves this morning. First-day jitters, I guess."

A minute later, they arrived at Le Jardin Rouge, a popular Wall Street restaurant that was anything but French. As soon as they walked in, the din and clamor of spirited conversation floated around them.

Autumn looked around and Isaac could tell she wanted to cover her ears.

"You call this quiet?"

Isaac held up his hand as a waiter approached with a couple of menus.

"Mr. Mason, hello again. I have your regular table."

He led them through a narrow hallway, past the kitchen, to a single room in the back.

Inside was a linen-covered table with two chairs and a fire roaring in the fireplace. They hung their coats on the two porcelain-tipped hooks on the wall and sat down.

"Thanks, Eric. Give us a moment, will you?"

After the waiter left, Isaac smiled and handed Autumn her menu.

"All better?" he asked, gesturing toward the low flames roaring in the fireplace.

Autumn nodded and moved her chair into place. "Much. And I can barely hear the other customers all the way back here."

"Yes, I often bring clients by for lunch or when I need to get away from the office, I just come here by myself and work. It's got a ton of character, no?"

"It's lovely!" Autumn rubbed her hands together in front of the fire. "What's good here?"

"Everything, mostly. The butternut squash soup is my favorite, especially on a chilly day like today. It'll help warm us both up."

The waiter entered the room with two bottles of mineral water. Isaac ordered the soups and a couple of side salads.

"That was awesome what you did back there," Autumn remarked, unfolding her napkin. "For me and for that vendor."

She poured her water into her glass and took a sip. "And here I thought all men who worked on Wall Street were ruthless penny-pinchers."

Isaac felt the blood rush to the tips of his ears, something that happened whenever he was either very embarrassed or very angry. In this case, her compliment pleased him, but he merely shrugged.

He squeezed a lemon into his water. "Contrary to popular belief, I can be a nice guy. But in order to make money in this town, one can't be afraid to push past boundaries and take risks."

"Even when it involves breaking the law?"

Her question wasn't posed in an accusatory tone. Still, it was unsettling and left a metallic taste in his mouth. Isaac was glad when the waiter approached the table with a basket of bread and their salads.

When they were alone again, Isaac asked, "Have you ever heard of the saying 'Whoever controls the money makes the rules?'"

Autumn buttered her bread and nodded.

He took a deep breath. "Sometimes it's true."

And he was living it. Or at least he used to...

The meetings to which he was mysteriously not invited, the silence that often befell a room whenever he walked in, and the opportunities for new client business that lately seemed to go to someone else or he never even heard about in the first place.

He was the wealthiest senior investment banker on staff. In fact, he made more money in his yearly bonuses than in his regular salary. But, lately, it seemed as if everyone was treating him like some runny-nosed intern.

Isaac kept thinking the cold-shoulder treatment from Sterling and the other staff was because he was being groomed for the responsibilities of becoming an executive partner, where there was less day-to-day trading and managing clients and more focus on higher-level investment strategy for the firm overall.

There was something wrong going on at Paxton, something he didn't understand, but he wasn't ready to believe that the something wrong could be him.

"So are you saying it's okay to look the other way?" Autumn pressed. Her brown eyes seemed as intense as the flames warming the room.

"Sometimes," he cautioned. Autumn's eyes narrowed almost imperceptibly and she seemed disappointed with his answer. "But only until one is sure that pursuing it means a net gain for both parties," he added, not wanting to upset her.

Autumn rolled her eyes and speared a piece of romaine. "You sound like one of my old bosses. Every question I asked the guy, the answer he would give me would sound like it came out of a textbook for Economics 101."

Isaac laughed, almost spitting out the water he was in the middle of drinking.

"I'm that bad, huh?"

Autumn munched on her salad and nodded.

"In that case, maybe I should quit investment banking and become a professor."

She swallowed and pointed her fork at him. "Maybe you should," she advised, her tone serious. "But not before you tell me why you invited me to lunch."

Autumn pursed her lips into a pouty smile that nearly teased him to distraction, and he realized that he felt so comfortable with her that he'd nearly forgotten the reason he'd invited her to the restaurant in the first place.

"Ah yes," he said, as the waiter arrived with two steaming bowls of soup. "We have an assignment."

"What do you mean by 'we'?" Autumn asked. "I thought you said that the analysts and investment and trading guys never worked together. Something about conflict of interest?"

Isaac nodded. "We usually don't. But this assignment came direct from Sterling, so I don't ask questions. He must have his reasons for wanting to do it this way."

She blew on her spoon and swallowed some soup. "Mmm…this is delicious. Okay, so what do we need to do?"

Isaac ate a few spoonfuls of soup and wiped his mouth with his napkin. "Have you ever heard of Eleanor Witterman?"

"Sure. She's a New York City legend. The wealthy socialite who never married. She's had plenty of suitors, or so they say. How old is she now?"

Isaac thought a moment. "Late fifties, early sixties maybe? She's around the same age as Sterling. But from the photos I've seen, she doesn't look it at all."

Autumn twisted her lips to the side. "She must have her plastic surgeon on speed dial," she remarked. "What about her?"

He smiled and took a sip of water before continuing. "Sterling has been trying to get her to become a client for years, but she's never come on board. Seems lately she's had a change of heart. Recently she sold a large portion of her art collection for just over ten million dollars, and she came to Paxton seeking counsel on how to invest it."

Autumn's eyes widened. "That's great. Any reason why she sold all that art?"

Isaac shrugged and leaned back in his chair.

"Who cares?" he said with a smile. "We've got ten million dollars to play with!"

"Where do I fit in this game of real-life monopoly?"

"You and I are going to put together an investment package that Eleanor won't be able to resist."

"That sounds more up your alley than mine. I'm an analyst, remember? I'm the one who double-checks all the calculations making sure one plus two doesn't equal four."

"Right, but to get this deal, we're going to need your forecasting and predictive analysis skills, as well."

"You mean you want me to be a fortune teller?" Autumn replied drily. She grabbed her purse and pretended to be searching for something. "Nope, no crystal ball in here."

"Come on, Autumn. You know everyone on Wall Street relies on a little wizardry now and then."

"Which is why we've had a financial meltdown in the United States and around the world," she retorted, folding her arms.

Isaac's mouth dropped open. He hadn't expected any push back, especially from a new employee. Maybe he'd been wrong about Autumn. Sterling was obviously losing his Midas touch in terms of hiring suitable Paxtonites.

"Whose side are you on, anyway?"

He tossed his napkin on the table and gave her a pointed stare. "You work in this industry. You know the way things are. Millions of stocks are traded every day by computer algorithms, not people. It's the new world order."

Autumn held up her hands. "I realize that, okay? All I'm saying is that we all should take some responsibility for what goes on, and what goes wrong, in our industry."

Isaac felt the tips of his ears get hot, and this time he wasn't happy. This lunch meeting was not turning out the way he expected. Autumn was looking like she would be difficult to work with, and yet, he had no choice.

He leaned forward and said in a hard voice, "The only responsibility I care about right now is the one I have to Paxton. And as a new member of our team, I would have thought you'd have a better attitude about this assignment."

Autumn's eyes widened. "I'm sorry, Isaac," she said, frowning. "Sometimes I just get caught up in all the negativity that surrounds our industry that I lose sight of all the good, and I know Paxton is one of the good guys."

She swiped at her left eye with one finger and Isaac wasn't sure if she was removing a tear or a speck of dust. No way could he have a woman crying because of him.

That would not be a very good day.

He paid for the meal in cash and they retrieved their coats. He waited until they were outside until he spoke again. The mood between them, which had been friendly an hour ago, was as icy as the air.

"Look, Autumn, let me give you the lowdown on Eleanor," he said, softening his voice. "She's very old-fashioned. She doesn't want her money being handled by computers, but by real people. Any investments we advise are going to be backed up by real numbers, forecasted to predict the dividends she could expect to receive in x number of years."

Autumn nodded, looking contrite, and for a moment he felt guilty for getting so angry at her.

She tilted her chin, and he noticed she had a tiny mole on her jawline. "When do we get started?"

"Immediately. The presentation is in two weeks. I want you to begin looking into possibilities this afternoon. I have a full day of meetings tomorrow, so if you're available, I'd like to have an early dinner so we can review your initial recommendations."

Autumn buttoned up her coat. "There are hundreds of industries or companies she could possibly invest in. Any idea where to start?"

Isaac thought a moment. "How about with her best friends?"

Autumn gave him a quizzical smile. "And who might they be?"

"Diamonds."

She burst out in a deep, knowing laugh, which was definitely better than almost making her cry.

He wiggled his fingers at her. "Now let's bust open these hand warmers and get back to the office. We both have a lot of work to do."

As they walked back, hands stuffed deep in their coat pockets against the harsh January winds, Isaac knew the hardest part of the days and nights ahead would be trying to stop Autumn from getting under his skin, or into his heart.

Chapter 4

When they got back to Paxton, Autumn stopped at the restroom to freshen up. Just as she suspected, the tears she'd nearly unloaded on Isaac had taken a toll on her mascara. Of course, they weren't real. She'd only pretended that she was going to cry.

Deep down she hated to use such a manipulative trick, but it was the only way she knew how to get a sense of his character.

She wet a paper towel and dabbed at her eyelashes. When she was finished, she smiled at her reflection in the mirror. Thank goodness, Isaac had passed her test.

He cared.

She was impressed with how well he treated the street vendor and their waiter at the restaurant. He didn't have to give either man any extra change or tips, but he did.

And he didn't have to care whether her hands were cold, either. Her heart swelled remembering how he'd bought her the hand warmers. She couldn't remember the last time someone had done something so sweet for her, just to save her from discomfort.

And she was relieved because maybe, just maybe, he wasn't like all the other greedy, stingy, emotionally dead men she'd met—and busted—while working undercover.

In her experience, the maxim "the bigger the bank account, the larger the ego" was a reality. There was something about making a ton of money that made some men turn into arrogant egomaniacs who thought they were above the law.

It was true that Isaac didn't seem to be too concerned about how Wall Street sometimes negatively affected Main Streets all around the world. He was likely worried about his job, and rightly so; otherwise, Sterling wouldn't have hired her to investigate him.

If he didn't have the activist mentality that she did, perhaps it was because he truly believed he wasn't doing anything wrong. Autumn hoped that's what she would discover, too. All she had to do was remember to avoid letting her emotions get in the way of her case.

When she got back to her office, Isaac's door was open, but he wasn't there. Presumably, he was already well into his afternoon meetings.

She hung up her coat, walked to the desk and noticed a light blinking on her phone.

Oh joy, she thought, her first voice mail.

Twenty minutes later, she'd figured out how to retrieve the message. It was Sterling calling for an update. The man certainly didn't waste any time, she mused while locking her purse in her desk. Although she wasn't particularly afraid it would get stolen, she wasn't stupid.

Petty crimes in the workplace were a common occurrence—a box of binder clips here, a laptop there. She wasn't about to give anyone the rope of temptation. Plus, the location of her office was a little remote, which was likely the reason it was originally used for storage.

Autumn grabbed a pen and an index pad and headed down to Sterling's office. His secretary, Doris, a plump woman who somehow managed to look attractive even with a tiny gap in her front teeth, informed Autumn that Sterling was on a call and she would have to wait.

Ten minutes later, the woman ushered her into his office and Autumn almost burst out laughing when she tiptoed out. But when she saw Sterling's face, she knew why. The man looked like he could melt copper off a penny with his eyes alone.

She took a few, tentative steps toward his desk. "I got your voice mail. You wanted to see me?"

Sterling motioned her closer, waving his hands impatiently.

"Yes, yes. Come in."

Autumn parked herself in one of the maroon-tufted leather chairs fronting Sterling's enormous desk.

She gave him her sweetest smile. "Is there anything wrong?"

"The world's gone to hell, that's all," he barked, and

sat down hard. "I'm hoping you have some good news for me. What have you learned so far?"

That Isaac was as kind as he was cute, she thought, but she knew that wasn't the information Sterling was seeking.

"Not much yet," she admitted. "We went to lunch and he informed me of our assignment."

"And what do you think?"

"It's brilliant."

"I know," Sterling replied. "I thought of it, didn't I?"

Autumn wanted to gag at the air of superiority in his tone, but at least his eyes didn't have daggers in them anymore.

"You certainly did, and it's the perfect way for me to observe how Isaac prepares for a new client presentation from start to finish."

Sterling steepled his fingers. "I called you in here because I want you to know that this is a real assignment with a real client, not a decoy."

Autumn nodded. "I'm glad you told me. I was kind of wondering about that when Isaac indicated the client seems to be afraid of computers."

"Eleanor Witterman is not afraid of computers," Sterling corrected. "She simply doesn't trust them. Quite frankly, on days like today, I think she might be right."

Autumn raised an eyebrow, not knowing what he meant but gathering it had something to do with the world going to hell.

"Don't worry, Mr. Paxton. I'll do my best to make every investment we advise as transparent as possible."

"Good," he replied with a satisfied nod. "How do you like your office?"

"It's great. Nice touch on the old office furniture. Very film noir. I feel like Jimmy Cagney's going to show up at any second and offer me a cigar."

He snorted a laugh. The sound was like a street full of taxis honking in unison. "Yeah. I picked it out myself. Straight from the storage closet in the basement. My father started this business back in the early 1950s and he was something of a pack rat."

"Are the boxes in my office the files you want me to review?"

Sterling nodded, absently jingling the coins in his pocket. "There are about eight years of records contained in those files. The rest are electronic."

"And these are all the deals Isaac has been involved with since he's been employed here?"

"Yes. He interned here while he was an undergrad, and then I hired him full-time after he graduated from Harvard."

"What made you think he'd be a good fit for Paxton?"

"He's smart. Smarter than a lot of people around here initially gave him credit for."

She gave him a pointed stare. "Why? Because he's black?"

Yeah. I went there, Autumn thought as Sterling sat up in his chair, his pale face aghast.

"We don't condone, nor will we tolerate, any form of discrimination here at Paxton."

She thinned her lips and didn't back down. In order

to conduct her investigation, she needed to have all the facts. Even the ugly ones.

"However since you asked," Sterling relented with a shrug. "That could have been the reason initially, but it's certainly not the case now."

His broad smile should have been reassuring, but instead it made Autumn wonder if he was telling her the truth.

Sterling reached for his phone, effectively ending the meeting. "Please keep me posted on any new developments," he ordered in a brusque tone. By the time she shut the door, he was already engaged in another heated discussion. She flashed a sympathetic smile at his secretary and headed back to her own office.

Isaac's door was now closed. He had the little strip of glass next to his door, too, but she wasn't about to peek in and see if he was there. She did, however, take a moment to peel away the cardboard from the glass in her own office. Not only was it tacky, but she didn't want to appear as if she had something to hide.

Autumn shut the door and sat down at her desk, rubbing at her pulsating temples, a sure sign a headache was in the works.

Sterling seemed appeased for now, but he'd want action quickly. While she was eager to get started, she was also afraid that she wouldn't like the answers she found.

The first thing Autumn needed to do was access Isaac's files on the network.

She couldn't help feeling slightly disappointed that Sterling had sent the security credentials via email. Hacking into Paxton's computer system was infinitely more fun and challenging, but time was not on her side. With only weeks to complete her investigation, the pressure from Sterling to wrap things up quickly was real.

As she waited for her computer to boot up, she dug out two ibuprofen and a bottle of water from her tote bag. She washed down the pills and was just about to open up her email when there were three sharp raps on the door.

Her heart beat faster, and she hoped it was Isaac coming to check in on her. She spun around, trying to catch her reflection in the window, but all she saw was snow. Facing the door, she quickly smoothed her errant curls, praying she didn't look like she'd just stuck her finger in a light socket.

"Come in!"

Felicia sauntered in and put her hands on hips. "You'll be happy to know you're staying right here."

Autumn felt her headache immediately worsen, noting that Felicia looked anything but happy. The scowl on her face could make a clown cry.

"I've checked with my father and it seems he was the one who arranged everything, without clearing it with me."

"I'm sorry there was a misunderstanding," Autumn said, under the woman's glare. "Thank you for clearing it up."

Felicia gestured toward the brown boxes lining the floor, dismissing Autumn's apology. "And these are supposed to remain here, although I don't know what for, but Daddy instructed me not to remove them."

"Were you able to locate the other boxes that were here?"

"Of course I did," Felicia snapped. "And they are now in an undisclosed location."

Felicia glanced at the boxes again and her brow creased, which made Autumn wonder why she was so concerned about the dusty, old files.

"I think the reason those are staying is because Isaac and I are working together on an important new business presentation," Autumn offered, trying to distract her. "He wants me to review previous history to get me acclimated to the way things are done around here."

Felicia turned and gave her a smile that Autumn knew was not meant to be friendly.

"Sterling told me about the assignment, which is why you're in here, in this cozy little office, and not down there on the farm," she said, referring to the floor where all the other analysts worked in tiny cubicles.

Autumn noted that Felicia didn't add "where you belong" to the end of her statement, but she got the gist. The executive floor was her territory and Autumn wasn't welcome.

Still, Autumn knew she had to do something to appease her; otherwise, Felicia could become a hindrance to her investigation, like a cockroach she could never kill.

She pushed away from her desk and crossed her legs.

"Somehow it seems we've gotten off to a bad start, and I just want you to know that if you ever need anything, I'm here."

Felicia tilted her head, and a few blond strands wafted around her face, softening her appearance.

"That's very kind of you, so I'll offer you one piece of advice."

"What's that?" Autumn asked, thinking she was going to tell her that short-term disability insurance was a good investment.

Felicia glanced behind her shoulder and turned back. "Watch out for Isaac. He has a reputation around here that's not as glowing as you might think."

Autumn wanted to tell Felicia that talking about a fellow employee behind his back had to be against the human resources official code of conduct, but she remained silent. It wouldn't do her any good to invoke Felicia's wrath when, at some point in the future, she could prove to be useful for something other than idle gossip.

"Don't let his looks or his money fool you," Felicia added before walking out.

"And don't let the door hit you in the ass," Autumn muttered under her breath.

God, the woman was infuriating.

No doubt Felicia was outside peeking in Isaac's little window to see if he was there. Her warning about him didn't ring any serious alarm bells for now, although it did make Autumn question Felicia's motive for telling her. She made a mental note to closely observe any future interactions between the two.

After downing the last of her water, she opened her email.

The first was from Sterling and contained the credentials for the network, plus his cell phone number with instructions telling her he was available 24/7 for any updates.

While she appreciated his eagerness, this was a potential case of corporate fraud, not murder, and she hoped there wouldn't be a need for a late-night phone call. If the man sounded like he wanted to smash heads at one in the afternoon, she shuddered to think what he'd sound like at three in the morning.

The second email was from Isaac.

Lunch was fun. I look forward to working with you on the Witterman pitch.

Since we're on such a tight time frame, please feel free to call my cell at any time if you have questions or concerns.

—Isaac

Autumn's lips turned up in a smile as she programmed his number into her cell, thinking she would call just to hear his voice. She suspected his playful tenor could turn passionate with the right woman.

She closed her eyes as a part of her wished she could be that woman. The part that missed a man's awakening touch, his urgent plea between her thighs, the hush of early-morning loving and the tender kisses that would sustain her all day.

Opening her eyes, she leaned her elbows on the desk and put her hands against her flushed cheeks. Daydreaming about Isaac being the one who could lift her self-imposed ban on men meant that she needed to get back to work.

She glanced over at the boxes in the corner and wondered why she dreaded reviewing them all. She was a natural snoop, so normally she didn't mind digging through reams of paperwork and finding the evidence she needed to help bring about justice.

But this case was different because she didn't want to find out anything bad about Isaac.

Even though she didn't know him, when she looked into his eyes, something deep inside her only wanted to see the good. The complete opposite of what she was called to do as a private investigator. To uphold the law, she had to condemn.

With a sigh, she decided she would take a stack of files home every night where she could review them while drinking a nice, big glass of wine.

She turned her attention back to the case by researching Paxton's prospective client, Eleanor Witterman. The search netted a surprising number of results for the never-married socialite.

Most were news items about the recent sale of her art collection, which consisted primarily of works by French painters such as Degas, Monet, Renoir and others whose last names sounded equally romantic.

There was also an article where she admitted she was something of a Francophile, a person who just can't get enough of all things French, including in her own words "Frenchmen." And while she'd reflected she'd had many lovers, no one could make her forget the one who broke her heart.

I'm not rich, but at least my heart is intact.

Autumn counted herself among the lucky ones. She'd

never had her heart broken, likely because she never let anyone get close enough to have the chance.

In Isaac's case, she knew she had to keep her lucky streak going, not that he gave her any outward, public displays of interest. Although a few times today at lunch, she did catch him glancing at her as if he wished he could.

In his eyes, the desire was there. But so was the wall.

At least they had those two things in common.

Autumn redirected herself back to beginning her analysis of the investment market for diamonds.

Prior to bringing one company to its knees for securities fraud and before she started working as a private investigator, she was primarily involved in researching stocks and bonds. So she was surprised to learn that diamonds had outperformed equities in recent years. The risks were a market that was complex, unregulated and highly secretive. Certainly not advisable for the average investor, but for a woman with Eleanor's wealth, investing in the diamond market might make sense.

Still, it was important for any investor to have a balanced portfolio and Autumn knew she had a ton of research ahead of her so that she could make the best investment recommendations.

Although she thought it was odd that Isaac didn't suggest a discovery meeting with Eleanor so they could get a better understanding of her risk potential, that was really his call. She had no choice but to trust that he had his reasons for moving forward.

She glanced at her watch and saw that it was nearly five o'clock. She'd better get moving if she was going to leave the office before Isaac. It wouldn't do for him to discover that she lived in the same building as he did. In a city of eight million people, it was the best way to keep tabs on him, plus the view of Central Park was fabulous.

Autumn got up and walked over to the boxes. She knelt down for a closer look and was glad to see they were organized by year. She opened up the oldest one and selected as many files as she could hold in one hand, before standing up and stuffing them into her tote bag.

After packing up her laptop and fetching her purse, she buttoned her coat, cracked open the door slightly and frowned. Isaac's door was shut and the lights were off.

Her brow crinkled. When had he left for the day? She hadn't heard any sounds in the hallway.

She guessed it was because diamonds had a way of commanding her complete attention. Or maybe she was just trying to let herself off the hook, she chided herself and vowed to be more observant of Isaac tomorrow. She certainly didn't need any excuses to keep a close eye on his beautiful body.

Worried that Isaac would be standing at the elevators, she shut her door and leaned against it to wait for a few minutes, trying not to be upset that he didn't say goodbye.

Isaac heaved his backpack over his shoulder, trying to ignore all the work within it. He picked up the pizza from the counter, pushed open the door and joined the swarm of people on Madison Avenue.

Eager to get home to his children, he walked as quickly as he could through meandering tourists and hurried workers rushing to get to the subway. Thankfully, the ice on the sidewalk had melted, but with the temperature dropping again that evening, he knew it would be treacherous in the morning.

When he arrived at his building, he glanced up at the evergreen cloth awning with amusement. The name of his apartment building was The Staffordshire, a name he always thought was better suited to a country estate in England than a high-rise apartment building in New York City. Central Park was right across the street, so he supposed that counted as the "country," and although he owned his apartment, with the maintenance fees he was paying every year, he could have bought an estate fit for a king a long time ago.

Isaac nodded to the doorman, got in the elevator, punched in his code and rode to the penthouse level.

When he arrived, the apartment was oddly silent. Normally when he got home, the television was on and his children were plopped in front of it, zoned out like two zombies.

"Anybody home?" he called, setting his backpack on the floor. When he didn't get an answer, he walked into the kitchen and yelled, "I've got pizza!"

Like magic, his children materialized.

Devon, his twelve-year-old son, ran and slid into the room in his sock feet. His sixteen-year-old daughter, Deshauna, entered a few moments later with the unhurried saunter so typical of teenagers.

That five-letter word works every time, he thought.

"Hey, guys! I've got your favorite." He opened and presented the box with as much flair as he could muster. "Pepperoni, broccoli and onions!"

Deshauna took out her earbuds and made a face. "Um…the broccoli-and-onions part? That's your favorite, Dad."

"Yeah. I hate broccoli," Devon joined in. "But I like the onions. They're slimy and go down like worms," he added, rubbing his stomach with a satisfied grin.

"Eww, get a life, Devon."

Feeling an argument was about to ensue, Isaac quickly closed the pizza box and set it on the granite countertop.

"How about we all grab something to drink from the refrigerator and eat? Devon, you get the plates. Deshauna, you get the napkins and silverware."

While his kids set the table, Isaac made a salad by grabbing a bag of pre-mixed lettuce from the refrigerator and pouring the contents into a bowl. If only everything in life were this easy, he thought as he retrieved a couple of bottles of salad dressing, mentally bracing himself for the latest crisis that his kids faced that day.

Devon and Deshauna had grown up in a slew of foster homes, just like he did, and were having some trouble adjusting to a new, stable life.

He'd adopted them both as he couldn't bear for them not to be together. Although now, Isaac chuckled to himself, he had to break them apart on a daily basis to keep them from killing each other. The struggle to survive had transitioned into sibling rivalry, and he was still trying to figure out how to manage it.

Food was the great equalizer though, and he was glad when they were all sitting down and digging in.

"So," he said, passing the salad, "how was your day?"

"I got an A on my math homework!" Devon said, his lips greasy with pizza sauce.

"That's great. So all that hard work you did last night paid off," Isaac said, resisting the urge to tell Devon to wipe his mouth. A boy should be able to eat his pizza in peace during a moment of glory, right?

It was times like these that he wished he had a wife. She could be the etiquette cop in the household and the kids could blame her for spoiling all the fun, instead of him.

Yes, she'd be mad at him for a while, but he'd be sure to make it up to her in bed all night long.

An image of Autumn suddenly popped into his brain. She was lying in his bed in a sheer lace nightgown and he was kissing the pout off her beautiful face.

Why am I thinking of her now? he wondered, even as he realized he hadn't stopped thinking about her all day.

"What about you, Deshauna? Did you get a chance to talk to the guidance counselor?"

His daughter, who was a junior in high school, was just starting the process of looking at colleges. His heart pinched in his chest, thinking about her going away in less than two years, when he'd just found her.

Deshauna nodded, her bangs falling across her forehead. "I brought a bunch of information home. Some of the papers we need to have back to her by tomorrow. Will you have time tonight?"

Isaac thought about the slew of work in his backpack. It would be another late night, but his kids came first.

"Sure thing, honey. Let's take a look right after dinner."

Her smile quickly turned into a scowl when Devon grabbed another slice of pizza. "Do you have to eat so much?"

"I dunno," Devon shot back. "Do you have to FaceTime with that boy every day after school?"

Isaac stopped chewing and stared at his daughter. "What boy?"

With a mortified look, Deshauna tried to kick her brother under the table, but he scooted away just in time, nearly taking the tablecloth with him.

"Cut it out!" Isaac instructed, inwardly proud that he managed to sound calmer than he really was. Between the two of them, he'd be lucky if he made it to his forties without having a heart attack.

"Deshauna, we'll talk about this later." He piled a second helping of salad on his plate. "Now, why don't one of you ask me about my day?"

"How was your day, Dad?" they chorused.

"So much for following directions," he commented drily. "But since you both asked, it was great. A new employee started working at Paxton today. Her name is Autumn."

"Ooh…is she hot?" Devon said, gnawing on a piece of crust.

Isaac wanted to laugh at the cuteness of his voice, knowing that Devon was trying to sound cool and grown-up, even though he still liked to play with toys.

"She is, indeed," Isaac replied, playing along. "As hot as those spicy French fries you love to eat."

Deshauna smiled sweetly. "Then you should date her, Dad," she advised.

Isaac could hear in her tone of voice that she was not concerned about his love life, but that dating Autumn might keep him out of her business for a while.

He pushed his chair back and stood. "Sorry to disappoint you guys, but I don't date women I work with."

Devon slurped down the rest of his soda. "Why not?"

"The girl would have to quit when you broke up with her, right, Dad?" his sister piped up in a firm voice, drawing Devon's immediate attention. "And I mean, you would never do that and they would never fire you because you make too much money for them, right?"

Isaac leaned his knuckles on the table and looked at his children. He recognized the worried expressions on their faces as fear. No matter how many times he'd told them they were safe, that they wouldn't be thrown out onto the streets, deep down they still didn't believe him. He'd only adopted them a few months ago and he knew it took time to build trust, but it still hurt him to the core.

"Listen. My job is very stable and I would never, ever do anything to jeopardize it, okay?"

Both children looked relieved and Isaac decided to give them some free time before they started their homework.

When they were gone, he washed the dishes and cleaned off the table, his thoughts turning to the workday.

In all his meetings, where the attendees thought

they'd had his complete attention, he'd only been there in body. His mind had been on Autumn. His penis hardened and grew against the counter just thinking about her full lips, gorgeous hair and curvy breasts.

Just a touch. Just a taste. That's all he wanted.

But he knew he was lying to himself. Because if he was lucky enough or stupid enough to try anything with Autumn, he'd only want more.

When the kitchen was clean, he grabbed his backpack and checked his watch as he walked into his study, pleased to see that he still had time to decompress and come up with a reason Sterling needed to assign someone else to work on the Witterman pitch with Autumn.

Thank goodness, his children had made him come to his senses, he thought, before it was too late.

Chapter 5

At six-thirty the next morning, Autumn slipped a one-hundred-dollar bill into the doorman's hand, who tipped his hat and winked. The man had been true to his word, ringing her apartment when Isaac had gone for his daily jog, with no questions asked.

The brochure for The Staffordshire, home to some of New York City's wealthiest individuals, had boasted of the "utmost privacy afforded to its upscale residents." She got into the cab waiting at the curb and laughed.

They paid for secrecy and so did she.

Irony at its finest.

As the taxi wove down Broadway toward the Financial District, she sat back and yawned so loudly the cabbie gave her the evil eye in the rearview mirror. She'd reviewed files late into the night and wasn't used to so little sleep.

Autumn yawned again and rubbed her shoulders, wishing it was Isaac's hands trying to relieve the knots under her skin, instead of hers. But the ride was too bumpy and her hands were too weak, so she gave up. There'd be many more late nights, so she could probably justify hiring a masseur. Preferably a male with abs so tight she could bounce a quarter off them.

Twenty minutes later, she arrived at the Paxton Building. She stopped in the ground floor café for a steaming cup of green tea and made her way to her office, hoping that Felicia wasn't an early bird like her.

Autumn hung up her coat, replaced the files in the box and chose a new stack. She piled them on her desk and powered up her computer, with the plan to review some now so she wouldn't have such a big stack to take home later. It was just after seven so it should be quiet for a while, as the official work day didn't begin until eight o'clock.

She swiveled her chair toward the window to enjoy the view and sip her tea until her computer finished whirring.

The next thing she knew, there was a knock at the door and she woke with a start, realizing that she'd dozed off for a few minutes. Her face reddened with embarrassment and she quickly turned around just before Isaac cracked open the door.

"Good morning." He popped his head into the room. "Mind if I come in?"

At the sound of his voice, her heart beat rapidly, quickly chasing away any lingering drowsiness.

Without waiting for her answer, he left the door open and straddled one of the chairs in front of her desk.

Isaac glanced at her desk. "Looks like you're already pretty busy," he commented. "What time did you get in today?" Autumn's throat went dry. Had the doorman told him about their little deal?

"Just after seven, why?" she answered, pressing a button to wake up the computer. It had gone to sleep, just like her.

He whistled low. "You keep doing that and you're going to make me look bad."

He gave her a wide smile, his teeth as white as the snow that fell outside her office window, and she knew he was joking.

"I'd have to get here at midnight to make you look bad," she teased back.

His languorous smile was an acknowledgment that he knew he looked good, and he was glad that she noticed.

And, my oh my, did she ever.

He wore no suit jacket, so she had a better view of the way his crisp white shirt stretched over his expansive chest. Although he wore an undershirt, she thought she could still see the barest hint of his nipples through the fabric. And his gray tie? Well, that was like a one-way road to pleasure that ended at his belt buckle.

Isaac Mason was looking fine enough that morning to make her want to shut the office door and slam down his trousers.

There were a lot more interesting ways to conduct an investigation than reading a bunch of files.

The picture in her mind was so vivid her loins trembled and she crossed her legs. The friction it caused between her thighs made her stifle a low moan, which she covered up with a series of coughs.

Isaac tipped his chair against the desk. "Are you okay?" He grabbed the cup of tea from her desk and shoved it at her. "Here, drink this."

She nodded, took a sip and almost gagged. "Ugh. Cold!"

The temperature of the liquid doused the flame of desire in her body like a cold shower.

He took it from her hand. "Do you want me to get you another one?"

She stared at him with surprise. "Sure, that would be great. Green tea, no sugar."

"Be right back," Isaac said, before leaping off the chair and heading out of the office.

Autumn shoved the files into a drawer and took out a mirror, praying she didn't have a line of dried drool on her face. Everything was clear, thank goodness, and she carefully reapplied a light coat of lipstick to freshen up. Due to allergies, she never wore much makeup, so her morning routine was easy, especially since there wasn't a man around to hog the bathroom.

She opened up her email and saw that she had a request from Isaac for an eight-o'clock meeting this morning. It had been sent late last night and marked urgent. She had accepted it to clear the message from her inbox when Isaac stepped back into the room.

"Thanks," she said, taking the cup from Isaac. "I just accepted the meeting request you sent and, like magic, you're here!"

She smiled brightly, but Isaac did not return her smile. Instead, he stood in front of her desk, looking uncomfortable. "Listen, the reason I wanted to meet with you this morning is because I'm going to request that Sterling assign someone else to work with you on the Witterman pitch."

Her heart sank. What had gone wrong? Had Sterling decided to pull the investigation for some reason?

Wait a second, she quickly told herself. Isaac just said that he was going to request to be taken off the project. Nothing had been done yet. She still had time to not only find out why Isaac was so skittish but change his mind, as well.

She walked over to the door and leaned against it to shut it. The desire that had ebbed flamed once again as his eyes roamed up her legs all the way to her face like a white-hot spotlight. She curled her toes in her shoes, basking in his admiration, not willing to ignore it, if only for a moment.

Walking toward him, she decided to sit across from him in the other chair, instead of at her desk. She wanted nothing between them that could impede communication. Hopefully, their discussion would lead to information that would help her understand him better. Deep down, she knew that her need to know everything about Isaac Mason had nothing to do with the case and everything to do with her heart.

Crossing her legs, she gestured to the chair.

"Why don't you sit down and relax."

Isaac hesitated for a second, then straddled the chair as he'd done before.

"Tell me what's going on, Isaac. Is it my background that bothers you? I know I've job-hopped a lot, but I promise I'm not going to jump ship on you. I really think Paxton is good fit for me career-wise."

He regarded her for a minute, then shook his head.

"It's not you, it's me."

She wanted to laugh out loud. How many times had she heard that line before, but hearing it on the job was a first.

"What do you mean?" she asked. "Has something happened?"

"Yeah," he replied. His eyes caught hers, dropped down to her lips, and suddenly she knew.

She put her fingers to her mouth in shock.

"Don't do that," he commanded. "It only makes me want to kiss you more."

He reached for her fingers and clasped them in his hand, and it was warm and strong and rough all at the same time. And if their chairs had wheels, she was sure he'd roll her to him, bringing her close enough to feel the heat from his skin.

But both old-fashioned chairs stayed stolidly on the ground, while her heart pumped so hard that she was sure he could see it right through her sweater.

"I'm more attracted to you than I have a right to be," Isaac admitted, grasping her hand even tighter. "In fact, you're all I've thought about for the last twenty-four hours."

Autumn hitched in a breath at the combination of desire and worry in his voice. She opened her mouth to speak, to tell him that she'd thought of him, too, but she could only tremble.

"That's why I have to ask Sterling to reassign someone else for this pitch."

Isaac leaned in close and ever so slowly brushed his lips along the ridge of her knuckles, daring her with his eyes not to react, not to feel the complexity within that simple caress.

She closed her eyes and tried not to succumb to the river of tingles he was invoking along her skin. But Isaac's lips were so firm, yet gentle and insistent, as they dwelled in those moments upon a part of her hand that she rarely noticed but would never dismiss again.

Autumn heard herself moan softly and it was like a wake-up call she wished she never had. What was wrong with her? She was supposed to be investigating this man, not wanting him to make love to her. She sat back suddenly and Isaac dropped her hand.

"I'm sorry, I—" she sputtered, her head felt as if it was on planet WTF Just Happened.

"Did you enjoy that?" he asked, his tone hopeful, without a touch of ego. "I just had to touch you, and I wanted you to like it. Did you?"

She felt herself nodding. *Oh yes, very much,* she wanted to say, *but the knuckles on my other hand are jealous, can you take care of them, too?*

But instead, she grabbed her tea and shut up. She didn't want to give him any ideas that she hoped he'd take her up on.

"Good."

His smile was kind and it made her insides swoon even more. Then his voice dropped to nearly a whisper.

"Because it can never happen again."

Autumn stood up without looking at him and walked around the desk to the window. She knew what he said was true, but she didn't want to hear him say the words, didn't want to see the need disappear from his eyes.

There was something about a man wanting a woman, a man wanting her, that made a normal, dreary January day seem like summer was right around the corner. And maybe, just maybe, love was there, too.

She could feel his eyes on her back as she pressed her hands against the cold glass. The snow had ceased, leaving only droplets of water that showed a world upside-down.

How could she have lost control so easily?

She'd never given up on an investigation and she wasn't going to start now, no matter the outcome.

Autumn swiveled on her heel and faced him. "You're absolutely right, Isaac, and I agree with your recommendation. I think it will be better for both of us. When are you going to talk with Sterling?"

Isaac stared at her as if he was shocked by her sudden turnaround. He dug his phone out of his pocket and stood.

"In about fifteen minutes."

"Okay. Let me know what happens," she replied, indicating the door with her chin.

He took the hint a few seconds later.

"Guess I'll be having dinner with someone else tonight," she added with a wry smile, and from the look on his face before he shut the door, he didn't like the thought of that at all.

Autumn sank into her office chair and covered her face with her hands. She picked up the phone, with the intent of calling Sterling to warn and advise him how to handle the conversation with Isaac so he wouldn't accidentally blow her cover. The man seemed a bit overwrought, but she decided against it.

Although she didn't want Isaac to leave, the more normal things appeared to him, the better. Otherwise, if she pushed to remain on the Witterman project with him, she feared he might become suspicious. Or worse, he might figure out that she wanted him as much as he wanted her.

Thirty minutes later, she was logged in to the Paxton network, reviewing some of Isaac's most recent deals, when she saw an email notification pop up.

Guess what? You ARE having dinner with me tonight. Meet me at La Vie at 5:30.
—Isaac

She closed the email and smiled. The plan was still intact.

Attaboy, Sterling.

Isaac drummed his fingers on the table. Autumn was fifteen minutes late, and he was getting antsy. Not only did he want to see her, but he didn't have much time.

Luckily, Devon and Deshauna were both at a friend's house for dinner, but they would be home soon and he wanted to be there before they arrived.

He sat back and toyed with his drink, a club soda for now, wondering if Autumn had received his email. She hadn't replied; nor had she spoken to him again all day, even though he was in his office, with the door open for most of it. Her door had remained closed, making him wish he had X-ray vision so he could see what she was doing.

He picked up his phone and shook his head at the irony.

Autumn was the first woman in a long time that he was interested in calling, yet he'd forgotten to get her personal cell number. That was a sure sign he'd lost his touch since becoming a father. But he had no regrets about adopting his children. He wanted to give them the life he never had growing up. He just hoped Devon and Deshauna would grow to love him as much as he loved them.

Isaac scrolled through photos of his kids and was so engrossed that he didn't see that Autumn had approached the table.

She cleared her throat and he quickly slid his phone back into his pocket. Perhaps one day he could tell her about his children, but not now.

He stood up, his fingers grazing her soft red sweater as he helped her out of her coat. She shivered, but he wasn't sure if it was from his touch or from the wintery bluster from which she'd just escaped.

A waiter approached to take their drink order.

"Is a bottle of red okay with you? It'll go great with that sweater."

Autumn's smile alone made her worth the wait.

She nodded and settled back in her chair. "So, I take it that the reason I'm here is because the meeting with Sterling did not go well."

Isaac blew out a breath. "No, it didn't. I think he would have thrown me out of his office if he could."

"Wow," Autumn said, shaking her head. "Has he always been uptight?"

"Yes, but it's never been this bad," he admitted. "But I bet having Felicia for a daughter doesn't help."

Autumn tried to stifle a giggle and failed. "That's mean. And I guess since it's only my second day at Paxton I shouldn't agree with you, but I think you might be right.

"I probably have no right to ask you this," Autumn said, tilting her head. "But is there anything going on with you and Felicia?"

Isaac almost choked on his wine. "No, nothing," he lied, now sorry he'd brought up her name in the conversation. Lately, he'd started to believe that Felicia was the one turning everyone against him at Paxton, including Sterling. He just didn't have any proof.

Autumn's eyes seemed to twinkle with some secret knowledge, and it made him nervous.

"Why, did she say something to you?"

She took a sip and shrugged. "Not particularly."

He set his wineglass on the table and decided that Autumn was just being coy.

Perhaps, instead of having information, she was digging for some. Maybe because she was interested in whether he was available or not. If she was, then it would be more difficult than ever to work with her. Feelings would start to develop on his part, and then what would he do? What could he do but break her heart?

There was only one way to find out. Maybe it was time to take a risk on more than the stock market. Maybe now was the time to take a risk on Autumn.

"You look beautiful tonight," he ventured.

One look at her face told Isaac she was not fooled. "Thank you, but you're changing the subject," she said drily. "Besides, I'm wearing the same thing I wore today."

"I know and I wanted to tell you earlier, but you had your door closed all day, for one."

"And the other?"

"The office wasn't the appropriate time or place."

She smiled and glanced around. "And this is?"

"Maybe," he replied nonchalantly. "It depends on how you feel about me."

She didn't speak for a while, only sipped her wine, and he began to feel like a fool for putting himself out there.

She set her wineglass down. "Listen, we should probably talk about the pitch, before we say or do things we really don't mean."

Now he really felt like a fool. He was thankful that she was acting as if she hadn't just dealt his ego a huge blow. It made it easier to shrug off her reaction as if he didn't care.

"Sure, but let's order some food first. I'm starved."

Autumn perused the menu. "I'm not really hungry, but I could go for some appetizers."

They ordered Thai scallops on a bed of mixed greens and fried tofu with homemade peach chutney.

Autumn opened up her bag and pulled out her tablet. "Let me share what I've learned so far. I've actually started a rough draft of the presentation."

He nodded his approval. "You're very proactive. That's one of the many things I like about you."

"Isaac. We're supposed to be talking about the pitch," she replied with the barest of smiles, and he could tell she was trying not to look pleased.

He grinned. "What? There's nothing in the Paxton handbook that says I can't compliment a coworker."

"I haven't read it so I'll have to trust you on that one." Autumn laughed. "Anyway, I took a look at the diamond market and I think it may be a good opportunity for Eleanor."

Isaac rubbed at his jaw. "Hmm. That's great, because when I suggested it, I was only kidding."

She put one hand on her hip. "*Now* you tell me?" she said, putting her hand on her hip. "I've spent hours researching."

He held up his hands. "Sorry, okay? Just let me know what you've found out."

Autumn docked the tablet and pulled up the presentation.

"Diamonds really have been the investor's best friend." She pointed to a graph. "They've outperformed equities since 2000. Plus, there are some new funds cropping up that could provide a way to invest without going direct to the wholesaler."

Isaac folded his arms across his chest and leaned forward. "Interesting. What else do you have?"

Autumn swiped her finger across the screen to advance to another slide. "Despite Eleanor's aversion to technology, I think investment in that sector is still a smart move. Plus, anything that involves green technology, such as hydroelectric engineering, is really hot right now."

The only hot thing he cared about was Autumn. But she made it clear for a second time that she wasn't interested.

Isaac leaned back in his chair. "This is a good start and we have a lot more work to do, but I like what I'm hearing. Go ahead and flesh out your recommendations. I'll need a complete analysis of each one, plus projections on how they'll perform over the next two, five and ten years."

He thought a moment. "I know a few people we can get in touch with to learn more about green technology, so you can put together a brief, but as for the diamond sector, you're on your own."

The food arrived, so Autumn powered off her tablet and stowed it in her bag.

"That's fine. I can do all that," she said, unfolding her napkin. "But I have one question."

"What's that?" he asked, licking his lips in anticipation of eating. Once he got some food into his stomach, maybe Autumn's rejection wouldn't hurt so much.

"How are you going to handle your attraction to me?"

Damn, but she was bold.

"I don't know. Take a cold shower twice a day." He shrugged, putting a forkful of scallops to his mouth.

He chewed and swallowed and paused. "Or maybe I'll just imagine you as a frog."

Autumn looked up from her plate and gasped. "Why a frog?"

"So I can kiss you and turn you into a princess."

She rolled her eyes, but he could see the smile she tried to hide, and he realized she enjoyed their ease at flirting as much as he did.

Isaac checked the time on his phone and reeled backward with surprise. It was getting late, if one considered six-thirty late, and he had missed a text from Deshauna that they would be home soon. He ran his hand over his head, worried that they'd get there before he did.

"Listen. Something's come up and I have to go."

He heard the tone of his voice and knew his excuse was lame, but it couldn't be helped.

Autumn put down her fork, her brow knit together with concern. "Is there anything wrong?"

"No, there's just somewhere I have to be soon." He reached for her hand and motioned to the waiter for the check. "I'm sorry to cut our evening short." He looked down at her still-full plate. "You barely got to eat."

Autumn pushed the food away. "It's okay. I've actually got somewhere I need to be, as well."

Now it was his turn to wonder if she was available or in a relationship, but he didn't dare ask.

He helped Autumn on with her coat and his fingers brushed her soft curls. He only had a short time left with her and he wanted to make the most of it. So he put a hundred dollar bill under his wineglass, knowing it would more than cover the check.

They made their way through the now-crowded restaurant to the entrance and saw that the snow had picked up considerably.

Isaac put his hand on Autumn's arm as she slipped on some gloves. "Where are you headed? It may be hard to get a cab now, especially in this weather. We can share one."

She finished wrapping her scarf around her neck and hesitated, as if she were considering the idea. "I'm going downtown, how about you?"

He shook his head, hoping the restaurant's dim lighting hid the disappointment in his eyes. "Uptown. Let's walk one block over to a side street—it may be easier to get a cab there."

She nodded in agreement and they both took deep breaths before Isaac opened the door.

The sidewalks were slick with ice and snow, but thankfully the wind was calm. Isaac immediately offered Autumn his arm to hold on to, but she refused and stuck her hands in her pockets. He wondered if she was upset about something. It was dark and snow was steadily falling, so it was hard to see her face.

A few yards later, she slipped rounding the corner. He grabbed on to her hand just in time, almost hitting the ground himself. This time when he tried to pull away, she didn't let go.

They were about halfway up the block when Isaac

spotted a place where they could wait for a cab without getting wetter than they already were.

He tightened his grip on Autumn's hand and pulled her into the alcove of The Rose Garden florist shop. A sign on the door read Closed Until Further Notice. He guessed the owners wouldn't mind if they loitered there awhile.

Isaac kept his back to the wall, positioning Autumn right in front of him to try to shield her from the cold as much as he could. He didn't need a thermometer to know that it was at or below freezing outside. Although they'd only been outside a few minutes, their coats and hair already had a light dusting of snow.

"I've got a perfect view of the street here, so I can watch for a cab and keep you out of this nasty weather."

"Thanks," she said in a jittery voice. "I'm freezing."

She started to shake her head side to side, but he reached out and cupped her face in his hands.

"Don't do that," he said. "All those snowflakes caught in your curls make you look like a princess."

She lifted her chin, the tiny droplets of melting snow on her face seemed to glisten.

"How can this frog be a princess when she's never been kissed?"

That was all Isaac needed to hear.

He sucked in a breath, not giving his mind time to think or to worry or to even care about tomorrow.

"I can take care of that right now," he whispered.

He closed his eyes and slowly guided her face to his, relying on sense rather than sight to that first taste he knew he would never forget.

And Autumn did not disappoint. Her lips were soft and warm and surprisingly insistent upon his, and in the haze of their kisses, he felt her fingers on his chest, unbuttoning his coat. The shocking blast of cold made him lift his lips from hers. He gasped aloud, but it was quickly silenced by the mellow warmth of her body against his chest. He bit his lip, going rock hard as she snuggled against him.

His back muscles tensed under her roaming hands, the pleasure of her touch unfamiliar, and her fingers kneaded his flesh as if seeking answers. They stumbled against the alcove wall and he wove his hands in her hair, their breath intermingling in the cold air, eyes transfixed on each other. In their gaze, a message of truth. They knew what they both wanted, but there wasn't much time.

Then his tongue met flesh again, seared the inside of her mouth, and their lips moved together. They kissed and kissed, not devouring but savoring like a fine wine, not wanting it to end. This moment was as fragile as the snowflakes that swirled around them.

He felt her breasts rub against his chest, flaring his passions, and he yearned to touch them, but he didn't want to open her coat and have her get cold.

Angling his hands under her coat and beneath her skirt, he molded his hands around her buttocks. His tongue licked the corners of her mouth almost delicately before taking a surprise plunge into her mouth. At the same time, he cupped her round behind, lifting her up and securing her firmly against him.

With a low moan into his mouth, she wrapped her

legs around his waist and his fingers sank into her soft flesh. Her heat fanned invitingly against his trousers; his constrained penis thumped in the hopes that she'd let him in.

The sound of her panty hose ripping pushed him over the edge and he broke the kiss. Staring into her eyes, his torso involuntarily started to slowly pulse against her and into that coven of heat, as if there were no fabric there at all.

His pace steadily increased and she tightened her grip around his waist and found his lips again, an anchor point on which to suck and hold. With every hard and desperate grind of their bodies, she held on.

Oh, how she held on.

Isaac threw his head back against the wall, nearly losing his senses of time and place when out of the corner of his eye he saw a cab ambling down the road.

"Damn," he muttered, releasing her.

He ran out to the curb, almost slipping on the ice, lifted his right hand and waved.

"Taxi!" he shouted, breathing heavy, the flaps of his coat wide open.

He didn't know whether to be happy or mad when the cabbie pulled over.

Isaac turned just in time to see Autumn smooth her hand over her coat. She picked up her tote bag and gingerly stepped onto the sidewalk. When she reached the cab, her breathing was steady.

"Are you okay?" he asked, touching her arm.

Autumn nodded but didn't meet his eyes as he opened the door and she stepped into the taxi. A moment later, she was gone. As he trudged up the road to the subway, Isaac's heart squeezed in his chest, wondering how he was going to face her in the morning.

Chapter 6

Autumn scowled at the stack of files on her desk. She hadn't wanted to lug them to the restaurant last night, possibly inviting questions from Isaac, so she had double the number to go through today.

Thank God, it was Friday. She couldn't wait to go home, open up a bottle of wine and not think about paperwork or the Paxton investigation for a while.

But she knew she wouldn't be able to forget about last night.

She rose and closed the blinds against the sunlight streaming through the windows. When she turned, she saw that Isaac's door was still closed, his office dark. It was after ten in the morning.

The doorman hadn't called this morning, and when

she inquired why, he told her that Isaac hadn't gone out for his run, so there was no reason to contact her.

She almost asked him to go up and check on him, to see if he was there, but she didn't want the man to be more suspicious than he probably was. Free money only worked for a while. Eventually he would start to ask her questions or, worse, tell Isaac that she was spying on him.

Autumn sat back at her desk and wrung her hands.

Where was he? She couldn't help feeling something bad had happened to him.

She felt a pang of guilt remembering how he'd allowed her to take the first taxi. It was a sweet, chivalrous gesture, because she knew he had somewhere else to go, someone else waiting for him to arrive. When she looked back, he had already turned and was walking away, and there were no more cabs coming down the street.

Had he even made it home last night?

Calm down, she told herself. There must be a logical explanation for his absence. Perhaps he had a morning meeting with a client. She only hoped he wasn't avoiding her, because she needed to talk to him about last night.

In the heat of the moment, they'd both forgotten about the real purpose of working together, which was to insure Eleanor Witterman became Paxton's newest client.

And of course, while Isaac was kissing her senseless, the last thing on her mind was the investigation.

Sterling wouldn't be too happy if he knew either. In fact, he'd probably fire both of them.

Autumn twisted a curl around her finger.

"That can't happen," she said aloud.

Felicia suddenly appeared in the doorway. "What can't happen?" She stepped into the room and glanced around. "Who are you talking to?"

Autumn's stomach clenched. "Myself. Haven't you ever done that?"

"What? Talked to myself?" Felicia shook her head. "People might think I'm crazy."

"Not if you're telling the truth," Autumn replied.

Felicia's eyes narrowed. "Exactly what are you implying?"

"Nothing," Autumn replied. "I'm only saying that talking to yourself doesn't mean you're crazy."

Felicia looked Autumn up and down. "Humph," she snapped. "That's your opinion."

If Autumn wasn't the confident woman that she was, she might have felt like an ant under Felicia's scrutiny. However, she knew that the woman had something to hide and she was determined to get past her obnoxious attitude to the facts.

Autumn folded her hands on her desk. "How can I help you? I'm sure you didn't stop by my office for idle chitchat."

"Good. You are starting to get to know me and how I work. I do have a purpose for being here."

Felicia dropped her hands, slowly sat down and crossed her legs, like a beauty-pageant wannabe practicing how to be graceful.

"I understand you are working with Isaac on the Witterman pitch."

"That's correct. In fact, we had a dinner meeting last night to talk strategy."

Felicia's eyes darkened suspiciously. "Why dinner? You couldn't meet here at the office?"

"No, Isaac was in meetings all day and that was the only time he could get together."

"Well!" she exclaimed. "Sounds like someone needs a seminar on time management!"

"I'd love one, but I don't have time for it," Autumn replied with a giggle.

But Felicia wasn't smiling and Autumn's face burned with embarrassment.

She cleared her throat. "So what about the project?"

Felicia moved her chair closer to the desk. "I want you to keep a very close eye on Isaac," she revealed. Her voice dropped down to almost a whisper. "There has been some talk among the employees and something isn't right."

Autumn held back a laugh. She couldn't believe her ears. Felicia actually wanted her to spy on Isaac.

"But you're the director of human resources. Why not just come out and ask him yourself?"

"Because he reports to my father, that's why, who adores him and thinks the world of him. He'd be really upset if I did anything like that."

"I see. Well, I'm not sure if I'm comfortable with this. I mean, I just started at Paxton. What possible repercussions can I expect to my career here?"

Felicia sat back, her eyes widening. "Why, absolutely

none at all," she insisted, sounding appalled at the question. "You have nothing to worry about. All you need to do is watch for anything improper that you find that could hurt the company, and report it to me first, not my father."

Autumn hesitated. Had Sterling told Felicia that she was really a private investigator? Was that what this was all about?

"I don't know about this. I'm an analyst, not a private eye."

Felicia exhaled impatiently. "I know that, Autumn. That's why you're perfect. You can actually discover any wrongdoing."

Autumn blew out a breath, inwardly relieved that her cover seemed to be still intact. "And you expect me to go behind your father's back with any information and come straight to you."

Felicia nodded. "Maybe you won't find anything. But if you do, I want to know about it first."

She pointed her finger at Autumn. "One more thing. If you try to hide anything you find out, you'll get a chance to see firsthand just how brutal life at Paxton can really be."

When Felicia left, Autumn wanted to laugh at her attempt to frighten her, but instead she threaded her hands through her curls. Now she was working for Sterling and Felicia against Isaac, and neither of them knew about the other.

Isaac clutched the paper bag that held his deli sandwich and a bag of salt-and-vinegar chips that he always ate when he was having a particularly stressful day and strode into the Paxton Building.

It was nearly one o'clock and his stomach was grumbling as if it hadn't had food to churn in weeks. After a morning chock-full of off-site meetings, all he wanted to do was eat and catch up on email.

Riding up in the elevator, a part of him hoped Autumn was still at lunch. Isaac didn't want to avoid her, not that he could anyway. Quite the contrary. He just needed more time to figure out how to handle what could turn out to be an uncomfortable situation.

If she wanted an explanation of why he kissed her, he couldn't give her one. If she wanted an apology, he couldn't give her that either. He sure as hell wasn't sorry he kissed her. He was only sorry that their kiss had to end so abruptly.

On the executive floor, he walked down the hallway to his office a little slower than usual and then, deciding he was acting silly, resumed his normal pace.

Autumn's door was open, but from his vantage point he couldn't tell if she was there. But he knew that she could see him through the little glass window. That's how Felicia had spied on him, before she'd tried to seduce him just weeks earlier.

Isaac clenched his jaw in disgust at the memory. How long had Felicia been watching him?

He dug his key out of his pocket and took a deep breath to relax, thankful that the room where Felicia had tried to destroy him was now occupied by a woman from which he welcomed seduction.

"Hey, stranger," she called out. "Are you okay?"

Isaac's heart leaped in surprise. Instead of being upset, her cheerful voice sounded like she was glad he was there.

"Yeah," he grunted, fumbling with the keys. "Give me a second to unload this stuff."

Opening the door, he flipped on the light, hung up his coat and carefully put his lunch and laptop bag on his desk. Then he walked into Autumn's office, hesitating only a moment before shutting the door. Whatever was about to transpire between them, he didn't want anyone to hear or see. As far as anyone knew, they were simply discussing business.

Isaac pulled out the chair in front of her desk and sat down. His eyes traced her lips as she wiped her mouth.

"Tough morning?" she asked, replacing the plastic top over a container of half-eaten salad.

"Tough clients," he said and sighed, stretching his legs out in front of him. "I think investment banking is the only business in the world where the customer isn't always right, but that doesn't make telling them when they're wrong any easier."

Autumn poked a straw into a bottle of mineral water and nodded. "But all is forgiven when the money starts rolling in, right?"

He shrugged. "So far I've been lucky."

Autumn stood and walked around the desk. She tossed the salad container into the trash and he watched as she slowly walked around the desk. Her pale pink suit wasn't skintight but was perfectly tailored to complement her hourglass shape.

She sat down opposite him. "What's the secret to your success?" she asked, crossing her legs.

For a split second, Isaac imagined her legs wide open, and only for him. He swallowed hard to rid his mind of the fantasy, knowing that she could only belong to him in his dreams.

"Intuition, I guess."

Her eyebrows knit together. "What do you mean?"

He settled back deeper in his chair, trying to put some imaginary distance between them. "Knowing when to push and knowing when to pull back."

Autumn exhaled. "Ah. Like when you kissed me." Her eyes flitted briefly to the door and back to him. "Somehow you knew I wanted you, too."

Her confession of lust baffled his mind, but his flesh knew exactly how to respond. He shifted in his seat and said nothing, wondering if she was trying to trick him.

He'd been burned once before in this very office.

Never again.

At his silence, she pursed her lips. "Didn't you?"

Her tone was so playful and teasing that he realized he wanted to explore the meaning behind her words almost as much as he wanted to explore her.

"I didn't know," he replied, shaking his head. "I took a chance."

Isaac dipped his eyes to the single pearl nestled at the base of her neck. Her modest blouse revealed nothing but the memory of her breasts against his body.

"I didn't want to stop. Is that wrong?"

She closed her eyes briefly. "No, but that taxi came along at just the right time."

He reached for her hand. "I wish it hadn't."

Gently, he lifted her hand to his mouth, bent his head and moved his lips across her knuckles.

She whooshed in a breath and her eyes flapped open. "Th-that taxi probably saved our careers."

Autumn pulled her hand out of his light grasp. She laughed nervously.

"Or at least mine," she continued. "I mean, what would people think? I've been here barely a week and I— They'll think I'm trying to make a play for you when all I wanted was—"

"To be kissed," Isaac cut in, realizing that what he thought was a deep attraction to him was nothing more than a spur-of-the-moment mistake.

She folded her hands in her lap as if to dissuade him from touching her. "You know when you haven't done something in a while and all of a sudden you get the opportunity?"

Her eyes danced with excitement, but not for him.

"Sure, when you're with someone you feel in your heart is safe, you just go for it," he replied.

Was that why he felt so comfortable with Autumn, because something about her felt safe to him?

Autumn blew out a breath. "I knew you'd understand. From what I've read about you, you're at the top of your career."

She stood, her pelvis close enough to reach. Close enough for him to pull up that skirt she was neatly smoothing and allow his hands—and his mouth—to mess it up again.

"You wouldn't risk it all for an office romance."

Oh, wouldn't I?

He rose carefully, hating that his flesh didn't get the memo that Autumn was off-limits. Still, he didn't bother to conceal the bulge in his pants. Let her see, and then imagine, what she was missing.

Isaac pushed the chair back with his heel, to allow plenty of space between them.

"You're right, Autumn. Why take a risk when you already know it will fail?"

Her head jerked back as if his words stung something deep inside her. Rather than ask if he'd hurt her, he simply headed to the door, not wanting to hear the answer.

Isaac turned back to see that she hadn't moved from where she'd been standing.

"But hey," he retorted, knowing he was trying to sound a lot more macho than he felt at the moment. "If you ever want to be kissed again, you know where I am."

He walked out hoping she'd take a risk and knowing, for both of their sakes, that she probably wouldn't.

Chapter 7

When Autumn left work that afternoon, Isaac's door was closed. She had no idea if he was in there or not, and she certainly wasn't going to knock. Not that he wanted to talk to her anyway.

After she'd rejected him earlier, Autumn realized she had two choices: solve the case or fall in love. She was being paid to find answers, not hop into bed with Isaac. Although the prospect of hot sex with one of NYC's wealthiest men was beyond thrilling, she had a feeling one night with him would never be enough.

A relationship, even a brief one, wouldn't be fair to either of them. Besides, she was far too much of a free spirit to be tied down, and she never knew where or when her next case would come along. There was something about digging into people's lives to find the truth that eased her loneliness.

Most of the time.

Once outside the Paxton Building, she adjusted her tote bag, heavy with files she needed to review over the weekend. The sooner she discovered something wrong, some kind of misdoing to pin on Isaac, the better. But so far, the only thing he was guilty of was turning her on.

The subway uptown, always unbearable, was even worse on a Friday afternoon, with everyone jostling to get wherever they were going. Her nerves were frazzled and her back ached, but not as much as her heart. She couldn't wait to get home, relax and try to forget about Isaac.

Autumn moved with the flow of humanity up the stairs onto Columbus Circle. Upon arriving at her apartment, she wanted to scream in frustration. One of the elevators was out of order and the other one was already filled to capacity with residents.

Not including the penthouse levels, there were over fifty floors in her building. Autumn adjusted her bag, leaned against the mirrored wall and groaned. It looked like she was going to be waiting awhile.

A few minutes later, two kids approached the elevators. One was a teenage girl who wore a smirk instead of a smile. The other was a boy who lagged slightly behind carrying two grocery bags. Autumn could tell by the strained look on his face that they were too heavy for him. Both children wore school uniforms and pricey designer coats, not with haughty confidence but as though their bodies didn't belong in them.

The boy frowned. "What's wrong with the elevator?"

"Can't you read, stupid?" The girl scowled, pointing the sign. "It says it's out of order."

"Signs can't talk," he retorted. "So who's the real dummy?"

The two started arguing and the decibels started elevating and Autumn wished she knew how to whistle through her fingers to get them to stop. But she didn't. Nor did she have any experience with children. However, she did watch reruns of *The Facts of Life.*

Autumn held up her hands as if she was directing traffic.

"Children, children," she intoned in her best impression of a housemother's voice. "Now if you will just quiet down, the elevator will be here shortly, and we can all go home."

Even though she left out the milk-and-cookies part, which she knew was the standard bribe, they shut their mouths and stared at her.

"I know another way up," the boy blurted out, looking over his shoulder. "The doorman is busy. Let's go."

He was either really convincing or Autumn was just tired of waiting, but she followed them around the corner and down a couple of hallways that she'd never seen before, until they stopped at an elevator she never knew existed.

"What's this? And yes, before you get smart, I know it's an elevator."

"It's for the penthouse apartments only," he explained. "We never use it. Our dad won't let us. He makes us ride in the regular elevators with everyone else."

His sister clucked her teeth. "That's because we are like everyone else."

"No, we're not. Not anymore," he insisted. "We're rich!"

Autumn blew out a breath. "Congratulations," she interjected, not wanting to get in the middle of another argument. "Now, if you guys will excuse me, I don't live in a penthouse, so I think I'll just go back and see if the regular elevators are working."

She turned to leave and she heard the rustling of plastic.

"Wait," the boy called out, looping both bags through one hand. "Why don't you come up with us? My sister is making dinner for my dad tonight. He can't cook and sometimes we get tired of ordering takeout."

The girl rolled her eyes at her brother. "What would Dad say if you invited a perfect stranger into his home?"

"It's our home now, too," the boy corrected. "And I think he'd thank us."

Autumn raised an eyebrow, intrigued. "Why's that?"

"Because you're really cute, and he's really lonely."

She smiled at the sincerity in the boy's voice. He seemed so eager to please, while his sister seemed the total opposite.

"Stop crushing on her," she ordered, obviously trying to embarrass him. "Dad doesn't need you to play matchmaker."

"Why not?" he objected. "I'm a lot safer than a dating website and I don't require a password."

Autumn burst out laughing. "Thank you for the invitation, but I really must be going."

The boy shrugged and pressed the elevator button. "Okay. But if you change your mind, my name is Devon and this is my sister, Deshauna. What's your name?"

"I'm Autumn. Pleased to meet you."

For once she was glad her hands were full, so she wouldn't have to shake hands. Children were walking playgrounds for germs and she didn't have the time to get sick right now. As if she ever did.

The elevator doors opened and the kids got in.

"Good luck with dinner and thanks again," Autumn said patiently. By the time she finally got up to her apartment, she'd need two glasses of wine instead of one.

The doors began to close. "He's a nice guy," Devon called out. "And his name is Isaac."

Autumn's heart took a nosedive and she stared at the elevator in shock.

And my cover is blown.

Isaac rolled down the window and leaned his head against the taxi's backseat. He could have taken the subway but just didn't want to deal with the hassle tonight. At least here he could be alone and have a chance to think before going home and dealing with whatever challenges his children had faced that day.

The icy air hit his nostrils as the cab sped down the street. He breathed in deeply, trying to clear his mind of the woman who had so easily lit a fire within his heart and—just as easily—doused it that very afternoon. No woman he'd actively pursued had ever rejected him before. Why had she?

Turning his head, he stared out of the window at the shops rolling by as they traveled down Fifth Avenue. The fancy storefronts, all lit up and glittering like diamonds, were filled with things most people couldn't afford. They say money can't buy love, but he sure as hell would pay just about anything to be with Autumn.

It hardly mattered anymore. All he had to do was get through the Witterman pitch and he wouldn't have to work with her again. She'd move down to the floor where all the other analysts were and he would rarely see her. The constant temptation to kiss her, to touch her, would hopefully go away. Still, if the ache in his chest and the bulge in his pants were any indication, he was starting to get the feeling that there was nothing as painful as letting something go before it even had a chance to begin.

When he arrived at his apartment building, he paid the cab fare and greeted the doorman, instructing him to have his dry cleaning picked up early the following morning.

As he rode the private elevator to his penthouse, his heart was heavy with regret for even thinking that he could have any kind of relationship with Autumn. When the doors opened, he palmed the lower half of his face in exasperation. For the first time ever, he'd actually forgotten to bring home dinner!

"Hey, guys, where do you want to go to eat tonight?" he called out.

He set his laptop bag down on the marble floor and

wrinkled his nose at the scent of steak wafting through the air. And it didn't smell burned.

"Surprise!" his children shouted as he walked into the kitchen.

Isaac was astonished at the sight of the round glass table, beautifully set for three with the china plates he'd bought years earlier thinking someday he'd use them, plus real, not plastic silverware. In the middle, a giant pitcher of lemonade with the actual lemons floating in it was surrounded by little votive candles.

He turned his attention to his two children. "What is this?"

"We made dinner," Devon said. "Steak and mashed potatoes with gravy. A real man's meal."

Deshauna rolled her eyes and nodded. "Yeah. Having takeout all the time gets old. So we decided to change things up a little bit." She bit her lip and then said, almost shyly, "Is it okay that we did all this?"

Isaac's heart melted and he moved to wrap them in a hug. "It's more than okay," he assured. "It's fantastic."

Ever since adopting Devon and Deshauna, he worried constantly that he wasn't doing enough. Being enough.

But maybe he was. Maybe the knowledge that he was there with them and for them forever was finally sinking in. Isaac wasn't going away or abandoning them. Maybe that was all his children needed to finally realize that he loved them.

They were no longer foster—they were family.

He hugged them tighter. "I know I'm new at this father thing, and that one of those cooking shows would never hire me, but I'm so happy you guys are mine."

"We are too, Dad," Devon said, his voice muffled against Isaac's shoulder. "But I've got to get the steaks now."

"And you're ruining my hair!" Deshauna shrieked.

"Okay. Okay," Isaac acquiesced, releasing them. "But be forewarned, if the meal is real good, I just might want to read you two a bedtime story."

Devon and Deshauna groaned and then got busy putting the food on the table while Isaac sat down. When everything was ready, he bowed his head and said grace, thanking God for his wonderful children. In his mind, he asked for strength where Autumn was concerned, grateful that thoughts of her were put on hold for now.

Isaac cut into his steak and took a bite. It was surprisingly flavorful. The mashed potatoes were light and fluffy, and the gravy had just enough of a savory kick that he poured even more on his plate.

"This is awesome. I guess all those hours watching food shows finally paid off!"

"I have another surprise for you, Dad," Devon said through a mouthful of food. "We found you a girl to date!"

Isaac stopped chewing. "Who?"

Devon slurped his lemonade and set his glass down. "Her name is Autumn and she's really hot."

"Gross," Deshauna huffed in disgust. They started to bicker back and forth, but Isaac barely heard a word.

Devon couldn't be talking about *his* Autumn. Could he?

"Oh, really?" Isaac put down his fork and peered at

his son. "And where did you meet this gorgeous creature?"

"Right here in our building. She lives here. Isn't that perfect?"

Yes. Perfect.

He cleared his throat, trying to buy time as both children looked at him expectantly. He had to play this right. Since he'd become a father, there hadn't been a woman in his life. Yes, he wanted one. He wanted Autumn. But he had to play this right.

"What did she say when you told her about me?"

"She didn't say anything," Deshauna piped up. "She just ran."

Isaac raised an eyebrow. Surely his daughter was exaggerating. "She ran?"

"Well, not exactly, but Devon invited her to dinner and she said no," Deshauna explained. "Then she ran."

"She had pretty hair, Dad. It was all curly."

"Her hair was all right," Deshauna stated with a hint of jealousy. "It looked frizzy to me."

"It sounds like she wasn't interested, kids. Thanks anyway. But you know there's a lesson in all this. If someone runs away from you, you should run, too."

Too bad he wasn't going to follow his own advice.

Instead, he was going to follow his heart.

Later that evening after Devon and Deshauna were in bed, Isaac took a long, hot shower. Afterward he pulled on a white T-shirt and a pair of comfortable sweats and slid into his well-worn leather slippers.

He took the private elevator downstairs to the lobby

and spoke to the doorman. After giving the man a large tip, he got on the regular elevator up to the forty-eighth floor. He only hesitated a second before knocking on the door of apartment 3G.

Autumn opened the door and nearly took his breath away. She was clad in an ivory robe that only accentuated her already-gorgeous skin tone. He could see a hint of pale yellow lace as she crossed her arms over her chest.

"Isaac!"

She actually seemed surprised to see him.

He leaned against the doorway. "You opened that door pretty quickly. I hope you looked through the peephole. We do live in New York and you never know what kind of crazy could be lurking in the hallways."

Her hair was bunched up into some kind of messy bun. She tucked an errant strand behind her ear. "Of course I did," she retorted, sounding irritated. "What are you doing here?"

"I live in this building. Why didn't you tell me you did, too?" he demanded, his voice echoing in the hallway. He knew he was being loud, but he couldn't help it. He was angry.

Autumn placed a finger to her lips. "Shh…do you know what time it is?"

"Yeah. It's way past time for you to tell me the truth, and I'm not leaving until you do."

Autumn stared at him a moment and then stepped aside. "Come in. But you can't stay long."

She closed the door, locked it and put her hands on

her hips. "What makes you think I knew you lived in the same building as me?"

Isaac opened his mouth to speak but then shut it to ponder her very logical question. He knew she had a good point. It was almost as if he was accusing her of lying to him, of hiding something. But why would she do that?

"Let me guess," Autumn continued quickly. "Your ego is so big that you thought I moved in here to try to meet the wealthiest bachelor in New York City. You probably think that's why I wanted to work at Paxton, to get close to you. Didn't you?"

"No. I—I thought…" He ran a hand over his head, feeling like a fool. "Listen, Autumn. I don't know what I was thinking."

When Autumn furrowed her brow and looked at him like he was crazy, suddenly he knew the reason he was acting like a paranoid fool.

"Ever since Felicia, I—" he blurted.

"Felicia?" Autumn interrupted. "What does she have to do with this?"

Isaac cursed inwardly for even saying that woman's name out loud. Even though he'd made it clear that he wasn't interested in her, she was still causing trouble for him. She was like a curse.

"I think we better talk," she acknowledged, gesturing toward the living room. "Please have a seat."

Although Isaac was sure nothing good could come from talking about Felicia, he nodded and followed her across the room.

As Autumn cleared stuff from the couch, he admired

the way her robe cleaved to her hips and draped over her round bottom.

She stacked a bunch of files on the floor next to her, sat down and crossed her legs.

Isaac sat down carefully as he was starting to get a little aroused at the sight of her bare feet. Her toenails were painted a light pink and were almost begging to be sucked.

He stared at her, almost not believing he was in the same room with her. It was so different from seeing her in the office. He liked it. The playing field was leveled.

Here he was just a man. And she was just a woman.

A woman he wanted to know and to savor, and maybe…to love.

She narrowed her eyes at him. "You're staring at me. What did I do now?"

He exhaled and shook his head. "Nothing. It's just that you're even more beautiful at eleven at night than you are at eleven in the morning."

She put her hands on her hips. "Are you saying I look bad in the morning?" she huffed, not noticing that her robe had fallen open just enough to reveal the lush curves hidden beneath lace.

"No!" Isaac reached for her hand. "I'm saying I could look at you twenty-four hours a day. Is that wrong?"

She ignored his hand and instead pulled her robe closed again so roughly that a few tendrils of hair escaped from her bun and skimmed her shoulders.

"You don't have to flatter me, Isaac."

"I can if it's true and if it will bring a smile back to your face," he said warmly.

"I'm sorry." She closed her eyes briefly, then opened them and scanned the room. "You caught me at a bad time and this place is a mess."

"Working on a Friday night? Even I don't do that!" he teased, pointing at the stack of paperwork on the floor.

"Have you looked at a calendar lately, Isaac? The Witterman pitch is a week from today. I thought it best to keep the momentum going on it."

Isaac knew the timeline was closing in on them, which was part of the reason he was glad Autumn lived in the same building. It would make working on the project all the easier, plus the added bonus that he could be alone with Autumn without anyone knowing.

The other reason was that he had to convince her to keep his children a secret.

"I'm sure Sterling would appreciate all your effort if he knew," Isaac said.

"Well, I don't plan on telling him. I don't think he's interested in the mechanics of how it's put together. All he cares about is the end result, and that's what I'm going to deliver."

Isaac leaned back against the cushions. "You're going to deliver?" he said, aghast. "Aren't I part of this team?"

Autumn pursed her lips. "Of course. I didn't mean to offend you." She glanced down at her lap. "But after our conversation this morning, I just thought—"

"That I didn't want to work with you because you rejected me?" he offered.

She looked up and nodded, and Isaac could tell she was embarrassed.

"And I thought you didn't want to work with me." Isaac smiled. "I guess we were both wrong."

Autumn smiled back. "You mentioned Felicia earlier. Where does she fit in all this?"

"She tried to seduce me a couple of months ago and I wasn't buying it. Besides, she's Sterling's daughter. If I were to get involved with her, I might as well kiss my career goodbye."

He sighed. "Anyway, ever since that happened, I feel that she's out to get me."

"I see. And do you have any proof of that?"

"No, not yet, but if she found out I have children, I know she would tell Sterling, and he would not be happy. He's not exactly pro-family. He feels that work should come first, no matter what."

"What made you decide to adopt?"

Isaac paused and heaved a deep sigh. Under Autumn's inquisitive gaze, it wasn't easy to hide. So he decided to take a risk.

"I grew up in a foster home. I know what it's like to be a slave to the system that is supposed to help you. I have money. I have a nice home and I sure have enough love to give. When I met Devon and Deshauna, I knew they needed me, and quite frankly, I needed them, too. I can't let anything break us apart."

Isaac flattened his palms together and realized they were slightly clammy. Embarrassed, he rubbed his hands together until they were dry, rather than wipe them on his clothes.

Autumn smiled and seemed not to notice his discomfort. “That’s a wonderful story. And it sounds like everything worked out.”

“It has so far, but sometimes I get a strange feeling that things are about to change.”

Autumn shook her head. “Is that why you haven’t told anyone?”

He nodded. “Yeah. Besides the fact that it’s just wrong to keep them a secret, I’m supposed to claim them for health insurance purposes. But I’m afraid that if Sterling finds out that I have other priorities besides making money for Paxton, I could lose my job and my chance at making partner.”

“That would never happen. You’re the most successful investment banker he has on staff.”

“Oh no? He and I haven’t exactly been on good terms lately. It wouldn’t be hard for him to pluck a new graduate from Harvard Business School and groom him, like he did me, twelve years ago.”

Isaac inched his body closer and reached for her hand again. “If I promise not to flatter you anymore, can you promise me that you won’t tell my secret?”

She looked down at his hand briefly and laughed. “What if I like it when you flatter me?”

“Then I will just have to find some other way to convince you to keep my secret.”

Autumn lifted her eyes and tilted her head. “Sounds intriguing.”

The seductive lilt in her voice put him at ease. He leaped from the couch and pulled her up with him.

She giggled a little. “What’s going on?”

“Come with me. I want to show you something.”

Isaac held her hand and walked over to the floor-to-ceiling window that spanned the length of the living room.

"Now look outside," he commanded. "We're forty-eight stories up. What do you see?"

"Central Park West," Autumn responded, confusion in her eyes. "What's this all about, Isaac?"

He applied gentle pressure on Autumn's shoulders to turn her toward the window again. Wrapping his arms around her waist, he pulled her close to him until her soft buttocks connected with his torso. When they rolled against the hard ridge of flesh beneath his sweatpants, he bit his lip to stop from groaning.

He traced his lips along one ear and she trembled in his arms. "You want to know what I see?"

At her nod, Isaac placed his cheek next to hers.

"I see a city with a million secrets."

He moved his lips along the velvety-smooth skin of her jawline. "What's one more?"

She hitched in a breath as Isaac quickly untied the belt of her robe and slid it from her shoulders. The light swoosh as the garment fell to the floor was the only sound in the room.

Isaac grew even harder at the sight of the thin ribbon of lace covering her otherwise bare shoulders and the deep vee of skin on her back.

She was still facing the window as he kicked off his shoes and clasped his hands around her waist. At night, he wore no underwear under his cotton sweats so there was no mistaking his physical excitement, both by feel and by sight. When she wriggled her bottom against him suggestively and gasped, he knew she felt his need for her.

He pulled her even closer to him and now he freely groaned aloud, fighting the urge to bend her at the waist and make her his, right now. He wanted to go slow, but she had made him so hard.

Struggling to maintain control, Isaac decided he would explore her by touch first. He flattened his palms on her abdomen. It was taut and flat, just the way he liked it. He spread his long fingers wide until both hands nearly covered her middle.

As he scaled his hands down even lower, she moaned deeply, the vibrations rolling from her body to his, and his fingertips stopped their journey a few inches below her belly button.

Isaac patted the small mound of hair that tantalized him beneath her nightgown. The treasure of this woman would be his and his alone.

"Are you wet for me yet, baby?"

With a nod, Autumn whimpered and he reversed his movements, denying both of them. Slowly he trailed his hands skyward along her body until they enclosed her breasts, still trapped beneath the silky fabric. He didn't even have to look at them to know they were beautiful, because they felt beautiful, so large and full in his palms, complete with nipples as hard as pegs.

Isaac licked his lips at his discovery and circled each tip with the pad of his thumb, breathing hard as the surrounding areola puckered immediately at his light touch.

"Oh," Autumn cried out. She raised her arms above

her head and looped them around his neck, giving him easier access.

He bent his head and planted featherlight kisses down her neck as he massaged her breasts until she arched her back away from him and thrust her nipples into the air.

Still standing behind her, Isaac lifted her nightgown to her waist. He slid the index finger of his left hand down the cleft of her buttocks and then, reaching around her waist, he slid the fingers of his right hand between her legs. She was slick and hot and ready.

My God, he thought, thumping his penis gently against her soft ass, she's so wet, so wet.

She dropped her arms from his neck and moaned, and he used that opportunity to remove the nightgown. Tossing it behind him, he moved in front of her, watching her eyes move down his body and widen at the sight of his penis tenting forth in his pants.

Autumn, her eyes glowing in the dim light, was now naked before him, and his mouth watered at the sight of her luscious body and all the curves and the shadows and the secret places he'd yet to explore.

The fact that they stood before windows that spanned the entire length of the room added to the excitement of the moment for both of them.

Autumn reached for him, touching the tip of his flesh jutting under his sweats, and that was enough for him to cave.

Isaac pulled her into his arms and kissed her deeply, and his heart pounded when her tongue slipped into his mouth first. He allowed her to take the lead for a while as she threaded her hands through his hair and kissed him with a fervor that left him gasping for breath.

When he broke away, her eyes were ablaze with the kind of heat that he knew he would always strive to attain.

Grasping her by the waist with both hands, Isaac bent his head to her breast. He flicked his tongue at one nipple, bouncing the stiff peak between his lips before launching into a full-on suck that had Autumn thrashing about in his arms.

She held on to his head as he traced his hands from her waist to her ass. He held on, wedging his mouth and tongue underneath her heavy breasts, before planting a soft kiss on her navel. Moving his hands to her slick inner thighs, which were quivering from his touch, he knew it was time.

Isaac sank to his knees on the carpet and buried his face in the heat of Autumn's wiry curls, inhaling her earthy scent. Carefully, he spread her moist outer lips with his fingers until he exposed the sensitive core of her desire.

Licking slowly, his tongue discovered every juicy curve and fleshy mound, while she writhed and moaned and at times cried out, bending and succumbing to the most secret of pleasures.

And at that moment, neither cared about the aftermath of their passion. It was hidden in the subtle glow of streetlights, the seedy darkness of alleyways, the pulsing music of an after-hours club and the tangled sheets of a lover's bed.

Chapter 8

Autumn awoke the next morning so drowsy she couldn't even remember how she'd got into bed. Then her thighs began to tingle and the memories came flooding back. Erotic ones that made her burrow under her covers and wish the pleasure never had to end.

Isaac.

What that man could do with his lips, his tongue and his mouth should be illegal.

Even though she was a private investigator, after last night, she'd break every law in the book to feel that way again.

She yawned, and the fantasy was broken as she realized how close she'd come last night to revealing the truth about herself.

When she'd met his kids, she was sure her cover

was blown and that Isaac would somehow know why she was really at Paxton. But as soon as he appeared at her apartment, she knew that, logically, there was no way he could know. Her assumption had been the result of panic.

Thank goodness she'd realized that in time; otherwise, she might not have had the fortune of a night she knew she'd never forget.

It was clear that he wanted her and that she wanted him. But even after she'd decided to play along in their game of desire, she hadn't expected Isaac to take himself out of the equation and focus completely on her needs.

Her body still thrummed from his gift, orgasm upon orgasm, until she thought she'd go mad. No man had ever done that before so willingly, so expertly. And yet, she knew her satisfaction would not be complete until she was one with him.

But that hadn't happened. When she'd collapsed in his arms, shaking and nearly incoherent, Isaac had carried her into her bedroom and held her until she fell asleep. Why hadn't he made love to her then, when he had ample opportunity? She found it noble that he refused to take advantage of her, and yet it raised her suspicions, too.

She stretched and the covers fell away. Her skin had goose pimples in the cool air and she rubbed her bare shoulders, having forgotten to set the thermostat to her normal bedtime temperature. Just as she'd forgotten that she was supposed to be working on busting Isaac.

She sat up and threaded her fingers through her hair,

recalling Felicia's request that she keep an eye on Isaac, drawing further suspicion that he'd done something wrong.

Now she understood why Isaac was concerned Felicia would find out about his children. Turns out he was right to worry. The woman obviously didn't take rejection well.

It was clear to her that Felicia's request would ultimately lead to revenge. As a high-ranking Paxton executive, it was entirely conceivable that she had access to some kind of information that she could use against Isaac.

Sterling's motive, on the other hand, appeared to be simply proactive. All he wanted was to protect his company's and his shareholder's interests. There was nothing bad or harmful about hiring an auditor, like herself, to check and recheck the accounting records. In fact, it was the smart thing to do.

Sterling had told her that he opted not to bring his fears to the attention of the accounting firm that was already on retainer. Autumn knew that if they were doing their jobs—and probably being paid millions in fees to do it—they would have already discovered something was wrong.

Still, maybe they had found something and informed Sterling, but Autumn doubted it because he had given her nothing to go on but a hunch and some old files.

If Felicia had proof of fraud, did she share it with Sterling and all Autumn had to do was find it and vet it? Or were father and daughter each working alone?

And here she was caught in the middle, not making

millions in fees but instead dreaming about Isaac making love to her. If anything, last night was proof that her motives were definitely in the wrong place.

Autumn swung her legs off the bed. Things were moving too quickly between her and Isaac. She had to put a stop to it. Before she fell in love with him and couldn't let go.

Her work had always come first. Her dedication to rooting out the corporate bad guys was what kept her getting up in the morning and why her clients kept calling.

She'd inherited the cop gene from her father, a well-respected New York City detective, who had also graciously bestowed on her the tenacious work ethic that had eventually driven her mother away. Her father had been divorced for over twenty years and, from what she gathered, was happy living alone.

Autumn had never been married and the dates were few and far between. For years, plunging headfirst into case after case had always kept her from feeling she was missing out. Until last night, when Isaac showed her so lovingly what she had been missing. She could only imagine what it would be like for him to completely own her—body and soul.

Her mind knew what she had to do, but her heart wanted something different. It felt like lead in her chest, and at that moment she didn't even want to get out of bed.

Autumn recalled her surprise at learning he was a father and she wondered why he'd decided to adopt instead of marrying and having some children of his own. Adolescents and teens were difficult to place with adoptive families. The majority of them wanted newborn babies, so abandoned teens often went through their entire lives in foster homes.

Yet, Isaac had welcomed them into his home. He was a good person and she respected that he was obviously trying to be a good father to his children. If Isaac was engaged in fraud, they had nothing to do with it. They'd only be victims of the fallout.

Isaac's secret was safe with her, but she felt a pang of guilt knowing that keeping his secrets would help her continue to gain his trust. That's what a good undercover investigator was supposed to do. Work to gain the alleged perpetrator's trust over time, and when enough evidence was gathered, move in for the kill.

For this case, time was working against her, but her growing feelings for Isaac were, too. She was really starting to care about him. How was she going to put all that aside?

The only way to avoid both of them getting hurt was to wrap up the case as quickly as possible. Starting today, she was devoting herself again to her own personal work ethic: no more fun and no more pleasure. By this time next week, she'd be on a plane on her way to her next client. Why start something that only had to end?

Autumn slipped out of bed and padded into the bathroom, intent on a hot shower and a strong cup of tea afterward. Both should make trying to find something to ruin Isaac's life go down a little bit easier.

* * *

Two floors up, Isaac slept soundly, oblivious to everything but his dreams where his mouth was sealed on Autumn's wet flesh, his tongue probing and searching, as she bucked in his arms. Her screams broke through the fog and he awoke with a start.

He propped himself up on his elbows and cursed. He was hard as a rock and the woman who'd made him that way wasn't there.

Reality sucks, he thought, just as the door suddenly opened. His head snapped up to see Devon barreling through his bedroom at high speed. Just before he pounced on the bed, Isaac had the foresight and the quick reflexes to bring his knees to his chest. Otherwise, his ability to have children of his own would have been seriously compromised.

"Hey, Dad!" he shouted.

He grabbed at his son and put him into a loose headlock. "What up, D?" Isaac responded with a smile. "Are you practicing to be a linebacker?"

"No, just trying to wake you up." He laughed as the two play wrestled for a few minutes.

Isaac bopped Devon on the head with a pillow. "You're just about the most dangerous alarm clock on earth. I'm not even about to hit the snooze button!" he joked.

Devon grabbed the pillow from Isaac's hand and bopped him back. "What are we going to do today?"

Isaac held in a smile. That was his children's second favorite question. The first was, *What are we having for dinner?*

"You promised we'd do something fun today, remember?"

All Isaac remembered was that his laptop bag, still where he left it in the foyer, contained a ton of work that had to be completed sometime over the weekend. Not to mention the work he had to do on the Witterman pitch. He couldn't let Autumn do everything, plus it would give him an excuse to see her again.

"I don't know about today, Devon. I've got a ton of work I need to catch up on."

"But, Dad, you promised."

Isaac started to shake his head no but stopped when he saw the look of disappointment on Devon's face. He was still getting used to the fact that he wanted the memories of his children to be so much better than his own.

"What's the weather like?"

Like his kids, Isaac wasn't going down without a fight. Devon jumped out of the bed, parted the curtains and peered out the window. "It looks cold, but at least it's not snowing."

He stifled a groan.

Kid 1—Parent 0.

The temperature he could deal with, but he hated the snow. Trudging around the city battling millions of white flakes, as beautiful as they were, was not his idea of fun. Although he would love to have a snowball fight with his kids one day.

As a foster kid himself, he'd missed out on all kinds of silly but memorable things. But more importantly, he missed out on the unconditional love of a parent.

He'd always wanted two, would have settled for one, but ended up getting none.

Thankfully, something within him, some kind of inner strength helped him hold on. He'd made it through his lonely and often chaotic childhood, graduated at the top of his class at Harvard and was now considered a "success."

Not bad for someone most thought would never even graduate from high school.

Being a foster kid with no one to love and no one to truly love him had affected him. It had made him tough in the wrong place, his heart.

Although Isaac was a single parent, the one thing besides money that his kids would never have to worry about was love.

He couldn't say the same for himself.

Last night, he realized how much he needed a woman in his life and how much he wanted that woman to be Autumn.

Suddenly, he had an idea.

"Devon, go grab my wallet off the dresser."

The boy retrieved the wallet and brought it back to Isaac. He fished out a one hundred dollar bill and gave it to Devon, who stared at it, his eyes like saucers.

"Go down to the flower shop on the corner and get me the biggest bouquet they've got. You can keep the change."

Devon nodded and was out of the room almost as fast as he'd come into it.

"And put your coat on before you leave," Isaac yelled. "We're about to go on an adventure."

Isaac only hoped that the trip would pay off.

Autumn had just poured her second cup of tea when she heard a sharp knock at the door. She ignored it because, in her heart, she knew it was Isaac.

She'd hoped that she would have some time to craft a plausible excuse of why they had to back off from each other. But she knew the reason was right in front of her.

Her heart raced as her eyes skittered to the kitchen table where Isaac's old files were spread out in plain sight. To have to collect and hide them would put her behind on the audit again. But she couldn't let him see them, either.

There was no way she was letting Isaac into her apartment.

The knocking was louder now, though, and more urgent. Isaac or whoever was out there was not going to go away.

She slowly moved to the door and looked through the peephole, breathing a sigh of relief that no one was there.

Just as she turned and was about to walk away, another knock sounded. She opened the door and, instead of Isaac, there was Devon with a bashful grin on his face and a big bouquet of flowers in his hand.

"Wow!" she exclaimed, when he didn't say anything. "Are those for me?"

"Yeah," Devon responded, shoving them forward so hard he almost punched her in the stomach by accident.

Autumn sidestepped Devon's fist and took the collection of roses, daisies and snapdragons decorated with ferns and baby's breath. A few of the ribbons that held the bunch together were so long they almost trailed to the floor and she realized they must have come loose somehow.

She buried her face in the bouquet and inhaled the incredible scents. "They're beautiful, thank you!"

Devon bowed awkwardly. "My father requests the pleasure of your company at our afternoon adventure."

Autumn raised an eyebrow. "Adventure? Where are we going?"

He straightened and shrugged. "I don't know. But my dad is rich, so it could be anywhere." Autumn heard the excitement in his voice, and she wondered if he knew how fortunate he was to have a father like Isaac.

She leaned against the doorway, knowing that she didn't have it in her to refuse. Flowers were her weakness.

"He's also very sweet. Please tell him that I accept his invitation," Autumn replied, her nose still in the flowers.

"Okay. Meet us in the lobby at 1:00 p.m. sharp. Later, yo!"

"Later!" she called after Devon, who was already down the hall and getting into the elevator.

Autumn closed the door and walked into the kitchen, where Isaac's files were practically calling her name. She didn't want to know what was in there even though she'd been hired to find out.

But wherever they were going this afternoon, maybe

Isaac would reveal something that could help her investigation so that she could say goodbye before either of them got hurt.

Or maybe spending a Saturday afternoon with Isaac would make her fall in love with him. She plunged her nose into the bouquet again, inhaling the scent not of flowers, but of fear.

Chapter 9

Autumn spent another hour poring over files, trying her best to concentrate and failing miserably. Every few minutes she would glance over at the flowers, now sitting in a vase on her kitchen counter, wondering what was behind Isaac's kind gesture other than the fact that he'd sent his son to deliver them.

She hated that she was being so suspicious, but it came with the territory. Her undercover work investigating corporate criminals so they could be brought to justice didn't exactly inspire instant trust.

And while she wanted to believe that the same man who denied his own needs to pleasure her all night and then had flowers delivered in the morning was innocent of any wrongdoing, all of it could be a ruse.

Until her investigation was complete, she resolved

again to be on her guard for any sign of an ulterior motive.

With his searing touch and mind-blowing kisses she swore she could still feel, Isaac had already proved how easily he could melt her ironclad will.

I'll just have to be stronger, she vowed as she cleared the kitchen table. The files had revealed nothing, but she was convinced she was missing something or maybe she just didn't want to see it. Even more reason to let things cool with Isaac.

After changing into her favorite skinny jeans and dressy top, she pulled on her black leather boots. The heels weren't too high, so she wouldn't almost fall on her face on the ice like she had so embarrassingly the other night when Isaac had kissed her for the first time.

Autumn donned her pale blue cashmere peacoat and pulled a wool hat over her curly hair. She clutched the handrail as she rode the elevator downstairs, her heart thumping in anticipation of seeing Isaac again. Her heels tapped on the marble floor as she walked to the front of the lobby.

When she arrived, she saw Isaac speaking to the doorman and she brought her hands to her chest in fear. Hopefully, he wasn't telling Isaac about how she was bribing him for information. When he tipped his hat in Autumn's direction, Isaac quickly ended his conversation and greeted her with a lazy smile that made her heart flip.

"Hello, stranger. Long time no see."

Isaac strolled over, so sexy in dark indigo jeans, a white button-down shirt and a black leather coat that looked buttery soft. She gulped down a breath trying to forget how much she wanted to explore him and the searing orgasms he'd given her only hours earlier.

He reached for her arm and leaned in close. "You're still as beautiful as ever."

The heat of his touch radiated through the heavy fabric of her coat. She started to wrap her arms around his waist, but out of the corner of her eye, she saw his two children lift their heads from their phones.

Her cheeks burned. "Thank you," she whispered, hoping she didn't sound out of breath. Isaac had heard her gasping enough last evening.

Autumn took a quick step back as his children approached.

Devon gave her a friendly wave. He had a round face that always looked cheerful. Deshauna wore a nasty glare that almost made Autumn cringe and wonder if accepting Isaac's invitation was a huge mistake.

Spending the afternoon with two teenagers and their mind-blowingly hot dad. What was she getting herself into?

Despite her jitters, she gave both kids a warm smile.

"Where are we going?" Devon asked, addressing his question to her.

Autumn shrugged. "Your guess is as good as mine."

"How about we just stay home," Deshauna said sulkily, still glaring at Autumn. "Whose dumb idea was this anyway? It's freezing outside!"

"The cold air is invigorating," Isaac interjected. "It'll give you guys plenty of energy to tackle your homework later on tonight."

Both kids groaned. They had started to pull out their devices in defeat when the doorman walked up and cleared his throat.

"Your car is ready, sir."

Devon ran to the lobby door and pushed it open. "That's not a car. That's a limo!" he said, his voice cracking with excitement.

"Sweet," Deshauna said. Her face brightened as she stepped outside and got her first look at the sleek black vehicle.

"Can we get in now, Dad?" Devon asked. The chauffeur opened the door and Devon was in the limo before Isaac could respond.

Deshauna stepped in next and plopped down next to her brother. She immediately went to the mini-refrigerator and grabbed a can of soda as if she'd ridden in a limo a million times.

Autumn ducked in advance of the low ceiling and could feel Isaac watching her climb in. His eyes met hers briefly as he slid into the seat beside her.

"Dad, can I have one of these for prom next year?" Deshauna asked, after a sip of soda.

Devon was busy pressing every button he could see. "Can we keep it?"

Isaac laughed. "No, we can't keep it. It's just a rental. But we can have fun in it today. Only the best for my family."

Both kids pouted for a few seconds but then forgot about the sulkies as they checked out the limo's luxurious features.

Autumn quietly inhaled the smell of Isaac's cologne

through her nostrils. The scent was even stronger now that they were in closer quarters. Not overpoweringly so, but just enough to make her want to bury her head in his neck. Like forever.

After a ride through Central Park, the limo emerged onto Fifth Avenue and parked in front of the Metropolitan Museum of Art.

"Dad," Devon whined as he clambered out after his sister. "I thought you said you were taking us on an adventure."

Autumn was equally surprised at Isaac's choice for a Saturday outing. She thought for sure they were headed to something more testosterone based, like a hockey game or maybe even bowling. Isaac never failed to intrigue her, and strange as it might seem, his being into art was a turn-on. She couldn't wait to explore the museum with him at her side.

By the time Isaac climbed out of the limo, Devon and Deshauna had already started up the stairs to the entrance. "This place has something from every culture in every part of the world. You don't call that an adventure?" he called out after them.

He reached for her hand and held it tight as he helped her from the limo. Their eyes locked and his smile warmed her in a way that made her feel she was curled up in his arms. And Lord help her, she wished that she could be.

The wind whipped her curls across her face and Isaac gently brushed them away with his right hand.

He stepped closer and cupped her chin lightly, as if he was going to kiss her.

"I'm glad you're here."

Her heart fluttered in her chest, and for a moment she didn't speak—she just panicked. She wanted him to kiss her but not in front of his children. She didn't want it to appear as if she and Isaac were in a relationship when they were really just friends. If he ever found out she was investigating him, they'd turn into enemies real quick.

Autumn stepped back far enough that it forced him to drop his hand from her face.

"So am I," she admitted truthfully as she withdrew her hand from his.

She hugged her arms around her chest and shivered. "Let's get inside. It's freezing out here."

Isaac nodded and they walked up the stairs to the museum, where they met up with Devon and Deshauna.

Once inside, Autumn gaped at the immensity of the lobby area while Isaac went to pay the admission fee. Although hundreds of people milled about, it didn't seem at all crowded.

Isaac returned shortly and after they checked their coats in, he handed each of them a paper ticket.

"Peel the sticker off carefully and stick it to your shirt," he instructed.

He then gave Devon and Deshauna one map to share and kept the other one for himself.

Isaac unfolded the map and Autumn held one corner of it so that she could look at it, too.

"Where would you guys like to go first?"

Devon piped up first. "Arms and Armor!"

"Boys and guns. So typical!" Deshauna muttered and rolled her eyes. "I want to see the costume exhibit."

"That sounds like fun. I love fashion, too," Autumn said in a friendly tone.

Deshauna clicked her tongue against her teeth and gave her a nasty look. "What do you know about style?" she retorted in a snippy voice.

Isaac's head snapped up. "Chill out, Deshauna. Autumn is our guest today and you will treat her with respect. Is that clear?"

Deshauna slanted her eyes in Autumn's direction and nodded reluctantly.

Poor kid, Autumn thought. Deshauna obviously felt threatened by Autumn for her father's affections. She wished she could reassure her that she had no need to worry. Autumn knew she would never have a permanent place in Isaac's heart.

Isaac turned to Autumn. "What would you like to see?"

She quickly perused the map. "I'd love to see any paintings and sculpture from Europe."

Deshauna took the map from her brother and folded it. "Dad, can we split up?"

Devon nodded. "Yeah, can we?"

Isaac frowned. "I was hoping we'd explore the museum as a family."

"We'll be good, we promise," Deshauna replied in a sweet voice before elbowing her brother. "Won't we?"

"Ouch!" Devon rubbed his side. "Yeah. So what do you say, Dad?"

Isaac sighed. "Okay, but be sure and stay with your

sister. Let's all meet back here in an hour and we can check out some of the other exhibits together."

His children didn't even wait for him to finish his sentence before they half walked, half jogged away.

Isaac turned to Autumn. "So much for a family outing," he said with a dejected shrug.

"They're teenagers. Don't take it to heart. When I was their age, I didn't want to hang out with my dad either."

They walked to the escalator that would take them to the second floor where some of the Met's vast collection of European paintings were located.

"What does your father do?" Isaac asked as they rode. "Does he work with money all day long like we do?" he teased.

Autumn hesitated a moment, unsure whether to answer what was otherwise a normal question. Even though she knew Isaac would be unable to trace her real identity, she was still fearful. To her, that was just another indication that she still wasn't used to her new life. But even if she could, she wouldn't change a thing. Her former employer's fraudulent accounting practices had bilked thousands of shareholders out of millions of dollars. Exposing these actions had cost Autumn her name, her reputation and career, but it had ultimately led her to Isaac.

"No. He busts bad guys for a living."

She paused a beat, watching Isaac's face for any kind of unusual reaction, but there was none, and she exhaled lightly with relief. "He's been a detective for the borough of Manhattan for over twenty years."

"Well, I hope if I ever meet him, he's not packing metal," Isaac joked.

His broad smile turned grim and his voice was so low Autumn could barely hear him.

"Unlike my son, I don't have a fascination with guns. I don't have anything against them. It's just that when I was growing up, they almost destroyed my life."

Isaac's stark honesty made Autumn's heart squeeze and her legs felt shaky when they disembarked from the escalator.

Without speaking, they wandered through the gallery and gazed at the priceless European paintings, both hoping that the other would break the uncomfortable calm between them.

Finally, Autumn reached out her hand and grasped Isaac's arm.

"Do you want to tell me what happened?" she asked softly.

Isaac looked around, as if to make sure his kids or any other people weren't in earshot.

"My father shot my mother and then killed himself."

His response was blunt, yet it didn't detract from the unmistakable pain etched in his eyes.

Horrified, Autumn breathed in so sharply and loudly that a few people in the room turned in her direction.

Without thinking, Autumn wrapped her arms around Isaac's neck.

"Oh, my God, Isaac. I'm so sorry," she managed to choke out.

He shrugged nonchalantly, linking his arms around her waist. "That's how I ended up being a foster kid.

And when I learned that the same thing had happened to Devon and Deshauna's birth parents when they were little, I adopted them. No kid should have to go through life alone."

She hugged Isaac even tighter, as if doing so could erase anything bad that had happened, and she realized just how much she was starting to care about him.

"I think what you did for Devon and Deshauna is amazing," she whispered into his ear. "You're a very special man."

Autumn knew adoption took a certain kind of selflessness. Plus Devon and Deshauna were victims of the same unconscionable violence he'd experienced as a kid. Raising them had to bring back painful memories of his own traumatic childhood.

She squeezed him even harder. How was he coping?

"Hey, go easy on the neck," he said tersely, disentangling himself from her grasp. "I can barely breathe."

Autumn dropped her arms to her sides. Her face prickled with embarrassment. What had caused her to hold on to him so tightly that she didn't want to let go? It was crazy. Especially when she knew very well that any kind of relationship with him was not only temporary—it was a mistake.

"Sorry," she muttered. "I was just trying to make you feel better."

Isaac sighed and ran one hand down his face. "No, I'm the one who should be sorry. I didn't mean to bite your head off."

Autumn nodded and started walking away, pretending to be deeply curious about the paintings that lined the wall.

Pretending she wasn't falling in love with Isaac.

She stopped in front of *Venus and Adonis.* She read the little sign on the wall and learned that it was a work by Peter Paul Rubens, a Flemish artist who lived during the late 1500s, early 1600s.

Isaac caught up to her and before he could say anything more, she pointed at the painting. "That's Adonis to the left. He's the god of beauty. Venus, the god of love, is to his right. Little Cupid is holding on to Adonis's leg."

"The chubby little guy probably wants his bow and arrow back," Isaac joked.

Autumn rolled her eyes. "I took an art history class in college and I remember that my instructor taught us that this painting is about Venus trying to prevent her lover, Adonis, from going into battle." She paused and shrugged. "Or maybe it was hunting. I forget."

"Why would she do that? The man was probably trying to put food on the table for his family."

She crossed her arms and looked deeply into his eyes. "Because she didn't want him to get hurt."

"So what happened?"

"According to myth, he ignores her pleas and ends up getting killed by a wild boar."

"Wow." Isaac shook his head. "I guess he should have listened to his woman."

They both stared at the painting for a moment.

Venus, her skin milky-white, her form Rubenesque. In today's world, she would be called fat, but Autumn thought she was beautiful. Adonis, clad in an orangish-red tunic, with his long hair and thickly muscled body, was a mythological romance hero. Their figures twisting into each other, toward a fate that was at that point unknown.

Isaac suddenly turned to her. "Will you be my Venus?"

Autumn felt her skin prickle at the heat of his gaze. "Do you mean your lover or your protector?"

He put his hands on her shoulders and touched his forehead to hers. "Both. I want to make love to you, Autumn," he said softly. "And in the morning, I want you to hold on to me tight, like you did a moment ago."

"Before you go into battle?" she whispered. At his nod, she asked, "What are you fighting against, Isaac?"

"Certainly not wild boars. Sometimes I think I'm fighting against nothing. Sometimes I think I'm fighting against myself." He paused and when he spoke again, his low voice caressed her ear. "I want you, Autumn. Last night was wonderful, but it wasn't enough for me. Not even close."

Autumn bit her lip and looked up at him. "I want to…but we work together. Things could get complicated very quickly. If Sterling or Felicia ever—"

Isaac laid his finger on her lips. "Shh…they won't. We'll be careful. I promise." He kissed her forehead. "Just think about it, okay?"

She nodded and moved her hands up his muscular back and clung to his shoulder blades as he kissed her nose and finally her mouth. Tilting her body against his as he stroked her hair, she opened her heart to him and, in her mind, they were alone as one. In those moments, she felt as priceless as the paintings on the wall.

Isaac's phone buzzed and reluctantly they drew apart. He ran his thumb over the screen. "It's Deshauna. They're downstairs waiting for us by the escalator."

She looked up at him, her lips still burning from his kisses, her mind in a whirl. "I guess we'd better go meet them."

As they made their way to the escalator, the floor seemed to be swaying dizzily under her feet and she stopped, trying to gain her footing.

Isaac, thinking she was right behind him, had already started to descend. When he noticed she wasn't there, he turned around and bolted up the moving stairs.

Autumn stepped back from the escalator. "I don't know why, but I'm feeling a little disoriented."

"I'll help you." He stretched out his hand. "Just grab me and hold on tight."

His hand clasped hers, its masculine grip so warm and strong that Autumn felt nothing bad could ever happen to them. But as they stepped onto the escalator together, she knew she was wrong, and that whatever she decided would only result in one thing: heartbreak.

Chapter 10

Isaac stifled a yawn and leaned back in his chair, trying to decide which was worse. An eight o'clock meeting on a Monday morning or a meeting with Felicia. Unfortunately, he was experiencing both.

His eyes drifted around the room and he noted that there were people from all levels of the organization in attendance. He wondered how many of them really wanted to be there. While participation was "voluntary," the unspoken word was that if you were invited yet didn't show up, you were not a team player. At least in Felicia's eyes.

The same verdict held true if a man, namely him, refused her advances.

Felicia rapped her pen on the boardroom table and

called the inaugural meeting of the Paxton Employee Satisfaction Committee to order.

Isaac straightened but pressed his back into the chair. This was one meeting that he wished he hadn't been invited to.

"Ladies and gentlemen," she began. "I've called us together this morning because it has come to my attention that we have a serious morale issue at Paxton that needs to be addressed." She paused and let her gaze roam around the table. "This committee is going to be responsible for brainstorming ways to fix these issues so that all employees will be happy in their careers at Paxton."

Isaac stared straight ahead and pretended to be engrossed in whatever Felicia was rambling on about next, but his mind was on Autumn.

The kiss they shared at the art museum had done more than just stimulate his body. It also made him think.

Oh…the possibility that he could have Autumn. It wasn't just the physical stuff, although that was very important to him. It was everything else that he wanted to share with her but didn't know where to start.

He hadn't been this excited about the future since he'd started at Paxton, fresh out of Harvard with no goal other than to make money, and lots of it.

Now, he had the money and two kids to share it with. But he knew that wasn't enough. He wanted a partner, a woman who was committed to a career and to building a life with him. The only thing he didn't know was if Autumn wanted the same thing.

He'd meant to sneak out of his apartment on Saturday evening sometime, but Devon got sick soon after they arrived back from the museum. Thankfully, he felt better on Sunday. But by then both kids were busy trying to avoid doing homework, so he spent most of the day encouraging and monitoring them through it while catching up on work of his own.

Now, Isaac was stuck in the meeting from hell.

All of a sudden, he noticed the room was totally silent and everyone in it was staring at him.

His back went ramrod straight, having no idea what was going on.

"Can you repeat the question?" he ventured.

Nobody spoke for a moment and all that could be heard was the faint sound of traffic fifty stories below.

"So let me bring you up to speed," Felicia said scathingly. "We were discussing some of our employees' biggest complaints."

She pointed to a man sitting right across from Isaac. He worked for the information technology department, informally known as PGS, Paxton Geek Squad. Mostly he answered help desk calls, but occasionally when things were really busy, Isaac had seen him around the office troubleshooting and fixing computer issues.

"Jonathan was inquiring why a new employee analyst was given an office when most people, other than executives, are assigned to a cubicle."

It was obvious that Felicia was referring to Autumn having the office across from his, a fact over which he had no control. Still he was secretly glad she was there and as far as he was concerned, he didn't want her to move.

Isaac narrowed his eyes. What did she have up her sleeve now?

Jonathan fiddled with his tie. "Y-yes," he stammered, looking down at the table. "People are upset. It's not f-fair."

Isaac leaned forward in his chair. "I can't answer that question for you. I'm not responsible for work space arrangements." He turned to Felicia. "Quite frankly, I'm confused as to why this issue even concerns me."

"Because our employees have the perception that our executive team has special privileges, which could be why morale is lower at the company overall."

Isaac opened his mouth to argue, but he quickly shut it as he realized what was happening here. Felicia was trying to pin the blame on him for two things that were out of his control: office morale and Autumn's work space.

Isaac glanced around at the other employees sitting at the table; some he knew, but most he didn't. Many of them wouldn't even look him in the eye. What kind of lies had Felicia been feeding them?

He wouldn't be surprised if she'd met with each person secretly to come up with some kind of accusation to level at him.

There was no way he was going to be a punching bag for their frustrations.

He took a deep breath. "Look, I don't know why morale is down at Paxton. In terms of perks, there is nothing unusual outside of my compensation package, which is, of course, strictly confidential."

Felicia cut in. "This isn't the place to—"

"Let me finish please," Isaac said. "If you are personally unsatisfied in your job, voicing your complaints in a meeting such as this isn't going to help. Review what you want, compare it against what's lacking in your job, and discuss your concerns with your supervisor. Otherwise, this committee is little more than a group gossip session."

When Isaac was finished, he saw a few heads nodding in agreement. Felicia glared at him, but addressed the group.

"Thank you for that insightful career advice. We'll adjourn the meeting for now and reconvene next week."

Not if I can help it, he thought, as people began filing out of the room.

As he stood up to make his own escape, his phone vibrated, a signal that his next meeting was due to begin shortly. If he hurried, he could go see if Autumn was in the office yet.

When Isaac walked by Felicia, she reached out her hand and touched him on his arm. Revulsion sifted through him. Despite his anger, somehow he managed to keep his tone light.

"What is it? Haven't you done enough to try to ruin my day?"

Isaac was beyond tired of Felicia's little games and they had to stop. It was time he took his own advice. He had to go to Sterling with his concerns. But he couldn't until after the Witterman pitch. It was more important than ever that he win the business. Maybe then, after signing the elusive multimillion dollar prospective client, Sterling would listen to him.

Felicia tossed her blond hair to one side. "All is fair in love and war." She squeezed his forearm and her voice was razor sharp. "And if I can't have love, then..."

Isaac didn't give her a chance to finish her sentence. He surmised what Felicia was hinting at even though she let it dangle. He shook his arm free from her grasp and strode out of the door.

If this was war, then Isaac knew he needed to prepare for a battle. He hurried down the hall in search of the only person he wanted by his side.

Autumn sat alone at a table in the corner of the Paxton cafeteria, nestling a fresh cup of tea in her hands. Her thoughts were a whirlwind of Isaac, the investigation and something else she couldn't quite pinpoint.

She stared down at the white plastic lid and realized how fluid and simple her life was now. She could go anywhere. Do anything. With her government-issued identity, she had no past and no future. She had only the present.

Yet, like the liquid in her cup, she was constrained. By virtue of necessity, whether it was for a particular case or for her own protection, she was held back from doing what she loved out in the open. In the pursuit of the truth, her real self was hidden from others. Her biggest fear was that someday she would look in the mirror and she wouldn't recognize the person staring back.

With a sigh, Autumn brought the cup to her lips and

her stomach clenched when she noticed Sterling walk through the cafeteria door heading for her.

"We need to talk," he ordered, pulling out a chair opposite her own.

Although there was no one sitting within hearing distance, several people glanced in her direction. Autumn made a mental note to remind him that they needed to meet in his office from now on.

Autumn took a sip of tea and set it down, unperturbed at Sterling's gruff tone.

"How was your weekend?"

"I was here the entire time, but never mind that," he retorted. "I stopped by your office on Sunday and saw that some of the files were missing. Do you have them?"

"Yes," she replied. "I took them home to review them over the weekend. Why?"

"The Witterman pitch is this Friday. I had high hopes that you would have found something by now," he sneered. "I guess I was wasting my time…and my money."

Autumn tightened her grip around the cup, bristling inwardly at Sterling's implication that she wasn't doing her job, when nothing could be further from the truth.

She'd combed through Isaac's files and client records, dating back to when he started with the company, and she only had a small batch to go.

The time she'd spent with Isaac these past few days were a part of her surveillance efforts. She was supposed to get to know him, closely monitor every move of his taut, muscular body and record any and all interactions with him.

But I wasn't supposed to fall in love with him.

A burst of panic made her grip the cup tighter. The thought seemed so loud in her mind that for a moment she feared Sterling could hear it. The notion that she could have any feelings for Isaac beyond simple lust was highly illogical, not to mention potentially detrimental to the case.

She couldn't ever record how Isaac had pleasured her in her apartment a few nights earlier, although the memory was forever seared in her brain. She couldn't stop thinking about him, and yet she wasn't supposed to be thinking about him.

Not like that anyway.

"It's not because I haven't been looking," she insisted, trying her best not to squirm under Sterling's harsh glare. "Are you sure you've given me every file?"

Sterling cast her a withering look. "Are you questioning the way I run my business and accusing me of losing crucial information?"

Autumn held up her hands. "Not at all. I was just putting it out there. Things happen sometimes, that's all."

He crossed his arms and huffed. "Not at Paxton, they don't."

Autumn nodded. "Initially you refused to tell me why you were having Isaac investigated in the first place."

Sterling wrinkled his forehead. "What difference does that make?"

Autumn flashed him a smile even though she wanted to gag. For a man responsible for the care and feeding of millions of other people's money, Sterling sure didn't have much common sense.

"Knowing all the facts could assist the investigation," she replied patiently.

Sterling unfolded his arms and leaned close to her. "Let me tell you something, Ms. Hilliard. When I invest money in a particular stock, I don't know all the facts."

He coughed and continued. "Sure, I can read the prospectus and see how the company has fared over a certain period of time, but in the end, investing is a high-stakes guessing game. I'm working off a hunch and I've made a living hedging bets."

At his words, the bitter acid from the tea rose in Autumn's throat. Didn't Sterling realize that there was more at stake here than money? There was Isaac's career and the children no one at Paxton knew about except her.

"And what if you're wrong? About Isaac, I mean."

Sterling opened his arms wide, as if he were Moses parting the Red Sea. "Look around you, Autumn. Does it look like I'm ever wrong?"

Autumn coughed back her disgust. "No, sir."

"Good." Sterling dropped his arms and stood. "I've got another meeting. But I expect a full report from you no later than a week from today."

He took a few steps but suddenly turned back. "Oh, and by the way, when you discover that my hunch is correct, Isaac is going to wish he never set foot inside these doors."

Autumn slumped in her seat, knowing his threat was genuine.

Obviously Sterling had never heard of the maxim "innocent until proven guilty."

She wondered what had caused so much friction between them, but it didn't matter at the moment. Her father told her repeatedly, "You're only as good as your last case, so…"

"Don't burn bridges," she muttered, echoing her dad's solemn voice in her head.

Her reputation and her career mattered more to Autumn than a man. Or at least, that's what she told herself, every night she turned on her side and no one was there.

Autumn got up and walked over to the garbage can. As she tossed in her empty cup, she vowed to set aside the romantic feelings for Isaac that had already started to grow inside her. At least for now, and perhaps, forever.

Later that morning, Autumn walked out of the restroom, drying her hands on a paper towel, and nearly bumped into Felicia. However, from the fake surprise look on her face, Autumn knew the chance meeting was no accident.

"I'm glad to see someone at Paxton taking hand washing seriously."

Autumn balled up the paper towel in her hand and shrugged. "I'm not a germaphobe. It's just good hygiene."

Felicia clapped her hands together. "I knew we had something else in common." She produced a small bottle and held it out to her. "Sanitizer? It's lavender scented."

Autumn shook her head and felt like telling Felicia to use it on herself, even though no amount of the clear gel would be able to wash off the sleaze.

"I'm glad we ran into each other." Something flashed in Felicia's eyes and Autumn instantly knew she was lying. "Do you have time for a chat?"

Without waiting for Autumn's response, Felicia grabbed her elbow and pulled her into a room that was reserved for nursing mothers. Luckily, it was occupied only by a couch that appeared sturdy though in need of newer upholstery.

Felicia locked the door and gestured to the sofa.

Autumn shook her head. "I'll stand. What's going on?"

"I just wanted to say that whatever you're doing, keep doing it. The natives are restless!" she squealed.

"Natives?" Autumn echoed, confused. "What are you talking about?"

Felicia rolled her eyes. "I'm talking about the fact that we had our inaugural meeting of the Paxton Employee Satisfaction Committee. Everyone is up in arms about the fact that you have an office."

Autumn dropped her mouth open. "But, Felicia, you know I had nothing to do with that. Your father gave me that office."

"I know and initially I was really upset about it," Felicia admitted. "But now it seems to be working to your advantage. Everyone is blaming Isaac, which is exactly what I want."

Despite her will to stand, Autumn found herself sinking to the couch. "But why? It's not his fault, either."

"That's where you're wrong," Felicia replied, turning to the mirror. She smoothed a hand over her blond hair. Today, her style was less severe, but the calculated smirk on her face was all that was needed to make Autumn's stomach knot with worry.

What had Isaac done to make Felicia so vindictive?

"Do you know how long it took me to get my own office?"

Autumn shook her head and resumed watching Felicia primp in the mirror.

"Three years." Felicia turned on her heels and held up her fingers. "Three years! And I'm the boss's daughter!" she exclaimed. "I know what people say about me, but it's not true."

"So your father has made you work to get where you are today."

"Yes," Felicia cut in. "I followed in his hallowed footsteps and now I can barely get him to answer an email."

Autumn ignored the long look on her face. If Felicia wanted sympathy, she wasn't going to get it from her.

"What's that got to do with Isaac?"

Felicia put her hands on her hips. "Let's just say that when I get through with Isaac, he won't be able to show his face ever again in Manhattan."

Without another word, Felicia unlocked the door and stalked out.

Autumn rubbed her eyes in confusion. To her, Felicia's mini-rant sounded a bit like professional jealousy. But since Isaac was involved somehow, this was a lot more complex than mere envy. She had to find out what, if anything beyond her attempt at seduction, had occurred between them.

And even though Autumn couldn't claim Isaac as her man, she had to do it without getting jealous herself.

Chapter 11

Isaac hurried down the hallway toward Autumn's office, hoping to catch her before she left. He'd been wanting to see her, but meetings had kept him busy all day and he kept missing her. What he had to say couldn't be done in an email. He needed to be close to her, perhaps for the very last time.

When he arrived, he stopped just before the thin floor-to-ceiling window and inclined his head. The door was closed, but he could hear the faint tap of her fingers upon the keys. He took a deep breath and knocked on the door before opening it.

He popped his head into the room. Autumn looked up and her lips curved under the spotlight cast by the old-fashioned desk lamp. As she leaned back against her chair, her face was thrown into semidarkness but, thankfully, her smile was still there. His heart lifted as if it was eighty degrees and sunny rather than the frigid cold that awaited them both outside.

"Hey, it's after five. I thought you'd be gone by now."

Autumn shook her head and motioned him forward. "I just finished the presentation and was trying to email it to you, but it bounced back."

"Hmm…maybe I can help."

He stepped into the room and closed the door. "You wouldn't know it by looking at me, but I'm a closet geek."

Autumn gave him a quizzical look and her eyes zeroed in on his chest. He took a deep breath as his skin warmed under her gaze.

"Oh really? Where's your pocket protector?" she teased.

Isaac felt her eyes on his body as he walked around her desk. He placed his hands on the back of her chair.

"I could tell you," he replied, standing behind her before swiveling the chair so she faced him. "Or I could show you." Isaac watched her eyes flick down and graze over his torso. The moment lasted only seconds, but it was enough to make him hard. His penis throbbed and his mind warned him to back away from this woman, but his body yearned for something else.

He stepped closer, placed his hands on the armrests of the chair and bent at the waist.

"Which would you like?"

Her eyes rose, darkened and met his.

He sensed that she wanted him, but something was holding her back.

She folded her arms as if to ward him off or maybe to stem the flow of her own feelings. "What I want is to get the presentation to you without it blowing up my system."

"Why don't we go over it together? I could order in some dinner and—"

Autumn shook her head. "What about your children? Don't you have to get home to feed them?"

He released his grip on the chair. "First of all, they hate when I cook. They go into hiding when they hear me in the kitchen."

Autumn giggled. "That bad, huh?"

"Unfortunately, yes," Isaac said with a nod. "Second of all, they are with friends tonight." He lifted a tendril of hair from her face. "So I'm all yours."

Her eyes flicked past him to the window. "We may even be snowed in tonight."

Isaac looked over his shoulder and saw a mass of flurries against the glass. He turned and traced a finger along the apple of her cheek. It was as soft as the curve of a pillow.

"Would that be so bad?" he asked.

Autumn's eyes slid shut for a moment as if she were reveling in his touch. "No." Her eyes flapped open and she whispered, "I've missed you."

At those three words, Isaac placed his palms against the cold black leather on either side of her head. The chair rolled back, metal scraping against wood as he engulfed her mouth in a kiss.

Autumn opened her mouth to accept his tongue, her deep moan bubbling into his throat, and he retreated for only a second before plunging and swirling, wanting them to drown in each other.

But it was she who came to her senses first, albeit slowly. Hesitantly. Her palms flattened against his shirt and moved over the hardened muscles, her lips twisting and reaching for him even as she pushed him away.

He stepped back and groaned as he wiped his lips. The emptiness left in his heart by the sudden lack of her touch was something akin to torture.

"Isaac," she began, trying to catch her breath. "We can't do this."

His heart sank and his eyes roamed her face. "You said that you missed me. Did you really mean it?"

"Of course, I did. But before we go any further, we need to talk about Felicia."

Isaac sighed and stepped back. "What do you want to know?"

"What's going on between the two of you?"

He leaned his head back against the wall and stared at the ceiling. "Nothing. But that's not what she wants."

"You told me that she's been making your life at Paxton here a living hell lately."

Isaac leveled his gaze at her and nodded. "I think she's turned Sterling against me. He's not acting the way he normally does with me and he's always in a bad mood."

Autumn twisted her lips to the side. "I thought that was just his personality."

He couldn't help but laugh. "No, not at all. It's just lately he's been treating me differently. More like an outsider than a confidant."

"Don't you think you may be blowing this out of proportion?" Autumn asked gently.

Isaac scratched his chin. "I used to think so until today. Felicia has me on this committee that is supposed to be a nonconfrontational sounding board for employee grievances and how to resolve them, but instead she threw me under the bus. Everyone is blaming me because you have an office, and they don't!"

"I know," Autumn replied quietly.

He pushed himself away from the wall. "You do? How?"

"Felicia told me this morning. She practically accosted me outside the women's restroom."

"That b—" He swallowed the word just in time. "What did she say?"

"The same thing you just told me," Autumn replied, tilting her head. "But with a little added bonus."

Isaac raised his brow, urging her to continue.

"She wanted me to keep an eye on you, and report back anything I find."

"Anything you find? What do I have to hide?" Anger sipped through his veins and he struggled to keep his voice down. "I can't believe she is trying to turn you against me, too."

Autumn clucked her tongue against her teeth. "Really?"

Isaac grunted. "You're right. This is Felicia we're talking about." He shook his head. "You haven't worked here that long and you've already got her pegged for what she is. A sneaky, conniving, little you-know-what who—"

"Has your briefs in a bunch," Autumn cut in. She stood, walked over to the window and faced him. "But what you're not telling me is why all this matters."

"It matters because it's my livelihood," he retorted.

"But you're one of the highest paid and most profitable brokers on Wall Street today. I'm sure you have nothing to worry about."

"Nothing except losing my job." He ran his hand over his head in frustration. "If Sterling or—worse—Felicia, ever finds out that I have two children now, they'll be more than just pissed."

She put her hands on his shoulders. "Isaac, they can't fire you because you adopted two children. I'm not a lawyer, but that sounds like it would be a clear case of discrimination."

Autumn hesitated and he could practically see the wheels turning in her head. "I guess they could reprimand you in some way for withholding information."

"Or find a reason to fire me."

Autumn dropped her hands from his shoulders and leaned against the opposite wall. "The best thing to do would be to tell them about Devon and Deshauna right away."

Isaac paced in front of the window. "But I can't. Not until after I'm made partner. I don't want anything screwing up what I've worked so long and hard to attain."

He snapped his fingers and turned to her. "That's it, isn't it? That's why Felicia asked you to spy on me.

She's building some kind of case against me in order to convince Sterling to let me go. Am I right?"

Autumn shrugged. "I don't know, Isaac. I have no idea what her motives are."

"I do! She's out to destroy me," he insisted as he paced back and forth again.

She reached out her hand and grabbed his arm. "But that's what I'm trying to tell you. She won't. She can't."

He stopped in his tracks. "How do you know?"

"Because I told her no," she said emphatically. "I told her that I refused to spy on you."

Isaac put her hands on Autumn's shoulders and peered into her eyes. "You did?"

She nodded and he pulled her into his arms.

"Thank you. I knew you weren't like everyone else," he whispered against her curls. "So many women I've met in the past were backstabbers. I couldn't trust them with my time, let alone my heart. But you're different. I trust you."

"I'm flattered, Isaac. But you hardly know me. Why me?"

He cupped her chin in one hand. "Maybe it's because Sterling trusted you first. You know the Witterman pitch is a big deal. He wouldn't have given you the assignment if he didn't think you could handle it."

"But, Isaac, that's business," she insisted. "And this is—"

"Personal. I know," he muttered low. He leaned in, took a chance and pecked her lips. "And I want us to get even more personal. So close we won't know where you start and where I end. What do you think?"

"I think we should get back to work on the Witterman presentation."

Isaac groaned and leaned his forehead against hers. "You're no fun."

"But I am efficient and efficiency—"

"Is one spoke in the Paxton wheel of fortune, blah, blah, blah. I can't believe you actually read the employee handbook!"

"Way to kill a moment, huh?" Autumn mused, her eyes twinkling.

Isaac laughed. "Don't worry. If I have anything to say about it, there will be plenty more."

Autumn pulled away and smiled, but he could tell there was something still bothering her. He hoped that in time she would trust him enough to confide in him.

"Why don't you pull that chair around so we can both look at the monitor together?"

Isaac glanced at the door, puzzled. Her drop into business mode was as unexpected as the stock market he played in all day. The trouble was, he knew how to win the market.

He had no clue how to win her.

"But I was going to order in dinner."

"There's no need." Autumn shook her head. "This won't take long. I want you to get home to Devon and Deshauna as soon as possible."

Isaac shrugged, not bothering to remind her that his children were with friends for most of the evening.

He pulled a chair around next to Autumn. Once he was settled in, she put the presentation in full-screen mode and began to walk him through it.

"First, we'll lay some groundwork to make Ms. Witterman comfortable with the organization by reviewing our long history of successful investing, et cetera."

With her right hand, she clicked on the mouse and kept talking, but the only thing Isaac noted was her fingers. They were long, manicured and completely bare. In spite of his fear of the altar, he imagined a ring on one of them. A nice big, ridiculously expensive rock, but not necessarily from him.

Autumn had the kind of raw, earthy, back-to-Eve beauty that a man would have to be a fool to let get away.

She had to have someone in her life.

Suddenly, he felt an elbow in his rib cage.

"Isaac. Are you listening?" Autumn demanded.

His mind drew a blank on everything but her sexy little nose. It had a slight crook in it that he longed to trace with his finger.

"Yeah, I'm down with that," he finally muttered. Although he didn't even know what he'd just agreed to do, he hoped it involved the tearing off of clothes.

She gave him a quizzical look. "So you'll review the accuracy of the corporate backgrounder, correct?"

"Of course! I'm sorry," he said with a grin. "I was just mesmerized by the beauty of the graphs."

Autumn gestured to the screen. "But I haven't even gotten to the data portion of the presentation yet."

Isaac held up his hands. "Okay. You busted me. I was mesmerized by the beauty of you."

She stared at her lap and Isaac saw a crease of a smile.

"We're supposed to be working on the presentation, remember?"

Isaac twisted in his chair and she looked up. "I haven't forgotten."

He placed two fingers under her chin and gently lifted. "But this is more fun. Tell me something. Why did you agree to come to the art museum with me?"

"That's easy. Their collection is unparalleled and my tour guide was utterly charming."

"Even though I don't know a thing about art?"

Autumn nodded and they burst out laughing.

"Wow, since you have so much confidence in me, I have some other things I'd like to show you."

Autumn cocked her head to one side. "Right now?"

Isaac stood up and, with his foot, pushed his chair against the wall. He took her hand and quickly pulled her to her feet.

"Yes, right now."

Without letting her hand go, he slid past her and sat down in her leather office chair.

"Hey!" Autumn exclaimed in protest and leaned against the desk.

He uttered a mock sigh of satisfaction. "This is much more comfortable than that old wooden thing." He looked from side to side and frowned. "But there's no place to put my arms."

Suddenly he pulled her into his lap, hardening instantly at the feel of her soft buttocks on his thighs.

"There. That's better. Sitting next to you was too tempting."

He wrapped his arms around her and pulled her even closer.

She trembled and exclaimed, "But what about the Witterman presentation?"

"It's not going anyplace," he soothed with a kiss on the tip of her nose. "But right now, you belong here. Where I can do this..."

Gently, he tucked a few curls over her right ear and kissed her earlobe.

"And this..." Isaac moved his lips along her jawline.

"Autumn, I want us to be as close as we can get for now."

He molded his hands around her waist and slowly moved them up her back. "Because now is all we have."

Isaac nuzzled her neck and the sound of her moan tickled his lips. "I just want to feel you."

He quickly unbuttoned her silk blouse and eased it down over her shoulders. "You're so beautiful," he whispered low. He stroked his fingers over the fabric of her bra, then traced his finger along her exposed skin.

"How'd you know I wear briefs?"

"Lucky guess?"

Her voice caught in her throat as he began to massage her breasts.

Isaac looked up and flashed her a devilish grin. "You wanna find out for real?"

Autumn straddled him firmly and then reached back and unclasped her bra. "Does this answer your question?"

As she slowly slid each strap from her shoulder, Isaac

hitched in a breath. The fire in her eyes and the sound of her bra hitting the floor only magnified his desire.

His eyes dipped down to her breasts, which seemed even larger and more luscious than he remembered them. Before he knew what he was doing, he reached out and cupped her heavy flesh in his hand, flicking one nipple gently until it stiffened at his touch.

Isaac placed his hands underneath her skirt and lifted her bottom slightly to move her even closer. He wanted to feel the heat between her legs and he wanted her to feel him getting harder and hotter.

Autumn sighed and her eyes slid shut. "More," she uttered through parted lips. "Please, Isaac."

Isaac swiveled the chair around so her back was against the edge of the desk. He gripped her waist and his mouth watered in anticipation as she clutched his head and slowly guided him toward heaven.

Felicia locked her office and shouldered her purse, glad to finally be heading home. Most days she was counting the minutes till five o'clock. But she had two new hires with paperwork that needed to be processed and that took time.

It wasn't like she had anyone at home waiting for her, she thought bitterly. While she was very attractive, she refused to date because the only man she wanted was Isaac. Trouble was, he didn't want her.

And for that, he would pay.

Since she was a little girl, her father had always taught her that she could have whatever she wanted, whenever she wanted it. Most of the time, she didn't have to work for what she wanted.

Sterling had given her this job, and even though she hated it, she stuck with it because it was easy and she got paid enough to buy everything her father wouldn't outright give her.

The only thing he couldn't give her was Isaac. They had nothing in common except the pursuit of money, but from the moment she met him, she was obsessed. She almost went so far as to install a hidden camera in his office, but she was afraid Sterling would somehow find out. So she was forced to keep her attraction to Isaac a secret, especially since at Paxton relationships between coworkers were strongly discouraged.

Perhaps her desire for Isaac was because she was white and he was black. Or maybe it stemmed from the need to pursue something she knew deep down she'd always wanted but would never have. Like her father's love.

Unlike her, Isaac couldn't be bought. He couldn't even be seduced. She'd tried and failed miserably.

But he could be fired.

And when that day occurred, Isaac would finally realize that he needed her because she was the critical link to Sterling. He would come to her, on his knees, begging for his job back, and she would make damn sure that their first meeting would occur in her bedroom.

Felicia walked down the hall to the elevator, idly thinking about calling a friend for dinner so she wouldn't have to eat alone again.

She checked her watch, squinting at the dial. It was

after six o'clock and, on orders of her father, many of the overhead lights were automatically dimmed to save money on electricity. Sterling wanted less of Paxton's profits in the hands of Con Edison and more in his pockets. Plus, going green and reducing Paxton's corporate footprint was a smart business and public relations move.

As she walked past the last hallway before the elevator, she noticed a small wedge of light in front of Autumn's door and stopped in her tracks. According to the security tapes, Autumn had already developed a habit of leaving around four-thirty, which was totally ballsy considering the Paxton work day ended at five o'clock. That was another reason Felicia didn't like her and she was happy to make note of Autumn's leave time in her personnel file.

Isaac normally left around five-thirty, although he used to stay much later. Still, it worked in her favor, as she regularly snooped around in his office and those of other employees. She had keys to every room and every office at Paxton. It always amazed her the types of things people would keep in their desks, naively assuming no one else would ever discover them, or use it against them.

Felicia started down the corridor, for once grateful for the carpeting that her father had installed years prior. It was ugly but it sure came in handy for sneaking around.

As she approached, she didn't hear a sound but looked behind her once just to be sure she was alone.

She stopped short of Autumn's office door and took a deep breath before peeking through the little window.

At the sight of Isaac's lean muscular body folded over Autumn's exposed skin, her eyes widened. When Autumn arched away from the ugly metal desk, Felicia clenched her fists into a ball.

Isaac's hand slowly caressed Autumn's abdomen and Felicia felt her knees weaken. But like a tree with roots gnarled into the ground, she stood firm and watched the scene unfold as if she were in a trance.

Not wanting to see, but not having the strength to tear her eyes away from the sight of Isaac's bent head, she watched his large hands knead Autumn's skin and his full mouth roam everywhere it could reach. Lips she had so desperately wanted on her own body were now hungrily seeking and sucking—someone else.

In that moment, the lust she felt for Isaac was instantly replaced with a deep hatred that seeped through her veins like a sieve.

Fingers raked Isaac's bare back, and limbs Felicia wished she could snap in two hugged his trim waist, when through the thunder roaring in her ears and the jealousy burning in her heart, there suddenly came the muffled cries of a woman in love.

Chapter 12

Autumn tapped her foot on the marble floor of the apartment lobby. If Isaac didn't hurry, they were going to be late for the meeting with Ms. Witterman.

But in reality, punctuality was the least of her problems.

The doorman winked at her as if he could read her thoughts and she pasted a nervous smile on her face. She didn't know which was worse: keeping a secret or the desire to expose it to the world.

Or at least to the man you loved.

Autumn faced the mirrors that lined the walls and fiddled with the collar of her coat.

Love. Was that what she felt for Isaac? Or was she simply playing a role that would result in heartbreak for both of them?

Right now, all she was sure of was that she desired him more than she had any other man. Her need fueled her dreams and also stoked her fears.

More than anything, Autumn didn't want to hurt Isaac.

Knowing that her every thought, touch and kiss was hinged on a lie was getting to be more than she could bear. She was getting in too deep and it was time to step back. Loving Isaac was bad for her, worse for him and potentially disastrous for the case.

Being alone with him earlier in the week had made her come to her senses, and she knew she couldn't be alone with him like that again.

They'd almost made love that evening, right on the top of her desk, which was about as comfortable as that long-ago night when she'd camped in the desert and just as hot. The memory of his hands and tongue on her skin was so real that it made her blush, as if he were right there in front of her, covering the sounds of her climaxing with a kiss.

And when she had begged Isaac to go on, he'd told her it wasn't the right time and seemed content to pleasure her in his arms.

As it turned out, Isaac was right. Time was definitely not on her side, and the more time she spent with him, the deeper she would fall. So she started to edge away, or tried to at least.

For the rest of the week, Autumn insisted that they meet at a local coffee shop in the evenings to review the presentation, instead of in her office or apartment.

Isaac protested at first, but eventually, they came to

a silent understanding and settled into a routine where they were able to focus on the task at hand.

They both knew the importance of this deal.

If all went well today, Autumn would be able to present her findings to Sterling on Monday and that evening be on a plane to her next case.

After extensive research, she had found no evidence of any wrongdoing on Isaac's part, which was great, but it didn't make leaving him any easier.

At the sound of the elevator bell, Autumn checked her appearance in the mirror. She could hear Devon and Deshauna arguing even before the door opened. The two were still going at it when they walked out, with Isaac following close behind.

"I told you not to go into my backpack," Deshauna hollered.

Devon shrugged. "I needed a pencil. How was I supposed to know you kept your diary in there?" He turned to Isaac. "Do you think she really kissed James?"

Deshauna gasped in horror and dropped her backpack to the floor. "That's my private business." She lunged for her brother. "I'm gonna knock your—"

"Whoa! Hold on," Isaac commanded, stepping in between the two just in time. "Nobody's kissing or knocking anything. We'll talk about this tonight. Now you guys better get to school before you're late."

Devon made a quick getaway while Deshauna picked up her bag, her brow still furrowed in anger.

She started to head for the door but stopped when Isaac put his arm around her shoulder.

"I'm sorry that happened. Boys are stupid sometimes. Trust me, I know." He gave her a gentle hug. "Your secret is safe with me."

Deshauna smiled shyly. "Thanks, Dad." She broke away from his embrace. "See you later."

When she was gone, Isaac turned on his heel and walked the short distance to where Autumn stood waiting.

She smiled. "You really handled that well."

Isaac set down his briefcase and buttoned his coat. "Thanks. But I've still got a lot to learn about teenagers, sibling rivalry and first kisses."

"Well, at least you've got the kissing thing down pat," Autumn blurted out, immediately regretting voicing her observations.

"I do, huh?" Isaac replied with a sexy smile. "Care to try again and make sure?"

Autumn hitched in a breath as he wrapped one arm around her waist and pulled her to him. "I didn't get a chance to run this morning and I need something to wake me up."

"But you run every morning. What happened?"

He dropped his arm from around her waist. "I don't recall telling you that. How did you know?"

"I—uh," she stammered as the doorman went outside to flag down a cab. She pointed at him. "He did."

At that was partly true.

There was no point in mentioning the money she paid the man for that initial tidbit of information and for calling her every morning when Isaac left for his run, so that she could get out of the building before he came back. Now that Isaac knew she lived in the building, her money stayed in her wallet where it belonged.

Isaac placed his hands on his hips and stared at the doorman. "Billy? So much for privacy. I think it's time for a little talk."

Autumn reached for his arm as he started off. The case was almost complete. She didn't need Billy blowing her cover and ruining everything.

"No, it's time for us to leave for the presentation. The man made a little mistake. Let it go."

Isaac looked toward the door and then back at her. "You're right. He's a good guy."

Billy strode in their direction. "Cab this morning, sir?"

Isaac nodded and picked up his briefcase. Billy held the door and whistled for a taxi at the same time. Seconds later, one arrived and they got in. Their backs pressed against the seat as the taxi suddenly lurched away from the curb.

Autumn shivered and rubbed her gloved hands together. "Another cold morning in New York," she complained.

"I can't control the weather," Isaac replied, as he put his left arm around her. "But I know something that will warm you up."

He reached around and caressed her cheek with the palm of his right hand, the semi-rough texture heightening every stroke upon her soft skin. She leaned into his embrace and lifted her chin.

Isaac traced the shape of her lips with the tip of his finger. Her insides quaked at the tender gesture and she leaned into his embrace, forgetting that she wasn't supposed to want more.

"You're really special to me. Do you know that?"

She gulped in surprise at his words. "No," she admitted. He lifted her chin, forcing her to look in his eyes. "Then let me show you."

Isaac's lips trailed slowly over hers, one corner to the other, as if discovering their taste, so gently that he nearly brought her to tears. She reached up and grasped the back of his neck and pulled him closer, opening her mouth to accept his tongue.

Autumn kissed him back with a fervor that would later on astonish her. But, for right now, everything blurred and nothing mattered except for the moment they were creating together.

He groaned as he probed the inside of her mouth, his lips grinding against hers. With every kiss, their passion increased and so did the desperation to capture and hold on to it, each knowing that it had to end.

Still, they held the kiss and each other as the taxi raced over bumpy roads and swerved through honking traffic, each not caring about the final destination.

The taxi stopped suddenly, breaking their embrace and bringing them both back to reality.

Isaac exhaled deeply and grinned. "With a kiss like that, I'll never have to drink coffee again."

Autumn nodded distractedly and barely heard his statement. She was worried that Sterling was in the lobby, waiting for them. If he had seen them kissing, she knew he wouldn't be happy, plus it would destroy any trust he had in her to conduct an impartial investigation.

She grabbed her purse and quickly exited the taxi. She smiled at the doorman, who already had the lobby door open for her, and she was relieved that Sterling was nowhere in sight.

Isaac caught up and reached for her hand, but she took a few steps back, avoiding his touch.

He gave her a strange look. "Are you okay?"

She briefly touched her lips, still burning from his kisses, and nodded.

"Yes, I just want to get this presentation over with, know what I mean?"

Before she could walk away, he ran his hand slowly down her arm, the heat of his palm somehow searing through the heavy fabric of her wool coat, and she felt her knees weaken.

Isaac took a step and closed the gap between them. "And when it's all over, what are we going to do then?"

His voice was low and her loins tightened at his question, a hidden promise of continued passion.

"I guess we'll have to wait and find out."

But Autumn already knew the answer. She was leaving Isaac forever.

Isaac examined Autumn's face as they rode the private elevator to Eleanor Witterman's penthouse apartment.

She seemed to want to be with him, but the abrupt change in her demeanor led him to believe she was holding something back, too. The passion for him was assuredly there. He felt it in her kiss, heard it in her cries when he'd pleasured her to orgasm in her office, and that memorable first time in her apartment.

Still, there was an inexplicable hesitation on Autumn's part and before they moved to the next level in their relationship, Isaac knew he had to put her at ease somehow.

He had to tell her his feelings about her even though he was still trying to figure them out himself. It wouldn't be easy, for he realized he wasn't a very outwardly emotional man. But inside, the intense feelings she invoked in him were raw, powerful and very scary.

The elevator doors opened and Sterling greeted them.

"Here they are, Eleanor. We were wondering what happened to you both."

Isaac and Autumn stepped out onto the marbled floor.

"We left in plenty of time, but crosstown traffic was a mess this morning," he lied.

A tall woman with a regal air walked toward them, holding a small dog in her arms.

"Not to worry, dears. Sterling and I have been having a grand time catching up on old times. Haven't we?"

"Old times?" Autumn asked in a confused voice.

Sterling appeared embarrassed. He put his hands behind his back and cleared his throat. "Eleanor and I are old friends, and I'm hoping that after today, I'll be able to call her a client, too," he said tersely.

The latter statement was obviously directed at Isaac and Autumn and was followed by a yip from the dog.

"We'll do our best," Autumn replied hastily, cutting her eyes at the bundle of fur.

"I'm eager to hear where you think I should invest some of my money. It was a good thing Sterling called me when he did," she added. "I was ready to leave it all to my little Pookie."

When Ms. Witterman pursed her lips and started making obnoxious kissing noises at the little fur ball, Isaac glanced over at Autumn, who appeared to be struggling not to laugh.

"What do you say we get started then?"

"Great idea," Sterling replied hastily. "We're going to be meeting in the media room. Eleanor, will you direct us?"

She nodded and set Pookie down on the floor, and they all followed her to a room on the farthest edge of the luxurious penthouse. When she opened the door and Isaac took one look at the movie-theater-like setting, complete with a popcorn machine on wheels, he knew he had to have a similar room in his own apartment.

"This is fantastic," Isaac commented, setting his briefcase on the floor. "It would be great for watching sports or movies with my k—" He stopped himself just before saying the word *kids*. "I mean friends."

But thankfully, Sterling and Eleanor weren't even listening. They were busy getting Pookie settled. Apparently the dog had his own booster seat.

He turned to Autumn, shaken inside at his near error. Now wasn't the time to reveal to Sterling the fact that he had two children and the reasons he chose to keep them a secret.

"That was close," he whispered, shrugging out of his coat and laying it over a nearby seat.

She unzipped her laptop bag and nodded. "I know."

She squeezed his hand, her touch instantly calming him.

Autumn handed him the laptop. "Let's get the computer set up. The sooner we get this over with, the better."

Isaac kept his eyes on hers as she took off her coat, hoping she could see the grateful look in his eyes.

Turning away, he located an elaborate console in a small closet. In just a few minutes, he was able to figure out how to get the presentation to display on the large plasma screen.

When Isaac joined Autumn in front of the room, Sterling and Eleanor were already sitting in the second row, with Pookie in the seat between them happily gnawing on a small bone.

He dug his small laser pointer out of the inside of his suit coat, smiled at Autumn and then at the group in front of him.

"Ms. Witterman, thank you for having us here today. Autumn and I are excited to represent Paxton Investment Securities to discuss our plan to grow your capital through a sound investment strategy that we predict will result in long-lasting and profitable dividends."

"Show me the money!" replied Eleanor enthusiastically, backed by Pookie, who looked up from her bone and yipped in agreement.

Three hours later, Isaac and Autumn emerged from Eleanor Witterman's penthouse apartment exhausted and unsure.

While their potential client had listened intently and had asked a ton of questions, which they and Sterling had taken turns patiently answering, neither knew if she was on board.

"She really had her poker face on," remarked Isaac. "I think that was one of the most stressful presentations in my entire career."

"It was pretty nerve-racking," Autumn agreed as she slipped her arms into her coat. "But that damn Pookie dog sure made out like a bandit. Did you see how many biscuits Witterman fed him?"

"Yeah," Isaac agreed, laughing heartily. "I think he wanted us to convince her to invest in the pet industry instead of diamonds, technology, health care and wind engineering."

Autumn cracked up and they were both laughing as they made their way to the lobby door.

"Isaac! Autumn! Wait!" Sterling called out.

They turned and watched as he strode quickly to them.

"I'm glad to see you're both in a good mood. I have news."

Sterling slapped Isaac on the back. "She loves the strategy you guys presented. Congratulations, we won!"

Isaac and Autumn turned to each other, wanting to embrace with joy but knowing they couldn't.

"That's wonderful," Autumn replied.

Isaac added, "Coming out of the meeting, we weren't sure. It was hard to gauge her reaction to our ideas."

Before Isaac could ask if Autumn would be involved, Sterling stuck out his hand. Isaac shook it, followed by Autumn.

"Great job, both of you. She'll be in our offices sometime on Monday to sign the contract. Isaac, be sure to clear your schedule."

Sterling checked his watch. "It's way past lunchtime, plus it's Friday. Why don't both of you take the rest of the day off. You deserve it."

"Thank you, sir," Isaac replied. "Are you headed back to the office now?"

Sterling shook his head and adjusted his tie. "I'm going to go back upstairs and try to convince Eleanor to go to lunch with me."

"Good luck," Autumn said.

Isaac and Autumn watched as Sterling hopped into the elevator and smoothed his hair. Just before the doors closed, he gave them the thumbs-up.

They walked outside, where a taxi sat idling and the long Friday afternoon stretched pleasantly before them. The sun was shining, making it seem warmer than it really was, and Isaac felt like a heavy load had been lifted from his shoulders.

Winning the Witterman pitch was the last hurdle to his becoming a partner at Paxton. Once that happened, he'd be able to tell Sterling about his kids and he would have achieved everything he'd ever wanted in life.

There was just one thing missing. The love of the woman standing before him.

Autumn looked back at the building and shook her head in amazement. "Now that was really strange. I don't think I've ever seen Sterling so happy. He's normally such a grump."

"Me neither," he responded, belatedly shrugging into

his coat. "And I don't think winning the deal had anything to do with it."

She turned back as he was picking up his briefcase and he smiled at the curious look on her face.

"What do you mean?" she asked.

His eyes floated slowly over her beautiful face, the lithe body that, ever since he'd met her, he craved night and day.

"Let's go home and I'll show you."

Isaac reached for her hand and his heart lifted in his chest when, this time, she took it willingly.

Chapter 13

The cab eased away from the curb and Autumn knew there was no going back.

Her bare hand, still firmly clasped in Isaac's, and the utter calm she felt in the depths of her spirit, were both proof that she was about to risk everything for what lay ahead.

The silence between them gave her time to think, and she idly wondered if she was being foolish or, worse, naive. But Autumn forced those thoughts from her mind. If she had to, she would admit to being a lot of things.

Ambitious.

Willful.

Defiant when she had to be. Harsh, too, although the barbs she dealt were primarily directed at herself.

Some people would call these personality flaws; she preferred to think of them as her protection. Her dad had taught her to never let her guard down, for right around the corner, waiting in the dark and ready to leap, was the unknown.

Thus, naïveté didn't fall into the realm of her existence. Her new life as a private investigator was far too unpredictable for her to be anything but completely confident in her decisions.

She looked out the window and squeezed Isaac's hand. A tense and palpable excitement hung in the air around them, waiting to be unwrapped and explored. In her mind, she cursed the lumbering midday traffic and urged the taxi to drive faster.

When they finally arrived, they hopped out and Isaac suddenly turned and pulled her aside, and she almost slipped on a patch of ice.

She opened her mouth to protest, but he leaned his cheek against hers, his breath hot in her ears. "I want to make love to you, Autumn."

Isaac's voice was low and urgent. "Really make love to you."

He caressed her earlobe with the edge of his mouth and she shivered against his overcoat. "And I don't want you to say anything. Just follow my lead, okay?"

Autumn knew it was crazy, to be at this man's bidding. But, without a moment's hesitation, she found herself nodding her head.

Some would call her decision selfish, since she was leaving town in a few days. But she didn't think it was wrong to take one afternoon of passion with her. Memories were the only things that lasted anyway. Relationships sure didn't. They only got in the way of, well, everything.

This was the right decision, for it would protect both of them from eventual and mutual heartbreak.

Isaac draped his arm around her shoulder and they walked inside the building. As they rode the private elevator up to his penthouse, he pressed his body against hers and kissed her gently.

The doors opened and he backed her into the foyer, his lips never leaving her mouth.

She dropped her purse and he let go of his briefcase, not caring at the moment if the laptops and cell phones within suffered any damage when they hit the marble floor. Their only concern was the inner world of pleasure they were in the midst of creating for themselves.

Autumn's hands drifted up Isaac's back, the heavy fabric of his coat tickling her palms, while he got busy unbuttoning her coat. He eased it over her shoulders and she shivered and broke out in goose bumps in spite of the heat between them.

"Cold?" he asked, shedding his own coat.

She nodded, feeling as needy as a child yet wanting him like a woman.

"I know just the thing that will warm you up."

He led her to the master bathroom and started the water in the huge Jacuzzi tub.

She stepped out of her shoes, trembling in anticipation. As the water ran, he quickly undressed her. She thought it was odd that he did not caress her skin and she found herself yearning for his touch.

When he began to undress, she started to turn away, her nipples puckering painfully in the cool air.

"Watch me," he commanded.

She felt his eyes on her face as he undid his belt and his trousers fell to the tile floor, revealing the bulge of his erection, the outline so deliciously apparent in his white briefs that she bit her lip and prayed he removed his underwear next.

She let out a low groan of frustration when, instead, he slowly unknotted and removed his tie, and then his blue oxford shirt to reveal a muscular frame that seemed even more imposing and sexy in broad daylight.

Finally, Isaac slid his briefs down over his thighs and she gasped as the length of his penis sprang forth.

He placed one hand and ran it up and down the shaft. "Do you like what you see in front of you?"

She pursed her lips and nodded in response.

"So do I. You're beautiful, Autumn. Do you know that?"

It was a good thing he'd commanded her not to speak, for she didn't know how to answer his question. She never thought of herself as beautiful. Pretty, maybe, but never beautiful.

Autumn held her breath as Isaac went to her, his penis jutting out between them, and cupped her face in his hands.

"If you don't think you're beautiful, you will soon," he said urgently.

After grabbing a couple of towels, he turned off the water, took her hand and helped her step into the tub.

"Wait," he said, stepping in after her. "Before you sit down, there's something I need to do. Turn around with your back to me."

Autumn did so and when Isaac traced his finger down the hollow of her spine, from her neck to the crest of her ass, she began to shudder uncontrollably and put her palms against the wall to steady herself.

He ridged a finger against the soft folders of her outer lips and the intense rush of pleasure she experienced as he slid it back and forth made her hands curl into fists.

Isaac sucked in a low breath. "Already wet. Good." He pulled her up against him, and she felt his hard penis roll against the small of her back. "I knew you wanted me."

He wrested her gently around to face him. And she saw that his eyes were as dark and as wanton as his actions.

I do! she wanted to cry out as they sank on their knees into the warm water. Her unsaid thoughts were quickly forgotten by the pressure of his mouth against hers, while their tongues entangled in a lush firestorm of intense need.

Their kiss seemed to last forever, and when Isaac broke away, she whimpered a little and reached for him again. He placed a finger upon her lips to shush her and she stuck her tongue out and licked it in defiance, enjoying his wide-eyed look of surprise.

Autumn gladly complied when Isaac motioned for

her to sit astride his lap, facing him. When her buttocks touched his hard thighs, he moaned and clutched each cheek in his hands, drawing her even closer.

She wrapped her legs around his waist and she didn't have to look down to see just how much Isaac wanted her. The evidence was pressed against her abdomen, taunting her. It took all her strength and will to not lift her hips and slowly guide him inside her.

Instead, she closed her eyes, leaned in and nuzzled at his neck. Inhaling Isaac's dense, spicy-musk scent made her feel more alive than she had in a long time. The slightly rough texture of sponge he used to gently wash her back and arms only added to the pleasant sensations. She couldn't remember the last time she'd felt so cared for by a man.

When he was finished, Isaac cupped her shoulder blades and leaned forward so her back was submerged in the water, washing the soap away. Without thinking, she tilted her head back, dampening her hair, and unwittingly exposed her breasts to the air.

His tongue flicked at one of her nipples and she yelped, and then moaned when he did it again. And again.

Isaac cupped and lifted her flesh in his hands. "Your breasts are so—"

He never finished as she held on to his head, keeping her abdomen tight so she wouldn't fall back into the water, while his tongue curled around each stiff tip, never yielding, never lifting. So warm and wet and steamy.

Finally, he broke away and caught her bottom lip in his teeth. "Let's get out of here."

Isaac exited the tub first and wrapped a towel around his waist. He smiled when her eyes locked on his torso where the fabric wasn't smooth.

When she managed to stand, she found that her legs were rubbery and she almost fell down. But Isaac grabbed her hand, wrapped her in a towel and swooped her into his arms.

The bedroom was only a few feet away and Isaac laid her on his enormous bed before slipping away to draw the curtains shut. He lit two candles on the dresser before returning to her side.

Isaac unwrapped her body from the towel and drew in a breath. She closed her eyes while he stood over her and rubbed her dry with the towel.

When he was finished, Autumn turned on her side and balanced her head on one elbow. His eyes were questioning when she reached out her finger and crooked it between the towel and his waist. With a just quick snap of her wrist, the towel was on the floor and his shaft was throbbing before her. She sat up and slipped him into her mouth, almost to the full hilt of his length, still moist from the bath.

He tilted his hips and groaned as she savored his length with her tongue, enjoying the thick fullness of his skin in her mouth, so velvety soft yet so virile. Capable of creating life and giving pleasure.

His groans became more guttural and he wove his hands through her curls as she sucked hard on the core of his strength. Teasing and taunting him to release, to expend the power he had over her, which she was now controlling with such acute mastery.

Finally, he clasped her cheeks in his palms, breathing heavily and she released him. Smiling, she fell back on the bed and stretched her arms over her head. Without a word, he slipped his hand under the small of her back and clutched at her waist, moving her farther up on the bed. The weight of his body upon hers made her yearn even more to be connected to him.

"Autumn, you drive me crazy enough to tell you that I think I'm falling in love with you."

She opened her mouth, dumbfounded at his confession and was just about to speak when he covered her lips with his own.

Edging her legs apart with his knee, he broke away and whispered in her ear. "Now just let me show you how much I love you."

Autumn gasped as he slid inside her easily and she wrapped her arms around his torso while he rocked his hips and her entire world.

Back and forth they moved together, the bedspread rippling underneath and around them. Isaac nipped at her breast, and her arm muscles tightened as she clenched the little dunes of fabric. She discovered that holding on only intensified the sweet agony, so she held on tighter.

Autumn lifted her head from the bed, hair matted against her neck. "Isaac! Oh, God. Please. Don't. Stop."

She folded her knees to her chest, inviting him to

plunge deeper. He did and, within moments, dove deeper still. The heavy weight of his testicles slapped between her thighs and against her moist outer lips until she thought she'd go mad.

As Isaac increased his pace, so did the fierce whirlwind of emotions that surrounded them, until release poured forth from a cloud of ecstasy.

Eyes wide open, hearts on fire, time forgotten.

Chapter 14

Autumn plopped down on her sofa, limbs extended like a scarecrow, and rubbed her eyes. She had read once somewhere that Sundays were either a time for reflection or regret. Today, she'd experienced plenty of both.

Her eyes welled with tears, still overwhelmed at Isaac's admission of love. Part of her wished his words were only a result of the heat of the moment. The other part prayed they were true.

He'd told her before she left on Friday that he was taking his children on their first ski trip. So, other than a few text messages, she hadn't been in contact with him all weekend. Maybe that was a good thing. He would get used to her not being around and she would get used to missing him terribly.

Autumn wiped the rag in her hand across her forehead, not caring at the moment that it was full of dust, and gazed out the window. It was already dark, the oppressive blue-black wintery hue that made her gloomy mood seem all the more real and her present situation downright inescapable.

Was this how a woman in love was supposed to feel?

Autumn didn't think so. Nor did she think she could face Isaac again, not when she'd betrayed him.

He didn't know that yet, but that's what she did.

Tomorrow morning, she was going to walk into Sterling's office with the final report of her investigation. As far as she could surmise, Isaac was innocent. And now that she knew him and loved him, she realized that there was nothing else he could be but completely free of wrongdoing.

She was the only one who had committed a crime whose only sentence was a broken heart for both of them.

Autumn straightened and leaned over to dust the coffee table. She saw her reflection in the glossy surface and wondered how she was going to explain to Isaac that she was leaving New York in two days.

To tell him the truth, she'd have to reveal the reason she was hired at Paxton in the first place.

To spy, to lie and to betray.

Not to love and then to leave.

But that's exactly what she planned to do.

Autumn moved her bare feet against the edge of the couch and felt something hard.

She slid to the floor and saw her favorite slipper, which had been missing for over a week.

"So that's where you've been!" she scolded, wedging her hand underneath the sofa to retrieve it. And with it came a set of papers, stapled together, that she hadn't known were there.

Autumn backed up against the sofa and sat cross-legged on the floor. The paper was a detailed report of a recent investment transaction conducted by Isaac for one of his clients. It was dated six months earlier, and attached was a copy of the check the client had given as payment. After flipping back and forth through the pages, she could not find any record that the client's payment was applied to Paxton's account.

She threaded one hand through her hair. She'd reviewed hundreds of similar documents for the past two weeks, and somehow she'd missed this one. It must have slipped under the couch on one of the many nights she'd fallen asleep there.

No big deal, she thought as she stood and walked into the kitchen. She would simply follow the same process she'd used with all of the previous reports and check it against the Paxton's accounting system.

She sat down and quickly logged into the Paxton financial network, yet after a few minutes of searching, she could find no record of the transaction.

With a ball quickly forming in the pit of her stomach, she logged out of the Paxton network and logged in to Isaac's personal bank accounts. After an advanced search, she discovered the exact amount of the client's check appeared as a deposit in one of Isaac's accounts.

Autumn's heart sank and she banged a fist on the table, wishing she'd never found the missing document. How could he have done it, she thought. How could he have stolen all that money?

No matter how she felt about Isaac, keeping this information to herself wasn't an option. She had to tell Sterling.

Autumn thought about calling him right away, but she'd already emailed him earlier that she had good news. There was no use in spoiling the man's evening when she could ruin his Monday morning.

She calmly packed up her laptop and slid the report into her bag. Her phone buzzed and her pulse quickened when she saw it was a text from Isaac. She slid her thumb over the top to read his message.

Back home. Missed you. Still cold from skiing.
Can I stop by so you can warm me up?

Autumn stared at the letters for a while before she turned off the lights in the rest of the apartment and headed to the bedroom. It was only when she'd gotten under the covers that she deleted Isaac's text and cried herself to sleep.

The next morning, Autumn left early to avoid running into Isaac and had breakfast at a diner. The pancakes were delicious, but so large that she knew she'd be in a carb coma before ten o'clock. She was on her second cup of tea by the time she arrived at Paxton and she went directly to Sterling's office.

His door was open, but she rapped on it anyway.

Sterling looked up, his brows knit together in a way that made him look instantly angry.

"Looks like the yen is going to ruin my Monday again," he muttered irritably.

"At least the Dow closed on an upswing last week," she offered. "And we closed the Witterman deal."

Sterling looked thoughtful, and then sighed. "Sometimes I wonder why I got into this business."

"To make money?" she offered, wishing he would stop waxing philosophical so she could tell him the bad news.

"No, Autumn. To change lives. Money can do that, you know," he instructed with a wan smile.

"It can also ruin lives," Autumn replied, pulling out the report she'd found last night.

"What's this?" Sterling asked, putting on his reading glasses.

"This is a report from approximately six months ago, a client by the name of Ginsaro."

Sterling reached for the report and she handed it to him.

"Yes, what about it?" he asked impatiently.

"I discovered client funds were never entered into the Paxton financial system. Instead they were deposited into Isaac's personal checking account the same day."

Sterling laid the paper on his desk and glared at her.

"In your email last night, you indicated that your investigation was complete and that you found no potentially criminal evidence."

Autumn nodded. "At the time, that was correct. But

late last night, I discovered this document underneath my couch, and then I logged on to the network and—"

He waved his hand, cutting her off. "Are you sure about all this?"

"I wish I could say no, but I can't."

Sterling nodded grimly and picked up his phone. He stabbed at the buttons. "Felicia, get in here," he barked.

Autumn's stomach clenched. If Felicia was being called into the meeting, that could only mean one thing.

She approached his desk and hoped she wouldn't sound like she was begging. "I think you should give Isaac a chance to explain. There must be a reason or perhaps a misunderstanding."

Sterling raised an eyebrow. "Don't worry, Autumn. We have procedures in place to deal with these kinds of situations." He checked his watch. "He should be here any minute. If you recall, we were scheduled to talk at nine-thirty about finalizing the Witterman deal. Eleanor will be here just before noon to sign all the paperwork, which in light of your discovery, I will now personally handle instead of Isaac."

Felicia stalked into the room without knocking and without acknowledging Autumn.

One of the perks of being the boss's daughter, Autumn thought.

She tossed her blond hair over her shoulder. "What's going on, Daddy? I'm in the middle of something important."

"I need you in here for a meeting that I'm having with Isaac in just a few minutes."

Felicia cocked a brow and stared at Autumn. "Isaac?

I just saw him running down the hall to his office. Do you want me to go get him?"

"No need," Sterling replied. "I'm sure he'll be here soon. You two might as well sit down and wait."

Both women settled down into chairs at a small conference table that was located diagonally from Sterling's desk. Autumn wished she could stare at the buildings outside rather than at the door, but her back was to the windows.

There was a tense silence in the room, as they waited for Isaac. No one bothered to make small talk.

Through the corner of her eye, Autumn caught a glimpse of Felicia, who was watching her intently. More than anything, Autumn wished she could wipe the smug look off her face. The witch knew something. It was almost as if she was expecting trouble and was getting ready to enjoy it.

When Isaac arrived, Autumn drew in a sharp breath.

"Good morning, Sterling. How was your weekend?" he said cheerfully, walking in.

From the doorway, the two women weren't visible, but as Isaac approached Sterling's desk, he turned his head.

Autumn's heart beat faster as he caught her eye and nodded, his eyes lighting up in a way that was only meant for her.

The memory of those same eyes squeezed shut as he kept pace with the urgent rhythm of his lovemaking scraped through Autumn's mind and her body warmed at its most intimate core.

"I'm sorry, I didn't see you ladies there. What is this? A party?" he joked.

"I'm afraid not," Sterling replied, his tone anything but funny. "Please sit down."

Isaac edged a quick glance at Autumn. Somehow she was able to keep her face unchanged, although inside she wanted to scream. At herself mostly, because she was powerless to warn him about what was going to happen next.

He sat and crossed one leg over a knee. "Sure, what's going on?"

Sterling pulled his chair closer to the desk and folded his hands. "It has come to my attention that some client funds are missing from the Paxton accounts. The money was deposited into a personal bank account, instead of ours."

Isaac looked confused. "So, what's that got to do with me?"

Sterling glared at him. "The client is yours and so is the bank account."

Isaac slowly put his foot on the floor. "What are you talking about? What client?" he asked, leaning forward.

"Dr. Ginsaro," Sterling replied.

"But he passed away months ago. I've been trying to get in touch with the lawyer handling his estate, but no luck."

"That's a very convenient excuse," Sterling snapped. "A game of phone tag doesn't explain how $100,000 ended up in your bank account and not ours."

"But I don't know what you're talking about!" Isaac

insisted, raising his voice. "I've never even seen the check."

"First of all, watch your tone. Second of all, as of right now, you are suspended without pay, pending further investigation of these allegations."

"B-but, I didn't do anything wrong!" Isaac sputtered.

"Felicia!" Sterling said, ignoring Isaac. "Call custodial services and get Isaac a box so he can take his personal items with him. You have thirty minutes to leave the premises."

Isaac leaned forward in his chair, looking as though he wanted to throttle Sterling's neck.

"But this is bull! What evidence do you have?"

"We have certain documentation, which will be shared with you upon approval of our counsel. May I suggest you retain your own attorney?"

"I'm not going anywhere. I didn't do anything!" he raged.

His eyes caught Autumn's again, and this time they were frantic. She shook her head, almost imperceptibly, hoping he would avoid further trouble and just go. Although she yearned to speak up and defend him, she couldn't deny what she'd found, any more than she could deny her feelings for him.

Felicia got up and walked over to Sterling's side. "Don't make me call security," she warned.

Isaac flattened his palms on his thighs and stood abruptly. With his chin high, he stalked out of the room.

Felicia followed him to the door and Autumn heard her mutter "Good riddance" under her breath as she shut the door. She sat in the chair Isaac had just vacated.

"Do you want me to prepare the termination papers?"

Sterling didn't glance up from his computer, where he was already typing away as if nothing had happened. "Hold off until I tell you to move forward."

Felicia folded her arms and huffed. "But why? We have everything we need to fire him."

Sterling stopped typing and stared at his daughter as if he was seeing her for the first time. "Not quite. Hold off. End of discussion."

"Well, at least tell me why Autumn is here. For legal purposes, we have rules around who is supposed to be present in the room when someone is reprimanded or terminated. Only you and I should have been in this meeting."

"Autumn is here because she *is* the law," Sterling responded grimly.

Felicia turned around and Autumn enjoyed the look of shock on her face. "You're a cop?"

"No, I'm a private investigator under contract with the U.S. government, to investigate suspected cases of corporate fraud."

She faced Sterling. "Daddy, how did you know?"

"I had some suspicions and I hired Autumn to look into things more carefully."

He stared at his daughter, and Autumn detected a hint of challenge in his eyes.

"I may be getting old, Felicia, but I'm still aware of everything that goes on, and goes wrong, in my company."

Yikes! Autumn thought, quickly planning her escape before she became embroiled in a father-daughter battle.

She stood up and put her coat on. "If you don't need anything else, I've got to get home and pack."

Sterling walked around his desk. "I appreciate everything you've done," he said, extending his hand.

Autumn nearly winced at his strong grip. "No problem at all."

"When are you leaving town?"

"I fly out late tomorrow evening for another case."

Sterling looked impressed. "The government must keep you pretty busy."

"There are plenty of greedy people out there."

Sterling laughed, unaware that her comment was directed toward him.

"Anyway, please feel free to call me if you need anything further," Autumn continued.

She turned to Felicia. "I believe I may have left one of my favorite scarves in my office. Under the circumstances, I don't think it's wise that I go and get it myself."

Sterling's face had a sober expression as he turned to his daughter. "Go check on Isaac and make sure he doesn't take his laptop with him. There's obviously a lot of data on there we don't want him to have access to for now."

He walked back to his desk and sat down. "Felicia will locate your scarf and mail it to you. Thanks again and good luck."

Autumn nodded and walked out of the room, heading in the opposite direction of her former office, for the stairwell. If Isaac was still here, she didn't want to risk running into him at the elevators. She was almost there when she felt a hand grasp her arm.

Before she even turned around, she knew who it was.

"Thanks for not ratting me out in front of my father."

Autumn shrugged. "He's the one paying the bill."

Felicia laughed softly. "Yes. Thank goodness." Her eyes narrowed. "I'll be sure to take good care of Isaac. He'll need someone to turn to now. Someone other than you."

"There's nothing between us, Felicia."

She raised a brow. "Oh no? Well, in that case, I trust you won't have a problem with me satisfying his needs on something other than some old desk."

Autumn felt her cheeks get hot with embarrassment.

"That's right, Autumn. I did a little spying of my own."

"You're sick," she spit out.

Felicia looked thoughtful. "Perhaps, but then again, I'm not the one who has to screw people to get information out of them."

Autumn turned her back, pulled open the door and started her way down the steps, irked that Felicia was right. Dishonesty was at the root of her undercover work. She'd lost count of all the nights she'd lain awake contemplating the irony.

Still, she loved what she did and couldn't fathom doing anything else, regardless of the duplicitous things she needed to do or say in order to get the job done.

Deep in her heart, though, she knew there was nothing false about her love for Isaac, her need to be close to him, but now there was nothing she could do to tell him the truth.

Like her true identity, she had to hide her feelings for Isaac to protect him, as well as herself.

Felicia stood at the door, frowning as she listened to Autumn's heels clanging down the metal stairwell. She was glad that Autumn was out of the way, but she didn't appreciate being played for a fool.

Neither would Isaac once he learned the truth.

She turned and set off for Isaac's office. Autumn was sneaky, conniving and now totally unable to defend herself. Felicia knew this was the right time to reapproach Isaac to lend her support.

When she arrived, Isaac was just locking his office.

"Did you leave your laptop in there?"

"I'm not even going to justify that question with a response."

She ignored his glare and held out her left hand. "I'll take those."

He dropped the keys into her cupped palm. "This is all a sham, Felicia."

She flashed an innocent smile and leaned one shoulder against the wall. "Even if that's true, and I'm not saying that it is, you're not the only one at Paxton who has been deceived."

"I highly doubt that," he retorted.

"We've both been played by the same woman."

His face contorted. "Who? What do you mean?"

"You'll never guess," Felicia said with a drawn-out smile, enjoying the discomfort in Isaac's eyes. "Autumn

Hilliard. She's a private detective, not an investment analyst, as you and I both originally thought."

"What kind of craziness are you peddling now, Felicia."

"It's true. My father hired her to investigate you. She's a fraud." Felicia shrugged, keeping her eyes pinned on his. "I guess that's one thing you both had in common."

His eyes widened in shock and he looked over at Autumn's office. "You're wrong!"

Felicia put her hand on her chest and adopted a solemn tone. "I wish I was. I feel horrible. I mean, if word gets out that I allowed a private investigator to be hired, even if it was by my father, the other departments at Paxton will lose trust in my abilities as a human resources professional."

Isaac shot her another glare. "It's always about you, isn't it?"

Felicia laughed and tossed her blond hair. "You're very astute." She stepped toward Isaac and ran a finger down the lapel of his coat. "But I'm more than happy to make this about you...and me."

"Cut it out, Felicia."

He pushed her hand away and her stomach clenched in anger.

"You know, you really should be nicer to me. After all, I didn't tell Sterling about your little tête-à-tête with Autumn in her office. In case you forgot, we have strict rules here at Paxton about public displays of affection."

"That didn't stop you, did it?"

She laughed again and wrapped her arms around his neck. “When I see something I want, I always get it.”

He twisted away, breaking her hold. “I said, cut it out. I don’t want you,” he retorted in a disgusted tone. “I want—”

Isaac looked again at Autumn’s closed door and Felicia enjoyed the pained expression on his face.

“What you want, Isaac…is a lie. Don’t you see that?”

She felt vaguely satisfied when he didn’t say another word and instead walked away.

He’ll be back. I’ll make sure of it.

There was nothing better than betrayal to cause a man to flee…right into another woman’s arms.

Chapter 15

Isaac rubbed his eyes and yawned as he waited for his children in the kitchen. A cup of coffee, long since gone cold, was the only remnant of a sleepless night. Normally, he would have made an attempt at cooking breakfast, but not this morning when all he wished he could do was to talk to Autumn.

She hadn't responded to texts or phone calls, and when he knocked on her door last night, she didn't answer. To add to his frustration, the doorman wouldn't say if she'd returned to or left the building.

The woman he loved, and who he thought perhaps loved him, seemed to have disappeared into thin air. She was as elusive as the feelings they once shared.

Isaac leaned over the table and stared into the coffee cup, as if it would give him an answer to his biggest question.

He was innocent. Why would she investigate a sham?

All he wanted from her now was an explanation, and maybe a little help in clearing his name.

Isaac lifted his head and checked the time on the microwave. "Kids! Hurry up or you're going to be late for school," he said in a halfhearted yell.

Deshauna sauntered in, touching her hair to make sure her style was still intact. She hoisted her backpack over her shoulder and eyed the table. "I don't want cereal again this morning. Can I have some money to grab a bagel on my way to school?"

Isaac nodded. "There's a ten-dollar bill on my dresser. Don't spend it all at once."

"Thanks, Dad," she called back, already halfway to his room. "I'll see you later."

"Wait a minute. Aren't you going to wait for your brother?"

But his question fell on deaf ears because a moment later, he heard the door slam.

Isaac sighed. As much as he wanted Devon and Deshauna to stick together as before, the pair had become much more independent since the adoption. That was a wonderful thing, but it also meant that he had to worry more about them. New York City had a lot of tempting people, places and things for teenagers, and not all of it was good.

Devon ran into the room, jolting Isaac out of his thoughts.

"Hey, Dad." He stopped just before he got to the table. "Why are you still in your pajamas?"

He was glad at least one of his children had noticed that he wasn't in his normal attire for a Tuesday morning.

"I'm not feeling well this morning, son."

Devon glanced outside and shrugged. "Oh. I thought it was because we had a snow day."

"Sorry to disappoint you, bud, but snow days are pretty rare in NYC."

"I know, Dad, but I can still hope, can't I?"

Devon sat down and poured some cereal into a bowl. He was the only kid Isaac knew who ate cereal without milk.

"So what's wrong, Dad?"

His son's earnest tone made him thankful once again that he decided to adopt. Isaac rubbed at the stubble on his chin. "Well. Something that I thought would work out…didn't, so I guess I'm feeling a little down this morning."

He didn't bother mentioning the fact that, for the time being, he also no longer had a job.

"You know what, Dad? Before you adopted us, I was ready to give up." He finished munching on some cereal and swallowed before continuing.

"We'd been waiting so long for someone. But the evening before we all first met, I told myself that I wasn't going to quit hoping. And as soon as I started believing that in my heart, everything fell into place."

Devon looked around the room, as if he couldn't believe his good fortune. The brightness of his smile could have powered a small city.

"It works, Dad. You should try it!"

Isaac glanced around, but all he saw was expensive cabinetry and appliances he barely knew how to use.

He grinned wide, even though he didn't feel like it. "That's great advice, Devon."

"When I grow up, I want to be a good guy. Just like you."

Isaac felt the corners of his eyes smart, which happened whenever he felt like crying, but he held them back.

He reached over and patted his son's head. "Thanks, bud. I have no doubt you will."

Isaac leaned back and rubbed away the emotion from his eyes. "Better get going before you're late for school."

Devon nodded and jumped out of his chair. With a final wave goodbye, he ran down the hall and out the door.

Isaac slumped in his chair. He needed a fresh cup of coffee badly, but he didn't feel like making any; nor did he feel like getting dressed to go out and buy one.

A few minutes past nine, his phone rang. His heart raced as he reached for it and then fell in disappointment. It was Sterling.

"Good morning, Isaac. How are you?" Sterling bellowed.

"I've had better days," Isaac muttered, holding his phone away from his ear.

"I was wondering if you had lunch plans," Sterling continued, not missing a beat.

"Well, I was going to catch up on my favorite soap opera, but I just learned it was canceled three years ago, so I'm free," Isaac replied.

"Wonderful." Sterling gave him the name of a restaurant on the Upper East Side. "I'll see you at noon."

"What's this all about?" Isaac cut in, but Sterling had already ended the call. He stared at the phone for a second, wondering if he should call his lawyer, before sliding the device across the table in disgust.

Yesterday around this time, Sterling was busy accusing him of one of the worst crimes in business. Now twenty-four hours later he was inviting him to lunch?

Isaac rubbed the bridge of his nose trying to erase the memory of the compliment his son Devon had given him earlier. It was untrue and one that he didn't deserve. Would a good guy let the best job and the best woman he ever had in his life slip away?

With a resigned sigh, Isaac got up and walked down the hall to the bathroom for a shower. He might feel like a bum, but he didn't have to look like one.

Three hours later, Isaac and Sterling sat in a booth at Rudy's, an upscale sports bar and restaurant at 90th and York. The room was crowded with people trying to escape the workday grind if only for an hour, wishing it were three. Many were drinking beer.

Isaac looked around at the wide-screen televisions and neon liquor signs. "I didn't know you were into sports, Sterling."

"I'm not," Sterling huffed. "I had a meeting in the

area and with what I want to discuss with you, it's important that we have some privacy."

Isaac met his eyes. "Well, if it's anything like what we discussed yesterday, perhaps I should start drinking now."

He lifted his hand to call over a waiter.

But when the man arrived, Sterling beat him to the punch.

"We'll have two club sodas with lime and two chicken Caesar salads."

"Good thing I like salad," Isaac muttered as the waiter walked away. "So if you won't let me drink or order my own food, why don't you tell me why we're here?"

Sterling loosened his tie and looked uncomfortable. He cleared his throat. "For an apology."

A sudden roar of laughter erupted from the next table over.

"Excuse me," Isaac said. "I don't think I heard correctly."

Sterling cleared his throat again and leaned against the table. "I'm here for an apology." He held up a hand. "Not yours, mine."

"I don't understand," Isaac replied.

"The document that Autumn found is a fake."

"That's what I was trying to tell you yesterday," Isaac retorted in an exasperated tone.

"But what you don't know is that I planted it."

"You did? Why?"

"I was trying to help my daughter. I knew it was her

that was running an internal smear campaign against you."

"I'm not surprised," Isaac said. "She was constantly trying to throw me under the bus."

"Even worse, a few weeks ago she gave me some trumped-up documents, similar to the one that Autumn found, to prove you were guilty of securities fraud," Sterling continued. "I knew when I hired you ten years ago that you were above reproach, and I still believe that so I brought Autumn on board to prove us both right, and in the meantime, I hoped that Felicia would realize what she'd done."

Isaac sat back in his chair, incredulous at what he was hearing. "So you try to help Felicia by ruining me? That doesn't make any sense, Sterling."

"I know," he admitted. "But I had hoped that she would confess to everything yesterday. That's why I invited her to the meeting. When she didn't, I had to go through with the charade of dismissal."

"Charade?" Isaac swallowed hard. "Does that mean I have my old job back?"

Sterling nodded. "If you'll accept my apology, that is."

Isaac knit his brows. "There's always a catch with you, isn't there?"

Sterling chuckled and waited to speak until the waiter had set down their beverages.

"Then let me sweeten the deal. There's a little thing called a partnership at the end of this rainbow. Does that make accepting my humble apology more palatable?"

Isaac stirred the ice cubes in his glass of club soda

with a straw, buying time. Sterling's offer seemed genuine, but with everything the man had just told him, he still wasn't sure.

"Do you think I'm ready for the responsibility of a partner?"

Sterling nodded. "You've been ready for months, Isaac. You're the best investment analyst on staff. You've got the keenest eye for the moneymaker stocks and clients love you. What more could I ask for?"

"Oh, I don't know. Maybe a son-in-law for Felicia," Isaac replied with a shrug.

Sterling nearly choked. "What?"

"Your daughter has the hots for me, and I'm not interested. If I come back, I need you to tell her to lay off."

"That won't be necessary," he assured, sounding relieved. "I fired her this morning."

Isaac tipped his chair back, almost hitting someone at the opposite table. "You fired your own daughter, why?"

"Because somewhere along the way, I failed her, which was likely the reason she tried to destroy you. If I don't get her some help now, I could be next."

Isaac blew out a breath. Being offered a partnership at Paxton, the firm he'd given so much of his time and talents to, was a dream come true. All his sacrifices would pay off. But he had some confessing to do of his own.

"You know, a part of me almost understands why you felt you had to give Felicia every chance to make things right because I'm a dad, too. I adopted two teenagers about six months ago. Their names are Devon and Deshauna."

Isaac paused a beat and waited for Sterling's reaction.

"I know."

Isaac folded his arms. "How?"

"I make it a point to know everything about my employees, even some things they are trying to hide. That's why I knew you couldn't be deceitful. Anybody that could give up his freedom to become a father to two teenagers is a man I know I can trust."

"It was kind of scary at first, being a dad. And I'll still make a ton of mistakes. But I love them and they love me."

"Now you need to take the same leap with Autumn."

"You know about her, too, huh?"

Sterling nodded. "You think she let you down, but in all truth, she didn't. I urge you not to let pride get in the way of love. I did and for twenty-five years I've regretted it."

"Ms. Witterman?"

"Isn't she a beauty?"

Isaac laughed. "I wish you both the best of luck."

Sterling pushed back his chair and stood. "You can have your second chance, too, Isaac. The best way to win a woman's heart is to be the man she's always been waiting for. Just don't wait twenty-five years to do it."

"Any idea where I can find her?"

"She mentioned she would be moving on to her next assignment in a few days. That's all I know," he replied, shrugging into his coat.

The waiter approached with the salads they had ordered earlier.

"Wait. What about your food?"

Sterling pushed his chair back against the table and wrapped a plaid scarf around his neck.

"I'm having lunch with Eleanor. Take mine to go and share it with your kids." He started to walk away, but turned back to Isaac. "See you at 8:00 a.m. sharp tomorrow?"

Isaac smiled gratefully. "I'll be there and thanks for everything."

As soon as Sterling was gone, Isaac instructed the waiter to package up both salads. With a very busy afternoon ahead, there was no time to spare. He needed to track down Autumn before he lost her for good.

Autumn kicked her sneakered toe against the front of her suitcase. Her flight to Seattle had been delayed for a few hours and rather than suffer at the airport, she had decided to wait it out at her apartment. The doorman was in the process of getting her a car service to JFK and would call her with the details.

The travel delay was annoying for sure, but she was also grateful for it for no other reason than she hoped she would hear from Isaac again. She stared at the phone again, willing it to ring, and wanting to kick herself for not answering his calls and texts yesterday. Now the phone was silent, mocking her cowardice.

Sterling had kept his end of the bargain. He didn't let on who had found the report that got him suspended.

Now she had to uphold her part of the deal and get out of town, so she could bury her fears in her next case.

Autumn jumped at the sound of a knock on her door. "This is it," she muttered softly under her breath, stretching her arms against fatigue as she left the couch.

"What time is the car coming? The flight leaves in ninety minutes," she called out as she opened the door.

When she saw who was on the other side, she took a step back over the threshold.

"You're not going anywhere until we talk."

"Isaac! How did you know I was still here?"

"You're not the only one who can pay off the doorman." His lips curved into a smile, his eyes twinkling. "He's expensive, but very effective, don't you agree?"

Autumn felt her face burn, but she refused to acknowledge his comment. She dropped her hand from the knob and stepped aside so Isaac could enter the room.

When the door was closed, she leaned against it, glad for the support. He was wearing that cologne again. The same one he wore on the night they made love for the first time.

"I'm sorry about your suspension."

"You should be. You're the one who caused it."

Autumn's eyes dipped low and the blood rushed to her face. She started to open her mouth to explain, but Isaac held up his hand to stop her.

"Let me guess. You were only doing your job, right?"

She nodded, but then tilted her head. "Why don't you sound mad?"

He laughed. "Because we both got played…and it's wonderful!"

She shouldered off the door and stood before him. "What are you talking about, Isaac?"

His eyes bored into hers and there was a hint of seriousness in them. "Did I ever tell you how cute you look when you get confused?"

"You're a stockbroker, not a lawyer, so don't change the subject," Autumn warned.

"Felicia told me you're a private investigator."

Autumn cringed inwardly. "And I suppose you believed her?"

"At first, I didn't want to. I kept calling and calling to try to talk with you but you never answered."

"I'm sorry. I didn't know what to say. I didn't want to lie anymore and I couldn't tell you the truth under the terms of the contract I had with Sterling."

"I understand."

"You do? Well, how did we both get played then?"

"Sterling used both of us to try to convince Felicia to stop harassing me. He knew the document was fake because he planted it in the files himself!"

Autumn shook her head and then she started to laugh. "I can't believe it."

"Neither could I at first. Felicia had originally given Sterling some reports meant to incriminate me, but he was suspicious that she'd doctored them up somehow. So he hired you in the hopes that at any point during the investigation she would confess to what she'd tried to do. Yesterday was her last chance."

"Where is Felicia now?"

"On the unemployment line, I suppose. Sterling fired her sometime between yesterday and today."

"And what about you?"

"That's the best news of all. You're looking at the first African-American partner at Paxton Investment Securities!"

Autumn clasped her hands around his neck. "Isaac, that's terrific! Congratulations."

"You know what would be even better?"

She laid her head upon his chest and listened to his heartbeat.

"Coming home to you every evening and making love to you far into the night."

Autumn looked into his eyes. "I would love that, too, but I've accepted another assignment."

He clasped her hands in his. "Do you have to leave so soon?"

She stepped back, praying that her next words wouldn't hurt him. "But I love my career, Isaac. There's more crooks to catch and hopefully this time, they're real."

"I'm not asking you to give up anything." He dove into one of his pockets. "Just take this."

When Isaac opened his hand, there was a key in his palm. "You'll always have a home with us. When you come back, I'll be here. Waiting to show you how much I love you."

Tears sprang to Autumn's eyes and she had to fight to hold them back. "I love you, too." She took the key and held it tightly as she clung to him.

"Can I tell you another sec
my real name."

He smiled and stroked her hair. "
super sexy spy?"

"I'll tell you, but it's a crime if you k
answer," she teased.

Isaac's lips found hers. "Guilty as charged."

* * * * *

HER SOLDIER PROTECTOR

SORAYA LANE

As a little girl I begged frequently for a dog
of my own. Thankfully I only had to wait until
my seventh birthday before I was gifted an
eight-week-old Australian Silky Terrier named
Chloe. So this book is dedicated to my amazing
parents for giving this dog-loving girl her
dream come true!

CHAPTER ONE

LOGAN MURDOCH SURVEYED the waiting crowd. After years spent serving overseas, usually in the desert and lugging an eighty-pound pack on his back, he had no intention of complaining even if he had to wait another hour for his superstar client to arrive.

"Stand by for arrival in five minutes."

He touched his earpiece as the other security expert's voice came on the line.

"Cleared for arrival in five minutes," he responded.

Logan moved down the line, checking that all the waiting fans were securely behind the low, temporary fencing. A couple of policemen were on guard, keeping an eye on the large crowd, and he had a security team ready to help if he needed them. He reached down to give his dog a pat, before moving out with one minute to go to wait for the car. Logan had already led his dog around and inside the entire perimeter to check for explosives, and now their primary objective was to get the client safely from the car into the building.

"I have a visual on the car. Stand by for immediate

arrival," he said, before talking to his dog. "Stay at heel," he commanded.

His dog knew him better than any human possibly could, and the verbal command was just procedure. One look and Ranger would know what he was thinking.

The car pulled up to the curb—jet-black with dark tinted windows—and Logan stepped forward to open the back door. He'd researched his client, knew all there was to know about her in the public domain, but nothing had prepared him for seeing her in the flesh. For the slim, tanned legs that slipped from the car, the beautiful face turned up toward him or the star power she exuded from her small frame. She was gorgeous.

"Ms. Evans," he said, holding out his hand to assist her. "Please follow me immediately through the front door. Will you be signing autographs today?"

Her eyes—big blue eyes that were as wide as saucers—met his, and she shook her head. Logan might never have met her before, but something told him she was terrified.

"Yes!" someone from inside the car barked. "Candace, you're signing autographs. Go."

Logan tightened his hold on her hand as she stepped out, and suddenly they were surrounded by flashes that seemed like bulbs exploding in front of them.

"Easy," he told Ranger, his grip on the dog's leash firm. "Let's go."

He released her only when she loosened her hold, then he walked with his palm flat against her back, his dog on his other side. If she wanted to stop to talk to fans, then that was her decision, but anything that alerted him to a potential problem? Then he'd be the one calling the shots, never mind what her manager or whoever he was wanted her to do.

"Don't leave me," she whispered just loud enough for him to hear, a tremble in her voice.

"I'm right here until you tell me to go," Logan replied, moving his body closer to hers, realizing his instincts had been right. "I've swept every inch of this place, and my dog never makes mistakes."

Logan watched her nod, before bravely squaring her shoulders and raising her hand in a wave to her fans. The flashes from the paparazzi were still in full swing, and now everyone in the crowd seemed to be screaming out to the woman they'd queued hours to meet. He'd been doubtful that she needed such high-level security, but the worry in her voice told him that maybe it had been justified.

"Candace, over here!" one girl was yelling. "Please, Candace, I love you!"

Logan steered her forward, stopping only when she did. He noticed the slight shake of her hand as she signed multiple autographs, before angling her body toward the building. He took his cue.

"Autographs are over," he announced, at the same time as the crowd started yelling again.

They walked straight toward the door, stopping for a few more fans just before they disappeared inside.

Logan touched his earpiece. "We're in the building. Secure the exits."

As the doors shut behind them, Candace collapsed against the wall, her face drained of color.

"Ms. Evans?" he asked, at her side in a heartbeat.

"I'm fine. It's just overwhelming," she muttered, resting her head back against the wall. "I didn't think I was going to be able to make the walk from the car."

Logan dropped Ranger's leash and told him to stay, before crossing the room to fill two glasses of water.

"He won't hurt me, will he?"

Logan glanced back and saw that his dog was sitting to attention, ears pricked, eyes trained on her. Ranger was looking at her as though curiosity was about to get the better of him.

"Lie down," he commanded, smiling as Ranger did as he was told. "He's a big softie and he knows his manners. The worst he'd do is lick you if I let him, and he sure seems to like the look of you."

Her smile wasn't convincing, but she did seem to relax. He passed her a glass of water, trying not to look too intently at her bright blue eyes, or the long blond curls that were falling over her breasts. In real life she was beyond stunning—much shorter than he'd have guessed, and tiny, like a doll.

"Tell me why you're so scared," he asked. "I'm guessing it's more than just the bombings that have happened around the world lately to cause a seasoned superstar like you to panic."

Candace nodded, sipping her water before passing it back to him.

"I've received threats," she told him. "The first few to my house, then a package sent to my last tour bus and another to my manager. I was fine to start with, but it's starting to get to me."

Crap. He'd guessed there was more to this story, but the fact that he was head of security and hadn't been correctly briefed was a major breach of trust from everyone involved.

Logan kept his face neutral, not wanting her to see him as anything other than trustworthy and dependable. It wasn't her fault that not all the information had been passed along—he would save his anger for someone who deserved to be blasted. *Like maybe his boss or her manager.*

"I've worked with Ranger for five tours in warzones, so there is no chance an Improvised Explosive Device is coming anywhere near you without him detecting it," Logan told her. "The only thing you have to do is make sure your people keep me fully briefed at all times. No secrets, no lies."

The smile she gave him was shy, but it lit up her face, made her eyes swim to life. "Will you stay with me until I go on? I have an interview to do soon, but I'll be in my dressing room until the show."

"Yes, ma'am." There was no way he was going to walk away when he'd finally seen her smile like that.

"I don't even know your name," she said, pushing off from the wall she'd been resting against as her entourage came down the stairs at the end of the hall, having been escorted into the building through a separate door.

"Logan," he said. "And this here is Ranger."

"Call me Candace," she told him, her eyes never leaving his as they spoke. "If you're in charge of keeping me safe, you can at least call me by my first name."

Logan smiled at Candace and picked up Ranger's

leash, before following a few steps behind her. He might have moaned about being asked to work security by the Australian Army, but this job was turning out to be a whole lot more interesting than he'd expected. She was here to perform to a sold-out crowd and help promote Australia to the rest of the world at the same time, and being her private security detail might just prove to be the most enjoyable work he'd done in his career with the SAS.

Personally enjoyable, anyway. Not to mention it was a job that wasn't going to haunt him in the middle of the night like his last few assignments.

For the first time in weeks, Candace was relaxed. The tightness in her shoulders had almost disappeared, and she wasn't on edge, looking sideways to make sure no one was following her who shouldn't be. Ever since the letters had started to arrive, she'd hardly slept and almost cancelled the last leg of her world tour, but she hated letting anyone down.

And then Logan had escorted her past the waiting crowd and into the building, and the fear and terror had slowly seeped from her body.

She'd had plenty of bodyguards over the years, usually hulking guys who could deal with any physical threat. But with the latest spate of bombings around the world and the situation with the letters, she didn't just want men capable of brute strength around her. She'd asked for the best, and it looked like she'd received him.

"We'll take it from here."

She glanced across at her manager, Billy. He always

had her best intentions at heart, or at least she hoped he did, but right now she wasn't interested in doing what she was told.

"I've actually decided I want Logan to stay with me," she said.

Eyebrows were raised in her direction, and she almost laughed at the stern expression Logan was giving them in response. She doubted that he was easily intimidated, or that anyone here would have the nerve to cross him, especially not with his fierce-looking dog at his side.

"This way," Candace said, nodding toward the room with her name on it.

He followed, dog at his side, each of his footsteps covering more ground than two of hers. It was oddly comforting having his heavy boots thumping out of rhythm with the click of her heels.

"So are you in private security now?" she asked, wondering how someone who'd served in warzones was even assigned to work with her.

He chuckled. "Would you believe me if I told you I'm still SAS, but that the Australian government was so determined to have you here to promote their new tourism campaign they decided to send me here to head the security team?"

She shook her head, pushing open her door. Logan walked past her, his dog doing what appeared to be a quick check of the room.

"You're not kidding, are you?"

"Nope. But I can't say that I mind. After years on

patrol in the middle of nowhere, it's a nice change of pace before I retire."

She sat down on the sofa and gestured for him to do the same, unsure of whether she believed him or not. "What do you feel like? Sushi? Something more substantial?"

He raised an eyebrow. "You're ordering lunch for both us?"

"Ah, yes," she said, not sure why he found that so unusual. "Unless you do something different at this time of the day in Australia?"

He shook his head, a wry grin on his face. "If you're buying lunch, then I definitely have no complaints about this gig."

"I have a bit of a ritual that I always eat Japanese food before a show. I'm thinking sashimi and miso soup, but maybe you'd like something more."

"Candace, I'm used to eating dehydrated army food when I'm working, so if you feel like sushi, I say sure."

"That settles it then. I'll order." She stood up to use the phone, ordering way more food than they'd ever consume.

Candace turned back around, eyes locking on Logan's as he met her gaze. It wasn't something she was used to—a man not intimated by meeting her, not fazed by the circus they'd confronted when he'd escorted her from her car. *She* knew that she was no one special, but men usually reacted badly to her fame or her money, and the way Logan was behaving was the complete opposite. He was just staring back at her like she was… ordinary. Although she guessed a lot of it, dealing with the crowds and stress earlier, was more to do with his training than anything else.

"Can I ask you something?"

He shrugged. "Shoot."

"You're the first guy in years who's treated me like a regular woman and not a celebrity. Is it your training or just how you are?"

He leaned back, crossing his legs at the ankle and stretching out his big body. Logan was tall and fit, the T-shirt he wore snug to his athletic frame, pants stretching over his thigh muscles. She'd sure hit the jackpot where he was concerned.

"*Aren't* you a regular woman?"

She felt a blush crawl up her neck and heat her cheeks. It had been a *long* time since a man had drawn that kind of reaction from her, but he'd said it like it was the most logical answer in the world. Which she kind of guessed it was.

"Of course I am," she said, refusing to be embarrassed. "It's just that men usually avoid me, look at me like I'm some freak show because they've seen me on television or in magazines, or otherwise they're all over me. Even most of my bodyguards have never gotten used to dealing with the whole fan and paparazzi thing."

"Sounds like you haven't spent much time with real men," he said with a chuckle. "Or maybe it's just that Australian men aren't so easily intimidated. A pretty lady is a pretty lady, no matter who she is, and at the end of the day, I'd rather a camera in my face than a semi-automatic."

He thought she was pretty? "Well, maybe I should

spend more time *down under.* Is that what you call it here?"

"Yeah, that's what we call it."

Candace could tell he was trying not to laugh.

"So, are you going to hang around for the concert?"

"Is that an invite?"

"There's a VIP pass with your name on it if you want to stay. And I can't say I'd mind you hanging around, knowing that you're keeping an eye on things that could go boom."

"Sure thing. Can't say I've ever been given the VIP status before, so it'll be a nice change."

Candace cleared her throat. "Ah, do you have a partner or anyone I should add to the list, too?"

"Yeah, but he's probably not that interested in a show."

"Oh." He was gay? She sure hadn't seen that one coming, and it wasn't exactly easy to hide her disappointment. "If you're sure, then."

Logan met her gaze, his eyes dancing with what appeared to be...humor? "You've already met him, actually."

She swallowed, trying to figure out why he looked like he was about to burst into laughter again. "I have?"

"Yep. He's pretty big, beautiful brown eyes...and he's staring at you right now."

It took her half a second before she locked eyes with the dog staring at her, his black tail thumping against the ground as she showed him a hint of attention, like he'd figured the joke out before she had.

"That wasn't funny," she said, shaking her head and refusing to smile.

"Sorry, couldn't help myself."

"So, just the one pass, then?" she asked.

"Just the one," he confirmed, standing up when a knock at the door echoed throughout the room.

Candace watched as Logan accepted the food and kicked the door shut behind him. He wasn't hard to watch, the kind of guy she'd always notice no matter where she met him—tall, built and with close-cropped dark hair that matched his eyes. But he was strictly off-limits, eye candy only, because she was staying true to her promise not to get involved with anyone at the moment.

He paused, stood there looking down at her before crossing the room again.

"Candace, I won't be offended if you say no, but are you busy after your show?"

Why did he want to know, and why did he suddenly look so...staunch? "Why's that?"

Logan cleared his throat "I thought you might like a night out in Sydney, you know, to just have fun once you're done with work." He laughed. "I've been working around the clock for months, and I have a feeling you don't take much time off, either."

Candace stared at him, taken aback. He'd just managed to surprise her twice in less than a few minutes. "It's not that I don't want to, but it's just not that easy for me to hang out in public." Was he asking her on a date or did he think taking her out was part of his job description?

He put the containers down on the low table between the two sofas and sat down, leaning forward, eyes on hers. "You're in Australia, not America, and the places I'll take you, if it's just the two of us, no one will even realize who you are." Logan held his hands up. "But I have thick skin, so you can just turn me down and I'll forget I ever asked."

She took the plastic tops off the containers and reached for a pair of chopsticks, before looking up and seeing the serious expression on Logan's face. He was serious. And she had no idea what to say to him.

"You promise I'd be safe? That it would just be the two of us?"

"I promise," he said. "You'll just be a girl in the crowd instead of a superstar."

A shiver cascaded down her spine, spreading warmth into her belly. *Now that was something she liked the sound of.* "I'll think about it, but it does sound nice." It sounded way better than nice, but she didn't want to lead him on, not until she'd had time to think about it.

"Well, you just let me know when you're good and ready," he said. "Now it's time for you to tell me exactly what I'm about to bite into here, because I haven't ever seen anything that looks like this before."

Candace didn't usually even talk much before a show, tried to rest her voice, yet here she was chatting with a cute guy and thinking about going out with him. Maybe Australia was exactly the place she was supposed to be right now, to take her mind off everything that had been troubling her since...way too long.

* * *

Logan fought not to grimace as he held the chopsticks—awkwardly. He wasn't opposed to trying new things, but the food sitting in front of him looked downright scary. Not to mention the fact that he was more comfortable using a good old knife and fork.

"When you said Japanese, I was kind of thinking about the over-processed chicken sushi that I find at the mall."

Candace gave him her wide smile again, the one that was making him wish he'd met her under different circumstances. Although, someone like her wouldn't exactly have crossed paths with him if he hadn't been assigned to mind her. She was an international superstar and he was…a soldier turned bodyguard for a couple of days. Which was why he'd taken his chance to ask her out while he could. That would teach his friends for pestering him about being single too long and not enjoying enough human company—he'd stepped completely outside of his comfort level with Candace.

"So, I probably should have explained to you that sashimi is raw fish, huh?"

Logan raised his eyebrows and wrangled with the chopsticks some more, trying to mimic her actions. Except she was already dunking her first piece in the soy sauce and popping the entire thing in her mouth, which meant she was way ahead of him.

"Here goes," he muttered, leaning over the table so he didn't spill any, his other hand ready to catch anything that fell.

"What do you think?" she asked.

He swallowed. "I can't say I've ever wanted to eat raw fish before, but I guess it's not half bad."

"I do have one kind with a cooked prawn on top. Here," Candace said, opening another box and then pushing it his way. "Try this."

Logan shook his head. "I can't go eating your favorite foods hours before your big concert. I'm the help, not a guest."

She rolled her eyes. "If we eat all this I can order more, so just take whatever you like, okay?"

Logan stared at her, wondering if he was about to see her diva side firsthand. He had a feeling someone that beautiful and talented was bound to be difficult. "You're sure?"

"Look, most celebrities have a rider about exactly what they do and don't want backstage or in their dressing room. Me? I just ask to have someone ready to run out and grab me great Japanese food and bottled water, and I request good lighting for my hair and makeup team." She smiled, shrugging at the same time. "I like the fact that everyone thinks I'm easy to deal with, so trust me when I say we can order more. These people are used to divas requesting a certain number of candles with a particular scent, flowers, bowls filled with expensive chocolates and imported candy. You get my drift?"

Logan got the picture. "Okay, pass me the prawn one, then."

"That's more like it."

Candace pushed the container closer to him, as well as a cup with a lid on it.

"What's this?"

"Miso soup. You'll love it."

Logan took off the lid, staring into the brownish liquid. "You sure this stuff won't kill me?"

"Positive. Now stir it with your chopsticks and take a sip. The green stuff is just seaweed, and there might be a few pieces of tofu floating around, too."

"Tofu?" he asked, pausing before the cup touched his lips. "You're killing me. I don't even think Ranger would eat tofu."

As if he understood exactly what they were saying, Ranger let out a low whine that made Candace laugh.

"Tofu," Logan muttered, taking a sip.

It wasn't half as bad as he was expecting, so he had some more, careful to avoid anything solid that was floating around in the soup. He was probably the only person in the building who hadn't tried this type of food before, but he was a soldier and a rancher—he was more used to simple steaks, vegetables and fries than the latest cuisines. Not to mention he was having to act like a regular guy instead of one who usually couldn't go a day without exercising like a crazy thing—sprinting as hard as he could to outrun his demons.

"So, what do you think?" Candace asked, pulling her long hair from her face and throwing it back over her shoulders.

"I think," he said, clearing his throat and putting down his chopsticks, "that it's time I went and did another perimeter check."

He was starting to become way too comfortable sitting around with Candace, eating fancy food like he did it every day.

Smoke billowed around him, obscuring almost everything. He walked slowly, not able to see even one of his feet, but he never let go of Ranger's leash. And then he stumbled, looked down and realized he'd just walked over another human being, facedown in the sand.

Logan cleared his throat, pushing away the memories that always hit him when he was least expecting them. If he wasn't on duty, he would have changed his shoes and hit the gym. But today that wasn't an option, and neither was giving in to his memories.

CHAPTER TWO

CANDACE TOOK A deep breath, mentally preparing for the concert. She'd been given her sixty-minute countdown already, which meant it was time to start running through her exercises, have a little something to drink, stretching out so she was all limbered up and dressing in her first costume.

But preparing for the performance wasn't taking up all her energy like it should have been. Instead she was thinking about a certain man who'd as good as knocked the wind from her earlier in the afternoon.

She'd been single for so long, not to mention the fact that she hadn't met a man who'd even remotely interested her for close to a year. Maybe that was why Logan had surprised her so much. Because even if she stayed true to her promise to remain single, she could still appreciate a good-looking man. And Logan was a fine-looking addition to the male species.

Candace cleared her throat and was about to start rehearsing when there was a knock at the door. She didn't call out because she was saving her voice, but she did cross the room to see who it was.

"Hey."

The man she'd been trying her best not to think about was standing in the hallway.

"How did you get past my security detail?" she asked in a low voice.

Logan grinned. "It just so happens I know the boss."

She laughed and pulled open the door so he could come in. She was about to ask him in when he held his hand up and shook his head.

"I'm not going to disturb you, I just wanted to check that you felt safe," he told her. "I personally handpicked the men working tonight, so you've got nothing to worry about, and I'm going off duty now for a quick break."

Candace thought for a second before saying what was on her mind. "What do you think about escorting me to stage and watching from the wings?"

"Like my own private concert?" he asked, raising an eyebrow.

She grinned. The idea of having Logan close by in case something *did* happen would be reassuring.

"What if I made you a trade?" she asked.

He cocked his head, clearly listening.

"I'll say yes to the night out you suggested, tonight, if you look after me for the duration of my performance."

Logan didn't even blink he answered her so fast. "You're on."

Candace met Logan's gaze, determined to keep her head held high. He was a handsome man who happened to be protecting her, and one she'd agreed to go on a date of sorts with. It didn't mean she had to go all bashful and forget the confident woman she usually was.

"Well, that's settled then," she said. "I'm going to keep running through my routine, so if you could come back in about forty-five minutes?"

Logan nodded. "Yes, ma'am."

Candace forced herself to stop staring at the tall, heavily muscled hunk standing outside her door and shut it instead, slowly slithering to the floor once she did so, cool timber against her back. She was behaving like a silly girl, flirting with a man who probably had no interest in her other than to parade her around a few hotspots on his arm. How many times before had she had someone say to her that they wanted to take her on a quiet date, only to find the paparazzi tipped off the moment they arrived at a restaurant or club? Or a man pretending he wasn't interested in her fame, only to find out he was a wannabe film star or singer with a CD he wanted to slip her during drinks or over an entrée. *That* was why she'd sworn off men for the time being.

Deep down, she wanted to believe that Logan was different, but until he'd proven that he wasn't the type of guy she was used to, she needed to tread lightly. No falling for her bodyguard, no touching her bodyguard and definitely no letting herself think, at any stage, that he could be anything more than fun.

She'd tried serious, and it hadn't worked. She'd even tried marriage, too, and that hadn't worked out well at all. When it came to men, she'd realized that maybe she just wasn't good at picking them, and it was probably something she'd inherited from her mom. Her mom might have been an incredible businesswoman, but she'd also had to raise Candace singlehandedly because of her poor decisions when it came to the male species.

Candace sighed, reached out for her first outfit, ran her hands down the silk, shut her eyes and imagined herself on stage, wearing it. Listening to the crowd. Holding the microphone as the band started to play. Hair and makeup would be back any minute, and so would her stylist.

She could do this. She'd performed a hundred times before, and Logan had promised her that the venue was safe and secure. She needed to forget the stupid threats and just do what she did best. Because no matter what happened to her, no one could ever take away her love of singing. Performing was the love of her life and it always would be.

This was her time to shine.

"You a fan of country music?"

Logan glanced at the woman standing beside him, her headset pulled back so she could talk to him. She was holding a tablet, and until now she'd had her eyes glued to it and had been speaking intently into her headset.

"I can't say I've ever really listened to it before," he admitted. Truth be told, he'd never listened to it because he'd never really liked it before, but watching this particular performance was fast converting him to the genre.

"She's pretty incredible to watch," the woman said, pulling on her headset again. "I get to see a lot of performers, but she's hands down the most talented and nicest we've hosted yet."

Logan smiled in reply and turned his attention back to Candace. As the song finished she wowed the crowd with her mesmerizing, soft laugh, before turning around and waving toward the band so they could have their own round of applause. He was pleased that she'd asked him to watch, but he'd actually been employed to stay until the end of her concert anyway. He just hadn't told her that.

"Thank you for having me here tonight!" she told her fans. "Australia is one of the most beautiful countries I've ever visited, and I wish I had more time to spend here."

The applause was deafening, but Logan could no more take his eyes off her and walk away than he could stop breathing. If there was such a thing as star power, she had it—on stage she wasn't the sweet, soft-spoken woman he'd spent time with earlier in the day. Up there, her presence was almost overpowering, and the screaming fans only seemed to make her light up more in front of them, her confidence soaring as they encouraged her.

As she burst into another song, Logan leaned against the wall where he was standing. The past year had been nothing short of hard, unbearable, and being here tonight, watching Candace, was the kind of night he'd needed, even if it was technically work.

When Sam had died...*hell.* He didn't want to go back there. Losing one of his closest friends so soon after his parents' accident, then coming so close to losing another under different circumstances, not to mention deciding to retire—he'd only just pulled through. But the rush he'd felt when Candace had said yes to a night out with him had given him a much needed boost. He was ready to add some nice memories to his thought bank, and Candace was exactly the kind of memory he'd prefer to dwell upon.

He looked up as the next song came to an end, and the next thing he knew Candace was running toward him.

"What did you think?" she asked, eyes flashing as she glanced at him, a big smile on her face as she ran in her heels. "The crowd is crazy here!"

She kept moving, not pausing, so Logan spun and jogged to keep up with her, even as she was surrounded by a group of people who started to tug at her clothes and talk a million miles an hour.

"You were great out there," he managed when the crowd paused for a nanosecond.

"You really think so?"

There was an innocence in her gaze that made Logan smile, because this was the woman he'd glimpsed earlier. The one who was so used to being told by others what they thought she wanted to hear, that she no longer knew who to believe, who to trust. She wanted to know whether she could believe him—it was so obvious it was written all over her face, and he had no more intention of lying to her than anyone else.

"I know so," he told her honestly.

The words were barely out of his mouth before she disappeared into her dressing room, and Logan turned his back when he realized the door wasn't going to be closed. It seemed like only minutes later that she was running back out again, heading toward the stage, and instead of trying to keep up with her this time he just walked behind. She was still being plucked and prodded, her outfit pulled into shape and her hair fiddled with just before she was due back on stage. The woman with the tablet from earlier was flapping her arms at a group of dancers, before starting a countdown and sending them on as the music started again.

Just before she disappeared, Candace turned and locked her gaze on his, smiling for barely a second before throwing one hand in the air and returning to the stage.

There was no doubting she was a brilliant performer, but she was also like a little girl desperately in need of someone to look after her and trust in. To tell her the truth when she needed it, but also to shield her from harm.

"I'm not that person," Logan muttered to himself, even as his instinct to protect reared within him before he could stamp it out.

He'd protected and looked after people all his life, and still he'd lost those he loved. Some of the people he cared most about in the world, and some strangers whose faces he'd never forget until the day he died, too. Looking after Candace while she was on stage and during her press conference tomorrow was his job, and one he intended on doing well, and tonight was about having fun with a beautiful woman. There was no need to overthink the situation or turn it into something it wasn't.

He wasn't going to be the one to rescue her, because

he was still waiting to be rescued himself. Tonight was going to be great, but after that he'd never see her again, which meant she wasn't his to worry about. Or protect.

Candace took one last bow after her second encore song before walking from the stage. It had been the kind of night she loved, the type that made her remember how lucky she was to perform for a career, even though her nerves had jangled whenever she'd let her mind stray to the hate mail she'd been receiving. There were always those times when she wondered if that person was in the crowd, watching her, but with Logan standing in the wings and the security amped up for the evening, she'd tried to make herself just relax. And for the most part it had worked.

Her heart was still pounding, adrenaline making her feel a million dollars, as she disappeared into the darkness of the wings, her eyes taking a moment to adjust from the bright lights she'd been performing under.

"I think you've made me like country music," a deep male voice said.

She recognized Logan's Australian twang the moment she heard it, and her heart started to race a little more.

"I'd say I don't believe you, but I kind of want to," she said with a laugh.

"I'm actually thinking of joining your insane fans and lining up for a CD and T-shirt. It seems to be the thing to do."

She laughed, brushing her hand against his as she passed and then snatching it back like she'd connected with a flame. It had been a long time since she'd just touched someone impulsively like that, and it wasn't something she wanted to make a habit of. Especially not with a man, even if she was enjoying his company.

"You can have a free T-shirt, I'll even autograph it for you," she teased.

"So what time do you want to head out?" he asked, following her.

Candace took a slow breath, still energized from her ninety minutes on stage. She always felt amazing at the end of a performance, exhaustion never setting in for hours after she finished.

"We'll need to wait until the crowds die down. I don't mind signing a couple of autographs, but I'm not going to ruin my buzz by being mobbed. Not tonight."

Logan shook his head. "I think we're best to leave immediately, before anyone expects you to depart. My truck's parked around the back and we should be able to get in before anyone realizes it's you, so long as we move quickly."

Candace wasn't convinced, but then she also usually timed these kind of things all wrong anyway and ended up in the middle of a hundred fans, trying to reach her getaway car. Or else her manager set things up to happen like that for maximum publicity when she gave him explicit instructions to the contrary.

"I don't believe you, but I'm prepared to give you the benefit of the doubt," she said.

"Good. I'll go check the exit now and be back in ten minutes," he told her. "Shall we meet in your dressing room?"

Candace nodded. "Let's do it."

The idea of a night out was exciting—she'd become used to feeling fantastic, on a high from singing, then going straight back to a hotel room, alone. Most of the time she ended up ordering room service, watching an old movie and going to bed, before receiving her wake-up call and taking a car to the airport early the next morning. Before she'd become recognizable, she'd always had a fun night out after any gig, which was why tonight was like a blast from the past for her. Add the tourism campaign she was the face of, and she didn't have a hope of Australians not realizing who she was.

It was yet to be seen whether she could even manage to leave the building without being recognized or followed, so she could easily end up holed up in her hotel room just when she least expected it.

Candace closed her dressing room door the moment she stepped inside and slipped the feathery minidress off, letting it pool to the floor. She rummaged around in her case for the casual clothes she'd packed, in case she needed them, pulling out a pair of dark blue skinny jeans and wriggling her way into them. She didn't have anything other than a T-shirt to wear, so she flicked through the tops hanging on her racks, wishing they weren't all so costume looking, until she spotted a sequined black tank. Candace pulled it over her head, grabbed a studded leather biker jacket, and slipped into a pair of dangerously high heels she'd worn on stage earlier in the evening.

Glancing at the clock on the wall, she stopped, took a deep breath, then sat down at her dressing table. Her makeup was excessive—thick false eyelashes and sparkly eyeshadow—but she didn't have time to change it. Besides, Logan had seen her looking like this all evening. She did run her fingers through her hair to flatten it down a bit, teasing the hairspray from her curls so it felt like real hair again, so it was touchable.

There was a knock at the door. Candace jumped, glaring at her reflection at the same time. It was just Logan, and it wasn't like she hadn't known he was coming, but her nerves had been permanently on edge for weeks now. Maybe she could talk to him about it and see what he thought the best way to react to the threats was.

"Just a minute!" she called out.

Candace jumped up to grab her purse, checked her credit card, phone and hotel swipe card were all inside and swung open the door.

"Wow."

Logan's approving smile and the way he looked her up and down made her laugh. He seemed to say what he was thinking, and she liked the fact he was a straight shooter with her.

"Are we cleared to leave?" she asked, trying to ignore what he'd just said even though she couldn't stop smiling.

"I told your manager and the rest of the team that you're feeling ill, and you wanted me to escort you straight to the hotel. I said we'll be exiting from the side entrance, and I have a feeling there'll be a lot of fans waiting there, if you catch my drift."

"So we can't go?" she asked, hearing the disappointment in her own voice.

Logan gave her a wry smile, a dimple flashing against his cheek at the same time. "We're going out the very back. My vehicle's parked down the alleyway, so no one will see us."

"So you lied to everyone?" she asked.

"I expanded the truth," he said, winking as he gestured for her to follow him. "I have a feeling your manager is more interested in getting publicity than a quiet getaway for you, and given that I'm your head of security, all I care about is your safety. You say no fans or paparazzi? That's what I give you."

Candace shook her head. "I think I underestimated you," she said with a chuckle.

"I also told them that you'd be exiting in fifteen minutes, so if we're going to do this, I think we should hurry, just in case someone comes looking for you before we go."

He waited for her to nod, then clasped her hand firmly, walking fast in the opposite direction to which they'd arrived earlier in the day. Candace had to almost run to keep up with his long, loping stride, but she didn't care. Logan was going to get her out of here without being mobbed, without even having to come face-to-face with her manager, and she might actually have a drink at a bar before anyone figured out who she was. Adrenaline was starting to fill her with hope.

Her phone started to beep in her purse, and she managed to open it without slowing down. She glanced at the screen.

"It's Billy, my manager," she told Logan when he looked down.

"Text him from the car when we're driving away," he said. "You can tell him we've gone once we've hit the main road, but not before."

Candace slipped the phone back into her purse and hurried along with Logan, trying to concentrate on not falling off her stiletto heels. A few little white lies weren't going to hurt anyone, especially not her manager, who didn't seem to care that she'd spent the past few weeks frightened out of her own skin about the thought of being in public.

"So did you believe me when I said I'd get you out of there?"

Logan glanced over at Candace and saw that she was staring out the window, watching the world as it blurred past.

"No," she replied, sighing and turning in her seat to face him. "If I'm completely honest I didn't even want to let myself hope that I'd get out of there that easily."

"So I don't need to ask you if you're still keen for a few drinks and something to eat?"

Candace laughed and it made him smile. "I'll stay out until someone starts flashing camera bulbs in my face."

"You're on. The places I'm taking you no one will ever find us."

She was looking out the window again, and he took his foot off the gas a little so they weren't going so fast. For someone who hadn't found it easy being back or dealing with people, he was finding it weirdly easy to talk to Candace. She should be the one person he had nothing in common with, but for some reason he was drawn to the fact that she was an outcast just like he was, albeit a different one. It settled him somehow.

"That kind of makes you sound like a serial killer," she finally responded, like she was just thinking out aloud. "Which makes me wonder how I ended up letting you whisk me away from everyone who's supposed to be looking after me and keeping me safe."

"I'm the one who kept you safe today, so you don't have a lot to worry about," Logan told her, taking his eyes off the road for a second to make sure she was listening to him, looking at him. "If I'm perfectly honest, you have a manager who makes sure you get mobbed when he knows you hate it, and the rest of your entourage probably have way less interest in making sure you're kept out of harm's way than I do."

She shut her eyes and put her head against the rest. "I know you're right about my manager. Deep down, I think I've known it for a while. I just didn't want to acknowledge it."

He didn't answer. He knew he was right, but he didn't need to make her feel worse than she probably already did.

"Until you said that, I guess I've been trying to bury my head in the sand and pretend like everything's fine."

Logan fought the battle to bite his tongue and lost. "The guy's seriously bad news. How long have you put up with him for? I know you have more experience with the whole celebrity thing than I ever will, but that's a layperson's take on him."

Candace sighed. "He's been with me for years, and

he used to be a lot better than he is now, that's for sure," she muttered. "Things have kind of been going downhill for a while now."

"How about we stop talking about work and just have a nice night?" Logan suggested, wishing he'd just kept his mouth shut instead of insulting her people. For once in his life he wasn't screwing up—usually something he only managed to achieve in his work life—and he needed to just enjoy the company of a beautiful woman.

"You betcha," Candace agreed. "Hey, where's your dog tonight?"

Logan grimaced. "I left him at home. He was pretty pissed."

"You know, for a dog he's kind of nice."

"You're a cat person, aren't you?"

She laughed, like she was embarrassed. "Sure am. I was attacked by a German Shepherd when I was a little girl. In fact, I still have the scars to prove it. I've just never really warmed to dogs since. Stupid, I know, but just the way I am."

"Understandable." Personally, he wasn't fussed on cats, but he wasn't going to tell her that. "I've had dogs all my life, but then I've never had one be anything other than loyal to me."

"Back home I have a pair of Birman cats called Indie and Lexie, and if I'm completely honest they've probably done me more damage with their claws than your dog has probably ever done to you with his teeth."

They both laughed. Logan changed the subject for a second, wanting to point out to Candace where they were going.

"See just over there? That's Cockle Bay and it's where I'm taking you for dinner."

"I thought we were just going for drinks?" she asked, her nose almost pressed to the window, looking where he'd pointed.

It was the reason Logan had brought her here, because he knew how amazing the harbor was to visitors. Him? He'd grown up with it and was used to it, but every time he'd returned from a tour it had always put a smile on his face, told him he was home.

"If you're not hungry, we can always skip dinner."

"Don't be silly. After all that energy I used on stage, I'm famished," she admitted. "And dinner sounds great."

Logan parked his four-by-four and jumped out, grabbing his jacket and pulling it on. He walked around the vehicle and opened the passenger door, waiting for Candace to step out.

"Thank you," she said. "You know, it's kind of strange for me getting out on this side of the road."

Logan waited for her to grab her purse, before shutting the door and leading the way, walking slowly so she didn't have to hurry beside him.

"Your shoes are insanely high."

"I know, but aren't they fab? They were a gift from my favorite designer."

He raised his eyebrows. "You're talking to a soldier, sorry. But they do look cool, I guess, for a pair of shoes, that is."

Candace laughed. "I definitely need to spend more

time with real people. Of course you couldn't care less about my shoes!"

He shrugged and pointed ahead. "We're going to a place called Jimmy's and they have the best seafood in Sydney. Plus they're right on the water."

Candace started walking even slower, a smile spreading over her face that he couldn't miss as they passed a couple who didn't even look at them.

"You have no idea what it feels like to just walk along the street and not be noticed. I've missed this for so long now."

Logan looked up, taking comfort in the bright stars twinkling in the dark sky—the same stars he'd looked at every night when he was on tour even though he'd been on the other side of the world. When he was at home in the Outback, they always seemed brighter, but they were still just as pretty to look at in the city.

"When I was on my first couple of tours, white soldiers were pretty easy to notice. I remember the first time we went through a village, and the women were screaming out to us, begging us to help them. I couldn't understand what they were saying, but the pleading, desperate looks they were giving us told me that I was their last chance. That that's how they thought of us." Logan took a deep breath, wondering why he was even telling Candace all this. He hardly ever spoke about his tours, except with Brett, but for some reason he just needed her to know. "These little children were hanging on to us, grabbing us as we walked through on patrol, and we gave them all the food we had. It wasn't until the next day that we found out all the men had been killed by local insurgents, and the women were left to fend on their own, terrified that they'd be next, and with no way to provide for their children."

Candace had almost stopped walking now, her eyes like saucers, filled with tears as she stared at him. Her hands were clenched into fists at her sides.

"What happened to them?"

Logan shook his head. "I don't know. But I can tell you how awful it was to be recognized, as someone who those people thought could save them, when in reality all I could offer was some dried snacks and a candy bar. And it happened to us over and over again."

"So, what you're saying is that I need to stop caring about being recognized for who I am?" she asked, her voice soft.

"No, what I'm saying is that sometimes being recognized for the right reasons is okay. The people who want to see you just want a smile and an autograph, and they're things you can give them. It's when you're powerless that being recognized is something to be scared of."

Candace shook her head, a sad look on her face. "I sound like a selfish, self-centered idiot for even saying all that, when you compare it to what you went through. But I guess it's just that I struggle with the whole fame thing. I'm a singer and I love what I do. It's just the publicity that I find really difficult." She sighed. "Unfortunately one doesn't come without the other in this industry."

"No, Candace, that's not what I meant," he said as they started to walk again. "I guess I just want you to know that I probably understand some of what you go through on a daily basis, even though our worlds are light-years apart."

They walked in silence for a minute, almost at the restaurant. She knew what he meant, but she still felt stupid for moaning aloud about being recognized. She was lucky and she knew it, but lately being surrounded by fans had turned from flattering to downright scary.

"Have you ever tried Morton Bay bugs?" Logan asked, changing the subject.

Candace gave him a look like she was trying to figure out if he was joking. "I have no idea what you're even talking about, but they sound revolting."

He laughed. "Definitely not revolting, I promise you. They're kind of like lobster, but different. Better."

"You're serious, aren't you?" she groaned as he opened the door. "You're actually going to make me eat something called a *bug as punishment for the sashimi.*"

"It's a stupid name for what they are, but yeah, you're definitely going to be eating them." Logan chuckled as they stood and waited to be greeted. "Grilled with garlic butter, fresh bread on the side and..."

"Logan?"

He spun around, taking his eyes off Candace and her cute smile. "Hey, Jimmy."

His old friend raised his eyebrows, looking from him to Candace, before his eyes widened. Logan gave him a look that he hoped he understood, not wanting their night ruined before it even started.

"The kitchen's closing soon, but I can squeeze you two in if you order quick," Jimmy said, grabbing two menus. "How you been, anyway? I haven't seen you in ages."

Logan motioned for Candace to follow, touching his hand to her lower back and guiding her forward.

"I've been okay, can't complain. Especially since I'm back for good now."

Jimmy walked them through the restaurant and waved toward an alfresco table, complete with low candles on the table and a view out over the water. Even though it was dark, the water was twinkling under the lights from all the restaurants and the luxury yachts moored nearby. The night air was warm, slightly muggy still after the hot day.

"Do you even need these?" Jimmy asked with a grin, gesturing at the menus.

Logan grinned straight back at him, pulling out a seat for Candace. Jimmy obviously knew exactly who she was—maybe he was just too starstruck to remember his manners, or his job.

"Let's start with two buckets of prawns and sourdough bread, then Morton Bay bugs for two, and maybe a Caesar salad."

Jimmy was nodding, but he was also spending most of his time glancing at Candace, who was looking out at the water, her body turned away from them.

Logan leaned in closer to his childhood friend, giving him a playful whack across the back of the head.

"Don't you breathe a word of this to anyone until we're gone. No tipping the media off, no telling your girlfriend."

Jimmy made a face like his head hurt, but he was

still grinning. "Can I at least get an autograph before you leave?"

"Keep everyone else away from us and I'll make sure you get one. Deal?"

Jimmy's smile grew wider. "And a big tip, too, right?"

"You do know I have a dog that could eat you in a few mouthfuls, don't you?" Logan said in a low voice, smiling as Candace turned to face them.

Jimmy just laughed. "I'll get your order in and bring you some drinks. Champagne?"

Logan sat down and glanced at Candace. "Bubbly or beer?"

She made a thoughtful face before one side of her mouth tilted up into a smile. "Let's have a beer. Why not?"

Logan didn't let the surprise show on his face, even though he'd never have picked her choosing beer over champagne in a million years. "You heard the lady. Two beers, bottles not glasses."

Jimmy shook his head and walked off, leaving Logan to burst out laughing. Candace seemed to be finding the entire thing as hilarious as he was.

"He knew who I was the moment we walked in, didn't he?" she asked in a soft voice, like she wasn't in the least bit surprised.

Logan wasn't going to lie to her. "Yeah, he did. But there's no way he's going to make a fuss or say anything, okay?"

She nodded. "So you don't think it'll be in the papers that I was spotted out with a mystery man, knocking back beers? Knowing the paps, they'll probably say I was out of control and ready for rehab."

"You missed the part about us digging into two massive buckets filled with prawns, that we'll be eating with our fingers like barbarians instead of fine dining."

Candace dipped her head when she laughed, looking up at him like she wasn't entirely sure whether he was ever being serious or always joking. "And here I was thinking you'd brought me to a classy restaurant."

"Believe me, nothing in the world is better than fresh seafood eaten with your fingers, washed down by an ice-cold beer. We don't need five forks and silver service to eat incredible food."

"Well, I'll have to reserve judgment until I've experienced it, but I'm guessing you're probably right."

He leaned back in his chair. "See the beautiful super yachts out there?"

She nodded, following his gaze.

"When you come here earlier in the evening, there are waiters running back and forth from the restaurant to the boats, carrying silver trays of seafood and champagne. It's crazy, but a lot of fun to watch."

"I was right going with my gut feeling on promoting Australia to the world," she said with a laugh. "Next time I'm ready for a vacation, I'm heading straight back here."

CHAPTER THREE

CANDACE LOOKED BACK out at the water to avoid looking at the man seated across from her. There was something exciting about being out somewhere different, on the other side of the world, and with someone she hardly knew. And for the first time in forever, she actually felt like herself, like the old her, the one she'd started to slowly lose a few years earlier. When her marriage had started to crumble, so had her self-confidence, and then when her mom had died…she pushed the dark thoughts away and focused on Logan.

"Is this somewhere you come often?"

Logan leaned forward, both hands on his beer bottle. She took a sip of hers while she waited for his response.

"I've been coming here for years. Every time I came home from deployment, this was the first place I headed to for a meal," he told her. "There were three of us with a standing date."

"As in three soldiers?" she asked, curious.

Logan twirled his beer bottle between his hands. "Yeah."

Candace could sense there was something else going

on, something unsaid, but she didn't know him well enough to pry. She knew what it was like to want to keep some things private.

"It must have been a relief coming here for the amazing food after what you had to eat over there," she said, wanting to give him an out if he needed it.

Logan looked up and met her gaze. "It was. There's only so much dried jerky and dehydrated food a guy can eat, right?"

She laughed, but it died in her throat as their waiter approached the table with an enormous amount of food.

"No way."

Logan grinned and leaned back as two large silver buckets filled with prawns were placed in front of them. She'd never seen so much seafood in her life.

"You're telling me that this is just for starters?" she asked, groaning.

The waiter returned with two dishes of some kind of sauce and freshly quartered lemons, as well as a bowl of warm water, which she guessed was for them to dip their fingers in to after eating.

"In Australia, we have a saying that you can't eat enough seafood," Logan told her.

"You do?" Candace watched as he picked up one of the prawns and pulled the head off, before peeling the shell.

"No, I just made that up to make you think this was a good idea." He gave her a wink that made her heart thud to her toes. "If you don't want to get your hands dirty I can peel yours?" he offered.

"I appreciate the gesture but I think it's about time

I got my hands dirty." She was sick of people running around and doing everything for her, and tonight was about her just being her. "You show me what to do and I'll do it."

"You just have to grab your beer bottle between your palms so it doesn't get all greasy. Like this," Logan explained, demonstrating with a quick swig of his beer before dipping his prawn into the sauce.

Candace just shook her head, finding it hard to believe that she'd been performing live in front of twenty thousand people only an hour earlier, and was now sitting at a restaurant, tucking into a meal with the man who'd been assigned her personal head of security. Add to that the fact she hadn't been asked for even one autograph…it was insane. She shouldn't have trusted him so easily, but she hadn't been so relaxed in a long time. Maybe she'd wake up and realize it had all just been a dream, but if it had been, at least it had been a nice one.

She peeled her first prawn and dipped it in the sauce.

"Good?" he asked.

"Amazing," she murmured, hand over her mouth as she spoke. "You were right."

They sat in silence for a while, both eating their prawns and sipping beer. Something told her that Logan wasn't usually a big talker—that he was comfortable not saying anything at all, and she liked it. Where she'd grown up, the men had a motto of speaking only when they'd had something worthy of being said, but her adult life had been filled with men who couldn't say *enough* to make themselves sound important.

"So have you always lived in the city?" she asked.

Logan looked up, finishing his mouthful and dipping his fingers in the lemon water to clean them. She watched as he dried his hands on the napkin.

"I actually grew up in the Outback," he told her, finishing his beer before leaning back in his chair. "I'm based here a lot of the time, but when I'm not working I head straight back there just to be away from the city and out in the open air."

So, that's why she felt so comfortable around him. It had been a while since she'd hung out with a country boy.

"Your family all ranch out there?"

He grinned. "We call it farming here, but yeah, it's my family property."

Candace paused, slowly peeling a prawn. "So your dad runs the place or a brother?"

Logan took a deep breath, she could see the rise and fall of his chest, before he waved to a waiter and gestured for another beer. He glanced at her, but Candace shook her head—hers was still half-full.

He cleared his throat. "My parents both died a few years ago, and my sister lives on a farm with her husband," Logan explained. "The property has been in our family for generations, so I'd rather die than sell the place, but I've had to have a manager employed while I've been serving so the place can continue to run smoothly."

Candace sighed. "I shouldn't have been so nosey, Logan. I'm sorry."

"It's fine. Sometimes it's just hard to say out loud,

because admitting it makes it real, as stupid as that sounds."

She knew exactly how that felt. "My mom died a couple of years ago, and if I'm honest, that's why I've put up with my management team for longer than I should have. She was the one who dealt with all that stuff so I could just focus on singing, and I'm still pretty lost without her. She was the business brains and I was the creative one, and it had always been just the two of us. We made a good team."

Logan took the beer that arrived at their table, his eyes leaving hers to look out at the water. She did the same, because it seemed wrong to keep watching him when he was obviously troubled about what they were talking about. He was silent.

"I didn't mean to just unleash all that on you," she apologized. "I don't usually spill my thoughts so easily, but…"

"It's nice to tell someone who actually gets it, right?" he finished, gaze meeting hers again.

"Yeah," she murmured, "something like that."

"Losing a parent is tough, and it doesn't get easier, so don't believe anyone if they try to tell you otherwise," he told her. "But you do learn to live with it."

Their table was cleared then and within minutes two large white plates were placed in front of them.

"So these are the bugs, huh?"

Logan nodded, but he was more reserved now than he'd been before—his enthusiasm dulled.

"You just scoop the white meat out of the shell," he told her. "It's incredible."

Candace spread her napkin over her lap, smoothing out the wrinkles, before picking up her fork and following Logan's lead. He was right—again—the food was great.

"Thanks for a lovely evening," she told him when she'd finished her mouthful. "It was completely unexpected and I appreciate the gesture."

He gave her a weird look. "Sounds like you're ready to leave."

"No, I'm just grateful that I've actually enjoyed a night in someone else's company. You've given me some perspective at a time when I needed it."

Logan went back to getting every last piece of meat from the shellfish, and she forced herself to stop watching him and just eat, too. There was something so refreshingly real about him.

"Another beer?"

She looked at her bottle and was about to say no, before she changed her mind. "You know what? Yeah. I'd love another. Why not?"

"So, I told you where I grew up. How about you?"

"I grew up on a ranch, too. My parents split when I was a baby, so we moved to my grandparents' ranch. I used to ride my horse and sing into a hairbrush, pretending it was my microphone. I spent every day outside, even if it was raining, just making up songs and enjoying the fresh air." She smiled just thinking about it. "It was the best childhood I could imagine, and my grandfather made up for my not having a dad. He was great."

He chuckled. "Ever wish you could go back in time?"

"I don't know about back in time, but I'd love to go

back to living on a ranch. I have a place in Montana, but it's not somewhere I get to very often these days, so it's not really where I call home."

"Why don't you just make time?"

Logan's question was serious, his voice deep.

"That's a very good question."

"Candace, when do you fly out?" Logan asked.

She pushed her plate away and reached for her beer. "Day after tomorrow."

Logan pulled a bread roll apart and took a bite, looking back out at the water again. There was a lot going on his mind, she was sure of it, but it was like he chose his words carefully, thought everything through before he said it. Their Caesar salad arrived while they were mid conversation, but there was no way she was going to able to eat even a mouthful of it.

"Why?"

"I was just thinking that spending some more time in Australia would do you the world of good."

"Meaning that I need to unwind?"

His eyes were still on the water, looking into the distance. "Meaning that if you want to remember what it's like to just be a human being in the world, here's probably the place to do it. The Outback heals the soul, or at least that's what I've always believed."

"Is that what the Outback did for you?" she asked, studying his side profile, the angle of his jaw and the fullness of his lips.

She glanced away when he turned, catching her staring.

"Yeah, it did," he said. "The Outback saved me when

nothing else could, and every time I go back there it reminds me what life is truly about. I guess it's my place in the world."

Candace didn't know why, or how, but when she saw the hurt in his gaze, the honesty of what he was saying, tears sprang into her eyes. This man who'd been so kind to her, so polite and respectful, had a power of hurt inside of him, and even glimpsing it made her sad. Whatever he'd been through was more than just losing his parents—he'd seen pain, grief, like she'd probably never know. What he'd experienced as a soldier must have given him memories that he'd never be able to shed.

"Excuse me, I'm just going to find the ladies' room," Candace said, grabbing her purse, before crossing the restaurant.

A waiter pointed her in the right direction and she disappeared into the first restroom, locking the door behind her. Candace stared at her reflection in the mirror, studying her face, seeing the makeup, the woman she was on stage, and not the girl she felt like inside.

The past few months, she'd been miserable except for the few times she'd been on stage or in the studio. So unhappy that she'd clung to what felt safe, what she thought was right, but one evening in the company of someone like Logan and she was starting to question everything. Today had been full of adrenaline and anticipation, she'd been excited when she'd said yes to going out with Logan, and now she was starting to spiral down, like a party girl coming off a high.

Logan was kind and handsome, and in all honesty she was probably drawn to him because he was capable of protecting her. But in less than two days she'd be flying away from Australia and never coming back, which was why she should never have agreed to tonight. Men were supposed to be off her radar, and after everything she'd been through, that's where she wanted them to stay. So getting her hopes up about an Australian soldier who'd probably never even think about her again, who probably just wanted what every other guy wanted from her, was beyond stupid.

Candace reapplied her lip gloss and gave herself a long, hard stare in the mirror. The best thing she could do was call it a night, not get involved in any way with Logan. For her sake and for his. She'd been stupid to agree to it in the first place.

Logan stood when Candace reappeared. He knew he was frowning, but the look on her face wasn't helping him to stop.

"You okay?" he asked.

"I'm fine," she replied, but he could tell from the smile she fixed that it was a face she'd perfected to hide how she really felt. He'd spent most of his working life studying people and situations, and he doubted he was wrong.

"Are you ready to head somewhere else for a drink, or..." He paused, watching the way her gaze darted away, the change in her eyes. "You're ready to go back to your hotel, aren't you?"

Candace nodded. "I think maybe we should call it a night."

Logan hesitated before reaching for her hand, not sure what he'd done to upset her.

"Candace, if there's something I've done..." he started.

"No, it's absolutely nothing you've done," she whispered, but as she spoke tears glinted in her eyes.

"It's been a long time since I've made a girl cry," he said, doing the only thing he could think of and pulling her toward him for a hug. "Whatever it is, I'm sorry."

She hardly moved, but her hand did reach up and grasp his shirt as he put his arms around her, held her so she could compose herself.

"I don't know why you're being so kind to me," she murmured, just loud enough for him to hear.

Logan sighed, inhaling the fresh scent of her hair, the aroma of her perfume. It had been a while since he'd been with a woman, and being this close to Candace was something he was already starting to crave.

"You sure you don't want another drink? Something else to eat?"

She ran her hand down his arm as she stepped back, eyes fixed on his. Logan was watching her, waiting for her to reply, when a flash went off, followed by what seemed like a hundred more. Logan leaped in front of Candace, instinct warning him to protect her no matter what, anger burning inside him as he realized the threat was only a photographer who'd managed to find them.

"Crap," he muttered, taking her hand firmly in his.

"It's okay, it's just one pap," she said.

He didn't care if it was one or twenty, he was still pissed at the intrusion. The photographer was escorted from the restaurant within minutes, but Logan knew it had been enough to rattle Candace. He had his own personal reasons to hate the media, and he wasn't going to let them ruin Candace's evening, not when she'd been so excited about an anonymous night out.

"Word will be out soon, so I'll take you straight to the hotel," he told her, before remembering what he'd promised Jimmy. "Before we go, I did promise our waiter an autograph in exchange for his discretion. If he was the one who tipped that guy off, I'll kill him, but I think I made it clear enough already what the consequences would be, so I doubt it would have been him."

Candace's smile diffused his anger as easily as someone blowing out a candle.

"Logan, we've sat here alone without anyone bothering us for the best part of a couple of hours. I don't care about one photographer finding us, but you're right about word not taking long to spread."

"So you're not angry?" He was confused—and he was seriously pissed.

Candace plucked a pen from her purse and signed an unused white napkin on their table.

"This is for your friend," she told him. "Do you want me to settle the bill and give it to him?"

Logan was reaching for the napkin when he froze. Had he just heard that right?

"You're not paying the bill."

"Of course I am," she said. "I wouldn't have it any other way."

"I asked you out for dinner, and I don't care how PC

the world is supposed to be, but you taking care of the bill is ridiculous."

"Logan—" she started, but he cut her off.

"Do you really want to insult me?" he asked.

"I'm just used to…"

"Jerks, if they let you pay. I don't care who you are. The only thing I care about is that you're a woman and I'm a man, and that means I take care of our bill tonight."

He watched as she shut her mouth and shrugged, clearly giving in. "Well, all right then. Thank you for a lovely meal, Mr. Neanderthal."

Logan burst out laughing as they walked to the front of the restaurant. "I know I'm old-fashioned, but seriously. Just because you're famous doesn't mean you shouldn't be treated like a lady."

He paid and passed his friend the napkin as they said goodbye, before walking out the front door.

"And just because you're a soldier doesn't mean you have to…"

Her words faded as someone yelled her name, and Logan sprung straight into work mode, putting his arm around her shoulders and hurrying her forward. There were a couple of guys trying to get close with their cameras, but he ignored them and just focused on propelling Candace away.

"We'll be fine once we get to the car," he told her, his palm firm on her shoulder.

"They'll follow us straight to my hotel."

"You want to go somewhere no one can bother you?" he asked.

"Please."

"Then I'll give them the slip and we can head straight to my place. No one will ever find you there."

Logan didn't know why he said it, why he'd even thought to take her back to his house, but he had and now there was no going back. The last time he'd let a woman into his home had been…Logan swallowed and moved faster, listening to Candace's heels as they beat a rhythm against the sidewalk. When he'd admitted to his friends that it had been a long time since he'd let a woman into his life, he hadn't been exaggerating.

He'd enjoyed tonight because he hadn't let himself dwell on the past, and if he wanted to survive having Candace at his place, then that's what he'd have to keep doing. There was no point thinking about the woman who'd hurt him, or anything else about what had happened in the past few years.

For months, he'd been telling himself that it was time to move on with his life, to put his past behind him, but some things were easy to think and a whole lot harder to put into practice. Especially when the darkness of his memories crept into his brain just when he was least expecting them.

CHAPTER FOUR

CANDACE COULD FEEL her heart racing—it was like her pulse was thumping in her head it sounded so loud. Fleeing the paparazzi and heading for Logan's place had seemed like the safe option when he'd suggested it, but now she was starting to panic. It was one thing to have dinner with the man in a public place, but going back to his house? Not something she'd ever usually do, especially with someone she'd just met, without anyone else knowing where she was.

They pulled up in front of a row of two-story houses. There wasn't a garage, so Logan parked on the street, and she waited for him to come around to open her door. It gave her time to calm her breathing and think about how to handle the situation.

"We managed to lose all of them, and I doubt they'll come looking for you in the suburbs."

She stepped out of the vehicle and shut the door behind her, before following Logan to the front door of his house. Nerves made her stomach flutter, but she ignored them. It was time she started trusting her own instincts.

"I should probably call my manager, just to let him

know where I am." Candace didn't like the fact that no one in the world knew where to find her if they needed her. Although come to think of it, she did have a tracking device on her phone, so her manager could locate her if he made an effort.

"Candace, you can do whatever you like, but if it were me? I'd be telling him you were safe and that you'd see him tomorrow. Unless you're okay with that same shark frenzy we just escaped from turning up outside here with telescopic lenses."

She grimaced. "You really don't like him, do you?"

"If I'm completely honest with you, I have my suspicions that the hate mail and threats you've been receiving aren't real. I don't want to point fingers, but there's only one person I can see who could be responsible, if my theory is correct."

Candace was sick to her stomach hearing his words, but she also realized that Logan could be right. She'd never have thought it before, *had never thought it,* but she also wasn't prepared to defend Billy without looking into it further. Without her mom to guide her, she knew she could have overlooked *something,* but if Logan's hunch was correct...She swallowed but refused to push the thoughts away like she usually would. She had only herself to rely on now, and that meant investigating the situation thoroughly if she needed to.

"Say you're right," she said. "What do you think I should do about it?"

"Ask him outright. I bet you'll figure it out the moment you catch him off guard and see the look on his face. Just trust your instincts, because they don't often let you down when you listen to them."

It was a serious accusation to make, but she would do exactly what Logan had suggested. What did she have to lose if she was wrong?

Logan flicked the lights on as he walked inside and she jumped back as his dog came bounding toward them.

"Hey, boy, settle down," he instructed, bending to give his dog some attention. "You remember Candace?"

She stayed in place, back to the front door, not certain about the excited canine. He was sitting to attention, perfectly obedient, but she still wasn't ready to trust him quite yet.

"Look, I just know Billy's type, and I'm a pretty good judge of people," Logan said, which made her flip her attention back to him and away from the dog. "I've spent enough time with dogs to know that they sense things in people, and I've started to understand the signs."

"So you think I should get a dog and let him choose my crew?" she joked.

Logan smiled, but his expression was still serious. "No, I think you need to listen to your gut and trust your own instincts. If it's not him, you'll know."

Well, that was exactly what she'd done by coming here, trusting her gut, and she was already doubting herself.

"This is a nice place you've got," she said, changing the subject.

Tomorrow she'd figure out how to deal with her manager. Tonight, she just wanted to forget all the stuff that had been troubling her for so long. If she was going to start trusting her instincts, then she was going to start with how she felt about Logan.

Candace looked around, liking the white hall and the open-plan living space she could see into. Logan motioned for his dog to move away, and they all walked through the house.

"Have you lived here for long?" she asked.

Logan crossed the room to the fridge and she sat at one of the high-backed chairs at the counter that split the living room from the kitchen.

"I purchased this place soon after my parents died, but I'm not sure if I'll keep it."

He held up a beer and a bottle of water, and she pointed to the water.

"Are you planning on going back to your ranch?"

Logan shrugged. "I want to spend a lot of time there, but I haven't really decided what to do with myself. Once this job is finished, I should officially be discharged for retirement from the army, and so will Ranger."

She smiled when he passed her the water and she opened it, taking a sip. "I'm guessing you get to keep him?"

"Yeah. That grey muzzle of his means he's done his time. He's worked as hard as any human soldier since he was a couple years old, but the stress and discipline eventually gets to them, just like it does us. I paid to get him home, and my parents actually started a foundation to make sure working military dogs receive the retirement they deserve."

"I love feel-good stories like that. Working for charity means a lot to me."

They were silent a while, Logan standing with his beer in hand, looking at his dog, and Candace looking around at his home. She knew that soldiers didn't earn a heap of money, and his house was furnished beautifully in a masculine kind of way, which was making her realize that his family must have been relatively well off. It shouldn't have mattered, but it made her curious about who he was and why he'd spent so many years in the army if he hadn't had to, financially.

"Logan, why did you take me out for dinner tonight?" she asked, unable to keep the question to herself.

His dark eyes locked on hers, sending goose pimples across her skin, making every part of her body tense.

"There was something about you that reminded me of myself," he said, his voice an octave lower than it had been before. "I liked you, and I guess I also wanted to show you that you could just spend a night out in Sydney like a regular woman. But it kind of backfired in the end, because we never even made it to a bar."

Candace swallowed, not sure where her confidence was coming from but suddenly needing to know more, wanting to know what Logan thought of her. She knew it was needy, that she should have just shut up, but the way he was looking at her, the way she was reacting to him, was more than just platonic.

"So this wasn't technically a date?" she asked, dropping her gaze and fiddling with the label on her water bottle.

"Do you want this to be a date?" he asked straight back.

Candace didn't look up, not straightaway, but she heard Logan move, his boots echoing out against the timber floor until he was standing beside her. He reached for her bottle and pulled it away, sliding it across the counter just out of her reach. Then he took her hand, his palm closing over it, waiting for her to respond.

She forced herself to raise her chin, to meet his stare.

"Candace?"

"I don't know," she whispered, her voice cracking. "I honestly don't know."

"Do you want this?" he asked, bending slightly, his mouth stopping barely inches from hers.

Candace didn't say anything, *couldn't say anything,* because as badly as she knew she should say no, she wanted it. Her body was humming like an electric current was running through it, all her senses firing to life, desperate to connect with Logan.

He paused for what felt like an eternity, before cupping her cheek and touching his lips so gently to hers that she almost didn't feel it. His lips hovered, pressed lightly, before his entire mouth moved against hers. She matched his pace, loving the feel of his warm, soft lips, the touch of his palm against her skin.

Candace sighed as he pulled back, like he was giving her the chance to change her mind, and she reached for his shirt, pulling him back toward her. His mouth was firm to hers again, tongue softly teasing hers, desire making her stomach flip with excitement as Logan's hands skimmed her waist before settling on her hips. His fingers were still then, the only part of his body moving was his lips, and Candace wanted more. She was hungry for him, craving the kind of contact she'd avoided for so long.

Candace ran her hands down Logan's chest until she reached the hem of his T-shirt, slowly touching beneath it, connecting first with the waistband of his jeans and then with bare skin. She let her fingertips explore his rock-hard abs, the warmth of his skin and the hardness of his muscles, making her moan into his mouth.

She had half expected him to pull back, to tell her no, but there was nothing about Logan's body language that was saying *no.* His hands matched hers, disappearing under her top and touching *her* bare skin, the slightly rough edge of his fingertips making the sensation even more erotic.

"Logan," she moaned, knowing she should stop but giving it only a fleeting thought.

His mouth became more insistent, crushing her lips before he started kissing down her neck, to her collarbone, his tongue tracing across the tops of her breasts.

Candace fisted her hand in his short hair, fingernails scraping his scalp.

"You want me to stop?" he mumbled, lifting his head to look into her eyes.

She shook her head. "No."

Logan didn't need any further encouragement. His mouth met hers in a wet, erotic kiss, before he scooped her up into his arms as if she were weightless, carrying her through the kitchen, marching down the hall. Candace sighed against his mouth, her lips moving in a lazy movement in time with his, their kiss less intense now but still making her belly flutter with anticipation.

It had been so long since she'd kissed a man, since she'd been intimate, and instead of being scared of it like she'd thought she would be, she could feel only a burning sense of desire. That even though she'd never had a one-night stand in her life, been with a man she wasn't in a committed relationship with, there wasn't a bone in her body that didn't want this right now. She was always the good girl, the one who stayed out of the media and never made a wrong step, but she was on the other side of the world with a man who'd shown more interest in keeping her away from the limelight than trying to be in it himself. So if she was going to do something reckless, then why not with Logan?

She'd tried marriage, tried settling down, and it had been disastrous. But this? This felt right in every way possible.

"Candace, we don't have to do this," he mumbled, walking with her in his arms until he could set her on the bed.

"I want this," she whispered as he covered her body with his, her legs looping around his waist so he couldn't get away, locking him in place.

"I'm not going to ask you again, but I will stop if you ask me to," he told her, propping himself up on his elbows and looking down at her, his hazel-brown eyes like pools of the darkest chocolate in the half-light. "You just say the word, and I'll stop, okay?"

Candace nodded, suddenly feeling vulnerable with this gorgeous, big man lying on top of her, yet being so careful with her at the same time. The last man she'd been with had never put her first, had hurt her with his mind and with his fists, which made her even more attracted to Logan. The fact that he was so strong yet so gentle told her that she'd been right to trust herself, at least in spending one night with him. In letting him be the first man to get close to her since her divorce.

"Thank you, Logan," she whispered.

His eyebrows shot up. "For what?"

"For just letting me be me tonight."

He dropped a slow, careful kiss to her forehead. It shouldn't have, but it felt more intimate than all the touches, all the kisses, they'd already shared.

"I haven't been me in a long time, Candace, so this is a first for me, too."

She had the feeling like they were two lost souls who'd found one another, two people who'd crossed paths for a reason, if only for one night. Logan had shared some of what he'd been through with her, and she'd hinted at her past, too—just enough so they both understood that they were the way they were for a reason.

Logan stared at her, his gaze unwavering, until she arched her body, stretching up to catch his mouth, to start the dance that they'd started in the kitchen. His gaze went from thoughtful to something that scared and excited her in equal parts, his mouth insistent, his hands even more so as he pushed up her top, sliding it up high so he could touch her stomach and then her breasts, his fingers teasing her nipples through the lace bra she was wearing.

Candace was just as desperate for him, wanting his bare skin against hers, needing to feel his naked body pressed to her own. She wanted Logan to make love to her, and she wanted it now.

Logan was trying hard to hold back, to let Candace set the pace and not push her, but after months serving overseas and hardly even *seeing* a woman, having Candace beneath him was sending him stir-crazy. She had a body like he'd never touched before—her waist was tiny, her limbs long and slender, and her breasts… He stifled a groan. They were full and luscious, and he wanted them free from the scrap of lace she had them covered with.

When she arched her body into him this time, her chest pressed to his, he took his chance to reach behind her and unhook her bra. He wanted to touch her, taste her, feel every part of her. And his impatience was starting to get the better of him. It wasn't often he could block everything out—his past, the memories—but with Candace, right now he couldn't think of anything else.

"Candace, you're so beautiful."

Her shy smile spurred him on even more because it was so unexpected.

"You're sure you want this?" He had to ask, needed

to make sure she'd thought this through. "I don't want you to regret anything in the morning."

Candace reached for him, cupped her hands around the back of his head and pulled him lower, her lips warm and pillowy as they traced his mouth.

"No regrets, Logan," she murmured. "I want you to make love to me."

Logan groaned as one of her hands left his neck, her fingernails trailing lightly down his skin, pushing at his jeans like she was as impatient as he was.

This time, he wasn't holding back, wouldn't push her away or ask her if she was sure. He'd given her a chance to say no, and she'd made it perfectly clear what she wanted. Now, he was going to give her exactly what she'd asked for.

Logan stroked Candace's long hair, gently fingering the curls that were splayed across his chest. They'd been lying in silence for a while, just lying in the dark. It wasn't a silence he wanted to break, either—she seemed as comfortable as he was with saying nothing at all, bodies pressed together, his fingers caressing either her hair or her skin.

He shut his eyes, starting to drift into sleep.

The sound of a plane's engine, the dark silence as it stalled and started to spiral, falling toward the earth.

Logan blinked and went back to stroking Candace's hair, touching a strand of it to his face as he focused on her again and stamped the dark thoughts away. He was not going to ruin this perfect moment with lurching back into the past.

"Logan, can I ask you something?" Candace's words were soft and husky.

He stopped twirling her hair and brushed his knuckles softly across her cheek as he propped on one elbow to look at her. She was lying on her back, and now he was on his side, facing her. Staring into her eyes seemed to help him to forget everything else.

"You seem to find it easy to talk about some of the things you've been through, and I guess I…" Her voice trailed off. "I guess it's just unexpected from someone who's been through what you've been through."

Logan wanted to look away but he didn't. "What I've told you is a very small part of what I've been through, Candace. There are some things I'll take to my grave that I should probably talk about but never will, and other things that I *can* talk about for reasons I don't understand." What he didn't tell her was that his head so was full of his memories that he wouldn't even know where to start.

She reached for his hand and linked her fingers with his. "So why did you tell me what you did, about being on patrol, being recognized, all those stories?"

He dropped his gaze to their hands, craving the contact, the touch of her skin to his. "There's something about you that reminds me of, well, me," Logan tried to explain. "I've been through a lot, and I saw something in you that made me want to talk to you. I don't know why. I've never wanted to before, but…"

She turned and snuggled into him. "You don't have to explain. I shouldn't have asked."

Logan dropped a kiss to her forehead, moving to her lips when she tilted her face up to him.

"That's the crazy thing. I'm usually so protective over my past, yet with you I wanted to talk." It was strange, because she also helped him to forget.

She laughed, just a soft, husky giggle. "Yeah, that's probably because you know enough about me to hold me for ransom over your secrets."

Logan raised his eyebrows. "Meaning I could sell all our sex secrets and whispered conversations to the media?"

"Exactly," Candace confirmed.

Logan just smiled and pulled her into him, lying back on the bed and shutting his eyes. He didn't need to say anything in response, because if she didn't trust him, it wasn't something she'd joke about. And there was no way he'd ever spill the beans on anything about Candace, or any other woman he'd ever been with, for that matter.

The last woman he'd shared his own bed and memories with, so many years ago, had hurt him beyond belief. She'd betrayed him when he'd trusted her, made him wary of any other woman and what she could do to him if he let her close. But Candace, she was different, because she felt she had too much to lose to betray him, or his confidence.

It might only be one night, he might never see her again, but it had been worth it. Because Candace had shown him that he wasn't the only damaged person in the world, and it had done him good to see the world through someone else's eyes for once. Or maybe it was because he knew it was only one night that he'd allowed anything to happen at all.

Candace lay awake, her head on Logan's shoulder, hand resting on his chest. She was listening to his breathing, feeling the gentle rise and fall of his chest, as she thought about what she'd just done. She had no regrets and doubted she would, but there were so many things running through her mind that she knew she'd never be able to fall asleep, even if she was exhausted.

Logan had shown her what it was like to just be a woman attracted to a man. She had no intention of making one-night stands a habit, and it wasn't like she'd ever had one before, but tonight had been…just what she'd needed. Her body was relaxed and satisfied, but her mind was working in overdrive, thinking about all the things she needed to do to get her life and her career back on track. And what he'd said about her manager—she didn't want it to be true, but Logan's words had made her wonder. Deep down, she wasn't even that surprised, in fact, if it was true she'd almost be relieved that there wasn't some psycho out there wanting to kill her! Ever since her mom had passed away, she'd ignored the fact that she no longer had someone she could trust in her life, to make all the big decisions for her.

But she was also thinking about the fact that she needed a getaway plan—she'd probably never see Logan again, and she didn't want things to be awkward between them when he woke up. Better to have a beautiful memory of what had happened than an awkward parting, or at least that's what she was thinking as she lay beside him.

"No!"

Candace jumped, pushing away from Logan as his body convulsed. She pulled the sheets up to cover her naked body, eyes trained on the man she'd just been cuddled up to. She'd been lying in the almost dark for so long that her eyes were fully adjusted, and she could see the sweat that had broken out across Logan's forehead, his hands clenched at his sides like he was about to start a fight. What the hell was happening?

"No!"

His voice was loud this time, the order clear, and Candace had shivers working like propellers down her spine, the familiar taste of fear like bile in her mouth. She knew it was a dream, probably a night terror that had something to do with what he'd been through, but she was still scared. Because she'd seen a violent man up close and personal, and it had terrified her.

What if he hurt her? Candace jumped clear off the bed. A whining noise made her spin, her heart still racing, but she realized it was only Ranger, and he had absolutely zero interest in her. He had run to Logan, was sitting beside the bed, head cocked to the side, emitting a low whine. Maybe he was used to his master's behavior? Or maybe he was just as scared by what was happening as she was.

Candace knew it was stupid, but she also knew what it was like to be on the receiving end of a man's fist, of being hurt by someone she'd never expected to hurt her, so she wasn't going to stay too close to Logan. And she definitely wasn't going to risk waking him. She'd seen enough television shows about soldiers with post-traumatic stress to know she could end up with his hands wrapped around her throat if he mistakenly thought she was the enemy.

"I'm sorry, Logan," she whispered, dressing in the dark as he continued to toss and turn, the sheets starting to tangle around him. She should have tried to help him, but she didn't, *couldn't.*

Candace found her shoes, slipped them on, then disappeared out into the living area. She pulled her phone from her purse, saw she'd missed a heap of calls while it had been on silent, but ignored them all and went online instead. She searched for the name of a taxi company, found out Logan's address, called to order a cab, and sat down on the sofa while she waited.

Running out on Logan wasn't something she'd wanted to do. It wasn't something she'd ever done before to any man, but she'd set the wheels in motion now and there was no turning back. What they'd shared had been incredible, a night she'd never forget for as long as she lived, but they'd made each other no promises, and now it was time to head back to the real world.

Even if right now that world held little appeal.

CHAPTER FIVE

LOGAN STRETCHED AND threw one hand over his eyes to block out the sun. He went to pull the pillow over his head instead before he realized what had woken him.

Bloody phone.

He reached for it, sitting up as he also realized that he was alone in his bed when he should have had a gorgeous blonde tucked up beside him. Where on earth had she gone so early in the morning?

"Hello," he muttered, shutting his eyes again as he hit the pillow.

"Tell me the media have gone crazy and lost their minds?"

Logan groaned as he recognized his best friend, Brett's, voice, before sitting back up again and pulling his jeans on so he could see if Candace was still in the house. He tripped over his dog, who was looking at him like he was the crazy one. He did that a lot lately, especially in the morning, and he had no idea why.

"Logan?"

"Sorry. What have you seen?" He checked the kitchen and living area, before ducking into the bathroom. All empty. *Crap!* How had he managed to sleep through her leaving?

"Oh, you know, just you leaving Nick's Seafood restaurant with Candace-*freaking*-Evans, and then her spotted arriving back at her hotel at about three this morning looking mighty disheveled."

Double crap. Logan swallowed the expletives that he would like to have yelled out. At least it was Brett telling him rather than some stranger confronting him.

"Are you sure she was seen at the hotel?"

His friend laughed. "You mean you lost her? Hey, Jamie, he didn't even know where she was, so they must have gotten the whole one-night stand thing wrong."

Logan grimaced as he listened to Brett call out to his wife. If it was all over the news, then there was little chance of anyone else believing that nothing had happened, and the last thing he wanted was the whole world to know what Candace had been doing the night before. He couldn't care less what anyone said about him, but he knew that she wasn't exactly the kind of woman used to making headlines for being scandalous.

A noise made him look up and Ranger let out a loud bark.

"Look, I spent the day with her yesterday…"

"And the night?" Brett was laughing, like he found the entire thing beyond hysterical.

"Oh, man!" Logan ducked out of sight when he saw that the front of his house was surrounded by a bunch of guys with cameras. The last thing he needed was to be photographed bare-chested in jeans he hadn't even buttoned up properly.

"What?"

"There's bloody paparazzi outside my house. How did they find my place?" Not to mention *why* they'd want a photo of him when they knew Candace wasn't even with him.

"From the fierce looks you gave them last night it's a wonder they wanted to go near you again."

Logan went around the house pulling all the blinds and drapes down so no one could see in.

"Look, she's a sweet girl and we had a nice night together. *End of story.* Now I have to go and make sure she's okay, because she obviously slipped out on me in the night."

Brett laughed again. "Guess that serves Jamie right for telling you it was time to meet a woman. We just didn't expect you to set your sights quite so high."

Logan was usually ready to spar with Brett whenever he became annoying, but today he wasn't going to take the bait. He could deal with his friend later.

"I have to go. I'll call you later."

"I'll email those pics through to you," Brett said. "You know, in case you want to check yourself out."

"Later."

Logan hung up and opened his fridge, pulling out a carton of juice. He managed to take a few sips before curiosity got the better of him, and he grabbed his phone again and checked his emails. Sure enough, Brett had already hit Send, because there was a link waiting for him to click on.

Naughty night out in Australia for America's sweetheart. Candace Evans waves goodbye to good girl reputation with mystery man.

Logan took a deep breath, refusing to let his anger get to him. He clicked through the shots and saw them leaving the restaurant together, a zoomed-in photo of them holding hands, one of them driving away in his car, then hours later Candace running into the hotel, her hair all messed up and one hand held across her face.

It wasn't like they'd actually caught them doing anything, but they'd built a story around nothing and put up a few photos together to try to prove a point. The worst thing was that she'd run from him, and he had no idea why she'd just disappear like that after they'd spent the night together. Had someone sent her the photos and spooked her?

Whatever had happened, he was going to make sure that she was left alone at the press conference this afternoon. Sure, the media might go crazy when they realized he was her bodyguard, but then again they might think they'd made a huge mistake and he'd just been minding her.

Either way, he was heading to the hotel now to see if she was okay.

His phone bleeped again, this time with a text. He flicked through to his messages, anger rising again when he read the words.

Looks like you had an interesting evening. Heads up that the press junket has been cancelled, so you're officially off duty on this one.

Great. Even his boss knew what he'd been up to, or allegedly up to, the night before. And Candace had obviously gone into hiding if she was giving up her afternoon appointment. Still, he was going to see her. If she was still in the country, he'd track her down. What Candace didn't know about him was that he wasn't exactly a one-night stand kind of guy, either, and he wanted her to know that he'd be there for her if she needed him, until her flight out.

Candace had made him see that he needed to move on with parts of his life that he'd ignored for so long, and for that alone he needed to thank her. Usually when he freaked out over anything, he went for a run or hit the gym. In fact, he usually did it every morning because his dreams freaked him out night after night, but today was different. Today he actually had to confront the problem head-on instead of try to outrun it.

Candace stared at her laptop screen. She was a sucker for punishment, and she still couldn't help clicking through and looking at each photo one more time. She'd looked before her shower, and now she was sitting on her bed, hair wrapped in a towel, torturing herself again.

She felt like a fool.

Being with Logan wasn't something she regretted, even if she did regret the paparazzi getting snaps of her and making it clear to the world what she'd been up to. It was the fact that it had taken Logan's comments for her to realize how bad her manager was—she'd hidden behind the fact that her mom wasn't around any longer, instead of dealing with something she knew was detrimental to her career. But those days were gone. The first thing she'd done in the taxi was text her manager and tell him she was okay, that she would be arriving back at the hotel within twenty minutes, and then when she'd arrived to quietly slip into her room, the place had been buzzing with photographers. There was only one explanation for it, and she was going to be giving him his marching orders and sending him packing before the end of the day, after she asked him whether he was responsible for the letters she'd been receiving.

Then she was going to figure out how to apologize to Logan for running out on him in the middle of the night, before figuring out what to do for the next few days. It was time for her to take a break, figure some things out, and find a beach to relax on where she wouldn't be disturbed. She didn't have any more concerts scheduled on this tour, and she'd been too busy for too long without taking time out for herself, punishing herself with work to avoid dealing with everything that had happened.

Her hotel phone rang but she ignored it, uninterested in whoever it was. She'd made it clear she didn't want to be disturbed, and she meant it.

Candace padded barefoot back into the bathroom and let her hair down, running her fingers through it and then working some product into the roots. She would do her hair and makeup, then deliver the verdicts that she'd decided upon.

It was time for her to take control of her own life, her own destiny, and that started today.

CHAPTER SIX

"LOGAN, IT'S CANDACE."

He stopped dead, flicking his phone off speaker and pressing it to his ear instead.

"Candace? I thought you were long gone."

There was silence for a moment, and Logan had to check that they hadn't lost the connection. The last thing he'd expected was for Candace to call.

"I was wondering if you had time to meet up," she asked, her voice low.

"Business or pleasure?" Logan cringed the second the words left his mouth. *Pleasure* hadn't exactly been the best phrase, given what had happened between them.

"Coffee," she said. "I'm at a different hotel, just down the road from where I was before."

"I can't believe you're still in Australia." *Unbelievable.* Almost two days later and he'd been sure he'd never hear from her again, especially when she'd never answered her door when he'd known she was in her room that next morning.

"You're still here, in Sydney, right? I mean, I thought you might have already left for the Outback."

"I leave tomorrow," he told her. "I'll head to you now, if that's okay with you?"

"Sure. Meet me in an hour at my hotel. I'll be in the café, and I'm wearing a short brown wig."

Logan said goodbye, zipped his phone into his pocket and tapped his thigh as a signal to Ranger. It would take him at least fifteen minutes to run home if he sprinted, but given that he was about to cut his workout short, he wasn't complaining. Ranger bounded along beside him and Logan tried not to overthink the phone call he'd just received.

He wasn't going to even bring up what had happened between them unless she did, and he was most definitely not going to offer to help her or take her out again. She had a bunch of professionals at the ready if she needed them, and he was done with the army and with working any kind of security, at least for now. From next week onward, he was just Logan Murdoch, civilian. He was going to spend time on the land, forget about the future for a while, and figure stuff out.

Or at least that was the plan.

He blanked everything out of his mind, focusing only on the soles of his shoes as they thumped down on the pavement. Logan concentrated on each inhale and exhale of breath, the pull and release of his muscles, his dog matching his pace as he ran directly at heel.

Exercise was how he kept in control, how he stayed focused, and it was the only constant he'd had in his life for a very long time. Candace might have rattled him, but he was going to stay in control and not let anyone distract him. And that included her.

Candace's legs were so fidgety she was fighting the urge to get up and start to pace. But then that would have only drawn attention to herself, and the whole point of sitting quietly and wearing her brunette disguise was so no one even thought to glance twice at her.

She still didn't know exactly what she was going to say to Logan, but starting off by thanking him for being so honest with her about her management team, and then apologizing for disappearing on him, was probably a good starting point. The guy had been nothing but nice to her, and he deserved an explanation about what had happened between them, and for how right he'd been about Billy. He'd set her on the right path and he deserved to know.

"Candace?"

She turned when a deep, low voice said her name. Heat flooded her body when she saw Logan, standing with his hands jammed into his jean pockets. There had never been any doubting that he was incredibly sexy, but seeing him in the flesh again brought back a certain amount of memories that she'd been trying to repress. Namely his mouth, his rock-hard abs, his…

Candace jumped up and kissed Logan on the cheek, stamping out those thoughts. "Hey."

"Wow, you look…" He hesitated. "Different."

"I don't know if I'm fooling the hotel staff, but so far no one has bothered me," she admitted. "It won't last long, but I'm planning on checking out first thing tomorrow."

Logan went to sit down, then stopped. "You want a coffee?"

Candace glanced at her empty cup. "Another chai latte would be great."

She watched as he crossed the room to order, rather than waiting for someone to come and serve them, before sitting down across from her. It was all old-fashioned decadence here, and big, strong Logan looked the completed opposite of the hushed-toned men in suits walking past. He looked relaxed in his jeans and shirt like only a confident, strong man could, and she liked that he had such a strong identity of who he was—or at least that's the impression he gave.

"Logan, I want to apologize for just leaving in the middle of the night. It wasn't something I've ever done before, and you deserved better."

She struggled to read his expression, but he didn't look angry.

"I'm not going to lie. I was looking forward to waking up to you beside me," he said, staring into her eyes and not giving her one chance to look away. "But I get it. You saw the photos and you freaked."

Candace took a slow, deep breath. So he thought she'd seen the pics on her phone and run. That she could live with. If he'd thought she was stone cold and happy to just bed him and then leave? Not something she'd have been able to swallow very easily.

"I'm just sorry that I dragged you into all this. You were just trying to be nice to me and..."

"Stop," he said, reaching for her hand then hesitating, like he'd acted before realizing what he was doing. "We had a great evening together and it didn't end quite as planned. We're both grownups and we never made any promises to one another. Right?"

So in other words he didn't care? Candace pushed aside the feelings of hurt, the emotion clogging her throat. This was why she wasn't a one-night stand regular, because she couldn't handle the blunt truth of a man being honest with her.

"Logan, I wanted to thank you for being honest with me," she started, reminding herself of the real reason she'd wanted to see him. "You were more honest with me than anyone has been in a long while, even though you hardly even knew me."

He raised an eyebrow. "This sounds serious."

She nodded, waiting for their coffees to be placed in front of them before continuing. "I fired my manager and pretty much everyone else I've been working with, and I'm going to take some time off before rehiring anyone. Just be me for a while."

He sat back, gaze fixed on her. "What changed? Why now, after all this time?"

Candace tried to relax, but with Logan staring at her she was finding it hard enough just to focus on breathing and saying what she'd rehearsed in her mind.

"I've used losing my mom as an excuse for too long now, and it wasn't until you read the situation for what it was that I realized I'd been putting things off for too long. I'm sick and tired of letting people make decisions for me, and you were right about everything. I've been spooked about those letters for so long that it was starting to consume me, and it was my manager all along." She blew out a deep breath. "All I've ever wanted to do, all my life, is just sing. But now that Mom's not here to cover my back for me, I need to step up and take more control of everything, rather than just burying my head in the sand."

He reached for his coffee cup and took a sip of the steaming black liquid. "For the record, I'm not one of those people who'd ever use you, and I will never talk to anyone about what happened between us. Or about the whole manager situation for that matter."

Candace couldn't help it—suddenly her eyes filled with tears and she was reaching for a napkin to blot them away.

"Candace?"

Logan was suddenly at her side, moving to the chair next to hers, his arm around her.

"Candace, please don't cry."

She shook her head and blinked the tears away, refusing to turn into an emotional mess.

"I'm sorry, it's just I'm not used to..." Her voice trailed off. "*You.* The way you are with me."

Logan kept his arm around her, and when she turned to him she could see confusion in his expression.

"I'm not sure what you mean?"

Candace looked up at the bright lights above, wishing she knew how to tell him what she meant.

"I'm not used to a straight talker, and I'm sure as heck not used to being with someone who doesn't have an ulterior motive. Who won't sell me out to the press."

She shrugged. "I'm just so tired of watching my back and not knowing who to trust, especially after what I've been through the past few weeks. I've been scared for so long, looking over my shoulder all the time, and it was just a ploy to create more press about me. Press that I didn't even want."

They were silent, just sitting there, Logan not saying anything in response for what felt like an eternity.

"Candace, I'm heading out with a couple of friends tonight. Why don't you join us?"

She knew she must have looked wide-eyed, but she could hardly believe what she was hearing.

"You mean to say you'd actually go out in public with me again? After what happened last time?"

Now it was Logan shrugging. "Look, it's no big deal. You can even wear your wig if you like. We'll just be heading to a bar for a few drinks, nothing too exciting, and I doubt we'll even be noticed if we're careful."

Logan dropped his arm and moved back around to his seat, his coffee cup in his hand again.

"You're sure your friends won't mind?"

"Brett has been my best mate for years, and I've known his wife almost as long. We're just hanging out for some drinks before I leave tomorrow. Catching up for a few hours."

Candace stared into her latte, wishing she'd been brave enough to just say yes from the start.

"If you're sure..."

Logan had no idea where that had come from. Why had he even asked her? The plan had been to see her, listen to what she had to say, then walk away. What happened to her not being his problem? To her not being part of his life? To not letting anyone too close?

"I'm sure," he heard himself say. "It'll be fun."

The words were just falling out of his mouth now like he had absolutely zero control over the link between his brain and his vocal cords, and that definitely wasn't something he was used to. He usually found it harder to talk than not.

"If anyone recognizes me or it becomes awkward, I'll just leave."

"Candace, it'll be fine. Want to meet me there or should I swing past and collect you?"

"If you wouldn't mind coming to get me?"

Her voice was low, a shyness there that made his protective instincts flare up, and told him exactly why he'd asked her. He liked her, sure, was beyond attracted to her, but he was also able to sense the vulnerability that for some reason she wasn't great at hiding around him. Anyone who saw her on stage or in public would think she was full of confidence, but he'd already seen firsthand that there was a lot more to Candace than met the eye.

"I'll pick you up at eight," he said.

Logan rose, unable to take his eyes off her. Even with a pair of crazy-high heels on she was still short beside him, and part of him just wanted to tell her to grab her things and come with him now so he could look after her. But he didn't. Because he had things to arrange for the morning, paperwork to deal with, and because he *did not* want to get involved.

Spending the night with a woman he'd never expected to see again had been one thing, but he knew he wasn't ready for anything else. There wasn't enough room in his mind or his heart to worry about another human being, to give what someone like Candace deserved. And besides, it wasn't like she'd indicated that she wanted anything else, either.

They could have another fun night together, and then they'd say goodbye for real.

"Thanks, Logan," Candace said, suddenly reaching out for him, her palm soft against his forearm as she stopped him from walking away. "After everything, just, thanks."

She didn't let go of him straightaway, and they stared at one another, not moving. Logan clenched his jaw as memories of their night together came flooding back to him—her hands on his skin, her body against his as he'd traced every part of her with his mouth and fingers. This girl.... God! She was under his skin and no matter what he tried to tell himself, being this close to her made it impossible not to want her.

"I'll see you tonight," he said, clearing his throat when he heard how husky his voice sounded.

"See you tonight," she repeated, slowly releasing him and taking a step back.

Logan gave her one last look, hesitated one second too long. Before he could even think through what he was doing, he'd closed the distance between them again, wrapping his arm around her so he could put his hand flat to the small of her back, lips closing over hers. It was a hungry kiss that he hadn't even known he'd been waiting to plant on her mouth, and she didn't disappoint. Candace kissed him back like she was as hungry for contact as he was, before raising her hand and placing it on his chest to push him back slightly.

"The purpose of the wig was to *not* draw attention to myself," she whispered, eyes dancing as she stared up at him.

Logan chuckled, shaking his head. What had Candace done to him? So much for being the guy Brett called Mr. No Emotion. He'd gone years without having any issues of self-control around the opposite sex, and now he was behaving like a deprived addict.

"I'll try to be on my best behavior tonight," Logan muttered.

Candace stroked his face, gently, like she was touching something fragile. She didn't, *couldn't,* know it, but that was exactly what he was. No one else saw it—everyone treated him based on his physical appearance and based on the rank he held—when inside he knew he was as vulnerable, if not more so, than anyone else. He just hoped she couldn't see too much of who he was, because he was certain the darkness of his thoughts, his memories, would send her running.

"I'll see you at eight," he said.

Logan backed away and turned, walking in a straight line toward the lobby and the front doors. This time he made it to his car, unlocking the vehicle and jumping behind the wheel. Ranger nudged him, dancing from paw to paw in excitement at not being left alone for too long.

"Don't ask," Logan muttered, giving the dog's head a scratch.

What he should have been concerned about was how much he was starting to treat Ranger like a pet instead of an elite military dog, and how easily they'd fallen into bad habits since they'd been home. Instead he was thinking about a blonde who'd looked just as sexy as a brunette, and who was starting to drive him crazy.

He picked up his phone and dialed Brett, hitting speaker and putting his phone on his lap.

"All set for tonight?" Brett said as he answered.

Logan fought the urge to thump his head on the steering wheel. Instead he yanked on his seat belt and started driving, needing to be distracted.

"There's been a slight change of plan," he told Brett.

"Don't even think about it. Jamie will kill you if you cancel."

"I'm not cancelling. I'm, ah, bringing someone."

Logan waited for the laughter, but all he heard was silence.

"Anyone I know?"

"Look, I need you guys to just not make a fuss. Just treat her like any other girl I might have met and brought along for a drink."

"Except you've never brought a girl along before," Brett said with a laugh. "In fact, I don't know when I last heard the words Logan and date uttered in the same sentence."

"I'm warning you…" Logan told him, knowing he could trust his best mate but going all stupid and protective over Candace anyway.

"No need. It'll be fun. Want to just meet us there?"

"Yeah, I'll see you there."

Logan hung up and let his head fall back against the rest. Asking Candace out had been crazy, but the fact he was heading out with Brett and Jamie would mean there was no pressure, that everything would be fine. So long as he didn't end up taking her back to his place again, it would just be a night out with friends.

Ranger whined and Logan took his eyes off the road for a split second to glare at him.

"I know, I know, but it's only one night."

His dog ignored him and stared out the window, and Logan tried to think about going back home to the Outback instead of what the night was going to be like. Because he couldn't convince his dog, and he couldn't convince himself that seeing Candace for a few hours over a drink was ever going to be enough. Or that he'd be able to hold back and not end up trying to make something happen between them again.

Weakness wasn't something he'd ever struggled with before. He'd had to fight a lot of other emotions, deal with loss and a lot of crap over the years, but no one could ever have accused him of being weak. Until a gorgeous, sexy country singer had walked into his life and turned everything he'd ever known, ever felt, up on its head.

Next thing he knew he'd be playing her music and singing along to her songs like a lovesick puppy.

Candace had a pile of rejected clothes strewn across the bed. After trying almost everything on, she'd settled on a pair of skinny jeans, a T-shirt with sequined sleeves and a pair of super-high stilettos. Logan was insanely tall and while she liked the fact that his size made her feel protected, she didn't like only reaching his shoulder if her shoes weren't high enough.

She fluffed her hair, tousling her curls, and applied one final brush of lip gloss. Candace was about to reach for her purse when her phone beeped. She grabbed it and scrolled through her emails, smiling when she read the first new message.

Candace Evans spotted getting cozy with mystery man in L.A.? Source sees her being rushed through customs and into the arms of another stranger.

She blew out a sigh of relief and flicked her phone to silent before jamming it into her purse. Her tip-off had worked, which meant no one would be expecting her to still be in Australia, and definitely not at a local bar hanging out with some regular people. She just had to hope that enough gossip sites passed around the message.

Candace left the light on in her room and turned the message on the door to Do Not Disturb, then headed for the elevator. Her heart was pounding, nerves making her hands damp. The anticipation of seeing Logan again was putting her more on edge than she ever was just before a concert. It was crazy, and she hadn't been like this around a guy for a very long time, but something about the sexy soldier-turned-bodyguard had her stomach doing cartwheels.

She'd promised herself that she wouldn't ever fall for a man again, that she was better off being single, but while that might have been easy before, it didn't seem quite so straightforward now. Because Logan had shown her that not all men were jerks, and no matter how hard she wanted to resist him, her willpower had failed her from the moment she'd agreed to go out with him the first time.

The elevator dinged and Candace took a deep breath and walked out. She hadn't bothered to put her wig on, but she did keep her head down as she walked toward the lobby doors. She doubted anyone would bother staring at her too hard, and all the excitement over her concert had well and truly died down.

"Candace."

She glanced up just as she almost walked straight into Logan, his deep voice stopping her. He was standing with his arms folded, waiting like he'd kill anyone with his bare hands if they so much as came near her.

"Hey," she said, wishing the sight of him had settled instead of unnerved her.

"I was half expecting a brunette tonight," he joked, turning so he could put his arm around her and walk them both out of the hotel. "It's kind of like the whole Miley Cyrus versus Hannah Montana thing."

His joke blew all the nerves from her body, somehow made her relax.

"How on earth do you know *anything* about Hannah Montana?" she asked, laughing as he opened the door to his vehicle.

Logan leaned in toward her, one arm braced on the

door. “Ten-year-old niece. I was trying to be a good uncle.”

Candace laughed to herself as he shut the door. *This* was why she liked Logan so much—being in his company was…refreshing. It made her feel like she was a world away from everything, and right now that was the best feeling she could imagine.

“So tell me about your friends,” she said, angling her body so she could stare at Logan. “Do they know you’re bringing someone along with you?”

He glanced at her before starting the engine, and she was just watching as his mouth opened to reply when—

“Argh!” Candace squealed and almost hit her head on the ceiling.

“Ranger!” Logan barked, pushing his dog back and reaching for her, his hand covering her thigh. “I’m sorry. I was just about to warn you and then…”

“Your dog stuck his tongue in my ear. Actually in my ear,” Candace complained, wiping at her face and glaring at the dog in the backseat. But her anger quickly turned to laughter when she saw the confused look on Ranger’s face.

“It’s fast becoming one of his party tricks,” Logan confessed. “We both apologize, don’t we, Ranger?”

Candace reached back and gave the dog a stroke on the head, finding it hard to believe that the dog had actually molested her, not to mention the fact that she was voluntarily touching him.

“It’s okay. I guess that was just him saying hi,” she said, not wanting to get the dog into trouble now that she was actually starting to like him. "Next time I suggest warning your passenger, though."

Logan stroked his hand across her thigh before putting it back on the wheel, and she wished she had the nerve to just grab it and put it back in place.

"He was all upset seeing my bags packed, so I told him he could tag along for the ride."

Candace leaned back in her seat, keeping an eye on the dog in case he decided to get frisky again.

"Anyway, you were asking about Brett and Jamie?"

"Yeah. Tell me about them."

Logan made a noise in his throat that made her think he didn't really want to discuss them, but then he took one hand off the wheel and seemed to relax.

"Brett is one of my oldest friends. We met our first day of training, and we both ended up going through to the SAS and then the doggies division."

"Has he retired now, too?"

Logan nodded. "Yeah, he was injured pretty bad on his last tour."

She watched as Logan's jaw tightened, a visible tick alerting her to the fact that this might not be something he was comfortable discussing with her.

"Is he, ah, one of the guys you mentioned the other night? One of the two that you used to meet up with at the restaurant?" Candace hoped she hadn't pushed him too far by asking.

Logan didn't say anything straight away, but he did put his fallen hand back on the wheel, the whites of his knuckles showing how hard his grip was. She wished she knew what was going through his mind, wondered if it was the same memories that he fought in the night.

"There were three of us. Brett, Sam and me. They were on tour together about a year ago, working a routine patrol, when an IED bomb went off and killed Sam."

Logan paused and Candace just stayed still, silent.

"Brett lost his dog in the blast, too, and he's so lucky to be alive himself."

She had no idea what to say. "Logan, I'm sorry."

He shrugged, but she knew he wasn't finding it easy to talk about, that it wasn't something he'd ever be able to truly shrug off, no matter how convincing he might look.

"When Brett came home, things kind of became difficult between us when he, well, he kind of fell in love with Sam's wife. His widow, I mean. It's all a bit of a complicated story, but at the end of the day it was the best thing for both of them."

Jeez. When Logan had said he'd been through a lot these past few years, he actually had.

"You must have found that pretty hard to deal with?" Candace said. "Understandably so, I mean."

"I was a jerk when I should have listened to them, but Jamie can tell you more about all that if she wants to. All I care about is that they're both happy now." He glanced across at her. "I'm not usually the guy who overreacts, except when it comes to the people I care about."

Candace shifted in her seat as Logan focused on the road again.

"And you," he added, his voice low.

She stopped moving, wondering if she'd heard him right. "Me?" Candace forced herself to ask.

Logan pulled over, parking the car, but she couldn't take her eyes off of him. What did he mean by that?

Once the vehicle was stationary, he turned his body to face hers, reaching for her hand. She let him take it, their fingers linking.

"There's something about you that I can't stay away from, no matter how much I tell myself I should."

Candace was like a spider caught in a web—Logan's gaze was impossible to escape from, and she didn't want to. It was like he was saying the words that were in her head, telling her what she was thinking.

"Meaning you wish you hadn't asked me out to-night?"

"Meaning," he said, cupping her face in his other hand, "that it probably would have been best for both of us if I hadn't, not that I didn't want to."

She knew exactly what he meant, because she'd been telling herself the same thing, knowing that it would have been best to move on and not think about Logan, let alone see him again. But like a bee was lured to nec-tar time and time again, so it seemed was she to him.

"You're leaving in the morning, right?" she whis-pered.

Logan nodded, just the barest movement of his head. "Yes."

"Then it's just one more night. We'll both be head-ing our separate ways tomorrow."

He leaned toward her, placing a feather-light kiss to

her lips. Logan didn't say anything, and he didn't need to. Whatever it was they had between them, whatever was pulling them together, wasn't something either of them seemed to understand. But by tomorrow, neither of them would have a choice.

"Let's go meet your friends," Candace said as he dropped his hand from her face.

Logan smiled and jumped out of the car, and Candace quickly touched up her lip gloss in the mirror.

CHAPTER SEVEN

LOGAN TOOK CANDACE's hand as they walked toward the entrance of the bar. He hoped no one made a fuss and recognized her, especially not after last time. All he wanted was a quiet evening with friends, a couple of beers and to make the most of his only night left with Candace. So much for telling himself that he was going to play the part of the perfect gentleman tonight. After what she'd said in the car, his mind was all over the "just one more night" line she'd given him.

"They're just over there," he said into her ear, pointing toward where Brett and Jamie were standing near the bar.

Candace squeezed his hand and they headed straight over. He could see the grin on Jamie's face even from across the room once she spotted them, and he knew it wasn't just because it was Candace he'd brought with him. She'd been trying to set him up with someone, *anyone,* for longer than he liked to admit, and even though he'd repeatedly turned her down she'd been pretty insistent that it was time he met someone. Pity he'd have to let her down gently that this wasn't a relationship that was going anywhere.

"Hey!" Jamie said, kissing his cheek and holding her hand out to Candace. "Great to meet you."

Candace smiled and shook hands with both Jamie and Brett, and Logan gave them both a hug.

"What do you want to drink?" Logan asked Candace.

Candace raised her eyebrows and looked at Jamie. "What are you having?"

"A mocktail because I'm driving. But whatever you do, don't let either of these boys talk you into a Long Island Iced Tea."

They all burst out laughing, except for Candace, who just looked confused.

"Come sit down and I'll tell you all about it," Jamie said with a grin, looping her arm through Candace's. "Logan, ask the bartender to make her something delicious. He's good like that."

Logan reached out and touched the small of Candace's back just before she walked away, receiving a sweet smile in response when she glanced over her shoulder. He stared at her as she moved, watched the gentle sway of her body, the long curly hair that hung like a wave down her back and that he was desperate to fist his hands in.

"Hey," Brett said, nudging him in the ribs. "You going to get these drinks or do I have to?"

Logan snapped out of it and stared at Brett.

"I'm losing it," he admitted. "I'm losing the plot and there's nothing I can do about it."

Brett sighed and leaned across the bar to order the

drinks, clearly deciding he was useless for the time being. "Next round's on you," he muttered.

"Brett, I'm serious. She's done something to me and I can't snap out of it."

"So you like her. What's the big deal?"

Logan put one elbow on the bar to prop himself up. "The fact that she's way out of my league, not to mention she leaves tomorrow." He ran a hand through his short hair. "And you know me, I'm just not interested in being with anyone after, well, everything."

Brett chuckled and passed him a beer. "You can pretend all you like, but you're interested in being with her. Otherwise you wouldn't be telling me all this. Besides, you can't dwell on the past forever, no matter how bad it is. At some point you're going to have to move on."

Logan raised the beer bottle and drained almost half of it. "She's under my skin. I want her but I don't, and…"

He had no idea what he was trying to say, because he didn't even know what he wanted. It was impossible to even think straight with her around. Deep down, he doubted he could give enough of himself to any woman, certainly not Candace, but he knew he was starting to think about her as more than a one-night thing. He'd be lying if he told himself he didn't want more. A lot more.

"Logan, she's a beautiful girl, and you've had fun with her. You telling me you want more than that, or are you just pissed that you can't have her in your bed for a few more nights?"

"Don't talk about her like that. It has *nothing* to

do with me just wanting her in bed." Logan knew he sounded angry, and he was.

"Whoa," Brett said, putting his beer down and holding up both hands. "I was just trying to make a point. You don't have to bite my head off."

"Well, don't," Logan grumbled, even though he knew it was him who'd been in the wrong.

"You remember when I was first with Jamie, and I tried to tell you how I felt about her?"

"Was that before or after I gave you the black eye?"

Brett punched him in the arm, but he was still grinning. "The point is, I felt differently about Jamie than I'd ever felt about another woman. I could have lost you as a friend just for telling you, for trying to explain, but she was worth it. *She's still worth it.*" He shrugged. "Your past is never going to go away, so you're just going to have to deal with it."

Logan watched as Brett glanced across to where the girls were seated, and he angled his body so he could see them, too. They were sitting together, heads bent as they discussed something that made them both burst out laughing. Jamie was one of his closest friends, and he'd been right to think that she'd be perfect for Candace to spend time with. And everything Brett was saying was right, even if it was blunt.

"Don't be so much of a hard head that you lose someone you feel that way about, that's all I'm saying," Brett said, picking up his beer bottle and another mocktail for Jamie. "Jamie was worth fighting for, and that would have been the truth no matter how high the stakes. You just have to decide if Candace is worth the fight, whatever that fight turns out to be."

Logan collected his drinks and walked beside his friend, knowing he was right. He often kept everything bottled up inside and refused to talk, but telling Brett what he was thinking had been the right thing to do.

"It's about time I told you I'm sorry for being a jerk when you tried to talk to me about Jamie," he admitted. "I should never have been so harsh on you, and every time I see the two of you together I know what an idiot I was. I hope you know that."

Brett just shrugged. "You were looking out for her, I get it. And you've said sorry enough times for me to believe you, so how about we just move on, huh?"

"Yeah, but until now, maybe I didn't know how you really felt. I meant it when I apologized back then, but all of a sudden I actually get it," Logan mumbled, eyes locked on Candace as he headed toward her. "As much as I want to forget about her, to ignore the way I feel..."

"You just can't," Brett finished for him. "Trust me, I get it."

"So what do I do?" he asked just before they reached the table. "What am I supposed to do?"

"Stop overthinking it," Brett said in a low voice. "If it feels right, just go with it. For once in your life switch that part of your brain off and just enjoy the moment."

"Hey," Candace said with a smile as Logan sat down beside her on the leather seat.

The table was tucked away, a low-hanging light casting warm shadows around them in contrast to the darkness of the bar.

"Try this and see what you think," Logan told her, sliding the drink across to her.

Candace grinned and leaned forward, at the same time resting her hand on his thigh. Logan stiffened, couldn't help how rigid his body went, like it was on high alert, but if she noticed she never said anything. What Brett had said had been right, trouble was that the last time he'd just lived in the moment, he'd had his heart ripped out and stomped all over. Add to that his fear of losing anyone he actually cared about again, and he was one screwed up individual, he knew.

"So what were you two busy talking about?" Brett asked, kissing Jamie when she turned to face him.

"Oh, you know, just telling Candace some stories about you two," Jamie responded. "It's always fun having someone new to share info with."

"I was telling Jamie about my fear of dogs, and how Ranger decided to make love to my ear with his tongue on the way here."

Logan just shook his head when the other two burst into laughter. He'd hoped they'd just be themselves around Candace, and they were, which was making the whole situation seem…like some sort of double date. They weren't treating her any differently than they would any other girl.

He cleared his throat. "I'm heading back home first thing tomorrow, Jamie, did Brett tell you?"

"Don't tell me you want me to babysit Ranger?" Jamie asked. "Or is that something Candace wants to do now that he's shown his love for her?"

Both Candace and Jamie giggled, and Logan exchanged looks with Brett. His friend was giving him a look he'd only seen when they'd been serving, a look that told him he had to do what he had to do. Before, it had been about war, about making decisions that could affect his entire team, and now it was about putting his own heart on the line and putting himself at risk. Which wasn't something he was comfortable with at all. Now, the decision he made was only going to affect his own life, which was why the whole thing was scaring him.

"What are your plans, Candace? You heading back to the States?" Brett asked, giving Logan a moment to gather his thoughts.

Candace was toying with her straw. She took a delicate sip before answering. "You know, I don't have any definite plans as yet, but I'm planning on staying in Australia for a few more days, maybe longer."

Logan almost choked on his beer. "You are?" He turned so he was staring straight at her.

She glanced across at him, her eyes not settling on his. "Yeah. You kind of convinced me that I needed a break."

"When you said you were going to take some time off, I didn't realize you meant *here.* I figured you were going back to your ranch in Montana."

Suddenly it was like there was just the two of them in the room, that Brett and Jamie weren't even part of the conversation. How had she not mentioned this earlier? Why hadn't he asked her?

"You're going tomorrow, and I didn't want you to feel like..." Her voice trailed off, her sentence unfinished.

"I could have changed my plans," he muttered. If

he'd known there was the chance of spending more time with her, of this being more than a one-night thing… he would have what? He still didn't know how he felt about Candace, what he thought, what he was capable of offering.

"Candace, you should see Logan's property while you're here," Brett said, interrupting them just as Logan was about to tear his hair out. "I know you've probably travelled to a lot of beautiful places, but there's nothing quite like the Outback."

An awkward silence fell over the table. Even the ever bubbly Jamie was quiet, which made the whole situation feel more pressure cooked than it was.

"I'd love to see it one day. I'm sure it's pretty special," Candace said, but she kept her head down, eyes on her cocktail.

"Brett, why don't we go get another round of drinks?" Jamie suggested, standing and tugging on Brett's hand.

"But we haven't even…" He stopped talking and just stood up when Jamie gave him a fierce look that Logan caught from the corner of his eye.

Logan let them leave before turning to Candace. His mind was jumbled, his thoughts all over the place, but he kept thinking about what Brett had said and he realized he didn't want to regret anything when it came to the woman seated beside him. It was time to man up and he knew it.

"You should have told me you were staying in Australia," Logan said, going to reach for her hand then hesitating, before forcing himself to get out of his comfort zone and just do it. "I just presumed you were heading back straightaway."

Candace's hand was warm in his, but her eyes were staring at their connection, not back into his. She was deep in thought and he wanted to know what was going through her head, what she wanted from him.

"Candace?" he asked, wishing he hadn't sounded so angry.

"I didn't want to tell you because I don't even know what this is between us," she said, finally looking up at him. "I couldn't exactly ask you not to go back home, to stay for another few days just to keep me company."

Logan's heart physically felt like it was going to stop. The pain he felt at seeing her eyes swim with tears was too much for him to handle, because it was him hurting her and that wasn't something he'd ever intended on doing.

"I have no idea what this is, either, Candace." It was the truth and he didn't know what else to say.

"A couple of years ago, I made a decision that I was better off alone than with a man in my life," she told him, still letting him hold her hand. "And then I met you, and I forgot all about the promise I'd made myself. I want you to know that I've never had a one-night stand in my life until you, Logan, and I'm fairly certain it's not something I'll ever do again."

Logan stared back at Candace, wondering what on earth she saw in him to make her want to spend any time with him at all. Why she trusted him, why they both seemed able to confide in one another.

"I don't have a lot to offer, Candace, not emotionally. But I'm not ready to say goodbye to you yet."

She leaned into him, her cheek to his chest. Logan circled his arms around her body, held her to him and shut his eyes, wanting to remember what it was like to have the tiny blonde against him. To be with a woman who made him feel things he'd never expected to feel again in his lifetime, to simply have Candace tucked against him. For as long as he lived, he'd never forget her warmth, the vulnerability he'd glimpsed—it was a comfort like he'd never experienced before.

"Come with me tomorrow," he said, his voice low.

Candace went so still he couldn't even feel her breathing.

"You mean that?" she asked, keeping her face to his chest.

Logan blew out a breath, not sure how he'd just ended up inviting a woman he barely knew back to his family home. But he had, and deep down he knew he wanted it more than anything. This time, he wasn't going to let his fears make decisions for him.

"Yeah, I mean it."

Candace eventually sat upright, one of her hands touching his face as she stared into his eyes.

"Screw doing what I think I should," she said, the corners of her mouth tipping up into a smile. "I think it's about time I just do what feels right."

He couldn't have said it better himself. Logan kissed her, forcing himself to keep his mouth soft to hers when all he wanted was to lose control. He usually hated any kind of public affection, but he wasn't exactly behaving like himself around Candace and there was no way he was going to *not* kiss her with her looking up at him like that.

"We leave you guys for, like, ten minutes, and already you're making out like a pair of lovesick teenagers."

Logan didn't pull away from Candace immediately, but when he did he glared at Brett. Trust his friend to push him in one direction then tease him about it as soon as Logan followed his instructions. But without Brett's chat, maybe he would have kept his mouth shut instead of taking a leap of faith.

"I think that round was supposed to be mine," Logan muttered, wrapping an arm around Candace and letting her snuggle under his shoulder.

"Yup. You owe me thirty bucks."

The drive back wasn't long, and in a way Candace wished it had been. The moment they'd buckled up, Logan had reached for her hand and held it, and they'd been like that the entire way back to her hotel. Even though they hadn't said a word, they hadn't needed to, and Candace had no idea what she would have said to him, anyway. They'd kind of said it all at the bar and the silence between them was comfortable.

"Here we are," Logan announced when he pulled up outside.

Candace reluctantly let go of his hand, wishing she'd just suggested they go home to his place.

"Do you want to come up?" she asked.

Logan stared straight ahead for a second, like he

wasn't sure what to say, or was having some sort of battle over what he wanted to say and what he thought he should say.

"I can't leave Ranger the whole night in here, but I'll come up for a little bit," he said.

Candace fought the heat starting to spread into her cheeks, finding it hard to believe that she'd been the one to ask a man up to her hotel room. Spending time with Logan was sure making her do a lot of things for the first time.

She jumped out and they both walked into the lobby, side by side but not quite touching. They headed straight for the elevator, and Candace toyed with the idea of putting her arm around Logan before deciding to just stand still and stop fidgeting.

"So this might sound like a weird question, but how exactly do we get to the Outback?" she asked, hoping that didn't make her sound like a dumb blonde. She had no idea whether it was two hours away or ten, and if she had to prepare for an insanely long drive or not.

"Not silly at all," he said, touching his fingers to hers when the doors opened. "I probably should have explained when I asked you."

"Don't tell me we have to go by bus or something?" She didn't want to sound like a princess, but…

"We fly," he said, stepping back so she could select her floor. "The catch is that I'm the pilot."

Candace spun around, her jaw almost hitting the floor. "No way." Logan sure had a way of surprising her when she least expected it.

He grimaced. "Yes way, but if it makes you feel any

better I've had my private pilot license since I was nineteen, so it's not like I'm trying to clock up flying hours just for experience these days."

She couldn't believe what she was hearing. "And the plane's yours?" she asked.

"It's not that unusual for a large Outback station to have a plane," he told her, clearly trying to be modest. "We have a couple of small helicopters based on-site for mustering, but I keep the plane here a lot of the time so I can go back and forth."

Okay, she thought. Maybe the reason he wasn't easily intimidated by her was because he had a lot more family wealth than he'd ever let on before. Either way it didn't bother her, but it did make her even more intrigued about the man she'd just agreed to go on a mini-vacation with. There was so much about Logan that was still a mystery to her.

"If you're comfortable taking me, I'm comfortable flying with you," Candace told him.

They exited the elevator when they reached her floor, stepping out side by side.

"Just in case you're getting any grand ideas, it's just a nice reliable four-seater, nothing over-the-top, so don't expect reclining chairs or champagne."

She smiled. "I don't care what the plane looks like, just so long as it gets us to where we need to go and safely."

A look crossed his face, either sadness or anger, she just couldn't quite put her finger on it, but something changed in him at that exact moment.

"We'll get there," he said in a quiet voice that she hadn't heard before. "Don't you worry about that."

Candace wasn't sure what she'd said, but something had rattled him, she could sense it. She wasn't going to pry, though—if he wanted to talk about something that was troubling him, then he could bring it up when he was good and ready. She hated being pushed when something was on her mind.

"So will I have Ranger strapped in beside me?" Candace asked as she swiped her room key. "Or will I be relegated to the back so he can have your wingman seat?"

Logan chuckled. "He's a seasoned flier after all the miles he clocked up in the army, so you don't have to worry about him turning into a quivering mess and wanting to sit on your knee. He knows his place in the back with his harness on."

They walked into the room and Candace dropped her key and purse onto the side table before flopping down onto the bed.

"Talk about a cheap date. Two cocktails and I'm buzzing."

Logan sat beside her, his thigh grazing hers. "So what did you think of my friends? They weren't too full-on?"

Candace lay back on the bed, kicking off her stilettos. "You're kidding me? They were fantastic. Jamie was hilarious, just the kind of company I've been missing. I really liked her."

"Yeah, she's a great girl." Logan was silent for a while, obviously thinking something over, when he suddenly turned to her. "Candace, I want you to know that I've never taken anyone I've been involved with to my family home before."

Candace went still, staring at the ceiling fan before pulling herself up and sitting back against the pillows. "You haven't?"

He shook his head. "I was dating someone a while back, someone I thought I was going to marry, but my parents died before I had the chance to take her there. I haven't been seriously involved with anyone since."

"I'm sorry," Candace said, wishing she could think of something more helpful to say and coming up with nothing.

"When they died, we'd already gotten engaged, and I was so angry that she hadn't met them, that we hadn't spent time together as a family. It seemed so stupid that I'd never made the time to take her home when it should have been a priority."

"So what happened?" Candace asked, her voice deliberately low.

Logan kicked off his boots and moved up the bed, lying beside her, his head almost touching hers. She waited, hardly breathing she was trying to stay so quiet.

"I've experienced a lot of loss, it's just part and parcel of what I've always done for a job, but losing my parents?"

Candace moved her hand so it was touching Logan's, her fingers linking with his, letting him know she was there for him.

"I still don't know how I managed to pull through.

And then the fiancée I thought was in love with me turned out to be a gold digger."

Now that was something she understood all too well, and why she rarely trusted her instincts when it came to men anymore.

"I don't know what to say, but I can say that I've been in that same position with a couple of men before. Nothing hurts more than that kind of betrayal."

Logan squeezed her fingers. "To be honest, that's why I'm telling you," he said. "Charlotte made a few comments that made me suspicious, that made my friends question her real motives, and so I told her that my parents had been in debt and there wasn't any inheritance left over once the debtors had been paid."

Candace sighed. "Don't tell me. She left straightaway?"

"Yep, she was gone from my life faster than I could blink. Her stuff was moved out of our city house within the week," Logan said, moving so he could put his arm around her. "So I lost my parents and my fiancée within a few weeks of each other."

Candace turned, too, so she could snuggle back into Logan. She'd been thinking about getting him into bed ever since he'd kissed her in the bar, but now that they were here, all she wanted was to lie in his arms. The fact that he trusted her enough to confide in her meant more to her than anything, especially when on so many levels she understood what he'd been through.

"Better to have her walk out before you were married, or after you'd had children. I know it's kind of a cliché to say that, but it's true."

Logan's hand tucked under her breast, keeping her close, the warmth from his body making her want to shut her eyes and just enjoy someone holding her, making her feel wanted.

"Logan, I don't know a lot about Australia, but I'm guessing your ranch is kind of, well, impressive," Candace said. "You're obviously in a—" she struggled to find the right word "—*comfortable* position."

Logan's breath was hot against her ear when he chuckled. "You want to know my net worth before you agree to spending more time with me? Is that what you're saying?"

Now it was Candace laughing. "I couldn't care less how much money you have, but from the story you've just told me I have a feeling you're a more eligible bachelor than you've let on."

"If I'm honest with you, we have one of the biggest privately owned Outback stations in New South Wales, and my sister and I inherited everything jointly," he told her. "It's something I'm proud of, but at the same time I'd rather slip under the radar without anyone taking any notice of me, if you know what I mean."

"And yet you've dedicated the last, what, ten years to the army?"

"Something like that," he said, his mouth against her hair. "I just wanted to prove myself, make my own mark on the world before I took over the day-to-day running of the station. It made my dad proud, and I'd always planned on working side by side with him once I'd finished with the SAS."

Candace kept her eyes shut, loving the feel of Logan

stroking her hair, running his fingers gently through her curls before starting at her scalp again.

"What Charlotte did to me, it screwed me up where women are concerned. I'm not the guy who'll ever settle down, because I couldn't ever trust anyone that much again."

That made her eyes pop open. It wasn't that she had any illusions about Logan wanting to marry her, but the fact that such a nice, genuine man was too afraid of being hurt to love again? It made her sad. She often had similar thoughts, but to actually believe that falling in love would never happen? That wasn't something she believed, no matter how disillusioned she felt sometimes.

"Logan, you deserve to have children one day, to carry on your family's legacy and be happy."

When he spoke, his voice was gruff. "My parents set the best example for what a marriage is, and they were the best parents a kid could ever wish for. If I can't be the same husband, and dad that my own father was to me and my sister, then I don't have any interest in trying."

She understood, but it didn't mean she agreed with him. To her he just sounded like a wounded person not wanting to admit that one day he'd be whole again.

"Can you stay a little while?" Candace asked as Logan's touch lulled her into a happy, almost asleep state.

He didn't say anything, but he didn't stop touching her, either. She should have turned to him, should have kissed him and enjoyed having a man like Logan in her bed, but she also didn't want to give up the feeling of simply having his arms around her. It had been a long time since she'd trusted someone as much as she trusted this man, and it was something she wanted to selfishly indulge in a little while longer.

"We leave at nine tomorrow morning," Logan murmured in her ear. "I'll be gone when you wake up, but I can either come back and collect you, or you can make your own way to the airport."

Candace was barely conscious she was so relaxed. "There," she murmured. "I'll meet you there."

She tried to stay awake, but as she was slipping into sleep she decided not to fight it. For all she knew, it might be the only time she was cuddled to sleep for a long time.

Candace woke with such a fright it was like a bolt of lightning had struck her. It took a moment, a split second as she struggled to remember where she was and figure out what on earth was happening, but when she did the panic was like a noose around her neck.

"Logan!" she gasped, trying to push herself up.

He was calling out, tossing and turning, the pain and desperation in his voice almost unbearable.

"Logan!" she called out, scrambling from the bed and landing on her feet.

One second Logan was thrashing, the next he was sitting up, looking disorientated, his hands above his head.

"Candace?" Logan's voice was rough, croaky.

She didn't say anything for a moment, just tried to catch her breath.

"Candace?" His voice was more panicked this time.

"Here," she said, leaning forward. "Logan, I'm right here."

He reached to flick the bedside lamp, illuminating the room so she could see him properly and him her.

"What happened?" he asked.

Candace took a big, shaky breath, before sitting on the edge of the bed.

"You were having one of your night terrors and I woke you."

Logan's expression changed, his face falling. "I'm sorry. I don't know what happened."

She reached for him, clasping his hand. "I think you might have these more than you realize," Candace told him, trying to be as gentle with her words and her touch as she could. "Logan, you, well, the other night when I left, it wasn't because I knew about the photos."

He pushed his legs off the bed, head falling into his hands as he sat there. Candace wanted to comfort him, but she also knew that talking about this probably wasn't something he was comfortable with. Wasn't something that would come easily to him.

"I've done this before with you?" he asked when he finally raised his head.

"The other night I woke to you thrashing around and I know I should have done something, but instead I just left," she told him. "I thought maybe it was a one-off thing, and I also didn't think I was going to see you again."

Logan stood, his body dominating the room with his size. "I don't know what to say. I shouldn't have fallen asleep, and I just, I mean..." His voice trailed off, like he was in pain. "I didn't realize that I ever lashed out when I was dreaming. If I'd known I would never have put you in danger like that."

"It's not your fault, Logan. And I'm here for you," she said, even if she *was* scared of it happening again. "I can help."

"Candace," he started, walking around the bed and dropping to his knees as she sat on the bed, reaching for her hands before gently touching her face and then dropping his head into her lap. "I'm sorry."

Tears flooded Candace's eyes, spilled over even as she tried her hardest to push them away. This man—this strong, big man—was literally on his knees before her, and it almost broke her heart.

"It's okay, Logan. Everything's going to be okay."

When he raised his head, she could see that his own cheeks were tearstained. He slowly rose to his feet, and she could hardly breathe, couldn't take her eyes from his face.

"I have to go," he said.

She shook her head but he just nodded, walking backward.

"You can stay," she whispered.

"No, Candace, I need to go. To think. I'm sorry."

Candace watched him leave then lay back on the bed and pulled the covers up, dragging them over her head and hiding away from the world. A part of her wanted to run after him, to grab him and tell him that he couldn't go, but she also knew that he wasn't the kind of man to be forced into anything. If he needed time, he needed time. End of story. He was a complicated guy and she understood that more than he probably realized.

If you love someone, you always need to be strong enough to let them fly.

It was a saying her mom had strongly believed in, and when she shut her eyes, she could hear her saying it, whispering it to her one night when she was a little girl. Then, it had been about her beloved dog, loving him enough to say goodbye the next day at the vet clinic. Now, it was about a man. The only difference was that this time, she wasn't ready to admit how she felt. Not yet.

Logan slammed his fist into his steering wheel so hard that the horn beeped loudly into the otherwise silent night.

All this time thinking no one knew about how much he struggled, about the memories that terrorized him, and there he'd gone and lost it in front of Candace. The fact that she'd seen him…it hurt. Because he'd always been so good at making people see what he wanted them to see, without admitting how hard it had been, coming back from war and losing his parents. Even Brett didn't know the full extent of what he went through every single day—the memories he lived with.

He reached for his dog and stamped out the thoughts that were trying to take over his mind once again, wishing there was something he could do to make them stop. When he was with Candace, his mind actually felt calm, which was why he'd never thought about how he might react in his sleep when he was beside her.

But he'd blown it now. There was no chance she'd turn up in the morning. He'd sealed his own fate there, so now he just had to live with the fact that his past was part of his future, whether he liked it or not. He'd tried to run away from it, and he'd found someone who made him forget, and it still hadn't worked.

Logan started the engine and pulled away, from the hotel and from Candace.

CHAPTER EIGHT

LOGAN TAPPED HIS thigh to tell Ranger to walk at heel, his bag slung over his back, heading for the plane. He'd hardly had any sleep last night, had lain awake thinking about Candace, about his night terrors...*everything.* But he still wanted to head home, and he wasn't so weary that he couldn't make the relatively short flight. Every time he got into the pilot's seat he remembered things he didn't want to recall, but each time he was also pleased that he hadn't given into his fears and stayed grounded. And if he was ever going to get himself together, he needed to keep facing his fears head-on.

He stopped and looked at the plane, prepped and ready for him to fly out in, and his hand fell to Ranger's head.

"Time to head home, buddy," he muttered.

"Logan!"

Logan stopped moving. He'd just presumed Candace wouldn't show, that whatever they had was over after what had happened, but...

"Logan!"

He spun around, not wanting to believe it was her until he could actually see her.

"Candace?" He murmured her name, eyes locking on her as she ran in his direction, her blond curls loose and flying out around her.

She had someone struggling to keep up with her, beside her, and Logan was pretty certain that it was probably a poor security guard who she'd managed to slip past.

"Sorry, Mr. Murdoch. She just…"

"It's fine," he said, once they'd reached him. "It's fine. Sorry for the inconvenience."

"You said nine," Candace panted, out of breath. "It's only one minute past and you'd already given up on me? Surely you know me better than that."

Logan shook his head, speechless. "I didn't expect…"

"You didn't expect me to turn up, did you?" she asked, finishing his sentence. "You thought a little scary dream was going to send me running for the hills?"

He shook his head. "I guess not."

"When we first met, you brazenly asked me out, and I did the one thing in the world I would never usually do," she said. "And that was say yes to you."

Logan stared at her, unable to take his gaze off her bright blue eyes—eyes that had only the night before been filled with tears and were now full of light.

"You pushed me out of my comfort zone, and if you hadn't done that, who knows how long I would have kept on going, stuck in the rut I was in."

"I still don't understand why you're here," Logan

said. Candace could be anywhere in the world right now, and she was waiting to board his plane with him?

"I'm here because the time I've spent with you has been amazing, and because I want to see exactly what this property of yours is like."

He relaxed as she reached for his hand, felt as if all the stress, all the fury that had been building since he'd left her, had just fallen away.

"I'm still invited back to your ranch, aren't I?" Candace asked in a quiet voice.

Logan bent down to kiss Candace's cheek, wishing he could come up with something better to say than simply *yes.*

"I was a jerk last night, Candace, and if I could take it all back, I would."

"You're human, and the thing is that humans make mistakes. Let's just move on from all that, okay?"

Logan nodded, drawing her in close so he could hold her in his arms, feel her soft, warm body against his. It was all he'd thought about as he'd lay alone in his bed, wishing she was still pressed back into him, letting him spoon her.

"Thank you," he whispered.

"There's just one thing," Candace said, hand to his chest as she leaned back and looked up at him.

Logan raised his eyebrows. "What's that?"

"I left a heap of luggage inside the terminal there. Would you be a darling and go grab it all for me?"

Logan burst out laughing and pulled her tight against him for another hug. Talk about surprising a guy in more ways than one.

"I'll get you and Ranger on the plane first, then I'll go back in," he muttered. "But you do realize that there's only so much weight a light aircraft can carry, right?"

She glanced over at his shoulder bag, forlorn on the tarmac, and he followed her gaze.

"Lucky you travel so light then, huh?"

Logan gave her a play punch on the arm and indicated for Ranger to walk with them, wanting her safely seated before he left her.

"I hope you're not this bossy once we get there."

Candace took his hand, her palm swallowed up by his when he closed his over hers. Next time he had the chance to open up to her, he was going to have to man up and deal with it instead of walking away. Because Candace deserved more, and if he was honest with himself, so did he. The fact that she'd turned up was a miracle, and it wasn't one that he was going to take lightly.

Candace took a deep breath as they started their descent. It had only taken a short time, and part of her wished they could have stayed up in the air longer. The view had been incredible the entire way, the day clear and fine, and flying across the Outback had been incredible. When she'd watched the movie *Australia* she'd thought the scenery had been manipulated to make it look so incredible, but she'd even seen kangaroos as they'd flown lower across the Murdoch property, hopping around freely in a way she wouldn't have been able to even imagine had she not seen it with her own eyes.

"You don't really eat kangaroos here, do you?" Candace asked, staring out the window, unable to look away.

"I don't personally, but yeah, a lot of restaurants here serve the meat now."

An involuntary shudder slid down her spine. "That's gross. I can't believe anyone would want to kill such a beautiful animal."

"It's even worse when you find a kangaroo shot by a hunter, or hit by a car, and there's a little joey alive in her pouch."

That made Candace snatch her eyes away from the view. "No."

Logan nodded, but his gaze and concentration never strayed from what he was doing. "Sad but true. When I was a kid I rescued one and she was like a pet for years. We pulled her out of her dead mother's pouch and she ended up being like one of our dogs."

Candace looked back out the window as they fast approached the ground. Logan sure had a way of surprising her.

"This should be nice and smooth, just a little bump when we first touch down," he told her.

Candace glanced over her shoulder at Ranger, sitting alert, his body braced by a harness that was keeping him secure and in place.

"Your dog is incredible. I can't believe he's so well behaved," she said, holding on as they landed and eventually came to a stop.

She watched as Logan flicked switches, looking completely at ease with what he was doing.

"The dogs that make it through SAS training have to be super canines," he said, stretching his arms out above his head. "Ranger had to be completely fearless, whether we were on patrol or being helicoptered into a situation. Sometimes he would be harnessed to my back if we weren't able to land, and we'd parachute to the ground together."

"No way!" It didn't even sound possible that a dog could do that kind of stuff.

"Yes," Logan said with a laugh. "I know it's crazy, but the dogs are probably worth more to the army than we humans are, because at the end of the day there are plenty of guys out there capable of doing our job, with the right training, but not many dogs who could make the cut."

Logan went back to unclip Ranger, and then he was opening his door and disappearing. The next thing, her door opened and he helped her down to the ground.

"You know, I'm almost starting to like dogs because of him," Candace said, stretching and looking around. Her eyes landed on two horses in a nearby field, their ears pricked, bodies dead still as they watched the plane and what was happening. "But I love horses *way* more."

Logan reappeared with some of her luggage, and nodded toward the house. It was a decent walk away, and she felt almost bad for having so much stuff.

"I'll take this lot and the butler can come get the rest."

"You have a butler?" she asked, rushing to catch up to him.

The look Logan gave her made them both laugh.

"Okay, I really fell for that one. But surely you have a trailer or something?"

He bumped his body against hers. “Don’t sweat it. I’ll come back with the quad bike later.”

Ranger ran off ahead and Candace was almost as eager, desperate to see the house that was obviously so special to Logan. She knew it was a big deal him asking her here in the first place, and if she was honest with herself, *not* turning up had never really been an option. Logan had probably been beyond embarrassed about what had happened the night before, and she didn’t want him to think he had to deal with his troubles alone.

“So who lives here when you’re not around?” she asked.

“We have a manager in a separate house, and his wife keeps the place tidy for me, stocks the fridge when she knows I’m coming back, that sort of thing.”

They crossed over toward the house and Candace couldn’t help but smile. “It’s beautiful.”

He was silent for a moment as they walked up to it. “Yeah, it is.”

She imagined it still looked the same as it had when his parents had been in residence. It was built from timber with a wide veranda that stretched around the entire house, the almost white paintwork in immaculate condition. As they stepped up toward the front door, Candace touched the handrail and let her hand stay on it until they reached the veranda.

“I can’t believe how beautiful this house is. I never realized it would be like this.”

Logan moved past her and opened the door.

“You don’t keep it locked?” she asked as she followed him inside.

"This is the Outback, not the city. We're miles from our closest neighbor and there's not really any risk of a break-in."

When he put it like that she guessed it made sense—it just wasn't something she was used to.

"So what's the plan for today?" Candace asked. "Horseback riding, a picnic, a swim in some amazing water hole?"

Logan chuckled and set her bags down in the hall. "I actually want to show you something. I was thinking we'd take a horseback ride there, if you're keen."

Was she keen? "I've been dying to get back in the saddle for months. Just give me a quiet horse, though, because it's been a while."

"That I can do," he said. "Now follow me while I give you a quick tour of the place."

Candace grinned and followed him, happy to look through the house. Taking the high road, and a risk, had been worth it, because she felt like the girl she'd left behind before her first album had launched, and she'd been missing that girl a lot lately. She just wanted to have fun, enjoy her life. It wasn't that she wanted to walk away from her career, because she could never stop singing, but creating a sense of balance was something she was determined to achieve.

"These are your parents?" she asked as they passed the hallstand.

Logan stopped, the smile that had been on his face dying. He touched the edge of one of the frames. "Yeah, that's them."

"Well, they look lovely," she said, touching his arm. "It's such a shame I couldn't have met them."

"My mom would have been in a huge flap if I'd brought you here when she was still alive. She'd have been baking up a storm and sending Dad to work in the garden, ordering him around like the queen was about to visit."

Candace liked the mental picture, had a feeling that she'd have probably loved his parents, too. Because that sounded a lot like her grandparents and her mom—just nice people who genuinely cared about their kids.

"So which room am I staying in?" she asked as Logan started to move again.

"That depends if you want to sleep in my bedroom or a guest room," he said, giving her a cheeky wink over his shoulder.

"Let's just see what happens today, shall we? I don't want you getting too cocky, soldier."

She was also a little scared of him having another one of his episodes, but she wasn't going to admit it, not to Logan. *And not one hundred percent to herself, either.*

"So what is it you want to show me?" Candace asked, loving the feel of the sun beating down on her shoulders and the gentle sway of the horse beneath her.

"We're almost there," he replied.

She admired Logan's strong silhouette as he rode slightly ahead of her, his big chestnut gelding tall and well muscled, just like his rider. Where she came from, men were always in the saddle, and it always made her laugh when city folk talked about horseback riding like it was a girls-only sport. Nothing made her admire a man more than one who could ride well and knew how to treat animals.

"Logan, I've been wanting to say that if you'd like to talk about what happened last night, I'm all ears," she said, wanting to get it off her chest to clear the air now rather than have it come up later.

"Can we just wait a minute?" he asked, his face not giving any hint of what he was thinking or feeling. "It'll all kind of make sense soon."

Candace didn't push the point, just accepted it and enjoyed the different scenery as they rode. Everything was so different to what she was used to, but the cattle grazing as they passed had the strange effect of making her feel like she was closer to home than she had been in a long while, even though she was on the other side of the world.

"It's in here," Logan said, heading toward a large shed.

She followed him and dismounted when he did, leading her horse closer and dropping her reins like he did. It wasn't something she was used to doing, but the horses seemed to understand exactly what was required of them.

"They won't move," Logan told her. "Come with me."

He bent down to put a key into the padlock that was securing the door, and she bit her tongue instead of asking why he locked this door in the middle of nowhere yet didn't bother with the house. She could see how tense his body was, that what she was about to see was something that meant a lot to him.

"Logan, what's in here?" she asked, curious and worried at the same time.

He yanked the door open and secured it back so that light flooded the big barn. Candace took a step inside, then another when Logan walked ahead of her. She watched as he dropped to his haunches, before looking back at all the metal and parts in front of her. It took her a second to figure it all out, but then she realized what she was looking at, what the wreckage had once been.

"This was a plane?"

She was staring at the back of Logan's head, waiting for him to explain.

"All my life, flying has been like second nature to me," Logan said, not moving. "I was up in a plane with my dad as soon as I was old enough to tag along, and I got my pilot's license as soon as I was old enough."

Candace swallowed, trying not to hold her breath as she listened to Logan. The way he was talking, the fact that they were standing in front of a wreckage, told her that this story wasn't going to end well. That what he was about to tell her was going to be hard to hear and even harder for him to say.

"Logan, what is this I'm looking at?" she asked.

"My parents died when the plane they were in crashed. My father had clocked up more hours flying than anyone I've ever met before, but the thing he loved killed him and my mom."

"Oh, Logan." Candace blinked away the tears in her

eyes and moved to stand behind him. "I don't know what to say."

"I'd just arrived back into the country when it happened, and even though they were supposed to notify next of kin first, the media got wind of who it was and I saw it on the news before my sister had a chance to phone me."

Now Candace *was* holding her breath.

"I dealt with the accident the only way I knew how, and that started with me insisting that I identify the bodies."

She listened as he sucked back a big breath before continuing on.

"They were badly burned, so..."

Candace put her arms around his waist and pressed herself to his back, just wanting to touch him, to hold him and let him know that she got how hard it was for him to talk, to share what he'd been through. That she was there for him.

"You had all the parts salvaged, didn't you?" she murmured against him.

"My training just kind of kicked in and I insisted on a second, independent investigation once the police one ended inconclusively. I just couldn't understand how a man like my father could be killed doing something he was capable of doing with his eyes shut. Nothing about it seemed right to me."

"Did they find anything?"

"Yeah, but it still doesn't stop me questioning everything, scouring through the report and then coming in here to go over every piece of the plane myself whenever I come home."

She released him enough that she could stand beside him, her arms still around his waist, head tucked against him.

"Yeah, but we can only deal with things the best way we know how."

"When I dream, the terrors I have at night, it's their bodies I see," he told her.

She moved around his body and watched as he shut his eyes, wished she could take away even a little of the pain he was feeling.

"I see them flying, then crashing, watch as they burn alive, and there's nothing I can do to help them. Then suddenly they disappear, and it's my friend Sam I see, being blown to pieces in front of me, his body burning and then somehow ending up alongside my folks, so they're all dead together."

"Have you talked to anyone about this before?" she asked. "Someone who could help you deal with what you're going through?"

Logan shook his head and gazed down at her. "You're the only person I've let close, the only person who's outright asked me about my dreams, and the only person I've ever opened up to about it." He paused. "But I don't want to talk about it anymore, Candace. I want to leave this in the past."

Logan hoped he'd done the right thing, but after so long carrying his pain on his own, it was almost a relief to finally get it off his chest. To show someone the barn he'd kept locked for so long, to talk about his memories. Because he couldn't hide his night terrors from Candace, not after she'd witnessed it firsthand, and he couldn't pretend like they didn't happen any longer, either.

"I don't know what to say, Logan, but I'm pleased you told me."

"It's been a long time since I've felt at peace with the world, but when I'm with you, I don't know. I just feel different."

"Me, too," she said, standing on tiptoe and kissing him. "This isn't something you need to deal with alone, and if you want to talk about your parents all night or not at all, it's fine by me."

Logan had a better idea. It was time he closed this chapter of his life, shut the doors to the wreckage and walked away from trying to find answers that didn't even seem to exist.

"You know, every time I fly my plane, I think about my dad up there in the sky, and I hope he didn't even know what happened when they crashed," Logan admitted, walking hand in hand with Candace from the barn and only dropping the contact to shut the door. "I get a bout of nerves every time I start the engine, but then that passes and I can hear his voice in my head, talking me through every step of the process."

Once he'd locked the door, he turned to find Candace standing as still as a statue, just staring at him.

"You okay?" he asked, forgetting his memories and suddenly worried about her instead.

"I'm fine. Better than fine."

"You know, when I'm with you, everything else just seems to fade away."

"Yeah, for me, too," she whispered in reply, tilting her head back so Logan had to kiss her, so that he couldn't think about anything else. "Everything else just seems to disappear."

"I can't make you any promises, Candace," he whispered, looking down at her. "I would never hurt you, and there is nothing more I want from you than just you, but I'm not…"

"Shhh," she murmured. "Just stop talking and let's forget. Everything."

Logan fell to his knees so he was directly in front of Candace, pulling her down then pushing her back gently until she yielded. He had one hand at her back to guide her down, cushioning her fall as she lay on the grass, rising so he was propped above her.

That was something he could do, something he *wanted* to do. He only hoped that she didn't expect more from him than he could give.

CHAPTER NINE

CANDACE STRETCHED AND pulled herself closer to Logan. She couldn't get enough of him—not his body, not his hands on her, not the feel of being cocooned against him. And now here they were, with hardly any clothes on, lying out under the hot Australian sun.

"We really need to cover up, otherwise we're going to fry like crisps," Logan said, but without making any attempt to move.

"But it feels so good," she murmured, shutting her eyes and basking in the warmth. "Just a bit longer."

"Candace, I don't want to ruin the moment, but I have this feeling that we're setting ourselves up for a fall."

She sighed, putting one hand flat to his chest and using it to prop herself up.

"Can't we just enjoy ourselves and pretend like everything's, I don't know, all going to work out."

Logan smiled up at her, and she leaned down to kiss him, loving the soft fullness of his mouth against hers.

"We can pretend so long as we both know that this is just a short-term thing."

"I know," she said, even though she was still trying to convince herself that she would see Logan again, that somehow they might be able to make something work. "I guess it's just nice to believe that things happen for a reason sometimes, that everything will work out for the best, in the end."

"This did happen for a reason," he told her, stroking a hand up and down her back. "You changed things that had been bothering you for a long time, and I finally showed someone what I've had hidden here. Opened up about what I've been going through."

A low bark made Candace jump. She looked over her shoulder and saw Ranger standing there, a stick dropped at his paws, and a curious look on his face.

"Is it weird that I feel funny about your dog staring at me when I'm practically naked?"

Logan sat up, reaching over for the stick and throwing it. "Yeah, that's definitely weird."

Candace play punched his arm but he just grabbed hold of her, a devilish look on his face.

"This is really bad timing, especially given the whole pretending we're in a bubble conversation we just had, but I had a message early this morning from my old commanding officer, and I have to fly out in a couple of days and head to base. After that, I'll receive my official discharge papers."

Candace shouldn't have expected more, had told herself time and again that this was just a temporary thing, something fun, with Logan. But knowing they only had a couple of days together still hurt.

"I guess I need to book my flight back to the U.S. then," she said, trying to keep her voice upbeat.

"Candace, if there was any way I could just hide out here for the next week, even the next month with you, I would," Logan told her, brushing her hair from her face. "If you want to stay here on your own for a little bit, I'll come straight back once I'm done with work. If you need a vacation where no one will find you, this place is perfect and you'll always be welcome here."

"I can't do that," she murmured, wishing as she said it that she'd just kept her mouth shut and nodded. "The longer I put off seeing my attorney back home and figuring out my management, the worse it'll all be. I've been too good at avoiding things for way too long and I need to head back and deal with it, no matter how good an extended vacation here sounds."

She leaned into Logan's touch, like a cat desperate to be petted.

"If we'd only met in another lifetime, or maybe in a few years…" Logan said.

Didn't she know it?

"You know, we're not so different, you and I," she said.

Logan laughed. "Yeah, except for the fact that I'm a soldier and you're famous."

She touched his cheek with her fingertips. "You might be a soldier, but you're also a ranch owner, and a kind, decent man. There's a lot about your family and your wealth that I think you've kept from me. And besides, I'm just a singer who got lucky. At heart I'm still just a country girl with a big voice, and in my mind that's who I'll always be."

Candace touched her forehead to his, eyes shut because she couldn't bear to look into his eyes.

"But we still come from different worlds. I love the Outback and I've waited my whole life to come back here, and you have a life in America," he told her in a quiet voice. "Even if we weren't so different, we still couldn't ever make this work. Believe me, I've thought it through. Too many times to count."

Hope ignited within her, a gentle tickle that turned into a full-on flip inside her stomach. *He'd actually thought about it?* Even if it was a lost cause, she still liked the fact that he cared enough to think about them being together. She knew it was impossible, that they lived on opposite sides of the world and couldn't possibly make anything long-term work between them, but it wasn't like she hadn't spent time wondering.

"So I guess we just enjoy the next two days and then part ways," she said, needing to say it out aloud to truly get her head around it.

Logan squeezed her hand. "For the record, I've been more content being with you than I've been, well, in forever."

Candace refused to become emotional, because they were both adults making an adult decision. She'd been with men who couldn't tell the truth, and she knew exactly what it was like to be lied to, so the fact that Logan was being honest and open with her wasn't something to mourn. He'd set the bar high for any other men she might meet in the future, and for that she needed to be thankful.

"Can I ask you one question before we stop talking about how little time we have together?"

Logan nodded. "Shoot."

Candace took a shallow breath and blew it straight back out again. "If we did live in the same country, if things were different, would you want to be with me? As in, in a relationship?"

She couldn't believe she'd even asked him that, but she had and she didn't regret it. She needed to know.

"Hell, yes," he whispered straight into her ear. "I can tell you, hand on my heart, that you're the only woman I've ever wanted to open up to. You're special, Candace, and don't let anyone ever make you think differently."

It was all she needed to hear. All the pain of past relationships, of men treating her like a free ticket to a life they wanted, it all just washed away. Because Logan was different, and she needed to make the most of every second in his company.

"Have I mentioned that my all-time favorite movie is *The Bodyguard?*"

Logan smiled as she looped her arms around his neck. "Any scenes you want to reenact?" he asked.

"Oh, there're plenty," she told him, pushing him down so she could straddle him. "In fact, we could role-play *those* scenes all day."

"I wasn't ever very good at drama at school, but I'm a pretty fast learner these days."

She laughed. "Then get ready to play my fantasy role."

And then all at once Logan had her arms pinned at her sides, mouth hot and wet against her skin. Maybe they could role-play later, because this wasn't something she had any intention of putting an end to.

Logan hadn't been so happy in years. Having Candace at home with him, on the property that was more special to him than any other place in the world, had been the best thing he'd ever done. It might only be temporary, but it had at least showed him that maybe he wasn't as screwed up as he'd thought. Damaged, sure, but maybe not beyond repair as he'd thought, *believed,* for so long.

"So what do you say to a walk down memory lane with me?" Logan asked as they rode back to the house, side by side.

Candace gave him a lazy look, like she was ready to fall asleep. Or maybe she was just feeling as relaxed and chilled out as he was.

"What do you have in mind?"

He chuckled to himself as he thought about what they could do, where he could take her. It had been a while since he'd just enjoyed the land he'd grown up on, reminded himself of why he liked the Outback so much. Wherever he'd been in the world, no matter how much pain he'd been in or how bad he'd struggled, this was the place he visualized.

"When we were kids, my sister and I used to ride bareback to a deep water hole, tether the horses and swim. Then we'd eat the lunch Mom had packed us and chill out in the shade for a while."

"Sounds like fun," she said, "although maybe we should stay out of the sun for the rest of the day and do it tomorrow."

"Deal," he agreed. He was more than ready to put his feet up and just chill for the rest of the afternoon and evening. "We can have a barbecue tonight and sit out on the veranda for a while. Listen to the wildlife."

Candace rode a little closer to him. "Speaking of wildlife, there aren't any crocodiles in that water hole, are there?"

He laughed. "We're in New South Wales, sweetheart. It's way too cold down here for crocs."

"Well good," she said. "The last thing I need to worry about is my leg being bitten off."

Logan chuckled and nudged his horse on when she tried to slow down and nibble some long grass. Candace had asked him before whether he'd want to be with her, whether they could have made things work if she lived in Australia or he in America, and he'd told her the truth. Maybe he wouldn't have been so open if there actually *had* been a chance of things working between them, but there wasn't, and he hadn't seen the point in not being honest with her.

Candace had been the breath of fresh air he'd been waiting for, and thinking of never seeing her again wasn't something he wanted to dwell on. All he cared about right now was making sure they made the most of the less than forty-eight hours they had together.

Because after that, she'd just be a memory that kept him going when things got tough.

The water was colder than she'd expected, but the feeling of swinging off an old tire that was attached to a tree overhanging the water hole was worth the initial shock factor.

"Ready to go again?"

Logan's enthusiasm was rubbing off on her, the smile on his face impossible to ignore.

"You're loving this whole feeling of being a kid again, aren't you?" she teased.

He responded by pulling her back farther than he had before, letting go so she flew out over the water. Candace screamed as she let go and landed with a plop, going completely under before emerging. She moved out of the way so Logan could do the same, launching like a missile into the deepest spot, his enthusiasm contagious.

"I can't believe how much fun this is," he said. "It's been years since I've even been down here."

She giggled. "My fans would be horrified that I'm such a kid at heart, but yeah, it's pretty cool."

Logan swam to her, blinking away the water that had caught on his lashes, his short hair looking even darker as it slicked back off his head.

"Would they be horrified about this?" he asked, clasping the back of her head and dragging her body hard to his.

Candace wrapped her legs around him, and her arms, making him tread water to keep them both afloat. "Oh, I think they'd definitely be horrified. Mortified, in fact."

"What about by this?" he asked, flicking the clasp on her bra so that the garment fell forward.

She slid her arms from the straps and watched the bra float away, wrapping her arms around Logan's chest so her bare breasts were against his skin.

"This swimming idea of yours was a pretty good one," she murmured as she kissed him again, nipping his bottom lip when he tried to slide the rest of her underwear off.

She refused to think about leaving, about the short time she had left with Logan, because she hadn't been this happy in years, and there was nothing she could do to stop the clock. All she could do was enjoy being in the arms of a man who was so different to any man she'd ever met before. These memories would last her a lifetime, of that she was certain.

"What say we paddle to shallower water, soldier?" she asked.

Logan tucked her under his arm like he was a lifesaver and headed for shore. "Done."

CHAPTER TEN

"THIS IS A pretty extravagant barbecue," Candace said, smiling up at Logan as he finished ferrying food over to the table.

"I only have one chance to impress you with my grilling, so I wasn't going to take any chances," he told her with a wink.

She laughed as she looked at her plate. "I probably should have made us a salad. You know, so that there was *something* green on our plates."

"What, you don't like my carnivore special?"

Candace looked at the array of meat on her plate and couldn't wipe the grin from her face. He'd done his best to impress her, but she was guessing that aside from grilling meat, he really didn't have any other culinary skills. She slipped Ranger a piece of steak under the table, no longer scared of the big dog's constant presence.

"It's really beautiful here, Logan. I never knew what an amazing country Australia was."

He leaned back in his chair, looking up at the sky. It was almost dark, but Candace could still see his face perfectly. They'd lit candles and placed them on the table, but it wasn't quite dark enough for them to need the extra light.

"It's paradise," he admitted. "Even when I stay here for weeks without leaving, I never stop appreciating how beautiful it is."

Candace wished she could have stayed longer, that she'd just taken Logan up on his offer to stay here while he was away, but she also knew that doing that would be putting off the inevitable.

She looked up at the sky, at the inky blackness peppered with white, and then turned her focus back to Logan.

"What do you say we finish dinner then turn in for an early night?" she asked.

"I think," he said, reaching for her hand across the table, "that you might just be a mind reader."

Candace was finding it hard to fall asleep. She'd snuggled up to Logan after they'd made love, and he'd promptly fallen into a deep slumber, but she couldn't stop thinking about leaving. About the fact that their holiday romance was almost over. Or that at any moment he could have one of his nightmares and end up thrashing around beside her.

She knew that he'd snuck out of bed the night before, because she'd woken to find him gone. He'd slept in another room, and then come back to their shared bed early in the morning. But tonight he'd fallen asleep without probably even meaning to.

Candace tried to shut off the overthinking part of

her brain and closed her eyes, listening to Logan's steady heartbeat beneath her, enjoying the warmth of his body. But just as soon as she'd relaxed, as if on cue, his heart started to race so loud that she could hear it. Before she had time to move, he was yelling out, his arm thrashing, smashing into her face as she tried to roll out of his way.

"No!"

"Logan, wake up!" she screamed, landing on the floor and yanking a blanket with her to cover her naked body.

Ranger was at her side, confused, and she held on to him as Logan leaped up, looking like a wild man in the moonlight spilling in through the windows.

"Candace? Where, what..."

Then he saw her and his shoulders dropped. He looked horrified at what he'd done.

"Sweetheart, I'm sorry," he murmured, walking around the bed and reaching a hand out to her. "I'm so, so sorry."

"Logan, you can say sorry all you like, but you need to do something about this," she murmured, knowing she couldn't just pretend like he was okay, act like everything would be fine just because he'd managed to talk to her about his nightmares. "You need help."

"It won't happen again, I can sleep in a different room, I..." He ran a hand through his hair before walking a step backward and sitting on the bed.

Candace stood up, her body shaking as she lifted a hand to her face, touching gently across her cheek.

"Logan, you hit me," she whispered, her voice cracking with emotion.

He stared at her, raised his hand then let it fall to the bed beside him. "Candace, I..." Logan took a deep breath. "Did I hurt you?"

"Logan, you need to talk to someone. If not me, then a professional, but you can't torture yourself in your dreams like that every night. It has nothing to do with you almost hurting me, and everything to do with you hurting yourself by not getting help. This isn't just going to go away."

"I don't have a problem and I don't want to talk about it. I can deal with this on my own," he growled out. "And for the record, what happened just now has everything to do with me almost hurting you. I don't care about me, but I *sure as hell do* care about what I could have done to you."

Candace closed her eyes for a beat. "Yeah, I think you do have a problem, Logan. One that could be fixed if you weren't so scared about facing your past."

He stood up, hands clenched at his sides. "This was a mistake. We don't even know each other and now you're trying to tell me...you know what, I think we're done here, Candace. I am who I am, and I can't change that."

Candace was done with being patient, because Logan was being a bullheaded macho male now, and she wasn't going to let him get away with it. She didn't care if she'd had a fantastic time with him—they also had to deal with reality. Maybe she'd been right to doubt her ability to make a judgment call when it came to men.

"I think you're right," she said, jutting her chin up and wishing she was taller. "Whatever this was, it's over."

Logan stood and stared at her, like he was going to reach for her, going to say something that would turn the entire situation around. She waited, never even blinking as she watched him for fear of crying, but in the end, he turned and walked out of the room.

"I think we should leave tomorrow," she said, willing her voice not to crack.

"Yeah, first thing in the morning."

She watched Logan go and didn't falter until he shut the door behind him. Then she collapsed onto the bed, face buried in the pillow and sobbed like she'd never cried before in her lifetime.

After so long protecting her heart, not letting anyone get too close to her, Logan had snuck past her defenses and managed to hurt her when she'd least expected it. When she'd thought there was nothing he could do to wound her. She should never have let herself be put in this situation, should have protected her heart instead of being vulnerable to Logan. Letting him get closer to her had been a stupid thing to do, and she should have known better.

Either way, there was nothing she could do to stop the pain shooting through her body like a drug being pumped through her veins. Whatever she'd had with Logan, it was over, and no matter what she tried to tell herself, dealing with never seeing him again was...

She swallowed the emotion that choked in her throat,

refusing to let it sink its claws in to take hold. But the pain was too much, the ache in her heart…

Unbearable.

Logan slammed his palm down onto the kitchen counter and hung his head. He was a total idiot. A bloody fool. And because he was incapable of dealing with his problems, he'd just walked away from the one woman he could have just been himself around. Who didn't care who he was, what his family name was, or what he'd been through. The one person who had simply been trying to help him.

Candace had given him a chance to open up and be himself, to acknowledge the nightmares that woke him almost every night, that haunted him, and instead he'd walked out on her and as good as told her it was over. All because she'd been brave enough to confront him, to try to get him to admit that he needed help.

Logan slumped forward, exhausted and unsure what he was supposed to do next. He should have turned around and walked straight back into his bedroom, begged for her forgiveness and just admitted he needed professional help, but his pride or some other stupid emotion was stopping him. He'd never acknowledged what he went through every night to anyone other than Candace, and talking to anyone else, dealing with it properly, wasn't something he was ready for.

He'd told Candace so much, had admitted so much to her that he'd hardly ever spoken to anyone else about, and yet when it came to admitting his shortfalls, acknowledging his true weakness…

Logan sat back, took a deep breath and straightened his body. The best thing for both of them was for this to end now, to stop things before they went any further when they both knew there was no future for them as a couple anyway. The whole idea of bringing her here with him had been stupid. Ridiculous even.

If that was true, though, then why did ending things with Candace seem like the stupidest thing he'd ever done in his life?

CHAPTER ELEVEN

"SO I GUESS this is it, then?"

They'd both been silent on the journey back to Sydney, and now they were standing outside the plane, Candace's luggage sitting on the tarmac. Logan had Ranger on his leash, at his side, and he'd asked someone to come and get all of Candace's things. Which gave them about another five minutes together.

"I'm sorry things had to end this way," Candace said, not taking her sunglasses off.

Logan didn't hesitate—he stepped forward, took her handbag and put it down, before wrapping her in a tight hug. He shut his eyes as she tucked into him, snuggled to his chest, her arms holding him just as tight around his waist. She probably hated him for what had happened, but he wasn't going to let her get on that plane without at least trying to show her what she'd come to mean to him.

"I'll never forget you, Logan. No matter what," she whispered, just loud enough for him to hear.

Logan kissed the top of her head, before putting his hands on her arms to hold her back. Her eyes were swimming with tears when he pushed her sunglasses to the top of her head, and if he wasn't fighting it so hard, his would be, too. All the times he managed to stamp out his emotions on tour, and here he was about to cry. Because this was about more than saying goodbye; this was about him being forced to deal with his past, with his terrors.

"One day, when you're old and gray, surrounded by ten grandchildren, you can smile and think about the naughty Australian vacation you had when you were a young woman," he told her, staring into her blue eyes. "Just promise me that you'll always remember me with a smile, because that's how I'll remember you, even if things didn't work out as, well, you know."

Candace shook her head, like she was trying to shake away her emotion.

Logan bent down to kiss her cheek, tasting the saltiness of her tears as she let him touch her skin.

"Goodbye," she said when she broke away.

Her bags were being loaded onto a cart behind them, and he knew it was time for her to go. They should never have even crossed paths in the first place, which meant they'd always been on borrowed time, and after the way things had gone last night, he was lucky she was even talking to him right now.

Logan watched as she gave Ranger a hug before straightening.

"You, my boy, are very special, you know that? I think I might just like dogs now that I've met you."

"Goodbye," Logan said as she walked away.

Logan waved then thrust his hands into his jeans'

pockets, eyes never leaving her as she turned and walked away. Candace was gone, and it was time for him to get on a plane himself and close the final chapter of his life as a SAS soldier. And maybe, just maybe, he'd think about what she'd said to him.

It was goodbye to the job he'd loved, and the woman he could so easily have fallen in love with, all in one day. Time to move on. Pity it wasn't as easy as it sounded. All he could do now was take his life one day at a time, and figure out what his future held. Because right now he was more confused than he'd ever been, and he also knew he'd been a jerk for not sucking up his pride and admitting his shortfalls to her. Because Candace had been there for him like no other woman probably ever would be.

Candace boarded the plane and smiled at the flight attendant who took her bag and put it in the overhead cabin. She took her seat, pleased she'd purchased both the first class seats that were side by side. The last thing she wanted was someone trying to make small talk with her, and she sure didn't want anyone to see her crying.

But there was something different about Logan, and she knew it. There was nothing she could think about him that would change her mind, and there was nothing she could do to pull herself from the mood she was in. After what had happened during the night, and then actually walking away from him…it was all too much. He'd behaved badly and she didn't regret what she'd said, but it still hurt.

"Would you like a drink before takeoff?"

Candace refused to take her grumpiness out on anyone else, so she forced a smile and nodded. She may as well drink something that would take the edge off her pain, or at the very least knock her out for part of the long trip home.

"Champagne," she said after a moment's hesitation. "Please."

Maybe she needed to celebrate the few days she'd just had, minus their argument. She needed to toast it and then forget it, because in the end Logan wasn't a man she could never have been with. Not when he refused to do something about a problem that was so serious, and not when they lived on opposite sides of the world.

"Here we go, ma'am. A glass of champagne for you."

Candace took the glass, shut her eyes and took a sip. It was heavenly. She had fourteen hours before she touched down at LAX, and a few more glasses were probably exactly what the doctor would order. She could pass out and sleep until the plane landed.

No more tears, no more feeling sorry for herself. She was a woman in charge of her own life now, she'd met a man who'd changed the way she thought about *everything,* and she was going home to start over. When she thought about Logan, she needed to learn how to smile instead of frown, and make the memories of her time with him last forever. She needed to simply remember the *good* times she'd had with him and forget the rest.

Today was the first day of the rest of her life. And if there was one thing Logan had taught her, it was that she had to trust her own instincts and learn to put herself first.

CHAPTER TWELVE

LOGAN STOOD OUTSIDE the plane and stretched. He was exhausted. Not the kind of bone-tired exhaustion that he'd experienced on tour, but he was still ready to collapse into bed and not stir until late the next morning. The smart thing to do would have been to stay in the city for the night, but he'd already let his apartment and his only option would have been to crash at Jamie and Brett's. He doubted any respectable hotel would have let him arrive with Ranger, even if he explained how highly trained he was, and he didn't want Jamie's pity. The way she'd look at him would only remind him of what he'd lost since last time he'd seen her.

"I'm getting old," he muttered to his dog, bending to give him a scratch on the head. "We were definitely ready to retire."

Ranger looked up at him, waiting for a signal that it was okay to run off, and Logan waved him on. He threw his pack over his back and headed for the house. *So much for planning to be gone only a few days, a week at the most.* He'd ended up being talked into spending time with some of the newer recruits in the K9 division, which he was pretty sure was his superior's way of trying to push him into a teaching position. It wasn't that he hadn't enjoyed it—he had, and Ranger had, too—but after so long thinking about coming back home, he was more than ready to make it happen. Not to mention the fact that he wasn't ready to make any long-term commitments just yet.

Logan stopped when he noticed a light on in the house. *Weird.* He hadn't phoned ahead and told the manager he'd be back a day early, which meant they wouldn't have bothered to go and turn lights on, and… *crap.* There was smoke coming from the chimney. Either his manager had decided to take some serious liberties and move into the main house, or there was a squatter or someone in there. His sister was away at a conference, and she was the only other person who had a key, and the right, to enter their house.

He broke into a jog, whistling out to Ranger to come back. His dog was trained to sniff out bombs, but he was also a lethal weapon when it came to providing protection when he had to be. Logan knew he was better with the dog at his side than a weapon, especially if there was an intruder.

He moved quietly up the steps, breathing slowly and filling his lungs as he trod, before trying the door handle. It was unlocked. Logan pushed it open, glanced at his dog and tapped his thigh so he stayed right at his side, and closed it behind them. He listened and heard only the low hum of the television, so he walked silently down the hall, pausing to listen before turning into the kitchen. There was a cup on the counter that he hadn't left there, and a couple of shopping bags sitting on the floor.

Someone had definitely been making themselves at home in his absence, and he wanted to know right now what on earth was going on.

Logan could see the television from where he was standing, saw the closing credits of a movie, but he couldn't hear anything else. He stepped carefully, not wanting to make any of the wooden floorboards creak, hardly breathing as he saw a foot sticking out. That someone was lying on his sofa.

"What the hell…" Logan's voice died in his throat as he leaped around the corner of the sofa.

No. He must be dreaming. Seeing things.

He bent to silence Ranger, still staring at the woman lying, asleep, her lips slightly parted, long blond hair messy and covering the cushions beneath her head and shoulders.

Candace. The woman he'd done nothing but think about these past two weeks was actually in his home, lying on his sofa. Logan had been so close to trying to track her down, but he hadn't even asked for her phone number before they'd parted ways, which he'd been telling himself had been smart, not having any of her contact details.

But now she was here? He couldn't believe it. *He didn't believe it.*

Logan bent to retrieve the television remote, hitting the off button, and disappearing to find a blanket. In his room the bed was slightly crinkled, and when he went to yank the comforter off, a hissing noise startled him. Then Ranger's low growl put him on high alert.

"Leave it," he ordered, wondering what kind of animal had gotten into his room.

A head popped out from between the pillows, followed by a yawn and a stretch. Candace was in his house, and she'd brought her cats with her? Logan pulled the comforter off despite the kitty's protests and put a hand on Ranger's head to settle him. The poor dog looked like his eyes were going to pop out of his head and he didn't blame him. Heck, *his eyes* had just about popped out of his head when he'd seen Candace.

"Easy, boy. It's just a cat. You're still the boss."

Logan returned to the living room, put a few more logs on the fire and stood above Candace, still wondering if he was imagining the whole thing. He was insanely tired, so it wouldn't be impossible for him to be dreaming, but...He reached down to stroke her hair from her face, smiling when she stirred slightly. There was no imagining that. Candace was on his sofa, asleep, and he wasn't going to waste any more time in joining her.

He sat on the edge of the sofa, gently scooped her and moved her across a little, then lay beside her, covering them both with the comforter and wrapping one arm around Candace. The feel of her body, the smell of her perfume, the softness of her hair against his face—they were things he'd tried to commit to memory and been so worried he'd forget.

Logan wanted to lie awake, or even better wake Candace up so he could find out what on earth she was doing back in Australia, but the desire to sleep was too strong to ignore. He relaxed his body into hers and shut his eyes, letting slumber find him. Tomorrow he could ask her all about it. Tonight, he was just going to enjoy having her beside him and falling into the sleep he'd been craving for hours. And after all the therapy he'd gone through, the therapy he'd finally admitted to needing, he was at least confident that he wouldn't hurt her.

Candace had the strangest feeling that she couldn't breathe. In her dream, there was something stuck on her chest, pressing her down, but when she opened her eyes the panicked feeling almost immediately washed away. *Logan.* Light was filtering into the room, so she knew it was early, which meant he must have arrived in the night and found her asleep.

She wriggled to move his arm down, the weight of it across her chest too heavy, and then turned on her side to stare at him. She had no idea what he was going to say or how he was going to react, and the idea of telling him what she'd done absolutely terrified her, but she was going to do it. *Fear was no longer going to stop her from doing what her heart told her was right.*

Candace touched one hand to Logan's cheek, trailing her fingers across his skin. He hadn't shaved for at least a day, so the stubble was rough against her fingertips. It took every inch of her willpower not to trace the outline of his lips, parted and full in slumber. But what was even more amazing was that they'd both slept—he hadn't woken like he had every other time she'd spent the night with him.

"Now that you've woken me, you'd better kiss me," Logan mumbled, eyes still shut.

She smiled, not surprised he'd tricked her and been awake, but she also did as she was told. Candace wriggled closer to him, their bodies intertwined, slowly touching her lips to his in a kiss so sweet it made her sigh. Logan's mouth moved slowly, lazily, against hers, like he was still half asleep, and it suited her fine to start things out slow, to just enjoy being this close to the man she'd thought of constantly since the day she'd left him.

"Now that's what I call a nice way to wake up," he mumbled.

Candace kissed him again, not so gently this time, one hand snaking around his neck and running through his hair as she pulled herself closer to him.

"Mmm, this morning just keeps getting better and better."

She pulled away only to look at him, to see if he'd opened his eyes, and he had.

"Hey," she said, staring into his hazel brown gaze.

"Hey," he said straight back, stretching his legs out and then slinging one over hers.

"Were you surprised to find me here?"

Logan chuckled. "Surprised would be putting it mildly."

She had no idea what he was thinking, but he hadn't exactly been opposed to her kisses, and he *had* cuddled up to her on the sofa while she was sleeping, which told her that he obviously wasn't unhappy to find her.

"I guess I should have called ahead first, huh?"

He raised an eyebrow. "It would have stopped me

from almost having a heart attack and thinking squatters were in my house."

"Sorry," she said, starting to wonder whether she had been crazy to just move in while he was away, without asking him.

"Then again, being exhausted and actually sleeping through an entire night with you by my side was worth the near-death experience."

Candace sat up, wanting to tread lightly with what she was about to say. "Logan, I can't believe you slept the whole night without…"

"Freaking out and having my terrors," he finished for her. "Yeah, it looks like I did."

She lay back down again, this time covering his chest, her cheek flat to his body.

"I can't believe it."

"Well, believe it," he said, rubbing her back. "You've changed me, Candace, in more ways than I'd like to admit. Because I finally got the help I needed."

She listened to him take a deep breath, his expression serious. "The way I reacted the other night when you confronted me," he started.

"Was a knee-jerk reaction to being pushed too hard," she interrupted, the kindness in his eyes making her want to just hold him and never let go. "I should have known that it wasn't something you could be pushed into dealing with."

"But pushing was exactly what I needed," he told her, stroking her cheek. "I was being pigheaded, and I owe you an apology."

"Can I tell you something?" she asked.

"Of course."

"I want to explain why I was so scared of you the other night," she started.

Logan frowned. "Because I understandably scared the crap out of you?"

She gave him a half smile, nestling in closer to him. "No, because the last man I was with, the one I thought was different than the rest because he wasn't interested in my fame or my money, he…"

Logan touched her hair, left his hand there and waited for her to continue.

"He was my husband, Logan, and he hit me, and when I went to leave, to call for help, he grabbed me so tight around the throat that I thought he was going to strangle me."

It was as if all the blood had drained from Logan's face when she glanced up at him.

"So when I struck out at you…"

Candace grabbed his hand and touched his fingers to her cheek. "You didn't even make a bruise here, Logan, but yeah, when I woke up to you going crazy it really scared me. Kind of brought a heap of memories back that I've been trying to forget. It was just all too much, one nightmare too many."

"No wonder we get on so well," he said, refusing to react to what she'd told him, to get angry when there was nothing he could do about what had happened to her. "We're both kind of screwed up about the past, huh?"

"I guess you could say that," she muttered, closing her eyes as he leaned down to kiss her. "I've met a lot of men that seemed so right at the start, but with every relationship that's failed, it's just made it so hard for me to trust in anyone. Because it's not just men who've used me, or tried to, it's been so-called friends, too."

"So you being here?" he asked.

Candace shut her eyes, knowing she needed to tell him what her being here actually meant. That she hadn't just flown in for a few days, that this was a whole lot more permanent than that. *If he'd have her.* That all she'd done since she'd left was think of all the reasons why she shouldn't have lost her temper with Logan, why she needed to take a leaf out of her own book and open up to him, to talk to someone about her past and why it haunted her so badly.

"Logan, I kind of took a risk just turning up like this, but something you said to me, something we talked about, just kept running through my mind after I'd left."

He was watching her intently, waiting for her to continue.

"I'm not just here for another vacation," she admitted.

"I kind of guessed that when I found one of your cats on my bed," Logan told her, his grin telling her that he knew exactly what was going on.

"When you said that if we lived in the same country, if we'd met at a different time or place, that things could have worked out between us..." She paused. "Did you mean it?"

He sighed and stroked her hair. "Of course I meant it."

"So, does the fact that I kind of just moved to Australia mean..." Candace stopped talking, knowing he knew exactly what she was trying to say to him.

Logan sat up, back against the armrest of the sofa. "You mean to say that while I was away working, you flew halfway across the world with your cats in tow to move into my house and surprise me?" He paused. "And forgive me?"

Candace's face flushed, the heat rising up her neck and into her cheeks. "When you put it like that you make me sound like a crazy person."

"You," he said, pulling her against him so she was firm to his chest, "are not a crazy person."

"So you do want me here?" she mumbled.

"Yes, I want you here," Logan said, squeezing her and dropping a kiss into her hair. "You and your crazy cats will always have a home here, Candace. Always."

From the moment she'd walked through the door with all her things, Candace had started to worry. What had seemed like such a great idea back in L.A. had seemed stupid and childish once she'd arrived, but having Logan by her side, seeing the look on his face when he'd woken with her in his arms, had made everything okay. It was the first time she'd ever taken a risk, except for the time her mom had forced a record label executive to listen to her songs, and both times they'd changed her life for the better.

"So now that you're here, are you going to be my barefoot housewife, cooking me three meals a day and tending to my every need?" Logan joked.

Candace laughed. "You wish, soldier. You wish."

Ranger came over and poked his head between them,

looking for some affection, and Candace stopped touching Logan and ran her hand across the dog's fur instead. She couldn't believe that after a lifetime of being scared of large dogs, she'd warmed to Logan's big canine so quickly.

"Poor boy was traumatized by your cats last night," Logan told her.

"Sorry, Ranger," she cooed. "Those mean old cats might try to take over, but you stand firm, okay?"

They sat in silence for a long while, Candace stroking Ranger's head and Logan running his fingers gently through her curls.

"I don't want to ruin the moment, but have you really thought about what it'll be like living here, when you're so used to such a, well, a glamorous lifestyle?" Logan asked. "And just because I've started to get help doesn't mean we aren't going to hit a few road bumps along the way." He paused. "I did dream last night, Candace, but it wasn't as bad and I was able to deal with it. To pull myself out of it somehow and use you to push the memories away and fall back asleep."

Candace's heart started to beat faster.

"So have you really thought this through?" he asked again.

Yes, it was *all* she'd thought about when she was trying to figure out whether moving was a good idea or not, but at the end of the day, she knew that having a partner in life was way more important than anything else. Her success as a recording artist wasn't going to keep her warm in bed at night, or give her someone to confide in and travel with, to start a family with. And the fact that Logan had actually done something about his terrors? That just made her decision seem all the more *right*.

"Logan, I've been performing for eight years now, and even though I love it, I don't think it's enough anymore."

"And you're sure this is what you want, though?" he asked. "Don't get me wrong, I want you here, but I don't want you to look back in a few months, or even a few years, and wish you'd thought it through more."

"I want you," she said, taking her hand off Ranger and pressing it to his cheek, looking up into his eyes. "It might mean a change of pace, but I'm okay with that. I'm *ready* for that. Because I honestly believe that this is where I'm supposed to be."

Logan's eyes crinkled ever so slightly at the corners, his smile making her entire body tingle.

"Why do I feel like you have this all planned out?" he asked.

She laughed. "Well, it just so happens that I've had a lot of time to think this through."

Logan groaned but she kissed him to stop it. He ran his fingers down her back and hoisted her up on top of him, letting her sit on top but taking charge of her mouth.

"Don't you want me to tell you all my great ideas?" she asked, pulling back.

Logan leaned up, cupping the back of her head and forcing her back down, kissing her again.

"No," he mumbled when she fought against him again, laughing. "Just let me enjoy being with you for a while before you map my whole life out for me. Unless, of course, you've written a song about me?"

"Yeah. I called it 'Bodyguard'," she joked.

"Oh, really?"

"Logan!" she protested when he tried to flip her beneath him.

He stopped, rolling to his side and dragging her with him. "Fine, go on then. I can see we're not going to have any fun until you tell me all your plans."

Candace laughed, but he was right—she did have everything all planned out, because planning had been the only way she'd been able to convince herself to take a risk, follow her instincts, and move halfway across the world.

"I figured we could keep a place in town, so we're only a short flight away from the city when we want to head in, but we'd obviously spend most of our downtime here."

"When you say downtime?" he asked.

"I have a tour next year that I can't cancel, so I was thinking that you could be my bodyguard," she said. "You *and* Ranger."

"Oh, you were, were you?" Logan muttered.

"It'll be busy at times, and I'll have to go back to L.A. to record another album at some stage, because I've already signed for one more, but after that we can decide on what works for us both, together. What do you think?"

Logan was trying hard not to laugh. As Candace talked excitedly, she reminded him of a little bright-colored parrot chirping a million miles an hour. It was impossible not to smile just watching her talk so animatedly, but his gaze was constantly drawn to her mouth, those pillowy lips of hers his weakness.

"Logan?"

He switched his gaze back to her eyes. "What was the question?" Logan had no idea what she'd even been talking about at the end there, but whatever she'd said he was inclined to just agree.

"I said does all that sound okay with you? I don't want to sound like I'm trying to organize your life, but it's going to take a bit of juggling at the start."

Logan smiled at the worried expression on her face, trying to reassure her. "Sweetheart, so long as I have you by my side and I get to spend a decent chunk of the year here at home, I'm happy. Everything else we can figure out as we go."

He'd never been more pleased to have his life organized for him, especially now that he was confident he could deal with his past, that he'd received the help he needed. And help was only a phone call away now, so he didn't have to burden Candace with everything when he needed to talk through his night terrors some more.

"You're sure?" she asked, bottom lip caught between her teeth.

"I spent the past couple of weeks in a foul mood even though I promised you I'd think about you and smile," he told her honestly. "I couldn't believe that I'd finally met someone I could actually be with, who I wanted to be with, and I only got such a short time with her. Or that I'd acted like such a jerk when I should have been taking care of her."

Candace seemed to melt into him, her entire body relaxing at hearing his words.

"Really?"

"Really." Logan pushed her up a little and hooked a finger under her chin, tilting her face up so he could look into her eyes. "You're the best thing that has ever happened to me, Candace, and I will do whatever it takes to make this work."

"Me, too," she sighed.

Logan was about to kiss her, but he hovered for a moment. "You do realize that Ranger has to come everywhere with us, though, right? I promised him a retirement by my side, and after what he did for me on the tours we went on, I can't go back on my word."

"Okay, so you *and* your goofy dog."

Logan broke their kiss as soon as he'd started it. "Who you calling goofy? Ranger has..."

"I know how awesome your dog is," Candace said with a laugh. "So just shut up and kiss me, would you?"

Logan didn't need to be asked twice. He kissed Candace slowly, groaning when she raked her fingernails through his hair, forcing himself to take things slowly. Because there was no rush now—they had all day together, and the day after that. *The month after that.*

He might have lost a lot, seen things that he'd never forget and that would haunt him for the rest of his life, but now he had Candace. And for all the darkness of his past, he now had her like a shiny bright light beaming into his future. There was no way he was ever going to let her walk away again, not if he could help it.

"I love you," he whispered as she pulled back, looking up at him.

Candace had tears swimming in her eyes, but her smile told him they were happy tears.

"I love, too, Logan," she whispered back.

Logan shook his head as he pulled her in for another kiss. How he'd managed to end up with Candace Evans in his life, in his heart, he'd never know. But he sure wasn't complaining.

EPILOGUE

"HAVE I THANKED you for being my bridesmaid?"

Jamie laughed, and Candace watched as she filled two spiraled glasses high with champagne.

"If you tell me one more time..."

"Sorry," Candace apologized, taking her glass and taking a nervous sip. "I just still can't believe that it's just the four of us here, that I'm about to get married."

"Stop," Jamie ordered, her hand closing over Candace's forearm. Her grip was light, but her intention was clear. "I don't want to see that panicked look in your eyes again, because I have no desire to chase you down the street if you go all runaway bride on me."

Candace took a deep breath, staring at her slightly shaking hand. "I just find it hard to believe that after so long, after everything, I'm standing here."

"Well, believe it," Jamie said, holding her glass high so they could touch them together. "I never believed that I would ever be with anyone ever again after my first husband died, but sometimes we just have to accept that things happen for a reason. Those men out there waiting for us?"

Candace nudged aside the blinds, searching for Logan. She saw his big silhouette almost immediately, sitting on the beach in just a pair of shorts. His skin was golden, his dark hair damp, off his face like he'd just run his fingers through it. She hoped he wasn't having any last minutes nerves, wasn't trying to devise a plan with Brett to make a run for it.

She pushed those thoughts away. It had been a year since she'd moved to Australia, and not once had Logan given her the impression that he was unhappy. It had been the best twelve months of her life.

"We're pretty lucky, huh?"

Candace blinked away the tears that had filled her eyes, wishing she didn't keep getting so emotional. Everything seemed to set her off these days—just the thought of standing in front of Logan and saying "I do" was enough to make her want to burst out crying.

"I was so lost when I met Logan, and he just took me under his wing like I was a broken bird in need of tender loving care. He healed me, Jamie," Candace said, tears now falling slowly down her cheeks. "I never thought anyone ever could, but he did it like it was the easiest thing in the world."

Jamie plucked a tissue and crossed the room to gently wipe her cheeks. "You know you saved Logan, too, don't you?"

Candace took the tissue and dabbed closer to her eyes and then her nose. "Logan was fine just the way he was. I was the fragile one."

She knew more than anyone else ever would that Logan had been suffering, that he'd been in so much pain from his past, but she also knew how strong he was. There wasn't a doubt in her mind that he'd have found a way to pull through and find happiness.

"No." Jamie shook her head, taking her own look out the window. "Logan has always been so good at hiding how he feels, making us all think he's okay, but the truth is that he's been hurting and alone for a long time. He didn't cope well when Brett and I told him we were together, and I'm not sure he's ever gotten over Sam's death, or what happened to his parents. Add his last tour to the Middle East into the mix?" Jamie sighed, before turning back around and reaching for her champagne flute. "We were worried about him. Until he met you."

Candace blinked away the last of her tears and sipped her drink to take her mind off everything. Deep down she knew that Jamie was right, but she was just so grateful for what Logan had done for her that it was hard to believe she could have done the same for him.

"I think we need to get dressed," she announced, putting her glass down and walking over to the wardrobe.

She opened the door and couldn't help the smile that spread across her face when she saw her dress. It was white, covered in the tiniest white jewels that caught the light like diamonds. Candace had already placed the same jewels in her hair, just a handful of them so they looked like raindrops against her blond curls, which were loose and tumbling around her shoulders.

"I still can't believe that you didn't even bring a makeup artist here," Jamie said with a laugh. "You're used to a whole entourage, and instead you've just got me."

"Well, believe it," Candace said, untying her robe and letting it fall to the floor so she was just standing in her underwear, before stepping into her dress. "The best thing we ever did was decide to come here, just the four of us. Although I'm sure we'll find out that there was a rogue long lens taking snaps of us when we get back."

"I don't care who takes a photo of me, I'm just in shock still that we're here," Jamie replied, zipping up the dress without having to be asked. "I still can't believe we have a butler just for our villa."

"It's Hayman Island, baby," Candace said with a drawl, imitating Logan when they'd first arrived. "Get used to living in the lap of luxury."

"And I will never stop thanking you for as long as I live. Seriously, I know you're used to the rich and famous lifestyle, but for us regular people, this is beyond incredible. It's the vacation of a lifetime for me."

Candace wriggled, getting her dress right, before spinning to look in the full-length mirror.

"Don't mention it. You deserved an amazing vacation, and for the record, I will never get used to coming to places like this. I still have to pinch myself." She sighed. "Besides, what fun would Logan and I have without you two? I foresee plenty of trips in the near future."

"Yes to that!"

Jamie took off her robe and slipped her dress on, and

Candace turned her back slightly to give her privacy until she felt her friend's hand on her arm.

"I think I also owe you thanks for letting me wear something beautiful. Last time I was bridesmaid I think the bride intentionally wanted to make us look terrible in case we stole the show!"

"Well, you do look beautiful," Candace told her, touching up her lip gloss before picking up the single, long-stemmed white tulip that had been resting on the bed.

They linked arms, took one final sip of champagne each, and stared at one another.

"Do you think they'll even be off the beach yet?"

Jamie laughed. "Sweetheart, those boys have spent all their adult lives in the military. There's not even a chance they'll be late to this."

Candace knew it was silly, and they only had to walk out the door and down the beach a little, but part of her was worried that Logan wasn't going to be there, that she'd just dreamed the past few months and reality was going to come crashing down.

"There he is."

Jamie's whispered words made Candace stop walking, clutching her friend's hand tight. She was right; he was there. Standing on the beach, barefoot, linen pants rolled up, wearing a half-buttoned loose white shirt and a smile that made her want to run into his arms.

"Oh, my gosh," she muttered, but the words just came out as one garbled sentence.

"Take a deep breath and just start walking."

Candace did as she was told, eyes locked on Logan's as they walked, even from this distance. She was aware that Brett was standing close to him, that there was a celebrant there, too, but all she could really see was the man she was about to marry. Tears welled in her eyes again, but she forced them back, wanting to bask in the happiness of being on an almost secluded beach, with the three people who'd grown to mean so much to her in only a year.

"I hope he knows how much I love him," she whispered to Jamie, still fighting the urge to run to him in case it *was* all a dream that she was about to wake up from.

"He does," she whispered back, "but tell him again anyway."

Logan took his eyes off Candace for a split second to glance at Brett.

"Do you think she's going to regret this? I mean, look at her."

"Sorry, mate. I only have eyes for the woman walking beside her," Brett said with a laugh. "But yeah, she probably will. I mean, you're just some commoner, right?"

Logan knew he should have waited, that he was supposed to stand with Brett until the girls reached them, but seeing Candace walk toward him was too much. He wanted her by his side, in his arms, and he wanted her now.

Thank God he was her bodyguard and had an excuse to be at her side all the time, because even seeing her walk alone made his protective instincts go into overdrive. He was so used to taking care of her when she was working that he couldn't stand to see her walking on her own.

"Where are you going?" Brett muttered as he left him.

Logan didn't bother answering, he just stared at Candace as he closed the distance between them, only stopping when he had his arms around her and his lips pressed to hers. Today was about telling the world she was his, that he was ready to be with her forever, and he was more than ready to stake his claim.

"Logan!" she exclaimed when he broke their kiss.

"What? I was impatient waiting down there."

He gave her a wink and took her hand, laughing at the eye roll Jamie gave him. Not that she could get away with teasing him after the way she behaved with Brett.

"You look absolutely beautiful, Candace," he told her, raising their hands to drop a kiss to hers. "And you, too, Jamie."

Jamie made a noise in her throat and joined Brett, and Logan kept hold of Candace's hand until they joined them. When they did, he took her other hand in his, so they were facing one another.

"Have I told you how much I love you?" Candace whispered, standing on tiptoe as she spoke into his ear.

"You can tell me those words as often as you like, because I will never tire of hearing them."

"Well, I do, and I'm so glad we decided to come here."

A noise made them both look up, and Logan gave the celebrant an apologetic smile.

"Can we just skip to the part where we say I do and I get to kiss the bride?" Logan joked. "No need to waste your time doing the entire ceremony."

Everyone laughed along with him, and he dipped his head for a sneaky kiss before their informal ceremony started. For a man who thought he'd never find happiness, would always be alone, life hadn't turned out half-bad. *In the end.*

"That," Logan said, kissing her mouth, "was," another kiss, "perfect."

Candace laughed, stretching out on the sun lounger before Logan held down her arms and lay down on top of her.

"Are you referring to our wedding or the amazing food?"

"Neither. I was talking about you and me being naked in the shower."

"Logan!"

"Honey, there's a reason we checked into a private villa. No one's going to tell me off for talking dirty with my wife, especially not at the per night price we're paying."

Candace swatted at him halfheartedly, at the same time as she stretched her neck out so he could kiss her. She groaned as his tongue darted out to trail across her skin, making every part of her tingle and think about exactly what they'd been doing in the shower only a short time ago.

"What you're doing to me right now definitely needs to stay private," she said with a laugh.

His hand skimmed her body, caressing her hip and running down her thigh.

"Logan!"

He raised his head, locking eyes with her. The stare he was giving her sent a shiver down her spine, a lick of pleasure that made her push Logan back up a little so she could run her hands down his bare chest. The physical reaction she had to her husband made it hard to concentrate on anything else when he was this close, and this bare, to her. But she wanted to tell him something that she'd been waiting all afternoon to share with him.

"Logan, there's something I want to give you."

He dropped a kiss to her lips before pushing up and moving back to lie on the lounger beside hers. The sun had almost completely faded now, but lying outside their villa was just as magical in the half-light as it was during the middle of the day.

"You do remember that we agreed on no gifts, right? This vacation is more than enough, for both of us."

Candace reached beneath the lounger, her hand connecting with a small box. She pulled it out and sat up.

"I promise that it cost less than twenty dollars, so you can't complain."

Logan's eyebrows pulled together, like he was trying to figure out what she could possibly have in the box. Her heart was racing, beating a million times a minute, her eyes never leaving Logan's. She still couldn't believe what she was about to tell him.

"Well, I would have guessed a snorkel or something

for our Great Barrier dive tomorrow, but that small? Hmm."

Candace passed the little box to him, wondering if she'd gone a little overboard by putting a bow around it. Maybe she should have just told him.

"Just promise me that you won't freak out," she mumbled.

Logan squeezed her hand, looking worried, as he reached for it. She looked at how tiny the little box was in his hand as he undid the bow and slipped the lid off.

"What...?"

She held her breath, barely able to even keep her eyes open as his face froze, recognition dawning.

"Is this what I think it is?" he asked.

Candace moved to sit beside her husband as he took the white plastic stick from the box as carefully as he would hold a broken bird, his eyes never leaving it. The pink word *pregnant* was bold, not something he could miss, although she got why he might not believe it straightaway.

"Logan?" she whispered.

He finally turned, the stick still in his hand. "We're having a baby?"

Logan's voice was deep, the emotion in his voice impossible to miss as he stared at her.

"It's very early still, but yeah," she replied. "We're having a baby."

He carefully put the test back in the box and put the lid back on, before slowly turning around and holding his arms out, pulling her against him.

"We're having a baby," he whispered, his lips against

the top of her head, kissing into her hair. "We're actually going to have a baby."

"Is that okay?" she whispered back, crushed against him.

"Hell, yes, that's okay!" he exclaimed, hands on her upper arms as he pushed her back, held her at arms' length. "Honey, aside from marrying you, this is the best thing that's ever happened to me. Honestly."

"Promise?" she asked, tearing up at listening to him say the words she'd been hoping to hear.

"I promise," he said straight back, lying down and pulling her on top of him so her body covered his. "Hand on my heart, I promise."

"At least we know why I've been so darn emotional," she joked.

"Come here, Mama," he said, yanking a strand of hair to make her lean down more.

"Logan!"

"Just shut up and kiss me," he demanded. "I only have, what, eight months of you to myself? That means I'm going to be making the most of every moment before I have to share you."

Candace crushed her mouth to Logan's, kissing him like she'd been deprived of his mouth for an eternity.

"So, you'd like more of that?" she asked, loving his hot breath against her skin, before touching her lips to his again and teasing him with her tongue.

"Yes," he murmured, "God, yes."

"Well, then, Mr. Murdoch, let's not waste a minute."

Candace shut her eyes, focused only on the feel of Logan's mouth pressed to hers, his hands as they roamed up under her dress, caressing her bare skin. They were alone on one of the most beautiful islands in the world, she was with the man of her dreams and very soon they'd have a family of their own.

Life couldn't get any better than this, and if it could, she didn't care. For her, this was perfection.

* * * * *

FINDING THE E

DEBRA WEBB

This book is dedicated to the outstanding men and women of the Chicago Police Department. Thanks for all you do!

Chapter One

The Edge, Chicago
Friday, May 4, 9:50 p.m.

"We're going to need more gurneys!" Dr. Marissa Frasier shouted.

Someone amid the fray yelled that more gurneys were coming. They had nine new victims besides the dozen already in the ER. All bleeding, some worse than others. All had been shot and all were armed. And every damned one sported white T-shirts with an odd circle inside a circle in the center and wore black beanie caps. Their shouted threats echoed like thunder, inciting fear. Thank God most of the other patients had been checked in and were either already triaged and stable or had nonlife-threatening emergencies.

Eva Bowman might have considered it just another crazy Friday night looming toward a code black if not for the three cars that had screeched into the ER entrance with those new victims. Several armed men had barged in, waving automatic guns and demanding help for their friends. The three apparently in charge had forced everyone in the waiting room onto the floor and sent the entire ER staff, including the receptionist and the two registration specialists, outside to help their friends.

In all the commotion, Eva hoped someone had been able to alert the police. One of the security guards had been shot. He and the other guard had been restrained and left on the floor in the waiting room, blood pooling around the injured man. One of the gunmen stood over the small crowd, his scowl shifting from one to the other as if daring someone to give him a reason to start shooting. Eva wished she was more knowledgeable about the tattoos and colors worn by the different gangs in the Chicago area, though she couldn't readily see how knowing would help at the moment. For now, she did what she was told and prayed help would arrive soon.

Eva pushed an occupied gurney through the double doors, leaving the lobby behind. All the treatment rooms were full so she found a spot in the corridor and parked. She ripped open the shirt of her patient. Male. Mid to late twenties. Hispanic. He was sweaty and breathing hard. He'd lost some blood from the bullet wound on his left side. Lucky for him the bullet appeared to have exited without much fanfare. Still, he was no doubt in serious pain. Whatever his pain level, he clutched his weapon and continued to bellow arrogantly at his friends as if a shot to the gut was an everyday occurrence. From what little she recalled of high school Spanish, he seemed to be claiming victory over whatever battle had occurred. If the group of wounded men who had been scattered on the asphalt in front of the ER doors were the winners, she hated to think what condition the losers were in. Didn't take much of a stretch to imagine they were in all probability dead.

An experienced registered nurse, Eva performed a quick assessment of her patient's vitals. Respiration and pulse were rapid. Though his skin was warm and moist, his color remained good. From all indications he was not critical, but there could be underlying issues she could not assess. He would need an ultrasound to ensure no organs were damaged, and the wound would need to be cleaned and sutured.

"Sir, can you tell me your name?"

The man stared at her as if she'd asked him to hand over his weapon. She decided to move on to her next question. "On a scale of one to ten, ten being the worst you've ever suffered, can you tell me how much pain you're in?"

"Cero."

She sincerely doubted that was the case but if he wanted to play the tough guy, that was fine by her.

Over the next few minutes her patient as well as the others were sorted according to their needs and ushered on to the next level of care. Some were taken straight to operating rooms while others went on to imaging for additional assessment. One nurse and a doctor had been allowed to treat the patients in the lobby. Eva remained in the ER helping to attend to those who had arrived and were triaged and assigned treatment rooms before the gunmen arrived and took over. The armed patients who didn't require further care were mostly loitering around the corridor waiting for the return of their friends who'd been sent off to imaging or to the OR. What they didn't seem to realize was that those friends wouldn't be coming back to join them tonight.

One of the other nurses had whispered to Eva that Dr. Frasier had initiated the emergency assistance protocol. The police had been made aware that the ER was under siege or under duress of some sort and required law enforcement intervention.

Once before she had found herself in a similar situation. Time was necessary for the police to arrive and assess the situation, then they would send in SWAT to contain the problem. She hoped no one else was hurt during the neutralization and containment of the gunmen. So far she had hidden three weapons. Two from patients who'd been rushed to the OR and one from the guy not a dozen feet away who claimed he was in zero pain. His pain had apparently been so nonexistent that he hadn't realized his fingers had loosened on the 9 mm he'd been waving around when he first arrived.

Dr. Frasier noticed what Eva was up to and gave her a look of appreciation. No matter that she had removed and hidden three weapons—there were still six armed victims as well as the three armed and uninjured men who had taken over the ER. Thankfully, the thug who appeared to be the boss had allowed the injured guard to be treated for the bullet he'd taken. The guard's injury was not life threatening. He and his partner for the night were now both locked in the supply room.

Eva glanced at her watch. Approximately ten seemingly endless minutes had elapsed since the police were notified of their situation via the emergency protocol. SWAT would be rolling in soon. She didn't have to look outside to know that cops would have already taken crucial positions in the parking area.

All handheld radios and cell phones had been confiscated and tossed into a trash can—except for Eva's. The only reason the pat down conducted by the shortest of the three jerks who'd taken over the ER hadn't revealed her cell phone was because she didn't carry it in her pocket or in an armband. Eva kept hers in an ankle band made just for cell phones. Her last boyfriend had been an undercover cop and he'd shown her all sorts of ways to hide weapons and phones. If she'd been smart she would have carried a stun gun strapped to her other ankle the way he suggested.

They might still be together if he had been able to separate his work from his personal life. It was one thing to pretend to be someone else to catch the bad guys but entirely another to take on a separate persona for the purposes of cheating on your girlfriend.

Apparently the guys playing king of the ER weren't savvy enough to be aware that, like gun manufacturers, cell phone manufacturers thought of everything when it came to keeping phones close to users. Whatever the case, Eva was grateful her phone was still right where it was supposed to be. All she needed was an opportunity to use it. Knowing the situation inside would be incredibly useful for the police, particularly in determining how they made their grand entrance.

Her cell phone had vibrated about twenty times. Probably her sister, Lena. An investigative journalist at a local television station, Lena had no doubt heard about the trouble at the Edge. The best journalists had good contacts within Chicago PD and the Edge always had news. A Level I Trauma test unit challenging the approach to emergency medicine, the Edge was the only one of its kind in the nation.

Eva glanced toward the rear of the emergency department and the door that led into the main corridor that flowed into imaging and the surgery suite, winging off to the Behavioral Unit on the left and Administration to the right. Then she surveyed the ongoing activity between her and the double doors that opened into the lobby area. The man in charge and his cohorts were in deep conversation with the three other patients who hadn't been moved on to another level of care. Dr. Frasier was suturing the wound of one while Dr. Reagan was doing the same with another. Kim Levy, a nurse and Eva's friend, was bandaging the third patient's closed wound.

Eva eased back a step and then another. Four more steps and she would be through the door and into the corridor beyond the emergency department. Slow, deep breaths. No sudden moves. Another step, then another, and she was out the door.

Eva whirled away from the softly closing door and ran to the ladies' room. She couldn't lock the door since it didn't have one—no one wanted a patient to lock him or herself in the bathroom. Inside there were, however, two stalls with slide locks.

She slipped into the second one and snapped the stall latch into place, then sat on the closed toilet lid and pulled her knees to her chest so no one coming in would see her feet. She tugged her cell phone from its holster at her ankle and saw four missed calls and six text messages from her sister. She didn't dare make a voice call so she sent a text to her sister and asked her to update the police on the situation inside the ER.

Three uninjured gunmen. Four injured with guns, five others currently unarmed and in imaging or an OR. One injured guard. Both guards incapacitated.

A few seconds later, Lena told her to stay calm and to keep a low profile. Help was already on-site. Daring to relax the tiniest bit, Eva slid the phone back into its holster.

All she had to do was stay calm. Easy enough. She stepped off the seat.

The sound of the door opening sent fear exploding in her veins. She flushed the toilet, took a breath and exited the stall.

The man she thought to be in charge waited for her. He leaned against the door, the weapon in his hand lying flat against his chest. She decided that all the intruders were under thirty. This one looked to be early twenties. Though he appeared younger than the others, he was clearly the boss.

Eva steadied herself. "This is the ladies' room." She stared at him. "*Baño femenino.*"

He laughed. "*Si.*"

Oh crap. She squared her shoulders and took a step toward the door…toward him. "I need to be back out there helping your friends."

He shook his head. "There is plenty help already."

Eva swallowed back the scream mushrooming in her throat. There was no one to hear. This jerk was slightly taller than her five-seven. He was heavier and more muscled than her for sure, and a hell of a lot meaner. But she might be able to take him…*if not for the gun.*

As if he'd read her mind, he smiled and pointed the muzzle at her head. "On your knees, bitch."

The shaking started so deep inside her that she wondered how she remained standing, yet somehow she did. "The police are coming." The words shook, too, but she couldn't keep her voice steady if her life depended on it. Right now the ability to continue breathing might very well depend on her next word or move. "If you're smart, you'll tell your friends and you'll run. *Now*, while you still can."

He nodded, that nasty grin still stretched across his lips. "Yes," he agreed, the word sounding more like *des* with his thick accent.

Since he made no move to rush to his friends and warn them, her advice had clearly fallen on deaf ears. "So you don't care if you get caught?" She shrugged. "You want to go to prison? Then *you* can be somebody's bitch."

He charged toward her, pinned her to the counter of the row of sinks behind her. Of their own volition, her hands shot up in surrender. "Just trying to help you out. You...you don't want the police to show up and find you distracted. If you go now, they won't catch you."

She hoped like hell the guy had enough self-preservation instinct to realize she had a valid point.

"You talk a lot for a dead girl," he growled as he jammed the muzzle against her temple now. "You give me some of *that*—" he slid his free hand down her belly, forcing it between her thighs "—with no trouble and I'll be gone so fast you'll still be begging for more."

Trapped between him and the counter with his damned gun pointed at her brain, she couldn't move, didn't dare scream. Her heart flailed against her sternum. *Stay calm. Your fear makes him stronger.*

"Okay, okay." This close she smelled the whiskey on his breath, could fully comprehend just how inebriated he was. Bleary eyes. Slurred speech. No wonder he wasn't worried about the police. She drew in a shaky breath. *Play along until you come up with a better plan.* "What do you want?"

He laughed. "Suck me."

She nodded as she slowly lowered her hands. The muzzle bored into her skull a little harder as she reached for his fly. He was fully erect, bulging against his jeans. Bile rose in her throat as she unfastened the button, then lowered the zipper. She told herself over and over she had no choice as she reached into his open fly. He didn't have on any underwear so he was right there. She closed the fingers of her right hand around him while somehow managing to restrain the shudder of revulsion.

In hopes of putting off what he really wanted, her hand started to move. He made a satisfied sound, his eyes partially closing. "Oh, yeah, that's a good start."

She worked her hand back and forth faster and faster, felt his body tense. Watched his eyes drift completely shut.

Now or never.

Eva ducked her head, jammed her left shoulder into his gut and pushed with every ounce of her body weight. At the same time, she released his penis and grabbed his testicles and twisted as hard as she could.

He screamed.

The weapon discharged.

The mirror over the sinks shattered.

He grabbed at her; she twisted her upper body out of reach, spinning them both around. The muzzle stabbed at her chest; she leaned away from the gun and rammed into him even harder. Another shot exploded into the air as they both went down. His head hit the counter, making a solid *thump* as his neck twisted sharply. They crashed to the cold tile floor. The air grunted out of her lungs. Eva was still squeezing his balls when she realized he was no longer moving.

Disentangling herself from him, she scooted a few feet away. His eyes blinked, once, twice…he mumbled something she couldn't comprehend.

Eva scrambled to her feet and backed toward the door. She should reach for his weapon…she should grab it and run…

The door burst inward, almost knocking her on top of the man on the floor.

Another of the gunmen stared first at her and then at the man on the floor whose fly was flared open with his erect penis poked out.

Before Eva could speak the man grabbed her by the hair with his left hand and the gun in his right shoved into her face. "What did you do to him?"

Shaking so hard now she could hardly speak, she somehow managed to say, "He tried to rape me, so I pushed him away and he fell…he hit his head."

The man shoved her to the floor. She landed on her knees. "Help him," he snarled.

Eva moved closer to her attacker. His eyes were open but he didn't look at her. When she touched his neck to measure his pulse he mumbled but his words were unintelligible. Pulse was rapid. His body abruptly tensed. Seizure. *Damn.*

"We need to get him into the ER now." She pushed to her feet. "He may have a serious head injury."

The man grabbed her by the hair once more and jerked her face to his. "Do you know what you've done?"

A new stab of terror sank deep into her chest. "He attacked me. I was trying—"

"If he dies," he snarled, the muzzle boring into her cheek, "*you* die."

Suddenly the gun went upward. His arm twisted violently. A *pop* echoed in the room. Not a gunshot… a bone…

The man howled in agony. His body was hurled toward the floor. He landed on the unforgiving tile next to his friend.

Eva wheeled around, readied to scream but swallowed back the sound as she recognized Dr. Devon Pierce, the Edge creator and administrator.

"Check the corridor," he ordered. "If it's clear, go to my office and hide. I've got this." The man on the floor scrambled to get up and Pierce kicked him hard in the gut.

When Eva hesitated, he snarled, "Go!"

She eased the bathroom door open and checked the corridor. Clear. She slipped out of the room, the door closed behind her, cutting of the grunts and awful keening inside. Her first instinct was to return to the ER to see if her help was needed there, but Dr. Pierce had told her to hide in his office. She didn't know what he was doing here but she assumed he was aware somehow of all that had happened. Perhaps the emergency protocol automatically notified him or maybe he had been in his office working late. Bottom line, he was the boss.

She hurried along the corridor, took a right into another side hall past the storeroom and the file rooms. Fear pounded in her veins as she moved into the atrium. Pierce's office was beyond the main lobby. She held her breath as she hurried through an open area. When she reached his secretary's office and the small, private lobby she dared to breathe, then she closed herself in his office. The desk lamp was on. Apparently Pierce had been in his office working. She reached for her cell.

Before she could put through a call to her sister, she heard rustling outside the door. The roar of her own blood deafening in her ears, Eva glanced quickly around the room. She had to hide. Fast!

With no other option she ducked under his desk, squeezed as far beneath it as she could, folding her knees up to her chin and holding herself tight and small.

A soft swoosh of air warned the door of the administrator's office had opened.

She held her breath.

The intruder—maybe Pierce, maybe a cop—moved around the room. She had no intention of coming out of hiding until she knew for certain. The sound of books sliding across shelves and frames banging against the wall clarified that the intruder was neither Pierce nor a cop. Footfalls moved closer to her position. She needed to breathe. She pressed her face to her knees and dared to draw in a small breath. Black leather shoes and gray trousers appeared behind the desk. Her eyes widened with the dread spreading inside her.

Definitely male.

The man dropped into the leather executive chair and reached for the middle drawer of the desk. His rifling through the drawer contents gave her the opportunity to breathe again. He moved on to the next drawer, the one on his right. More of that rummaging. Then he reached lower, for the final drawer on that side. She prayed he wouldn't bend down any lower because he would certainly see her.

She held her breath again. He shifted to access the drawers on the other side, and his foot came within mere centimeters of her hip. He searched through the three remaining drawers. Then he stood. Sharp movement across the blotter pad told her he was writing something. Finally, he moved away from the desk.

The door opened and then closed.

Eva counted to thirty before she dared to move. She scooted from under the desk and scanned the room. She was alone. Thank God. The books and framed awards and photos on the once neatly arranged shelves lay scattered about. Her gaze instinctively dropped to the desk.

I know what you did.

The words were scrawled on the clean expanse of white blotter paper. For ten or more seconds she couldn't move. She should go…get out of this office. Whatever that—she stared at the note—was about, she didn't want to get dragged into it. The men who had stormed the ER had all been wearing jeans or cargo pants, not dress trousers and certainly not leather loafers. *Just go!*

At the door, she eased it open and checked the administrator's private lobby. Clear. She'd almost made it out of the secretary's office when she heard hurried footfalls in the corridor. Renewed panic roared through her veins.

With nowhere else to go, she ducked under the secretary's desk.

The footfalls moved across the carpeted floor. She heard the sound of Pierce's office door opening. The man was popular tonight. Had the guy who'd written the note forgotten something?

A soft curse came from the general direction of Pierce's office.

Eva hoped SWAT was ready to storm the place. She would hate to survive a bunch of crazed thugs or gangbangers or whatever they were and be murdered by a man wearing dress trousers and black leather shoes.

"Eva!"

For a moment she couldn't breathe.

"Eva!"

Dr. Pierce. She scrambled out from under the desk. "Yes, sir. I'm here."

Fury or outrage—something on that order—colored his face. "The police are here. They'll need your statement."

Thank God. "Is everyone okay? The gunmen have been contained?"

He nodded, then frowned. "I thought you were going to hide in my office."

She shrugged and in that instant something about the expression on his face made her decide to keep what happened in his office to herself. "I heard someone coming. I freaked and hid under the secretary's desk."

"Someone came in here?"

He had to know someone had. He couldn't have missed the disarray in his office or the note on his desk.

She nodded. "I couldn't see what was happening, but I definitely heard footsteps and the door to your office opening and closing."

"You didn't get a look at who it was?"

She shook her head. Was that suspicion she heard in his voice?

When he continued to stare at her without saying more, she offered, "Is everything okay?"

"Yes." He smiled, rearranging his face into the amiable expression he usually wore. "It is now. Come with me. We should get this police business squared away so we can return to the business of healing the sick."

The walk back to the emergency department was the longest of her life. She could feel his tension in every step he took. She wanted to ask him again if everything was okay but she didn't dare stir his suspicions.

Right now all she wanted was for this night to be over.

Chapter Two

Magnificent Mile
Tuesday, May 8, 2:15 p.m.

Eva hurried up the sidewalk. She glanced over her shoulder repeatedly, checked the street over and over. She hated that her behavior no doubt looked entirely paranoid, but the truth was paranoia had been her constant companion for better than forty-eight hours. Since she received the first message.

Two men had swerved to the curb on her street as she walked home from the market on Saturday afternoon. She might have kept walking except the one hanging out the passenger window called her name.

Eva! Eva Bowman! He's coming for you, la perra. You killed his hermano menor.

The man who'd tried to rape her—the one who'd fractured his skull in that damned bathroom and then died—was the younger brother of one of Chicago's most notorious gang leaders.

Just her luck.

Eva walked faster. She hadn't meant to kill anyone. She'd been fighting for her life. He'd fallen...his death was an accident. An accident that wouldn't have happened had he not been trying to rape her.

The detectives on the scene had tried to make her feel better by telling her that Diego Robles—that was the dead man's name, Diego Robles—and his gang of nearly a dozen thugs had murdered six men and two women on Friday before overtaking the ER where she worked.

Except it hadn't made her feel better. Robles had been nineteen years old. *Nineteen.* He had an older brother, Miguel, who was thirty-five and the leader of the True Disciples, an extremely violent offshoot of the Latin Disciples. The brother had passed along his message to Eva on three occasions without ever leaving a single shred of evidence she could take to the police.

The first warning had come on Saturday afternoon via the two thugs in the car. Another had come when she walked out of the corner coffee shop near her apartment building on Sunday morning. Then, last night, another man had showed up at the ER asking for her. When she'd appeared at the registration desk, he'd waited until no one was looking and leaned forward to whisper for her ears only.

You will die this week.

With that he'd given her a nod and told her to enjoy her night.

She'd reported all three incidents to the police and all they could do was tell her to be careful. No one had touched her or damaged her property. She had no proof of the threats other than her word. But last night when she'd been too afraid to go to her car alone and then too terrified to go to her own apartment, she'd understood she had to do something. She worried the only evidence to back up her fears would come in the form of someone finding her body after it was too late.

Lena had demanded, to no avail, protection from the police for Eva. Kim Levy, her friend and another nurse at the Edge, had urged her to speak to Dr. Pierce. Kim had been in the ER on Friday night. She understood how terrified Eva had every right to be. But Eva couldn't stop thinking about the way Dr. Pierce had looked at her after the strange happenings in his office. She'd decided not to discuss that odd moment with Kim or anyone else. And she had no desire to discuss her personal dilemma with her boss. Still, Kim being Kim, she had gone to Dr. Pierce and told him what was going on. He had insisted on sending Eva to the Colby Agency. Eva had heard of the Colby Agency. Who hadn't? She'd certainly never expected to need a private investigations firm. Yet, here she was. She had an appointment at two thirty. Five minutes from now.

Almost there. The Magnificent Mile was always busy, even on a Tuesday afternoon with hours to go before the evening rush of commuters headed home. She looked at each face she met…wondering when one of *them* would appear.

She walked faster, pushing against the wind that seemed to want to blow her right back to where she'd parked her car.

No turning back now.

A shiver chilled her skin. It didn't feel very much like spring today. Barely sixty degrees and overcast. Just in case it started to rain again, she'd tucked her umbrella into the beige leather bag she carried. Her pepper spray was in there, too. She carried her life around in one of two bags: a well-used brown one for fall and winter and this tawny beige one her mother had given her for spring and summer. Life was complicated enough without changing the purse she carried more than twice a year. Eva went out of her way to keep life simple. She'd had enough complications her freshman year in college. She'd made a decision all those years ago never to allow those sorts of complications ever again.

Life was better when she stuck to enjoying the simpler pleasures. Like all the gorgeous tulips still in bloom and the trees that had gone from their stark winter limbs to lush and green already.

That was the ticket. Focus on the mundane...the normal.

The deep timbre of male voices was suddenly behind her. Fear crept up her spine like a cluster of spiders and her heart swelled into her throat. Her gait wavered, causing her to nearly stumble. A group of four men moved around and ahead of her. Despite the glaring facts that they paid her absolutely no notice, were dressed in business suits and kept moving at a brisk pace, her heart refused to slide back down into her chest where it belonged. The pepper spray in her bag felt wholly inadequate.

Damn, she was a mess.

It wasn't until she spotted the wide glass front bearing the address of her destination that she was able to breathe easy again. Her hands settled on the door and, despite her best efforts, she hesitated. Calm was the necessary watchword. If she went into this meeting shaken and panicky, she might very well meet with the same reception she'd received from the two Chicago PD detectives working the investigation.

Investigation. There were several aspects of the ongoing investigation. The clash between the True Disciples and another well-known gang with the resulting multiple homicides. The taking of an entire ER hostage. And the deemed justified homicide of Diego Robles. Both detectives, their captain and the DA had told her the events that happened in that bathroom were self-defense, completely justified. She had not intended to kill anyone. She'd only been trying to get away from him. The man's death was an accidental consequence of his actions.

But dead was dead.

Calm. Collected. Not your fault.

Eva squared her shoulders and pushed through the door. A wide, gleaming metal security desk curved around the center of the enormous lobby. Enough greenery to rival a small jungle softened all the glass and glossy metal.

"Afternoon, ma'am," the security guard said as she approached the counter. "You have an appointment?"

"The Colby Agency." She drew her wallet from her bag and produced her driver's license. "Eva Bowman."

The guard checked the computer screen, scanned her license into his system, then handed the license as well as a visitor's badge to her. "The elevators are to your right. Fourteenth floor is where you're headed. Your code for the elevator is on the back of the badge. Just drop the badge off here as you leave, Ms. Bowman."

"Thank you." As she moved toward the bank of elevators, she checked the back of the badge. Eight-two-six-seven. She clipped the badge onto the lapel of her sweater and tapped the call button.

The doors opened to a vacant car. Deep breath. She stepped inside and selected floor fourteen. The keypad warned that a code was required so she entered the necessary digits. When the doors closed she stared at her reflection in the mirrored walls of the elevator interior. She'd taken care to dress professionally. The soft blush color of her pants and sweater set complemented her too-pale skin. Matching leather ballet flats were easy on the feet. Her first month as an ER nurse had taught her to appreciate good shoes made for comfort. She'd swept her blond hair into a loose bun at the nape of her neck and she'd gone easy on the makeup. Just a touch of lip gloss and a swipe of mascara.

Calm. Collected.

The car bumped to a stop and the doors slid open to another lobby. A receptionist looked up from behind an opaque glass desk and smiled. "Good morning. Welcome to the Colby Agency, Ms. Bowman."

The next five or so minutes passed in a blur. After the offer of refreshments, which she declined, another receptionist appeared and escorted her to Victoria Colby-Camp's office, a large, elegant space with a wall of windows that overlooked the city from a prestigious Michigan Avenue address.

Eva had done an internet search on Victoria and her agency, but she hadn't been adequately prepared for the sophisticated woman standing behind the beautiful mahogany desk, the wall of windows a stunning backdrop. She wore her salt-and-pepper hair in a French twist. The turquoise suit fit as if it had been tailored just for her. Probably had been. Though she was no taller than Eva, her presence was commanding. The most surprising part was how incredibly youthful and fit she looked. According to Google, Victoria Colby-Camp was nearing seventy. Eva could only hope she would look that good in another forty years.

"It's a pleasure to meet you, Eva." Victoria smiled. "Please sit. Let's take a moment to get acquainted."

"Thank you." Eva settled into one of the two champagne-colored upholstered chairs in front of Victoria's desk.

"My intern, Jamie, will be joining us shortly," Victoria said. "I've reviewed your file. You're a nurse at the Edge. Dr. Pierce and I serve on Chicago's civic committee together. The Edge is an incredible step toward elevating emergency care to the highest level. We're all very proud and duly impressed by his advances in the field."

Eva nodded. "Dr. Pierce is an amazing man. His methods are changing the landscape of emergency medicine." The Edge was his brainchild. Whether it was a heart attack, a stroke or some sort of physical injury, the Edge was where everyone wanted to end up when an emergency occurred.

"You have family in the city?"

Eva smiled. Her first of the day. "An older sister, Lena. You may know her. She's an investigative journalist at Channel 7."

Victoria nodded. "I do, indeed. Lena Bowman is a household name in the city of Chicago."

Eva nodded. "She was determined to become one for as long as I can remember."

Victoria tilted her head ever so slightly, her expression turning somber. "I've also had an opportunity to review the Chicago PD's file on what happened Friday night. It's an outright miracle no hostages were killed. You and the others at the Edge handled yourselves extraordinarily well."

Eva nodded in acknowledgment of her kind words. "Since you read the file you must know about Diego Robles's death."

"Captain Cyrus explained what happened. He's very concerned that you've been approached and threatened. Dr. Pierce is immensely concerned as well. Why don't you start at the beginning and tell me what's happening."

As much as Eva had dreaded this part, somehow Victoria made her feel relaxed and comfortable—at least as comfortable as she could be under the circumstances. Eva started with what the second man who came into the bathroom on Friday night said to her. She moved on to the ones who'd shouted at her on the street on Saturday, the confrontation on Sunday, the visit at the ER last night and then to the carful of thugs who had followed her to the parking garage three blocks from here. Thankfully, they hadn't yelled more threats at her…they'd only watched her. Their hateful eyes on her had been equally threatening.

Victoria studied Eva for a moment after she finished recounting the events of the past three days. "I have full confidence the police are watching Robles's men, but they can't watch every move each of his hundreds of followers make—not with the budget cuts they've suffered recently. You haven't been assigned a protection detail for the same reason. Until a law is broken, the police can't afford to shift the resources."

"I might be dead by then." Eva hated to say the words aloud but they were true.

"Which is why we're here. We can fill that void." Victoria folded her hands atop her desk. "Since Dr. Pierce and I are well acquainted, he asked that I assign the very best to your security and he insisted that I send the bill to him."

"What?" Eva shook her head. She couldn't have heard correctly. "I'm prepared to pay for the services I need."

Victoria held up a hand. "I'm certain you are, Eva. But Dr. Pierce feels responsible. He would like to handle this and, frankly, he can easily afford to do so. Trust me, you should take him up on his generous offer."

Eva wanted to argue, but Victoria was right. She had scratched together the retainer but she would be hard-pressed to come up with more than a week's worth of the required fees. She wanted to be upset that Dr. Pierce had been brought into the financial aspect of this arrangement but she supposed it was the right thing to do. *I know what you did.* The note someone had left on his desk blotter flickered across her mind. She had no idea what the message meant or who left it. She had wanted to ask Dr. Pierce but with all that had happened that night and then the threats, she'd forgotten. In truth, she didn't feel comfortable discussing it with him after his reaction that night. She wasn't worried that he somehow felt she was involved or aware of who went into his office, but she couldn't quite dispel the idea that he'd looked at her with doubt for just a moment.

"I suppose I can do that."

Maybe when this business with Robles was behind her she would come clean and tell Dr. Pierce she'd lied about being in his office. *God, Eva, you're such an idiot.* It would have been so much easier if she'd told the truth in the first place, but it had felt so awkward in that instant. As badly as she felt about that decision, she had far more serious issues with which to deal at present.

"Good." Victoria picked up a manila folder on her desk and opened it. "When I assign one of my people to a case, I do all within my power to ensure I'm covering every possible need a client might have."

The door opened and a woman walked in. Blond hair, blue eyes. She was tall and thin. Very young. High school, maybe a college freshman. As young as she was, she held herself in a regal manner that reminded Eva of Victoria.

"I apologize for the delay." The girl smiled first at Victoria then at Eva. "I'm Jamie Colby." She offered her hand to Eva.

Eva shook Jamie's hand, noting the firm confidence in her grip.

"Eva, this is my granddaughter," Victoria said, pride brimming in her tone. "She's a sophomore at the University of Chicago and my intern two days a week."

"You look so young," Eva blurted before she could stop herself, "to have accomplished so much."

"Jamie is quite special," Victoria agreed.

Jamie smiled. "I took freshman classes my senior year of high school. It's not so unusual that I'm eighteen and a sophomore and certainly not special."

Her humility was refreshing. Eva said, "I'm certain your parents are very pleased."

"They certainly are." Victoria turned to Jamie. "All is in order?"

"It is," Jamie assured her.

"As I was saying—" Victoria turned to Eva "—I take great pride in assigning the best person for the job. Since your bodyguard—"

"Bodyguard?" Eva expected an investigator to help with the Miguel Robles situation, not a bodyguard.

Victoria and Jamie shared a look before Victoria's gaze settled on Eva once more. "We need to take this situation very seriously, Eva. Frankly, I'm surprised you're not already dead."

Eva's breath caught. She put her hand over her mouth too late to catch the sound.

"Ms. Bowman," Jamie said, turning in her chair to face Eva, "I've done extensive research on the True Disciples. Miguel Robles raised his younger brother since their parents were murdered fifteen years ago. He thought of Diego as more of a son than a brother. Typically when crossed, Miguel wields vengeance far more quickly and concisely. The idea that you're alive three days later tells us that he is planning to make some sort of example out of you. He wants you to know it's coming. He wants to watch your fear build. He wants a large audience and rumor on the street is that all eyes are on you right now."

Eva blinked repeatedly to hold back the rush of tears. "Wait, this is crazy. I didn't mean to kill his brother. He attacked me… I…"

When Eva's voice failed her, Victoria said, "I'm afraid it only gets worse. Chicago PD has a unit called

Gang Intelligence. Though they cannot provide any measure of security for you, they are watching. If you want my honest opinion, they're hoping Robles will come after you. If they can catch Miguel Robles in the act of trying to harm you, they can bring down a man who has slipped through their fingers repeatedly over the past two decades."

Oh God. "I think I see the whole picture now." Eve swallowed at the lump still lodged in her throat. "I'm bait. The police won't protect me—not because of budget cuts—but because they want to get this guy."

"In all fairness," Victoria reminded her, "no law has been broken—more or less tying their hands. At this time all anyone has are rumors and suspicions, and resources are stretched too thin already. I fully believe the police are doing all they legally can."

Jamie placed a warm hand over Eva's ice-cold one. "But we can take up that slack."

"Dr. Pierce has granted us full access to his facility," Victoria explained. "We'd like to provide around-the-clock protection until this situation is neutralized."

Round-the-clock? "Is that really necessary?" The moment the words left her lips she felt foolish for having said them.

Eva hadn't expected this insanity to consume her life. Her sister had told her it was bad. She'd spent the past two nights with Eva. If all that Victoria said was true, Lena being close put her in danger as well. Eva suddenly felt immensely grateful that Lena's boss had called about a hot-button issue in DC and wanted her there ASAP. Lena had nearly refused to go but Eva had promised she would be fine with the Colby Agency taking care of her. After considerable persuasion, her sister had reluctantly accepted the assignment. Eva now completely understood how important it was to keep Lena as far from this as possible…and to end this as quickly as possible.

"Okay," Eva heard herself say. "When do I meet this bodyguard?"

"As Victoria explained," Jamie cut in, "we take every precaution when making the selection. Your situation requires extensive training. The man we've chosen spent eight years in the military, six in the Army's Special Forces. He is an expert in all manner of defense and protection. His extensive emergency medical training will allow a smooth transition into your workplace. He's the perfect choice."

Victoria nodded her agreement. "You couldn't be in better hands."

Eva's head was still spinning. She could do this. It was necessary. Her boss understood. Lena would come unglued if Eva even thought of backing out of hiring the Colby Agency. This was the right step. *Just do this.* "All right. I'm ready to do whatever I have to."

"Before we ask him in," Victoria began.

Eva instinctively understood that something bad was coming.

"We've been made aware that there may be a stumbling block of sorts. Under normal circumstances," Victoria went on, "I never make assignments when there are personal connections. Emotions can often get in the way."

Eva shook her head. "I'm sorry. This is my first time here and I'm fairly confident I don't know anyone at your agency."

"Todd Christian."

Eva's head turned so quickly toward the woman seated next to her that her neck almost snapped. "Todd Christian?"

Impossible. Even as the word filtered through her, Eva comprehended it was not. Todd had gone straight from college into the military. She'd heard at some point later that he was in some sort of special something but she couldn't remember what. She had spent the past nine years blocking every single thing about him from her brain. Todd Christian no longer existed as far as Eva was concerned. She had worked extremely hard to make that happen.

Jamie nodded. "He is the perfect choice."

Eva shook her head. "No. Absolutely not." She could not—would not—spend one minute much less 24/7 with him. No damned way.

Another of those looks passed between Victoria and her granddaughter.

"Todd thought you might feel that way," Victoria offered. "Eva, let me just say that I've been doing this for a very long time."

"A seriously long time," Jamie echoed.

"I do not make a suggestion such as this lightly," Victoria continued. "I ask that you put your personal feelings aside for a moment before you request an alternate choice. Toward that end, Todd has asked if he might speak with you privately before you make your final decision."

"He's here?" Stupid question. He worked here. Of course he would be somewhere on the floor. Eva felt the heat rise in her face and then, just as suddenly, the color drain away, leaving her as weak as a kitten.

How could she face him? He was the last person on Earth she wanted to hear about her personal issues.

"With your permission, Jamie and I will wait in my private lobby while the two of you talk for a moment."

"There must be someone else." Eva shook her head again. This would never do. "You mentioned an alternate choice."

Victoria set her hands palms down on her desk and stood. "I pride myself in hiring only the best, Eva. Of course, there are others, but no one who would fit as seamlessly into your world. To make sure you are protected in such a way that the enemy will not simply lay low until that protection ceases, we must ensure they are taken by surprise. The last thing we want is for Robles to step back and wait out your resources. This is the only way to guarantee the outcome you desire in the quickest manner."

As crazy as it sounded, Eva had to admit that she could see her point. But could she do this? Could she allow *him* back into her life? Uncertainty and a new kind of fear coiled inside her like a snake ready to strike.

"I'll speak to him." Eva took a big breath. "I can at least do that."

Victoria nodded. "Excellent."

Jamie patted Eva on the hand and stood. "We'll give you a few moments, but we'll be right outside."

Eva tried to smile but her lips wouldn't make the transition.

When the door closed behind the two women, Eva stood and smoothed a wrinkle out of her sweater hem. Slow, deep breaths.

The door opened and she turned to face the man who had shattered her heart when she was barely old enough to understand what love was. He'd been a senior, she a freshman. She'd never lived anywhere but at home with her parents and sister until she moved into that college dormitory. Lena had gone to Europe for a year of studies abroad. And Eva had fallen madly, deeply in love with the man who taught her what a real orgasm felt like.

She might have been able to say the thirty-two-year-old man who walked into the room and closed the door behind him hadn't changed one bit except that would be utterly and completely wrong. He seemed taller somehow, his shoulders even broader. Her gaze moved down his torso, over the ridges hidden behind the crisp blue oxford she knew all too well. The long sleeves ended at his wrists where the wide hands and blunt-tipped fingers that had touched her as if she was all that mattered in this world to him didn't look as smooth as they once had. Long legs were camouflaged by navy trousers tailored to mold perfectly to the powerful muscles beneath. She blinked and shifted her gaze to the handsome face she'd dreamed of every night for years even after he left her. His face looked the slightest bit leaner, more angular, and there was a small scar on his right cheek. His lips…his pale, pale blue eyes— She shifted her gaze from his face. His brown hair was still more blond than brown and in need of a trim. So many little things had changed and yet her body reacted to his mere presence as if absolutely nothing were different. Fire licked a path along every nerve ending.

His lips—the ones that had instructed her in the true art of kissing—slid into a smile. "Eva… It's good to see you."

The hesitation after he said her name told her he was savoring it. Something else she'd yearned for night and day. The sound of his voice, the pull of every syllable he uttered. Chill bumps rose on her skin. The smile…the sound of his voice, his presence in the room even after all these years had the ability to make her nervous. Made her ache for things she couldn't name.

Eva commanded the butterflies that had come to life in her stomach to go away. She stared directly into those gorgeous eyes of his. "Is it true, what they say? That you can protect me better than anyone else employed at the Colby Agency?"

"You have my word."

Those four little words—damn him—sent another shiver racing over her too-hot skin. "I'll need more than your word, Christian." She refused to call him Todd. She could not. "You see, I learned long ago that your word is of little value."

"I hurt you, Eva," he confessed. "You haven't forgiven me and maybe I don't deserve your forgiveness, but if you'll trust me now I swear on my life that I will take care of this for you. Let me do that. Please."

The idea that she could spend the next few days making him damned miserable held some appeal. "Fine. I trust *your boss*. She says you're the man for the job. We'll see about that."

"Good."

She picked up her bag and slung it over her shoulder. "Make sure you remember that once we walk out of this building *I* am the boss."

He nodded his agreement, and just like that she jumped right out of the frying pan and into the fire.

Chapter Three

West Grace Street Apartments
5:50 p.m.

Eva didn't want him close. She'd insisted on driving separately to her building. He hadn't liked it but she'd given him no choice. He'd stayed right on her bumper on the drive from the agency to her address. Rather than warn him about the parking situation, she'd driven into the covered area for tenants and he'd had to fend for himself on the street. When he'd finally found a spot, he'd had to hurry to catch up to her before she reached the building.

Like it or not, that would not happen again. Next time they would be in the same vehicle *together.*

At the front entrance she entered the code for the door and walked in, letting go of the door as she did. The damned thing almost closed before Todd caught it. She didn't look back, obviously unconcerned as to whether he made it inside.

He hadn't really expected her to forgive him—not even after nearly ten years. Not ever, most likely. Under the circumstances he was hoping for some sort of cordiality or at least a temporary truce.

Inside, rather than going for the elevator, she headed to the door marked with the stairwell logo. No problem. He hefted his duffel onto one shoulder and followed her. His time in the service had taught him not to take his physical condition for granted. He stayed in the same shape he had when he'd been in active duty.

The climb to the third floor, however, gave him far too much time to focus on the sway of her hips. Someone else stayed in shape, he decided. He remembered her soft curves a little too well. Time had been good to her. She still looked like the nineteen-year-old he'd first met in the university library. He'd tried so damned hard to focus on the book he'd been reading for an English paper, only he couldn't stop looking at her over the top of the page. She had the blondest hair, still did. Every sweet hair on her gorgeous body was naturally blond. Her skin was the creamiest white, like porcelain. And those eyes, so green. When she smiled or got angry they shimmered like emeralds under a waterfall.

She exited the stairwell on the third floor, again without looking back or saying a word to him. He followed. This was another part they had to get straight. He went through any door first. She stayed close and behind him, preferably.

He imagined the real trouble was going to be in getting her to cooperate when he explained that she might be the boss but he was in charge.

At the door to her apartment he stepped in front of her. "I go in first." He held out his hand.

She dropped the key into his palm and stepped back. He unlocked the door and moved inside. He'd looked at the floor plans for her building. She had a one-bedroom. The entry door opened into a small hall. The living and dining space along with the kitchen were an L-shape, and then another tiny hall with doors to a linen closet, the bedroom and the bath. No balcony, but she did have two large windows. He motioned for her to come inside, but she didn't. She stared at the door across the hall.

"Something wrong?"

She shook her head. "Guess not." She gestured to the door she'd been staring at. "I thought my neighbor was going out of town." With a shrug she turned to her own door and stepped inside.

Todd closed and locked it. "Stay put until I have a look around."

She rolled her eyes and folded her arms over her chest.

The large window overlooking the street allowed plenty of light into the room. He was surprised there were no blinds or curtains. The Eva he had known before had been very shy and private. Another of those things that had attracted him. He was glad to see an upholstered sofa rather than leather since it would serve as his bed. A small cocktail table stood in front of the sofa and a side table sat between two comfortable-looking chairs. The upholstery and the throw pillows were soft, muted shades of blues and greens and yellows. A rug in the center of the room was scattered with two larger pillows. Didn't take much to imagine her on the floor curled up with a good book. Back in college she'd enjoyed reading romance novels when she wasn't studying. He'd often teased her about her secret hobby.

The kitchen was tiny with an even tinier dining area. Updated three-piece bath with lots of that subway tile people went gaga over. Big mirrors that made the space look a tad larger and more of those little bursts of color that adorned the main living space. He opened the door to the bedroom and the scent of her assaulted him and made him weak. The large window in this intimate space was covered with thick curtains, ensuring the room was dark. He flipped on a light, checked the closet that overflowed with clothes and shoes and then turned to go. The unmade bed and the nightshirt tossed onto the tousled covers made him hesitate.

Selfishly, he experienced a sense of satisfaction at the untouched second pillow on the bed. He scanned the walls and other surfaces for photos or signs of a boyfriend. The only photographs were of her and her sister, Lena, and their parents. Their father had died the year before Eva started college. She had still been struggling with the loss when they were together.

"Are you finished yet?"

He pivoted toward her voice, surprised she'd gotten as far as the door without him noticing. *Distraction is dangerous.* He knew better. "The apartment is clear."

"I noticed." She executed an about-face and stormed away.

Todd heaved a disgusted breath and plowed his hand through his hair. This might not be as easy as he'd thought. He had foolishly hoped they might be able to make amends. That maybe he and Eva could be friends now that he was back in Chicago. Guess not.

He exited the bedroom and took the few short steps to the kitchen. This place was considerably smaller than it looked when he reviewed the building's floor plan. Spending a lot of time here with her would prove less than comfortable. She opened cabinet door after cabinet door, then rummaged in the refrigerator, obviously looking for something to eat.

"We could have dinner delivered," he suggested.

She looked at him over the fridge door. "Yogurt and crackers are fine with me."

He gritted his teeth and restrained any response for a moment. Her plan was obvious—make him as miserable as possible. No problem. He deserved it. "Sounds awesome."

She blinked but not fast enough to cover her surprise. A carton of yogurt and an apple in hand, she left the fridge, grabbed a box of crackers from a cabinet and carried her haul to the counter.

He tossed his duffel on the sofa and watched as she carefully sliced her apple and arranged it on a plate, then added a handful of small crackers. With yogurt spooned into the center, she sprinkled a few walnuts on top. Spoon and plate in hand, she carried both to the made-for-two dining table. She poured herself a glass of water from the pitcher in the fridge, grabbed a napkin and then took a seat.

Todd ignored her indifference and made himself at home. He grabbed a plate, rummaged for a butter knife, found peanut butter and proceeded to slather it onto as many of the small crackers as the plate would hold. He added an apple, not bothering to slice it, poured a glass of water and then joined her at the small table.

"Looks like you predicted Lena's future correctly." He stuffed a cracker into his mouth, hoping the protein in the peanut butter would satisfy him. He was starving.

Eva licked the yogurt from her spoon. He stared at his plate, then went for the apple. Anything to avoid watching her tongue slide around on that spoon.

"Channel 7 loves her. The viewers love her." Eva nibbled on a cracker. "I'm really proud of her."

Todd knocked back a long swallow of water before placing his glass back on the table. "You haven't done so bad yourself. Pierce raved about you to Victoria."

"I'm happy." She reached for an apple slice.

She didn't ask about his career or whether he was happy or if his brother Kevin was okay. The only part that surprised him was Kevin. His brother had been just a toddler when their father abandoned them. Their mother had died a few months earlier and there was no known extended family. Kevin had been adopted quickly, but Todd hadn't been so lucky. He'd spent the next twelve years of his life in foster homes. It wasn't until college that his little brother found him. They'd been damned close since. Eva was the only woman he'd ever taken to Christmas dinner with Kevin. He had loved her. She always asked about Kevin after that…at least until Todd left. Then again, he couldn't really hold that against her since he hadn't exactly been around for her when her mother died. He pushed the sensitive memory away.

The rest of the not-so-yummy and definitely not-filling meal was consumed without conversation. She rinsed her plate and placed it in the dishwasher. He pushed in his chair and followed her lead with the cleanup. "If only we had dessert."

She didn't smile. Instead she walked to the cabinets,

put the crackers away and withdrew a tub of cake frosting. She shoved it at him. “Chocolate. Enjoy.”

Really? He put the frosting back in the cabinet and joined her in the living room. Since she obviously had no desire to catch up, he might as well move on to business. “How much do you know about the True Disciples?”

She curled up in one of the two chairs and started channel surfing with the sound muted. “Only what the police told me.”

He took the other seat. Since she kept the volume off he viewed that as an invitation to talk. “Miguel Robles’s father, Jorge, immigrated to Chicago in the ’80s. He became deeply involved in the Latin Disciples. About fifteen years ago, there was a falling-out between Jorge and the leader of the Latin Disciples. Jorge walked away, starting his own band of merry men. Five years later, Jorge found himself facing cancer, so he started the transition of power to Miguel. A decade from now Miguel, since he has no children of his own, would likely have been doing the same with Diego.”

With her sister’s channel on the screen, Eva set the remote aside and turned her attention to Todd. “He sees me as the person who not only stole his younger brother’s life but also as the person who turned his entire future upside down.”

The situation was far graver than she understood. “Avenging Diego’s death is a matter of honor, Eva. Whatever else happens, he has no choice but to kill you or lose face. Personally, I don’t understand why the police didn’t take you into protective custody.”

She glared at him as if he'd offended her. "Your boss said there aren't enough resources to go around."

Victoria was right about that part, but the sheer enormity of the situation should have prompted a stronger reaction. Not that he was suggesting the police didn't want to stop Miguel, but sometimes he wondered if their priorities were in order.

"That's true," he admitted. "But some cases fall outside the parameters of the norm. Those cases should be evaluated differently. Yours, in my humble opinion, is one of those cases."

She laughed. "You've never been humble in your life." With that announcement, she pushed up from her chair and walked to the window.

Maybe there was a time when her pronouncement was true, but not anymore. He hesitated only a moment before joining her. On the street below the traffic was heavy. The neighborhood was a nice one. Towering, mature trees lined the street. Much-desired shopping and restaurants were only a few blocks away. He'd driven past her building more than once since his return to Chicago last year. Mentioning that too-telling fact would hardly be a good thing, he decided.

"I'm sure you're aware that the police see you as their first real opportunity to get this guy."

She nodded. "Your boss mentioned it."

"I can understand how much they want him and the idea that using you as bait somehow serves the greater good, but I'm not them. My job is to protect you at all costs."

She glanced at him, the worry in her eyes tugging at his gut.

"So let's not make you an easy target by standing in front of this window." He touched her arm. She stiffened but he curled his fingers around the soft limb anyway and gently tugged her back to the pair of chairs they had deserted.

Rather than sit down, she stared up at him. She searched his eyes, worry clouding hers. "Do you really believe you can stop him?" She licked her lips, drawing his attention there. He remembered her taste as vividly as if he'd only just kissed her. "That all by yourself," she said, dragging him from the forbidden memory, "you can somehow do what the police haven't been able to do in what? A decade?"

No matter the seriousness of her question, this close he almost smiled at the small sprinkling of freckles on her nose and cheeks. She had hated those tiny freckles and he had loved them. This close he noticed there was a line or two on her gorgeous face that hadn't been there before, but those fine lines only added to her beauty. He wanted her to trust him. He desperately wanted her to believe in him again. Whatever else she thought of him, he would never lie to her. He hadn't lied all those years ago and he wasn't about to start now.

"First, I don't operate by the same rules as the police. Giving them grace, their hands are tied to some degree by the very laws they've sworn to uphold. Second, I can't promise I'll be able to stop Robles, but I can promise that I'll die trying."

EVA PULLED FREE of his touch and turned away from him. She couldn't bear the way he looked at her…as if he truly cared. Of course he probably possessed some basic human compassion for her as a person but otherwise she was nothing more than an assignment and maybe a potential opportunity for sexual release. Not that finding willing women would be an issue for him—it hadn't been a decade ago and it certainly wouldn't be now. He was still incredibly handsome and far too charming.

She closed her eyes. *So not fair, Eva.* She didn't know the man standing in her apartment right now. She knew the college guy he used to be. The super hot guy who seemed to show up in the library every Tuesday and Thursday evening just like she had. The guy with the beautiful lean, muscled body and scruffy, thick hair that made her want to twine her fingers in it while she traced every line and ridge of his healthy male body with her other hand. The guy who stole her heart and ruined her for anyone else.

Not once in ten years had she been kissed the way Todd Christian kissed her. Not a single time in the last decade had another man—not that there had been very many—made love to her the way Todd Christian had.

Eva hugged her arms around herself. What kind of fool permitted *that* guy back into her life?

A desperate one.

A *splat, splat, splat* echoed in the room. The window rattled in its frame. Eva instinctively backed up, her body bumping into his. Rivulets of red rained down from a cloud of red in the center of the window.

Todd pulled her behind the chairs. "Stay down while I have a look."

He moved across the room and took a position next to the window, out of sight from whoever was out there firing something at her window. Eva peeked around the chair and studied the damage to the window. It didn't appear broken or cracked. The splats looked like the ones made by a paintball gun.

Was this just another warning from the man who wanted his revenge?

"We need something to cover this window."

Todd was suddenly standing over her, holding out his hand. She ignored it and stood. "I have extra sheets in the linen closet."

He nodded. "You round those up while I give Detective Marsh an update."

"Are you working with the police?" She didn't know why she was surprised. The Colby Agency was a prominent firm. Her internet research had indicated that Victoria was known and respected by everyone who was anyone in Chicago. She'd been voted woman of the year more than once.

"Just keeping them up to speed on what's going on. If I play nice, hopefully they'll do the same for me."

She nodded. Made sense. While he spoke to the detective she went to the bathroom. She'd tried really hard the past few days to stay strong. To keep it together. The first day, Saturday, hadn't been so bad. Her sister had kept her mind off the horror of the previous night until Eva went unconscious from sheer exhaustion.

In the bathroom, she closed the door and sagged against it. But then the threats had begun. Eva was so thankful when Lena was sent out of town. No matter that her sister had wanted to stay and had insisted that she dove into the fray of danger every time she walked onto a hot news scene, this was different. Eva was the target. She felt certain this Miguel Robles would like nothing better than to use her sister to hurt her.

At least she didn't have to worry so much about that part right now. Lena would be in Washington, DC, for several days.

With her sister safely out of reach, Eva could focus on keeping herself alive.

The memory of her neighbor's door nagged at her. Mrs. Cackowski had mentioned going to New York to visit her daughter. The plan was she would leave today and spend the upcoming Mother's Day weekend with her daughter and her family. She would fly back next Tuesday. Mrs. Cackowski said flying on Tuesdays was cheaper. Eva wasn't entirely sure that was true but the idea appeared to make the older lady happy.

The trouble was, the No Solicitors magnet was not on her door. Mrs. Cackowski and Eva had a routine. Whenever her neighbor was away from home, whether for the day or for a week, she put the magnet on her door. When she returned, it was removed. This way, even if Eva missed talking to her she knew to keep an eye on the elderly woman's apartment. She usually left a key with Eva so she could water her plants if it was an extended vacation, but not this time.

Maybe her neighbor's flight had been changed at the last minute. If Mrs. Cackowski would break down and get a cell phone, Eva could call and check with her. She should probably call the property manager and tell him about the red paint—or whatever it was—all over her window. The two windows in her apartment didn't open so it wasn't like she could clean it up herself. Since she faced the street her neighbors wouldn't be happy about the unsightly mess.

A knock on the door had her jumping away from it. "You okay in there?"

Eva put her hand to her throat. "Fine. I just need a moment."

She went to the sink and turned on the water. How was she supposed to deal with all this? Her actions had caused a man's death. Shouldn't she feel something besides empty and cold about it by now? Last night a patient had required a psychological consult. After the doctor had assessed the patient, Eva had spoken to the psychiatrist briefly about what happened to her. He'd warned that she was in the shock and denial phase right now. In time the reality would hit and she might fall apart.

Start counseling now, he'd warned.

Like every other nurse and doctor she knew, the last person she wanted to spend time fixing was herself. It was far easier to take care of everyone else's problems. Funny how she'd worked so hard and long to keep her life simple. Work, eat, sleep and repeat. Once in a great while she bothered with dating.

How had her simple existence turned so suddenly complicated?

Maybe the shrink had been right about the shock and denial. She had pretty much been attempting to pretend Friday night never happened. She might have been successful if not for the continued threats.

After splashing some water on her face, she reached for the hand towel and dabbed her skin dry. At this point she didn't know if she had enough time left to reach the reality phase.

She could be dead before then.

Chapter Four

Wednesday, May 9, 8:15 a.m.

Eva scarcely slept at all. Between worrying about what the gang leader Miguel Robles might do next and the idea that Todd Christian was on her sofa, how could she hope to sleep? At some point after two this morning, she'd finally drifted to sleep only to dream about being chased by killers. She'd jerked awake in a cold sweat to the sound of the shower.

For the next several minutes she'd battled with her errant mind and its inability to control the wellspring of images involving Todd Christian naked in her shower. When he'd finished and she was certain he'd moved to the kitchen, she reluctantly headed to the bathroom. With the water as hot as she could bear it, she still couldn't wash away the scent of him...it clung to the tile walls, to the bar of homemade soap a friend had given her, insisting that no bodywash on the planet could compete. Despite rinsing the soap thoroughly, simply smoothing the bar over her skin aroused her. Shivers tumbled over her skin with every slow stroke. Her nipples hardened with the sweet ache of need and she once again found herself fighting to keep memories of their lovemaking at bay. How could those memories still be so vivid? So intoxicating?

Todd Christian was like an addictive drug. And like the wrong kind of drug, he was bad for her.

By the time she turned off the water she felt ready to explode with tension. Taking her time, she dried her skin and then her hair. By the time she finished, she had gone from the edge of orgasm to teeth-grinding frustration.

This arrangement was not going to work. No way, no how.

Shoulders squared, purple Wednesday scrubs and her most comfortable nursing clogs on, she walked into the kitchen to tell the bane of her existence he had to sleep somewhere else. She could not have him in her apartment like this. There had to be some other arrangement. Might as well get it over with now and salvage what little sanity she had left. The sooner, the better.

"Good morning." He smiled and saluted her with his coffee mug. "I scrambled a few eggs and popped in some toast while you were showering. Hope you don't mind."

If the scent of the freshly made toast and the coffee hadn't distracted her, she might have been able to hang on to her determination. Instead, her need for fuel took over and she decided she would tell him this wasn't going to work as soon as she ate. Why let the food get cold? The least she could do was be civil. If she let her frustration show she would only look immature. She would die before she allowed him to see how easily he could still get to her.

"Morning." She poured a cup of coffee and reached for a slice of toast.

The sheets they'd tacked up over the living room window last night blocked the morning light she usually enjoyed. The lack of natural light was a stark reminder that her life was a mess. She had killed a man.

She sagged against the counter. Didn't matter that she hadn't meant to kill him; he was dead just the same. Nineteen years old. A damn kid.

"Don't go there, Eva."

She blinked, his voice pulling her from the troubling thoughts. "I… I was just thinking about work."

He shook his head. "You were thinking about what happened in that bathroom on Friday night. The pain was written all over your face."

How the hell could he still read her so well all these years later? It wasn't fair. Just another reason he had to go. Today. She absolutely could not allow him back into her life. She'd thought she could handle this situation, but she couldn't. It was impossible. Unrealistic.

"You don't know me anymore, Todd." She set her cup aside and grabbed one of the two plates he'd placed on the counter. She raked a few eggs into the plate and snagged a fork. "I'm not the same naive young girl I was ten years ago."

He stared at her with that intensity she knew all too well. "No, you definitely are not."

She bit back the urge to demand what he meant by his statement.

He pushed off the counter on the opposite side of the island and reached for the remaining plate. She told herself not to watch every damned move he made but somehow she couldn't stop herself. It was like driving past an accident—no amount of willpower would prevent her from looking. His fingers wrapped around the fork and he lifted the eggs to his mouth. His lips closed over the silver tines. Her mouth watered and she forced her attention back to her own fork. She poked a bite of eggs and stuffed them into her mouth. Butter, eggs, cheese and pepper combined into an incredible burst of flavor on her tongue. Simple but so tasty. Most mornings she grabbed a cup of yogurt or a breakfast bar and devoured it on the way to work. A groan of utter satisfaction slipped past her lips.

"Thank you." He grinned. "You still love cheesy scrambled eggs."

The bite of toast she'd taken was suddenly like cardboard on her tongue. How could she have forgotten how he made eggs with cheese and toast for her every time she stayed over at his place? More important, how could he remember something as mundane as eggs and cheese?

She finished off her coffee and glanced at her watch. "I should go."

Before he could say something else she didn't want to hear, she disappeared into the bathroom, which also prevented her from having to look at him. She brushed her teeth and put her hair up in a clip, then stared at her reflection. It didn't take a shrink to narrow down the issue in front of her right now. Todd was the only man she'd ever loved—her first love. He'd taught her how to appreciate her body and to appreciate sex. How to fall completely in love with him. He'd allowed her to believe that what they had was never going to end.

Only it had.

She might have been able to forgive him, to put it

behind her and never look back, except that she hadn't been able to fall in love again. No one had been able to lure her down that path or even near it. No matter that an entire decade had passed, she could not feel for anyone else what she had felt for Todd Christian.

Staring at her reflection, Eva realized the one thing that really mattered in all this: staying alive. All this lamenting over how he left her and ruined her for any other man was ridiculous. A man was dead. She had killed him. And now his older brother wanted vengeance. Whining and complaining about the apparent best man to protect her until the situation was sorted out was ridiculous. Worse, it was childish and petulant. She was a grown damn woman. A nurse, for God's sake.

It was time she starting acting like a mature woman rather than a heartbroken college girl. And she would be damned if she would let him see just how much power he still held over her.

Summoning the courage that allowed her to work in one of the region's most demanding ERs, she walked out of the bathroom and grabbed her bag. "I'll see you at the hospital."

He dried his hands on the rooster-embellished hand towel she'd thought matched so well with the simple decorating scheme in her kitchen—the kitchen he had cleaned up after preparing breakfast. She ignored the gesture. What else was he going to do while he waited for her? The whole breakfast and cleanup thing was probably just his way of killing time.

"We should ride together, Eva. It's far more—"

"Then I guess you'll be riding with me." She headed for the door. He was not going to be in charge of every aspect of her existence until this was over. It was bad enough he'd invaded her home and her dreams. She wasn't giving him any more power.

She walked out the door and waited until he'd done the same. Once the door was locked she turned to head for the stairwell but hesitated. Still nothing on Mrs. Cackowski's door. She'd forgotten to call and ask the property manager if he'd spoken to her. *You're a bad neighbor, Eva.*

"Give me a minute," she muttered to her shadow. Without further explanation she banged on her neighbor's door loud enough to wake the dead. No answer. No TV sounds. Eva knocked again. An entire minute passed with no answer.

"I can open the door if you'd like."

She glared at him. "You're offering to break into my neighbor's apartment?"

He shrugged those broad, broad shoulders and smiled. "If you bang any harder you're going to break the door down anyway. Trust me, my way is a lot less messy."

"I can call the property manager." She frowned. "I should have done that already."

"Why waste the time? I'll only be a couple of seconds."

For three seconds she thought about telling him to screw off, but then she thought of the men who had followed her and made all those threats—the men who had killed no telling how many people already. What if Mrs. Cackowski was in there bleeding to death? "Okay. Fine. Open the door."

He stepped toward the door in question, forcing

her to back away. Another thought occurred to her. "This can't be legal."

That grin appeared on his lips once more. "Not in any way, shape or form."

Good grief. She knew this. No more pretending. Her cognitive abilities were officially compromised. "Then why are you doing it?"

"Because you asked me to."

"Just stop!" She could not think straight with him around. Damn it! She should just go to work and hope she didn't kill any patients.

"Too late." He gave the door a push and it swung inward.

For a moment Eva couldn't move. She felt frozen to the spot. This felt wrong. No, that wasn't true. Mrs. Cackowski's absence without putting out the damned magnetic sign was wrong.

"Would you like me to go in and check on her?"

His voice snapped Eva into action. "No. I'll do it." She glanced first right then left. Thank God none of her other neighbors were in the hall to see what they were doing.

Eva took a breath and crossed the threshold. Why not add the entering to the breaking? "Mrs. Cackowski, are you home?"

The living room was tidy as always. Mrs. Cackowski had told her how when she moved in years ago she had brought with her the salmon-colored sofa her husband had purchased for their tenth anniversary some forty years back. Three hand crocheted dollies lined the camelbacked sofa. The upholstered chair that swiveled and rocked in which her neighbor spent her days, the coffee table where she served tea every time Eva visited, all looked exactly as it should.

Except there was no Mrs. Cackowski. No sign of a struggle or any other untoward activity. She called her neighbor's name again. Still no answer.

Todd abruptly moved past her and checked the kitchen. Irritation nudged Eva. "Excuse me. This is my neighbor's home. What happened to me having a look around while you wait at the door?"

He shot her a wink. "I've never been a patient man."

Well, now, that was the truth...except when it came to making love. His ability to hold out, to restrain his own needs for hers, had seemed boundless.

No more thinking about sex, Eva. She followed him to the bedroom. No Mrs. Cackowski. Bed was made. He reached for the closet door. "What are you doing?"

He shrugged. "We've come this far."

She stormed up to the door. "I'm certain Mrs. Cackowski would be more comfortable with me checking her closet."

He held up his hands and backed away. "Whatever you say. This time," he warned.

She glared at him, then opened the door. The closet was as neat and undisturbed as the rest of the apartment. Her suitcase sat on the floor of the closet next to a neatly arranged row of practical shoes. Had she bought a new suitcase? Eva shook her head. Maybe the trip had been cancelled. Maybe her neighbor was merely at an appointment. Paranoia was obviously taking full control.

Eva slammed the door. "Let's just go before we get caught."

She walked back to the living room. Todd hurried around her and out the front door before she realized he was right behind her. She glanced back at her neighbor's favorite chair once more. Maybe the elderly woman's age was finally catching up to her and she'd simply forgotten to tell Eva her plans had changed. She turned the thumb lock on the knob. She couldn't lock the deadbolt without the key but at least she could secure the door.

Eva had the number for Mrs. Cackowski's daughter—maybe she'd give her a call today just to be sure. This Robles business was making her second-guess everything.

Once the door was locked again, they left. Todd entered the stairwell ahead of her, then gave her the all clear. Eva reminded herself that he was doing his job. The situation was serious so she should let him. Tamping down her frustration for now, she followed her bodyguard down the stairs and through the lobby.

As they exited the building the burst of fresh air helped her mood a little. The sweet smell of the azaleas lining the sidewalk lifted her spirits. She could make this a better day. All she had to do was keep the proper mindset. Focus on her work. Maybe tonight she'd go to the gym and run a few miles on the treadmill. Running always did amazing things for her outlook. She and her sister participated in a couple of 5k runs every year in memory of their mother and in support of breast cancer research.

Todd suddenly stopped. His arm went out, blocking Eva's path. "Stay behind me and call 911."

When she would have asked why, her gaze settled on her car. The windshield and the two windows she could see had been bashed in. Red spray paint or something on that order had been used to write a warning across the hood.

Death is coming.

Her heart started to pound.

Todd pulled her behind the nearest parked vehicle. “Stay down and make the call.”

Her hand shook as she dragged her cell from her bag. Her fingers turned to ice as she stabbed the necessary digits and put through the call. She watched Todd move around the parking garage as she answered the dispatcher’s questions. He carried a gun now. She hadn’t even realized he was armed. She provided her location and explained the situation. No, as far as she could see the perpetrators were no longer on the scene. Yes, the police needed to come. No, there was no need for an ambulance. The dispatcher assured her the police were en route. Eva ended the call and absently shoved the phone back into her bag. She stretched her neck in an effort to get a look around.

There was no one else in the garage except the two of them. At least if there was, he or they were hiding. She doubted the bastards would hide. They liked to show off…to inspire fear. Scumbags.

Todd returned to her car. This time he looked inside, though he made no move to open the doors. Preserving the scene, she realized. If he touched any part of the car, he might disturb fingerprints left behind by the bad guys. Even as she considered his reasoning, he walked to the rear of her vehicle. He leaned down to inspect something in the area of the trunk and the lid suddenly sprang open. Todd disappeared behind it.

Eva’s tension moved to a new level, sending her heart into her throat. She looked around. Still didn’t see anyone. Before she could talk herself out of the move, she stood and started walking toward her car. She opened her mouth to call his name but her voice deserted her.

No shots rang out. No sound of scuffling or fighting. Yet, she instinctively understood that something was very, very wrong.

As she reached the hood, Todd stepped from behind the open trunk lid. "Let's go back inside until the police get here."

He was moving toward her as the words penetrated the uncertainty that had paralyzed her ability to reason. When his hand landed on her arm, she trembled. Why was he trying to urge her back inside now? Why was the trunk still open?

Sirens blared in the distance. The police were almost here. They should stay put. Explain what happened.

"Eva," he said, his voice frighteningly soft, "I want to take you back inside."

She stared up at him. The blue eyes she knew as well as she knew her own showed no emotion…no indication of what the trouble was. And then she understood. He was hiding something terrible from her.

Her throat went as dry as bone. "What's in the trunk?"

Two police cruisers barreled into the parking garage and skidded to a stop.

Todd gripped her elbow and urged her in the direction of the nearest cruiser "I'll explain everything in a minute. Let's just make sure you stay safe until—"

Eva broke free of his grip and ran to her car. Her

heart thudded so hard in her chest she couldn't catch a breath.

"Eva, wait!"

She'd spoken to Lena yesterday. She was safe in DC. Eva rounded the back of the vehicle. Fear constricted her chest. She stared into the open trunk. At first what she saw didn't register. Pink dress…ghostly pale legs. Plastic that looked shrink-wrapped around the pasty skin of the woman's face. Gray hair. White cheeks…purple lips encircled a mouth that was open wide as if gasping for air. Dull, unseeing eyes.

Mrs. Cackowski.

Chapter Five

Chicago Police Department, 10:30 a.m.

Lorena Cackowski's daughter had been notified of her mother's death. She was on her way to Chicago from New York now. The preliminary conclusion from the medical examiner was asphyxiation. The murder weapon appeared to be the plastic. Manner of death: homicide.

Todd paced the corridor outside the interview room. The two detectives had insisted on interviewing Eva and him separately. He hadn't been happy about the idea, but she had assured him that she was okay with it so he'd backed off.

How the hell could Robles order the murder of a helpless, elderly woman like that?

Sick bastards.

The way Eva had trembled, the tears pouring down her cheeks, had torn him apart. He would make Robles pay for hurting her. As much as the desire to go after that revenge burned inside him, his top priority had to be keeping Eva safe.

The door opened and Detective Marsh stepped into

the corridor. "Almost done." He shook his head. "This thing is getting damned hairy."

"Who's the new guy?" Todd gestured to the interview room the man had exited. Marsh was the one to take Todd's statement but another detective had shown up for Eva's official interview. "He wasn't your partner the last time we had the pleasure of your company."

Marsh hitched his head toward the closed door. "Carter is from Gang Intelligence. He's been working this one behind the scenes since the war on Friday night. Until this morning he was more focused on what happened before Diego and his friends hit the ER. Everything's changed now."

Murder had a way of changing things for sure.

"This murder will draw a lot of press to the department," Marsh confessed.

Todd nodded. "Have the evidence techs found anything in the vic's apartment that ties Robles's people to what happened?"

For whatever reason, the usual gang markings hadn't been left behind in the vic's apartment or on Eva's car. It was possible that Robles considered this personal rather than gang business. Either way, he was behind the threats and now at least one murder related to Eva.

"Not yet," Marsh said with a weary sigh. "These guys might be thugs but the ones in charge aren't stupid. They know how to cover their tracks. Even if we're lucky enough to have witnesses we know for a fact were right there watching, they rarely talk. Too afraid, and who can blame them?"

Todd understood that the I-didn't-see-anything mentality in situations like this happened all too often.

Fear was the primary motive. "I spoke with my boss. We're taking Ms. Bowman to a safe house. You have a problem with that?"

Marsh shrugged. "I think Carter is making that offer as we speak. Yours, ours, wherever she is protected works for me."

Todd was glad to hear it. "We prefer our own place. No offense."

Marsh held up his hands. "None taken. Just keep us advised."

"Will do." Todd intended to leave that part in Victoria's more-than-capable hands. She had her own high-level sources inside Chicago PD. Todd had no reason to doubt Marsh's integrity or Carter's, for that matter. Still, he wasn't willing to take the risk that there could be a leak. Frankly, CPD had its share of problems, and he didn't intend for Eva to become a casualty of the department's recent highly publicized internal issues.

The interview room door opened once more and Eva walked out, followed by Sergeant Carter. The senior detective thrust his hand toward Todd. "We appreciate your cooperation, Christian. We'll have other questions, I'm certain. So keep us apprised of your location."

Evidently Eva had already told him the Colby Agency planned to take her to a private safe house. "You got it, Sergeant."

Eva only glanced at Todd as he spoke. Her eyes were red from crying. She kept her slender arms tight around herself. The mere idea that her life was in jeopardy was a painful reminder of just how fleeting life could be. He reached for her, placed his hand at the small of her back, hoping to convey reassurance as he guided her out of this place. The sooner they were as far as possible from the streets Robles influenced, the happier he would be.

When they had reached the lobby, he waylaid her at the main exit door and leaned in close. "Ian Michaels is picking us up. He'll drop us at the safe house. A new car will be waiting for us there. I guarantee Robles won't find us where we're going. You will be safe there."

She nodded.

Outside, Michaels waited at the curb in front of the main entrance. He glanced in the rearview mirror as they settled in the back seat.

Todd made the introductions.

"I'm aware this is a terrifying situation," Michaels said to Eva with another quick glance in the rearview mirror as he eased out onto the street, "but, rest assured, we will take care of the situation."

"Thank you."

Todd resisted the urge to scoot across the seat and put his arm around her. He was fairly confident she wouldn't appreciate the gesture however well he meant it. It would be in his best interest to stay out of her personal space for now. Keeping a couple of feet between them would be the smartest thing to do. His instincts went a little haywire when they were too close for too long.

He'd thought of her often over the years. Never expected to see her again. Even after he moved back to the Windy City, he hadn't worried. Chicago was a big place. No reason they should run into each other and be forced to deal with the lingering awkwardness. Not that he hadn't looked her up. He had. He'd checked up on her from time to time over the years before he returned to Chicago. He'd felt immensely proud when she graduated nursing school. Mostly he'd watched for an engagement announcement. Not that Eva was big on social media, but her sister, Lena, was. He'd admired the birthday pics Lena had posted each year since the last time Todd had seen Eva. He closely scrutinized the occasional vacation shot or night out on the town he ferreted out on social media. He'd scoured each one looking for the man who had taken his place.

That feeling—dread—he always experienced when he thought of her with someone else filled his chest now. *Idiot*. He'd left her because he couldn't handle where he felt the relationship was headed, and yet, he still couldn't bear the idea of her with anyone else.

He was worse than an idiot. He was a jerk.

Finding Michaels watching him in the rearview mirror warned his brooding hadn't escaped the older man's scrutiny. Ian Michaels had been with Victoria at the Colby Agency since she and her first husband started the agency. A former US Marshal, Michaels was particularly good at reading people. Todd figured the man likely already had a firm handle on how he was feeling right now.

Great.

Nothing like the world knowing how badly you'd screwed up whether it was yesterday or ten years ago.

He glanced at Eva and immediately turned his attention back to the street. He'd been a selfish bastard and he'd walked away from the only woman who had ever made him want more than right now.

Nothing he could do about the past. But he could make sure her future was free of thugs like Robles.

Bastard.

"Brace yourselves," Michaels announced. "We have a tail to lose."

THE CAR ROCKETED forward and fear trapped deep in Eva's chest.

Todd's hand was suddenly against her back, ushering her down onto the seat. He used his own body like a shield, hovering over her as the car swung from lane to lane. When he pressed more firmly against her, she started to demand what the hell he was doing, but the sound of glass shattering and metal popping silenced her.

"Hang on!"

The driver shouted the words and then slammed on the brakes. The car slid sideways. For an instant Todd's body crushed against hers, every rigid muscle cradling her. Eva's stomach lurched as much from his nearness as from the wild ride. Before she could catch her breath, the car was rocketing forward once more.

Another of those crazy sliding turns was followed by a roar of the car's engine as they zoomed through the city streets. Eva was grateful she couldn't see. No doubt pedestrians and other vehicles were scattered all around them. One wrong move and the crash would be horrific.

A moment passed with no abrupt moves and her respiration leveled out to some degree. She realized then that her fingers were clutched in the fabric of Todd's shirt. One muscled thigh had burrowed between hers, his knee anchored to the seat, holding her firmly in place. His other knee was planted in the floorboard and his upper torso shielded hers. The scent of his strong body, clean and vaguely sweet, filled her lungs and made her dizzy.

Pull yourself together, girl.

Eva took a breath and ordered her fingers to unclench. She was still working on the move when Ian Michaels announced, "All clear."

Todd's face turned down toward hers, making her breath catch all over again. "You okay?"

She nodded. Her fingers finally relaxed their death grip. Todd helped her upright once more and she struggled to right her clothes and her hair. She forced herself to breathe slowly and deeply until her heart stopped racing. She kept her gaze on the street. The rear windshield was shattered but, thankfully, remained in place.

Eva closed her eyes and told herself over and over that everything would be okay. Forty-five minutes later she still wasn't completely convinced as Mr. Michaels took an exit from I-94 toward Central Avenue in Highland Park. From there he drove to Egandale Road. Eva stared out the window at nothing at all until finally the car slowed and then stopped at a keypad outside an enormous gate. A high fence was almost completely camouflaged by mature trees and shrubbery. Michaels entered the code for the gate, rolling on through as it opened.

Todd glanced at her and smiled. "Don't worry. I've been here a couple of times before. It's not as uninviting as it looks from here. The security wall only makes it look like a prison."

As they rounded a deep bend in the long drive, Eva spotted the house. It sat in the middle of thick woods.

"Beyond all those trees," Todd said as if he'd read

her mind, "is Lake Michigan. The property includes a helipad as well as a boat dock. There are plenty of ways to escape trouble if the need arises. But it would prove extremely difficult for trouble to get into the compound. The walls around the property are lined with cameras. Anyone gets close, we'll know it. A state-of-the-art security system keeps the home secure. Robles's men won't be able to get to you here."

The car came to a stop in front of an enormous house that looked more like a castle than a home. Eva stared at the stone façade that might have looked cold if not for the lush border of flowering plants, climbing vines and shrubs. "Oh my God."

Michaels looked over the seat. "Call if you need anything else."

"Will do," Todd responded as he climbed out.

He was around the vehicle and opening her door before she had the presence of mind to grab her bag and prepare to exit the car.

Ian Michaels drove away in the car with its broken glass and bullet holes. Eva turned to the massive house, clinging to her leather bag as if it was the only thing left grounding her. At the moment she was pretty sure it was. This insane situation had taken her from her home, had kept her from work, and cost her neighbor her life. On cue, her head started to spin.

Todd's steady hand was suddenly at her back, ushering her up the stone steps. "All the windows are bulletproof," he explained. "A voice command can close the steel shutters over them." At the door, he placed his hand against a large pad. As soon as the system had identified him, the locks on the door released.

He opened the door and waited for her to enter ahead of him.

Inside, the home was large but warmly decorated. The layout appeared user-friendly. The floors were a smooth, rich wood that flowed forward in a welcoming path. The walls were coated in an inviting beige bordered by gorgeous ornate trim drenched in a gloss white.

"There's a six-car garage with a nice selection of vehicles, all well equipped for speed and safety if we need to take a drive. Whenever the house is not in use, the agency investigators take turns, on a rotating basis, spending weekends here for the sole purpose of driving the vehicles. I was here two weekends ago. The solitude is incredibly relaxing."

As imposing as everything about the house was, there was no denying its infinite beauty. Someone had gone to a great deal of trouble to create a luxurious getaway. "Has anyone ever lived here?"

Todd shook his head. "Victoria had it built to replace the agency's former safe house."

Eva took her gaze from the stunning view out the towering windows. "Former safe house?"

"She and her first husband built a lake house shortly after starting the Colby Agency," Todd explained, "but their seven-year-old son was abducted from there, so Victoria couldn't bring herself to live in that house again."

Eva's hand went to her throat. "How awful. Did they find him?"

Todd shook his head. "No. Twenty years later, he found her. Her first husband had died years before. But Jim, the son, found his way home. He and his family live in the old lake house now. And Victoria and Lucas, her second husband, live in a gated community near there."

Eva was glad the story had a happy ending. It was too bad that Victoria's first husband hadn't lived to see his son return.

"The kitchen is stocked with anything you could want." He turned to Eva. "If you'd like to eat."

"I'm not really hungry." How could she eat? Poor Mrs. Cackowski was dead. She squeezed her eyes shut. Murdered. It didn't seem real…except she knew it was.

"Understandable," he said, drawing her attention back to him. He gestured to the staircase that wound around the far wall and up to the second floor. "Your room is the second on the left. Anything you might need during your stay has been provided."

Eva nodded. She needed some time to gather her composure. "I think I'll lie down for a while."

"I'll be close if you need me."

She nodded before moving to the stairs.

"Eva."

She turned back to him.

"I wish there was something I could say to make this crappy day better. You're hurting, I know. Feeling guilty. Blaming yourself for Mrs. Cackowski's death. But this isn't your fault. You just happened to be in the wrong place at the wrong time and got caught up in a gang war. But this will all get better. I promise."

Eva wanted to cry but she felt all cried out. She nodded and trudged up the stairs.

How would she ever face her neighbor's daughter? What words could she say to explain that the woman's death was her fault? No matter what Todd said, it was true. If Eva hadn't moved in across the hall from the sweet lady…if she hadn't killed a gang leader's brother…

Tears burning down her cheeks, she opened the second door on the left and walked into the room. The sheer size of the space distracted her for a moment, but it was another of those towering windows that drew her across the lush carpeting to the other side of the room. The view over the courtyard made her smile even as more of those tears spilled from her eyes. A pool with a gorgeous waterfall surrounded by lush shrubs and flowers. Rock paths bordered by dense greenery circled and cut across the rear property, creating a maze. If she were on vacation, this would be the perfect place to get lost.

But she wasn't on vacation. She was hiding from a murderer. Her bodyguard was a few steps away. If only Mrs. Cackowski had had a bodyguard.

Eva scrubbed the tears from her cheeks and turned her back to the window. She walked to the first of two doors. She couldn't think about that awful truth anymore. She had to be strong. Had to do whatever necessary to make this right.

So she focused on the mundane. Her room for the next few days had a generous walk-in closet. Several outfits—jeans, sweaters, slacks, blouses with matching shoes—had been hung at eye level. An ottoman sat in the center of the room. On top were a couple of nightshirts and a selection of lacy panties and bras.

Eva shook her head as she touched the tags on the items. She would have been certain they'd raided her closet if not for the product tags. The agency had gone to the trouble to purchase a mini wardrobe just like one she would have bought for herself based on what she had in her own closet. Why hadn't they just grabbed some of her stuff?

Didn't matter.

The next door led to a bathroom that would wow the most discriminating of tastes. From the hairbrush to the beauty products, she could be in her own bathroom except her entire space would fit into the tub of this one. This was very nice of Victoria. She hoped the arrangement wasn't costing Dr. Pierce a fortune.

Eva stared at her reflection. An elegant hiding place. And that was what she was doing. Hiding.

Unless the police caught Miguel Robles—and they hadn't been able to do so in more than a dozen years—or Robles killed her as he intended, this would never be over. More people could be hurt or murdered... like her sister.

How could she possibly hide like this?

She couldn't.

She owed it to Mrs. Cackowski and to herself to make sure Miguel Robles paid for his crimes. He shouldn't be allowed to get away with murdering a helpless elderly woman or anyone else. Since the police hadn't been able to get him, maybe she could. After all, she had the right kind of bait.

She was the woman who'd killed his little brother.

Miguel Robles wanted to kill her, too.

Sticking to her routine, staying out there where Robles could find her was the only way to lure him. The realization settled onto her like a massive stone crushing her chest. It was true. All this time the police had been unable to find enough evidence against him, but she could draw him out, make him careless—because he wanted so badly to avenge his brother.

All she had to do was convince her bodyguard to go along with her plan.

Eva trembled at the thought of Todd. That part might prove the most difficult. She had noticed the look of guilt in his eyes more than once. He felt bad for having left her all those years ago. She'd gotten that message loud and clear. If he was looking to make up and to be friends, he could forget it. She could never be friends with him.

She couldn't trust herself.

Better to stay at odds with someone so dangerous to her sanity.

A pang of hunger vied for her attention. She should eat and figure out how to convince Todd that her plan was the right one. It was the least she could do for her sweet neighbor. Dr. Pierce had ordered her not to come to work today. That was okay. The truth was she needed to pull herself back together before she dared set foot out of this safe zone.

Not to mention she had her work cut out for her right here. As much as she would love to pretend she could do what needed to be done on her own, she was smarter than that. She needed Todd's full cooperation.

She smoothed a hand over her clothes, tugged the loosening clip from her hair and finger combed it. Steadying herself, she took a big breath and exited the luxurious bedroom. Downstairs she wandered from room to room until she found Todd. To her surprise, he was scooping vanilla ice cream into a bowl.

"I seem to recall you were a chocolate man." She

moved to the massive island in the center of the room and propped herself there.

"Don't worry." He licked the scoop and set it aside. "That's coming." He reached for a jar and spooned chocolate onto the mound of creamy vanilla ice cream. "Join me."

"I think I'll see what else is available."

He moaned, drawing her attention to his lips as he withdrew the chocolate-smeared spoon from his mouth. "You should rethink that strategy. The latest philosophy on the art of eating is that having dessert first is better."

"Maybe for a guy who's solid muscle." She opened the glass door of the double fridge. "Not for a girl who has to watch every ounce of fat she eats settle on her hips and thighs."

The salad fixings in the crisper drawer would work. She gathered the bag of greens, a basket of tomatoes and the vinaigrette dressing. She pushed the door closed with her hip.

"I don't see anything wrong with your hips or your thighs."

Eva looked from him to her lower anatomy. "I've come to appreciate how scrubs can cover a multitude of sins."

"Somehow I doubt there are any sins to hide." He shoveled another spoonful of chocolate-covered ice cream into his mouth. Chocolate dripped down his chin.

Looking away, she plopped her load on the counter and searched for a plate. As hard as she tried to focus on preparing her salad and ignoring him, her gaze kept shifting over to see if he'd swiped that chocolate from his chin.

Finally, when she couldn't take it any longer, she grabbed a napkin and walked over to him, then held it out. "You have chocolate…on your chin."

Rather than take the napkin he grabbed her hand—the one clasping the napkin—and swiped at his chin. The stubble there tickled her fingers and made her breath hitch.

"Did I get it?"

She drew her hand from the clutch of his long fingers. "Yes."

Leaving the napkin on the counter in front of him, she walked back to her salad.

"I'm telling you—" she glanced back at him as he spoke "—I don't see anything that's not exactly right with those hips."

She flashed a fake smile. "Thanks."

Determined to pretend his words, his voice—his mere presence—were not turning her inside out, she placed the grape tomatoes atop the bed of Italian mixed greens and then added the dressing. As she twisted the top back on the bottle, she realized she needed something crunchy. Crackers, croutons. Something.

A bag of croutons landed on the counter next to her plate. Todd grinned. "You always liked some crunch with your salads."

"Thanks." Evidently they both remembered plenty about each other. But there was one thing she could not afford to forget. Todd Christian had stolen her heart and then he'd left it shattered on the doorstep when he walked away.

She had every confidence she could trust him completely with her life...but he could not be trusted in any capacity with her heart.

Chapter Six

7:30 p.m.

Eva pushed to her limit. The grinding *whir* of the treadmill was the only sound in the room. She'd explored the entire house and decided a walk outside would do her good. Except Todd had insisted on accompanying her if she was setting one foot outside the house.

She'd wanted to shake him and inform him that her goal was to get as far away from him as possible. But that attitude wouldn't be conducive to cooperation.

A quick call to her friend Kim Levy had confirmed that they were shorthanded in the ER. Eva would use that as her first negotiating tactic. She doubted that particular tactic would carry much weight with her bodyguard, but it was a starting place. Then she had gone online and done extensive research on the True Disciples. She raised the incline on the treadmill and forced her exhausted body to comply. This well-equipped exercise room wasn't the only amenity in the Colby safe house. There was an office with three computers and the fastest internet access speed she had ever encountered, making her search all the easier.

She had discovered that Miguel Robles had been arrested no less than a dozen times but not once had the police been able to make it stick. He and his followers were thought to be involved in drug trafficking and gun smuggling across the northern border. Numerous murders were attributed to their ranks. Occasionally one or more of the followers would end up with a rap they couldn't escape. In each instance the gang member accepted his fate and never said a word. Deal after deal had been offered to lure in the "big fish" and not one of Robles's followers had accepted.

The elder Robles was more than the average thug. He was smart and he surrounded himself with above-average intelligence when it came to the highest level within or affiliated with his organization. Everyone from his CPA and his personal physician to the lawyers who represented him were from the city's most esteemed ranks. Just went to show what even an intelligent person with reasonable ethical standards would do for money.

Bottom line, she needed a better-than-average plan. An ordinary person like her couldn't hope to win a battle against Miguel Robles unless she had something extraordinary to offer.

Like the woman responsible for the death of his only brother.

She slowed the track speed and lowered the incline. Five miles was plenty to clock, particularly since she hadn't managed even a mile since last Friday. A few more minutes at a comfortable walk and her respiration was back to normal and she was ready to hit Stop. Eva grabbed her hand towel, patted her damp face and neck and headed for a shower. Maybe she would find an opening at dinner to discuss her concerns regarding her responsibilities at work. Other than her sister, her career was all she had. Though Dr. Pierce was onboard with her current dilemma, she doubted he would feel that way a month from now. He certainly wouldn't want to bankroll her situation forever.

Dragging out the inevitable wasn't going to alleviate this situation.

In the hall, she ran headlong into her bodyguard. She stumbled back in surprise, her fatigued muscles instantly reacting to the hard contours of his. "Sorry." She cleared her throat to buy time to steady herself. "I was lost in thought."

A bone-melting smile stretched across his lips. "Looks like you showed that treadmill who's boss."

"Ha, ha." She dabbed at her forehead.

His gaze slid down her body, lingering on her legs before returning to her face. The fitted running leggings were a little too well fitted, but there hadn't been anything else suitable for her workout in the provided wardrobe. The tank wasn't much better. Far tinier and tighter than she felt comfortable wearing with him around. The running shoes were high-end, and her size, and inordinately comfortable. As long as she was stuck here with him, she intended to spend as much time in the gym as possible. Alone, preferably.

Yet, deep down she understood that all the workouts in the world would not stop *this* inevitability either if she remained holed up with him for too long.

If she was lucky she would be able to talk him into going along with her plan sooner rather than later.

"Dinner's ready."

"You made dinner?" She didn't know why she was

surprised. He made dinner for her often…before. She'd assumed that was only because he had his own apartment and she lived in the dorm. Preparing dinner at home for a date was certainly cheaper than taking her to a restaurant. All that aside, he'd been a decent cook.

"Don't get excited," he warned. "It's only spaghetti."

"As long as there's a salad I'll be in heaven." At home and at work she popped more spaghetti dinners in the microwave than she would want to admit. It was the one surefire frozen entrée she could count on.

"Take your shower. I'll put together a salad and some garlic bread and track down a bottle of wine."

He flashed another of those charming smiles and goose bumps spread over her skin. She nodded and hurried to the stairs, putting distance between them as quickly as she could without breaking into a run. After finding Mrs. Cackowski murdered, the wine sounded like the best part of dinner. She could definitely use a glass to help her relax. But she had no desire to make herself even more vulnerable to Todd—especially *alone* with him.

Between the hard run and the luxuriously long shower, she felt immensely better. It never ceased to amaze her how much working out helped adjust her outlook. Hopefully, that good, confident outlook would help with what she had to do next.

Todd was heaping sauce onto a bed of noodles on a plate when she walked into the kitchen. He glanced up. "Have a seat. I'll serve."

A memory flashed through her mind, making her step falter. The image of her naked on his dining table, warm spaghetti sauce slipping down her skin, over her breasts…followed by his tongue lapping up the spicy sauce. He'd come to the living room to drag her to the kitchen to eat. She'd been waiting for him—naked and ready for more than just dinner. Together they'd removed his clothes on the way back into the kitchen. They'd had sex and eaten and had sex again…and snacked off each other's skin. He'd poured wine into her belly button and lapped it up, including the streams that slid well below her belly button.

Eva blinked away the memory and pressed onward to the table. This was not *that* table. This was not *that* house. Here and now was not who they *once* were.

He placed the loaded plate in front of her, then reached the wine bottle toward her glass and started to pour. "Say when."

She snapped out of her haze and held up a hand. "That's more than enough."

When he'd moved away, she reached for the fork and the small salad bowl he'd left by her plate. She picked at the one thing on the menu that didn't remind her of sex with Todd.

"Do you remember that time—"

"I don't know." Her gaze snapped to his.

He laughed as he filled his wine glass. "I haven't told you which time I meant."

She poked a forkful of greens into her mouth.

"We stood in line at that Italian restaurant in the pouring rain." He laughed. "It had just opened and everyone said it was the best in the country."

A laugh bubbled into her throat before she could stop it. She swallowed to prevent choking, then washed it down with a long gulp of wine. "I remember. I told you if it wasn't the best *bigoli* pasta I'd ever eaten I was going to make you regret that forty-five-minute, soaked-to-the-bone wait."

They both laughed for a minute but when their gazes locked, the laughter died. Their clothes had dripped onto the wood floor of the restaurant as they'd eaten. They'd laughed and stared directly into each other's eyes through the entire meal and then they'd hurried home to make love. Eva exiled the memories and reached for her glass again. A long gulp of wine later, she told herself to slow down. She picked at her salad a little longer before moving on to the spaghetti. It certainly did not help that images from their previous spaghetti-eating escapes kept flashing in her head.

"Did you discover anything interesting about Miguel Robles?"

Her head came up at his question. How did he know? "You monitored my online activities?"

He ducked his head. "It's my job. What kind of bodyguard would I be if I didn't pay attention to what you're doing?"

She wanted to be angry but couldn't muster up the wherewithal. "I learned more than I wanted to know," she confessed. She might as well say what was on her mind. "The police haven't been able to stop him or even come close to trapping him. Whenever they close in on some charge, someone else always takes the fall—if there's even a fall involved."

"Robles is no fool." Todd picked up his glass of water and downed a swallow.

Eva hadn't noticed until then that he had scarcely touched his wine, reaching for the water goblet more often than not. She felt a little woozy. Clearly that was what she should have done. She'd intended to keep a clear head…but those damned memories had taken her by surprise and dragged her down a too-familiar path.

"So," she set her fork aside, "what's the plan from here? If the police don't get him, and they haven't shown any sign of success so far, what do we do?"

"We've got people working on finding a weak link."

Eva wanted to believe that was good news but honestly she didn't see how. "I'm thinking he's the kind of man who either wins or he dies. No in between."

TODD STARED AT her and this time he reached for his wine. He knew better than to have even one glass when he was on duty, but he hadn't been able to help himself. She'd wanted some distance—that part had been clear. So he'd left her alone and watched over her shoulder via the sophisticated camera system in the house. He'd watched her search the web for information about Robles. He'd watched the worry on her face, the way she gnawed on her bottom lip as she read the stories that all—every damned one—ended badly.

Then she'd decided on a workout. He'd almost lost his mind watching her supple body move in that form-fitting outfit. Finding something to occupy his mind and his hands had been necessary. Somewhere in the back of his brain some neuron misfire had sent him down memory lane with an Italian menu. It wasn't until she walked into the kitchen that he'd remembered dripping that sauce on her bare skin and licking it off. Sitting at this table for the past half hour and remembering what they had done on his table had driven him out of his mind. He was so damned hard that at the moment he might not be able to stand without embarrassing himself.

He shrugged in response to her statement. "He's smart."

"We've established that he's smart," she sniped. "The question is, what are we going to do about it?" She finished off her wine. "I can't live like this forever. I have a career. I'm needed at the ER. They're short-handed today because I'm not there. And what about Lena? She'll be coming home in a few days. How do we protect her from this insane man?"

"I see where you're going with this." He stood and grabbed his plate. He'd lost his appetite as well as his raging erection.

By the time he reached the sink she was right behind him with her own plate in hand. "Then you know there's no other option. The police won't be able to stop him. You can't take down a bad guy without evidence. Their hands are tied. He'll just allow some low man in the gang hierarchy to take the fall for Mrs. Cackowski's murder—assuming his people can be tied to the scene. My sister, my friends—no one around me—will be safe until *he* is stopped. Mrs. Cackowski deserves justice."

He took her plate from her hand and put it in the sink with his own, then strode back to the table. His frustration level was way out of control. "What makes you think the Colby Agency can do anything—besides provide protection—more than the police are already doing? More important, what is it you believe you can do?"

"That's easy. The police want to charge him with one or more of his crimes. They want to prosecute him and see that he goes away for the rest of his life. We can help make that happen."

Todd's hands stilled on the bowl of sauce and the platter of pasta he'd intended to put away. His eyes fixed on hers. "You want to put yourself at risk."

She nodded, the move stilted. "Whatever it takes."

"Christ, Eva. You know we can't do that." He plopped the food back onto the table and set his hands on his hips. She was talking about sacrificing herself—sending a sheep to slaughter. "I don't ever want to hear you talk that way again."

"This is a war," she reasoned. "In wartime a soldier does whatever necessary to stop the enemy, right? This is the same thing. We have to draw him out or he'll just lay low and keep getting away with all manner of heinous crimes."

He shook his head. "Even in wartime there are rules of engagement, and protecting every single soldier in the field is priority one."

"If he isn't stopped, he'll just keep killing people. He won't stop until someone kills him. Since we can't exactly do that, we can at least help take him down." He opened his mouth to argue and she held up a hand. "I will not sit back and risk my sister's life or those of my friends. If that's what you expect—for me to do nothing and wait—then you can just take me home right now."

Rather than argue with her, he picked up the food again and headed for the counter. Maybe the wine had gone to her head. She damned sure hadn't eaten much today. He busied himself with putting the leftovers away and loading the dishwasher.

The problem was she was right. Miguel Robles would not stop until he'd accomplished his goal. That was his MO. He wasn't the sort of man to walk away.

Too much was riding on his ability to maintain a show of strength and power. The first sniff of weakness and his loyal disciples would eat him alive.

Eva watched him, her arms crossed over her chest, anger sparking in those green eyes of hers. "You know I'm right. All the police need is a decent opportunity to get to him. I can help make that happen. For Mrs. Cackowski." Tears glistened in her eyes.

"Let me think about it." The delay tactic likely wouldn't buy him much time, but it was the best he could do at the moment. He hadn't expected her to come out of the corner she found herself in wanting to dive into battle—at least not this early in the war.

Maybe she'd been right when she told him she wasn't the same naive girl she'd been ten years ago. He sighed. Which only made him want her more.

Idiot.

"You have until morning," she warned as she backed away from him. "FYI—tomorrow I'm going back to work. Hiding isn't the answer."

Chapter Seven

The Edge
Thursday, May 10, 10:00 a.m.

"Heart rate is 119. Respiration 39. BP is 90 over 60," Eva reported, her voice carrying above the sound of the gurney's wheels rolling as the EMT and paramedic pushed the patient through the emergency entry doors.

Dr. Arnold Reagan met them just inside. "Trauma room one," he ordered.

Another nurse, Kim Levy, as well as a respiratory tech joined Eva in trauma room one, taking over the patient from the two paramedics who'd delivered the young girl via ambulance. Kim checked the patient's airway and began the insertion of a trach tube.

"She's nineteen," the paramedic said as he backed toward the door. "She was walking to class. Witnesses said the vehicle carrying the shooter never slowed down."

"Alyssa Chavez," his partner added before they left to take another call.

Eva exchanged a look with Kim a split second before Reagan parted the already-torn blouse and had a look at the patient's chest. The bullet had entered center chest. Reagan swore. Their patient was in serious respiratory distress and profound hemorrhagic shock. If the internal bleeding wasn't stopped quickly, she would exsanguinate.

In the next two minutes the patient was readied and rushed to the OR. A surgeon was already standing by. Every second counted. Her life was literally slipping away in a far too rapid stream.

Eva stripped off her gloves, her adrenaline receding swiftly, leaving her weak.

The cell phone strapped to her ankle vibrated. She started to ignore it but decided it might be her sister. At this point she didn't dare ignore a call from anyone she cared about. Why hadn't she checked on her neighbor when she first noticed something was off? Maybe if she'd... *Stop, Eva.* It was too late for what-ifs. Finding justice for Mrs. Cackowski and all the others that bastard Robles had hurt was the one thing Eva could do.

A frown furrowed across her brow at the number on the caller ID. Not one she recognized. She answered with a tentative, "Hello."

"Alyssa Chavez is on you, Ms. Bowman. How many more do you want to die for you?"

The call ended.

Eva stared at the phone, her heart pounding harder and harder against her sternum. The caller had been male with a slight Hispanic accent. She stared at the blood-stained instruments on the tray...the pile of bloody gloves and sheets on the floor...the disarray in the trauma room that told the story of desperation.

A young woman was fighting for her life and that was her fault.

Eva wheeled and stormed out of the trauma room. This was enough. If that woman died…

"Eva."

She stalled and turned to the man who had spoken. *Dr. Pierce.* Her chest had grown so tight she could hardly catch a breath. "Sir?"

"When you've finished here, I'd like to see you in my office."

For a moment she wasn't sure how to respond. Flashbacks from those moments under his desk staring at the sleek leather shoes and the creased trousers joined the images of the man she had killed, her dead neighbor stuffed into her trunk and a beautiful young woman bleeding out on a gurney in front of her.

Please, God, don't let her die.

"Of course. Give me five minutes."

Dr. Pierce nodded and walked away. Eva stared after him, her head still spinning. When she'd managed to slow her thrashing heart, she washed up and headed to the station.

"You okay?" Kim glanced at her from the computer monitor she was bent over. "She might make it, you know."

Eva managed a stilted nod. "Hope so. Okay isn't something I'll be anytime soon." She heaved a big breath. "Dr. Pierce wants to see me in his office."

Kim considered her for several seconds. When Eva offered no further explanation, her friend and colleague said, "We're okay for now. See what Pierce wants and then take a break." She jerked her head toward the department exit. "Go."

"I'll be back in five."

She should let Todd know about the call. He would

need to inform the detectives on the case. Eva wasn't sure exactly where he was. He'd said he would be close, watching. There hadn't been time for her to wonder where or how he'd intended to do so. She hurried toward the corridor that led to the administrator's office. Her thoughts were rushing about in her head, a mishmash of worry and fear and desperation. The words the caller had said to her kept ringing in her ears. What she'd said to Todd last night had been right. Robles wouldn't stop unless he was behind bars—and maybe not even then.

How could she go on with her life and pretend Robles wasn't watching and waiting for the opportunity to snatch her or someone close to her off the street? If she persisted in her efforts to hide from him or to keep a stumbling block, i.e. her bodyguard, in Robles's path, he would only continue hurting innocent people like poor Mrs. Cackowski and Alyssa Chavez. Tears crowded into her throat.

Pull it together, Eva. She couldn't do what needed to be done if she fell apart.

Eva reached the lobby outside Pierce's office but his secretary was not at her desk. His door stood open so Eva walked to the opening and knocked once on the doorframe. Pierce looked up and motioned for her to come inside.

"Close the door."

Her hands shaking now despite every effort she attempted to keep them steady, she closed the door and crossed to his desk, then she waited for further instructions.

He glanced up, gestured to the chair in front of his desk. "Have a seat."

Had Pierce changed his mind about having her back at work? Had he already heard about the phone call? Impossible. She hadn't told anyone…but maybe the man who'd called her—presumably Robles—had called the administrator as well.

"Dr. Pierce, if you've changed your mind about my being here, I completely understand. Especially after what just happened." Eva squeezed her eyes shut a moment. "I am so sorry for what I've caused." More of that humiliating emotion gathered in her eyes. Where was her professional decorum?

He studied her for a moment, confusion lining his brow. "I'm not sure what you're talking about, Eva."

She met his questioning gaze. "A man called me right before you asked me to your office. He said…" She moistened her lips and wished she could swallow the lump of agony lodged in her throat. "He said Alyssa Chavez was on me." Deep breath. "It's my fault she was shot."

The tears burst onto her lashes and streamed down her cheeks before she could stop them. And she'd thought she was strong. Pierce grabbed a box of tissue and came around to sit beside her. He offered the box to her. "Have you notified Detective Marsh or spoken with Mr. Christian?"

Feeling more foolish than she had in years, she shook her head. "It just happened. I was going to after our meeting. I understand if you'd rather I didn't come back to work until this is…over."

Over? Would it ever be over as long as she was breathing?

"We need you here," he said, his voice uncharacteristically gentle.

Eva dabbed at her eyes. "My being here puts everyone in danger." She should have thought of that—she should also have realized that she was operating on emotion. Never a good thing.

"Your work here is what ultimately put you in this position, Eva. As a member of my staff I have an obligation to you. We've beefed up security. I can assure you that none of those thugs are getting in again. I'm fairly confident this Miguel Robles will keep hurting people in an attempt to get to you no matter where you are. If you'd been at home today that poor young woman may have ended up on your doorstep."

She couldn't argue with him there. Mrs. Cackowski was proof of his conclusion. The mere thought of how she'd looked stuffed into that trunk as if she were a worthless object rather than a lovely human being made her want to break down completely.

Eva took a steadying breath and gathered her scattered composure. "I appreciate your understanding. So, why did you want to speak with me?"

"I have a question about that night." The gentle tone was gone now. He sounded more like the commanding hospital administrator she had come to know.

"What would you like to know?" Her heart started that runaway galloping again. Did he somehow know she had lied to him about being in his office that night? Damn it, why hadn't she simply told him the truth in the first place?

You weren't thinking straight, Eva.

"You're certain you didn't see anyone come into or out of my office while you were in hiding?"

Damn. There it was. To reaffirm the lie was her first instinct. She hesitated. Lying to the man who was basically the only reason she had anyone watching over her in all this was simply wrong. She owed it to him to tell the truth. For what it was worth, at any rate.

"I wasn't completely forthcoming with you that night, Dr. Pierce." She shook her head and stared at her hands. "I was so shaken by what happened, I wasn't thinking clearly."

"I need you to start at the beginning and tell me exactly what happened after you left the ladies' room."

The sternness in his tone warned that he was not happy to hear her confession. Of course he wasn't happy. She had lied to the man who had given everything to designing and creating the most cutting-edge emergency department in the country. He had chosen his staff carefully and she'd just let him down. It would be a miracle if she still had a job when this meeting was over.

"I went into your office like you told me to do, but I heard someone coming so I hid in the first available space I spotted—under your desk." She braced for spilling the rest. "I hoped it was you coming to tell me everything was okay, but it wasn't."

He waited, silent, staring at her with an intensity that sent her composure fleeing once more.

"All I saw were his shoes and his trouser legs. Based on what I heard, he at first seemed to move around your office rifling through things, then he came to your desk. He opened each drawer and then I heard him scrawl something on your desk blotter." Her mouth had gone as dry as a box of fresh cotton balls.

"Did he take anything from the drawers?"

She shook her head. "Not that I saw. He pulled each

one open, rummaged through the contents and then pushed it close."

"Did it seem as though he might be photographing anything?"

Eva had to think about that one. "I don't think so. When he walked in he moved around the room without really stopping. He seemed in a hurry, maybe. At the desk… I suppose he might have photographed something during the few seconds before he started to open the drawers."

"He didn't say anything. Make a phone call?"

She shook her head again. "He just left that message."

I know what you did.

Pierce's silence added another layer of tension to the band already twisting tighter around her chest.

"Do you have any questions about that message?"

For the second time since she entered his office the urge to lie rushed to the tip of her tongue, but she resisted. "I'm certain you would tell me if there was a reason I needed to know."

"Eva." He exhaled a heavy breath. "When you create something everyone wants before anyone else can do so, you put yourself in a position to suffer extreme backlash and jealousy. Creating this unprecedented facility and launching a successful operation came at great professional and personal cost. Manufacturers of any medical product that is not used in this facility despise me. Most of the colleagues I once considered friends resent me. My efforts to do good have produced many enemies."

She'd had no idea how difficult his journey had been, though she did understand. Her sister's rising stardom as an investigative journalist had come at a high price. She'd lost lifelong friends and was as lonely as Eva. Just another confirmation that it was impossible to have it all. How sad that a man like Pierce had been forced to give up so much to create something so valuable to mankind.

"Don't waste your sympathy on me," he said, reading her face. "I executed more than my share of cutthroat maneuvers to make my success happen."

Eva felt so foolish now about the hasty decision she'd made to withhold the truth that terrifying night. "I apologize for not telling you everything. What I heard and saw didn't feel important considering the other events playing out so I dismissed the entire episode." A pretty pathetic excuse but it was the truth.

"Tell me about his shoes, Eva."

Surprised but determined to provide the best answer possible, she turned over the image in her mind. "Dark, black I think. Leather for sure. Not the off-the-shelf kind you find in a big chain department store. These were expensive shoes. The trousers, too. They were like a charcoal or dark gray color and creased as if he'd just, you know, gotten them from the cleaners."

"Tell me about his hand. You said you watched him open the drawers. Was he wearing a ring of any sort or a watch? Did you see his shirtsleeve? If so, what color shirt was he wearing? Cuff links?"

His rapid-fire questions reminded her of the interview with Detective Marsh and his partner. Had something else happened that may have been headed off if she'd told him the truth in the first place?

One more thing to feel guilty about.

Eva closed her eyes and replayed the moments in

her head. Light gray shirtsleeve to go with the darker gray trousers. She told Pierce as much. "There was a watch. No ring that I saw. No cuff links."

"What did the watch look like? Gold? Silver? An expensive brand?"

"Silver. Average size. Black face, I think. I couldn't see the brand but it looked heavy, expensive."

"Thank you, Eva. If you recall anything else, please let me know." He checked his cell. "By the way, the girl—Alyssa Chavez—is holding her own in surgery. I'll assign a security detail to her room when she comes out of surgery."

Relief swam through Eva's veins. "Thank God." She stood. "I'm not scheduled for the next two days. If you change your mind about me coming in on Sunday—"

"I won't."

"Thank you, sir."

As she exited the lobby area, Eva met his secretary, Patricia Ezell. The older woman smiled as if she understood the relief no doubt painting Eva's face. Once she reached the corridor she spotted the other possibility for the secretary's smile.

Todd Christian leaned against the wall, the nondescript tan scrubs taking not one ounce of masculinity away from him. How was it possible for any man to look that good in scrubs?

As she reached him, he pushed away from the wall. "I was hoping you'd give me a tour of the cafeteria. I hear it's the best hospital food in the city."

The tension that had held her in its ruthless grip as she entered Pierce's office eased, only to be replaced by a new kind of tension.

"It's good, yes. I just have to check in with the desk and then maybe I can take a lunch break."

He walked with her toward the ER. She tuned out the subtle scent of his soap. She should not have noticed the earthy, muted smell over the more potent odors of the hospital, and yet somehow she did.

"I received an unsettling phone call after the shooting victim, Alyssa Chavez, was taken to the OR," she told him, ready to get the painful business over. For the first time she wondered how Robles had her cell number? Who was she kidding? A scumbag like that probably had all sorts of unsavory resources.

"Robles?" He glanced at her, no surprise in his eyes. "I take it she was another message."

Eva nodded. "He said she was on me and asked how many more I wanted to die for me."

He stalled then, turned to her, one hand automatically going to her arm and squeezing reassuringly. "He wants you to feel as if this is your fault, but it's not. I'll call Marsh and let him know. Would you like me to take you back to the safe house? I'm sure Pierce will understand."

"No." She squared her shoulders and gave her head a quick shake. "I'm not going to be bullied by him. I'm here. I'm staying. Maybe before I come back on Sunday this will be behind me."

Those long fingers of his tightened on her arm once more. "We'll get him."

"Hope so."

They started walking once more and he said, "You were pretty awesome when the girl came in." He glanced at her, a big, wide smile on his face. "I liked watching you work."

"I didn't see you."

"I stayed out of the way. You were focused."

As they entered the emergency department, Eva couldn't deny a sense of pride at his words. "This is a good team. I'm lucky to be a part of it."

"I'm reasonably sure they know how lucky they are to have you as well."

She doubted Alyssa Chavez was feeling lucky. That massive cloud of doom that had disappeared for a few minutes was back. "Maybe."

Kicking aside the worry, she let Kim know she was taking an early lunch break. She and Todd could call Marsh together. Eva wanted to know what progress they had made on the case. The sooner they could tie all this to Robles, the sooner this would be over.

Except she wasn't holding her breath on that last part.

Robles wanted her and she had a bad, bad feeling nothing the police could do would change his mind.

This war was intensely private.

Eva had spent four years in college learning how and the past six working hard to save lives. For the first time in her life she contemplated the concept of taking one.

Chapter Eight

Colby Safe House, 9:30 p.m.

Todd did a perimeter check and then another walk-through of the house. Though it was doubtful anyone or thing could get past the security system without him knowing about it, another look never hurt.

Mainly because he needed to distract himself.

He'd spent twelve hours today watching Eva. Every move, every word...she didn't breathe without him knowing how deep. He'd kept as much distance as he dared, which was necessary on more than one level, but he'd stayed close enough to intervene if there was trouble. Other than the Chavez woman who'd served as a message from Robles, the day had been reasonably uneventful.

But watching her, listening to her voice, catching the occasional smile, had slowly but surely escalated the tension building inside him to the point of snapping. He had vivid memories of how her skin felt beneath his touch...how it smelled, tasted...but none of those memories held a candle to the real thing. Watching her was driving him out of his mind.

He shoved the last of the dinnerware into the dishwasher. When she'd announced that she was calling it a night early he'd almost hugged her in gratitude. Another few minutes and he would have undoubtedly said or done something he would regret. His self-control had long ago reached the breaking point.

Ten years was a long time to measure every woman he met, every kiss, every touch by the one he let go. He had no one else to blame for his misery...but he just hadn't been ready for the kind of commitment she deserved.

Or maybe he had been afraid he didn't deserve her.

What had a guy like him possessed to offer such an amazing woman? His parents had abandoned him and his little brother. His mother had died from the drugs she couldn't let go of and his father from a car accident—at least that was what he'd heard. He'd grown up in foster care. The last family who'd taken him in as a rebellious teenager had been good to him. He'd treated them the way he had all the others—with total indifference. Still, they hadn't given up. If he'd learned anything from those caring folks it was that his future was his to make. They'd drilled the importance of an education and a career into his head. With their encouragement, he'd made it to college. Then he'd met Eva and fallen head over heels...but how could he trust himself to do right by her when all that he'd known growing up was instability and one letdown after the other?

No matter that those last couple of years before college he'd found a good home, he could not trust himself to do the right thing. So he'd given every part of himself to her physically but he'd kept his emotional distance. Or so he'd thought at the time.

He had spent the decade since he left Chicago proving and establishing his worth. Achieving financial security. Devoted to his country at first, then back to the city that was home. As much heartache as he'd endured growing up in the Windy City, he had every right to walk away and never look back. But the truth was, Eva was still here. Not once in all this time had he admitted that part to himself. Building the life he wanted to share with someone one day had been his ultimate goal. The sad part was he hadn't found anyone else with whom he wanted to share that life. The past year he'd felt satisfied just sharing the city with Eva and waiting for her to marry some great guy who deserved her. Maybe then he could get on with his life.

Except she hadn't settled down with some other man.

When her file had been passed around at the agency's Monday morning briefing, Todd felt as if he'd been punched in the gut. He'd seen the news on Saturday about the incident at the Edge but her name hadn't been mentioned. As shocked as he'd been to learn she was involved and in danger, none of it had carried the impact of seeing her up close.

Yeah, he'd watched her a couple of times. Always from a safe distance. Educating himself on her life since he left her, keeping up with who she dated—none of it had adequately prepared him for standing in the same room with her. Watching her in the trauma room with that young woman who'd been shot had shifted something inside him. Her intense focus, capable hands and sincere care for the patient had made him fall for her all over again, only this time it was way beyond physical.

He now also fully understood he was in trouble.

He wanted to do far more than keep her safe. He wanted to touch her. He wanted to relearn every inch of her. He wanted to taste her…to hear her cry his name. He wanted her to belong to him.

Truly crazy, Christian.

An hour or so ago she had announced she needed a long hot bath and disappeared into her suite, and he had been trying to distract himself since. From time to time he checked the monitor. Looked without looking, so to speak. She was safe. In the bathroom there was no video, only audio. Just listening to her moans of satisfaction and the *drip, drip, drip* of the water had made him hard.

With the kitchen cleaned up, the perimeter and all egresses checked, he might as well hit the gym. Maybe he could burn off some of this excess adrenaline. Either that or he was going to explode. He hesitated at the door to her bedroom. His fingers fisted. She wouldn't want to hear about how badly he wanted her or how much he wished he could go back and have a do-over of the past.

He went into his own room—just across the hall—and peeled off his clothes. He tossed the scrubs on the bed and dug up a pair of running shorts and a tee. Once his sneakers were on, he hustled down the stairs. The best way to hammer down this kind of frustration was to run long and fast on an extreme incline setting. By the time he finished his body would be too physically spent for anything else.

He would defeat this need if it killed him.

EVA STARED AT her reflection as she set the hair dryer and brush aside. The ER had been hectic all afternoon. Nothing as serious as a gunshot but more than their fair share of automobile accidents, work-related injuries and falls. The last patient who'd come in, an elderly woman who'd broken an arm falling down the stairs in her building's stairwell, had kept Eva an hour past the end of her shift. The lady had wanted Eva at her side every step of the way until she was released. Eva wouldn't have left her for anything. She'd teared up more than once thinking about how she hadn't been there for her sweet neighbor.

Can't change that painful reality.

The best news of the day was that Alyssa Chavez was going to make it. The surgery had been a success. Her family had arrived to be with her. Between the newly increased security at the Edge and Chicago PD, no one other than staff and family were getting anywhere near her room.

Detective Marsh and his new partner from Gang Intelligence, Sergeant Carter, were less than thrilled with the news that someone—probably Miguel Robles—had contacted Eva and claimed responsibility for the shooting. She suspected their plates were already more than full. Piling on another incident, particularly a shooting, was not helpful. For Eva it confirmed her most troubling conclusion: Robles had no intention of stopping until he'd gotten his revenge.

She turned away from the mirror and the weary reflection there. She'd dried her hair and pulled on a pair of the provided PJs. These were comfortable lounge pants with a matching tank-style tee. The pale pink color was one of her favorites. She wished she had nail polish and a couple of emery boards and she'd give herself a manicure and pedicure. Not that she really needed one or even wanted one but it would buy some time. Still too early for bed. Mostly she was too keyed up to dare lie down now. Spending a couple of hours tossing and turning was her least favorite thing to do.

Maybe she should have spent a little longer on the treadmill. No matter that her arms and legs felt like limp noodles, especially after the hot bath, the tension and frustrating anticipation hung on like a bad migraine.

Surrendering, she decided to take her towel and the day's clothes to the laundry room and then she intended to find a bottle of wine. Going for something stronger wouldn't be smart. Wine would do the trick without making her potentially do something stupid—as long as she stayed in her room and clear of any possibility of running into him. Being locked away alone in a house with Todd was asking for serious trouble.

It was silent downstairs. Images played across the television screen but the sound was muted. The main hall that cut through the center of the house was cool and quiet. No sign of Todd. The kitchen proved the same. Almost there. The laundry room was deserted, too.

She sorted her laundry into the labeled hampers. A cleaning team came in each day and took care of laundry and whatever else was needed. She imagined a clearance and a thorough background search were required of the team. Just giving them access to the property meant they were above reproach. As much as she hated doing laundry, she wouldn't want to live like this. The house and property were beautiful but far too grand for her taste. She liked simple and homey.

The security part didn't actually bother her. Dr.

Pierce was equally careful with his staff at the Edge. No one worked there without a flawless background. She found it near unbelievable that someone had managed to reach his office without being stopped. Then again, security had been focused on the events unfolding in the emergency department. There were cameras everywhere as well. Why hadn't the intruder been captured on camera? Maybe that was the reason for all the questions about what he had been wearing.

Eva had a feeling the man and his message were intensely personal to Dr. Pierce. Whatever it was, it went well beyond professional. Not that she was in the position to judge. Her life was wacked out on all levels. Her primary goal at this point was surviving—what she knew she had to do in order to stop Robles.

Without incident, she found the wine cellar that wasn't really a cellar but a climate-controlled room. Wherever Todd was he had so far stayed out of her path. She was grateful. There were hundreds of bottles on display in the wine room. Control pads showed the temperature and humidity level in the various glass-encased storage shelves. She moved through the rows of white and blush wines until she found something sweet and bubbly.

Back in the kitchen she prowled through the drawers until she found a new-model corkscrew that made opening a bottle of wine easy. When the cork popped free, she grabbed the bottle by the neck and a glass by the stem and headed back to the stairs. She'd made it all the way to the bottom of the staircase when she sensed his presence. A shiver rushed over her skin.

"Taking a friend to bed I see."

His voice held a teasing quality but there was something else she couldn't quite discern. She glanced over her shoulder to say good-night but the sight of him stopped her. He wore nothing but running shorts. The loose kind that rode high on his muscled thighs and low on his lean belly. The tee he'd been wearing was wadded in his hand and serving as a mop for his glistening chest.

The bottle in her hand felt suddenly too heavy. Her fingers tightened around it. She did the same with the glass. "Good night," she somehow managed.

Go. Now.

The words were her mantra as she climbed the stairs. The need to look back at him burned in her brain but she refused. He watched her until she disappeared beyond his view. She didn't have to look back to know he'd been watching her. She'd felt his gaze burning into her…smelled the devastatingly sexy scent of his clean sweat.

The instant she was in her room with the door closed, she poured a hefty serving of wine into her glass and downed it. She did the same with a second glass and had just poured a third when she heard the door across the hall slam.

She closed her eyes and sipped at the third glass. However hard she fought to banish the images, the events unfolding across the hall slowly unfurled in her brain. She imagined him stepping out of the shorts and peeling off his briefs—if he bothered with any these days. Then he would reach into the shower and turn on the water. Muscles would flex and contract under all that damp, smooth skin. She remembered every ridge and plane of his muscled body. The memory cut right through her, made her weak. She raised her glass and tried to drown the images.

Didn't work.

Oh, yes. She definitely should have stayed on the treadmill longer and stayed away from the wine.

"Bad decision, Eva," she said aloud.

She crossed the room, left the bottle and the glass on her bedside table and grabbed the television remote with both hands. After scanning the entire channel grid, she gave up and tossed the remote onto the bed. Flashes of her bodyguard smoothing a towel over his damp skin kept flickering in her mind. Memories from their past lovemaking whispered through her, making her tremble with need.

"Enough." She did an about-face before she could change her mind and stormed out of her room, straight across the hall and into his room without knocking or stopping or even breathing. The water still raining down in the bathroom didn't halt her either. The door was open so she walked right on in.

Her determined gaze landed on more than six feet of stunning male and then she stopped stone still.

He was still in the shower.

He stood, utterly, gloriously naked beneath the spray of hot water…steam rose around him. He was as beautiful as she remembered. Sleek skin taut over all those perfect muscles. Damp hair clinging to his neck, blue eyes closed. The heat from the shower had him semi-aroused.

As if he'd sensed her presence those pale blue eyes opened. Her heart nearly stopped as he reached to turn off the water, his gaze never leaving hers. He grabbed the towel from the hook next to the shower door and flung it around his hips. His attention focused intently on her, he stepped out of the glass cage and moved toward her like a lion tracking his prey…and she was that prey.

"Are you all right?" His gaze swept over her from head to toe and back as if he'd expected to find a bullet wound or other trauma. The fingers of one hand raked the damp hair from his face. Water trickled down his skin, disappearing into the towel draped low on his lean hips.

For a single second she couldn't move or speak.

"Eva."

The sound of her name on his lips shattered the trance she had slipped into. She closed the short distance between them and stared straight into his eyes. "We should just get this over with so we can move on. Ignoring it is wearing me out."

Those blue eyes narrowed slightly. "How much did you have to drink, Eva?"

"Really?" Her hands went to her hips. "That's all you've got?" She grabbed his face, went up on tiptoe and kissed the hell out of him.

He held absolutely still the first few seconds, his powerful arms hanging at his sides. Her fingers forked into his wet hair and she leaned her body into his damp skin. He made a sound, not quite a growl. Still he didn't give in. She drew her mouth from his, allowed her fingers to trace down his magnificent chest, over mounds of rock-hard muscle. Her gaze followed that incredible path. A smile tugged at her lips when her fingers reached his naval and the swirl of golden hair there.

"Eva, we should talk about this."

"I don't want to talk." She stepped back, peeled off her now damp top and tossed it aside, allowing her breasts to fall free against her chest. Then she shucked the lounge pants, let them hit the floor in a puddle of silky fabric around her feet. Wearing nothing but lacy pink panties, she stepped out of that soft circle and toward him once more.

His gaze roamed down her body, burning her as if he were touching her. The slight hitch in his breath had her heart pounding even harder.

"Are you going to stand there," she asked, "or are you going to man up and do this?"

His jaw hardened and the purely female muscles between her thighs reacted, pulsing with need. Oh, he was angry now.

"You don't want to do this," he growled. "It's the wine."

She laughed. Even the sound of his voice made her nipples burn. "I'm not that naive little virgin you discovered in college. I know exactly what I want and right now it's you. If you think you can handle it, that is."

She sensed the moment he broke. He charged toward her and she lost her breath all over again. He pulled her hard against his body and allowed her to feel just how ready he was beneath that terry cloth. "Don't say I didn't warn you."

"Talk, talk," she accused. He held her so tight she could barely breathe the words.

He yanked the towel from his hips, the friction of it pulling between their bodies making her gasp. He shoved the door shut and trapped her against it. Her legs went around his waist. She pressed down against him, cried out in need.

"Not so fast," he snarled.

His right hand found that place between her thighs that ached so for him. He pushed aside the lace in his way and rubbed until she thought she would die of want and then he slid a finger inside, then another. She whimpered, her eyes closing with the intensity of the pleasure.

"No," he ordered. "Look at me."

She forced her eyes open, read the fury in his. "No more foreplay. Give me what I want. Now," she demanded.

"If we're going to do this we'll do it my way." The pad of his thumb nailed that sensitive spot once more while his fingers plied her body. "I want you looking at me when I make you scream for more."

She dug her heel between the cheeks of his muscled ass and rubbed. He gasped and his eyes drifted shut. "Now who's not looking?" she accused.

His fingers explored more deeply, stretching her, readying her for what was to come. Her breath caught as a ripple of pleasure shot through her. She clamped onto his fingers with those throbbing inner muscles and squeezed. "You keep playing and I'm going to remember I don't really need you to do this," she hissed.

He snatched his fingers away, stared at her, unmoving, his jaw pulsing with more of that fury. Staring into his eyes with matching defiance, she drew one hand from his neck and reached between their bodies. She rubbed that place he refused to assuage and her body tightened with growing desire. Harder, faster, she massaged that sensitive nub until her eyes closed and she moaned with the mounting pleasure. The first waves of orgasm spiraled from the very center of her being. Her body undulated against her hand, wishing it was his wide palm and blunt-tipped fingers.

Suddenly he yanked her hand away and plowed into her. She screamed with the exquisite pain of penetration. He groaned long and loud. For endless moments they didn't move, their bodies joined so completely and yet burning and pulsing for more. He shifted ever so slightly and a full body reaction pulsed through her, taking her over the edge. He stilled, waited, letting her go without him.

Just when she thought her mind and body couldn't take anymore, he started to move. Slow, shallow thrusts, his powerful hips rocking into her. His mouth closed over hers, kissed her, savored her, tasting her lips with his teeth and his tongue and then exploring deeper. His hands tightened on her thighs, pulling her more firmly against him, forcing his thick sex farther inside her.

"Say it," he murmured against her lips.

She bit his jaw.

"Say it," he commanded, nuzzling her cheek with his nose.

"More," she argued.

He thrust harder, deeper. She gasped.

"Say it."

She closed her eyes and lost herself to the new waves building from the inside out, tearing her apart. She arched to meet his powerful thrusts. Cried out with the pleasure-pain of just how deep he was inside her. Orgasm shuddered through her a second time, making her tremble.

He pressed his forehead against the door beside her head and whispered in her ear, "Say it."

She was too weak to argue but somehow she found the strength to cry, "More!"

He pulled her against his chest, flung open the door and carried her to the bed. They came down on the mattress together. One hand went under her bottom, and he lifted her hips to him, opening her wider as he plowed over and over into her. He squeezed her bottom.

She planted her heels on the mattress and met his deep thrusts. "More," she whimpered. Sweat coated their skin, the smell of it comingling with the sweet tang of her orgasms.

With his free hand he stroked her rib cage, trailed his fingers over her, bone by bone, until he grasped her breast. He squeezed, tempted her nipple. She bit her lip to prevent calling his name. She was too weak to fight anymore...too overwhelmed to beg. Her fingers twitched, her toes curled...almost there.

He roared with the orgasm finally overtaking him.

The new waves flowed over her, dragging her into that place of pure sensation a third time while he surrendered to his own.

He groaned a frantic sound as they collapsed together.

Eva closed her eyes against the burn of tears. She should have drunk more of the wine. She should have realized that there was no getting *this* out of the way.

This part of her still belonged to him...

Chapter Nine

Friday, May 11, 8:30 a.m.

Awkward was the word of the day.

Todd opened the fridge and put away the orange juice while plates and forks rattled in the sink. Eva had said exactly six words to him. *Morning*, when she first came into the kitchen. *Yes*, when he'd asked if pancakes would be okay for breakfast. And *I'll get the dishes* when she'd finished eating.

Last night he'd wanted to talk to her about what happened but she'd rushed away so fast he'd barely had time to get his head back down to reality. She'd wriggled free of his arms and left him spent across the bed. When he'd stumbled from the tangled sheets and dragged on his jeans, he'd knocked on her door but she ignored him. He'd heard the water running in the en suite bath. Apparently she couldn't wait to wash him off her skin.

Later he'd wanted to check on her via the security system but the idea had felt completely wrong. Instead, he'd crawled back into his bed and burrowed himself into the scent of her that was all over his sheets, all over his skin. He'd dreamed of their first time together—her first time with any man.

This morning he had awakened wanting more.

She clearly had not.

Their breakfast conversation had consisted of forks scraping against stoneware and coffee mugs settling on the counter. It would be easy to blame what happened on her. She'd come to him after all. But that wouldn't be fair. He was as responsible as she was and no amount of analyzing would change that cold, hard fact.

Dissecting what happened wouldn't alter the bottom line either: he was here to protect her, not take advantage of her vulnerability. Last night she had been vulnerable and he had taken advantage of that vulnerability.

"No work today, right?" he asked, his voice sounding particularly loud after the long minutes of silence. He knew the answer but it was the only conversation opener he could come up with at the moment.

"I volunteer at a walk-in clinic once a week." She dried her hands. "Today's my day."

He leaned against the counter, keeping at least a half dozen feet between them. "I'll need the address so I can decide on the best route to take and any other relevant info to pass along to Michaels."

Ian Michaels was his backup. Todd kept him apprised of their movements. The worst thing a protective detail could do was fail to report its movements. If communications were compromised, backup would have no idea where to start the search or where to send help.

"Warren Boulevard." She wrapped her arms around

her middle and met his gaze for the first time since she clambered out of his bed last night. "It's an old church at the intersection of Warren and Western. Anyone who needs medical attention is welcome. There's no charge. Church donations pay for the needed medical supplies. Several nurses and doctors donate their time. It's important work," she tacked on as if she feared he might debate the day's agenda.

"Maybe I can help, too."

She looked away. "Maybe."

It was highly probable that Robles had made it a point to learn her routine. "Have you been to the church since last Friday?"

"No." She straightened and tugged at the hem of her blouse.

"Good. Robles might not be aware you volunteer at that location."

Staying aware was key to navigating any area and the level of risk. Anyone looking to commit a crime would always single out a distracted victim over one paying attention.

Her destination was one with which he was familiar and, hopefully, Robles hadn't connected to her. "I'm ready when you are."

"I need to grab my bag."

He watched her walk away. The jeans and gray pullover shirt hugged every sweet curve he had traced with his hands and body last night. He closed his eyes and relived the moment when she interrupted his shower. He'd been done with the shower for a few minutes but he'd stood under the spray of water in hopes it would relieve the tension vibrating in his body. The water hadn't even come close to releasing his tension when she burst in. Watching her strip off her clothes and then stand before him in offering, he'd almost lost it.

She was still as beautiful as he remembered. Every inch of her was perfectly toned yet so damned soft. The first time they were together he'd been terrified that he would hurt her. She'd seemed so tender and fragile. She'd set him straight right from the start. Eva Marie Bowman was strong and tough and damned determined. She and her sister hadn't been shuffled around to foster homes the way he had, but they had experienced their share of tragedy and hard times. Like when their father died, leaving behind a wife who'd never been anything but a homemaker and two young girls who needed a college education. Their mom had worked three minimum-wage jobs to help get them through school. She had died a few years ago while he was still overseas. One of the first things he'd done when he got back to Chicago was take flowers to her grave.

Stella Bowman had liked him. Maybe she'd changed her mind after he left, leaving her daughter's heart broken. Learning to live with that prospect had been almost as hard as leaving Eva in the first place. Even if by some stroke of luck he was able to make amends with Eva, he couldn't change how her mother had gone to her grave feeling about him. Some things couldn't be undone. Yet another of those things was Eva's sister. He wasn't looking forward to running into Lena. Like most big sisters, she preferred to kick the ass of anyone who hurt her baby sister to talking things over.

"I'm ready," she announced.

He cleared his head and led the way to the garage. At the door he grabbed the keys for the Dodge Charger. He liked that it was black with heavily tinted windows and had an engine made for speed if the need arose.

"We'll take the Charger," he said when she stood at the front of the garage surveying the line of automobiles. He hit the fob and unlocked the doors of the sleek black vehicle that sat third from the right. He'd driven it several times. He felt at home behind the wheel of the Charger more so than the other vehicles.

While she climbed in he set the safe house security system to *away* using his phone. Once he was behind the wheel and had started the engine, the proper garage door automatically opened. As soon as he'd backed out, it closed once more. Five seconds later the garage went into the same *away* lockdown as the house.

For the first few miles he deferred to her decision to keep the silent treatment going. As a soldier in Special Forces he'd learned to wait out the enemies. Hours or days...whatever it took. He'd honed his patience and his ability to remain calm and steady with years of training and operation execution.

But he was no longer a soldier. This was a different world and in this world he was in charge. And he was frustrated and annoyed—mostly at himself.

"About last night—"

"I don't want to talk about last night." She stared out the window at the luxury estates set back amid the lush trees along the road.

Okay, so maybe his strategizing skills where these sorts of things were concerned were a little rusty. Maybe a lot rusty. The past decade he'd satisfied his baser physical needs with one-night stands and no-strings-attached encounters. He hadn't been in a relationship since...

Since he left Eva.

"We should talk about last night anyway." He slowed for a turn. A couple more and they would hit Central Avenue.

"We had sex." She stared straight ahead, her jawline rigid, her hands clutching the armrest as if she feared he intended to rocket into hyper speed. "What's to talk about? It was fine. Good...enough."

"Good enough?" A jolt of outrage joined his mounting frustration. Was she kidding? The sex had been mind-blowing...fantastic. A second's hesitation nagged at him. No way. She had been thoroughly satisfied. He knew the sounds Eva made when she was enjoying herself. She had enjoyed last night as much as he had.

"That's what I said." She released her grip on the armrest to bend forward and dig around in that enormous leather bag she carried as a purse. He was fairly certain it was the same one she'd carried in college. She called it her good luck bag. It was her last gift from her mother as she entered college. She jammed sunglasses over her eyes and returned her attention forward.

He did the same. The sex had been better than good. She was yanking his chain, trying to tick him off. He got it. Fine.

The truth always came out in the end.

Good Shepherd Church, 11:00 a.m.

"YOU'LL BE AS good as new in a couple of days." Eva smiled at the elderly man whose allergies were giving him a hard time. "Nurse James will give you the meds the doctor prescribed as you leave. Remember to go to the Imaging Center for your appointment for the chest X-ray. Dr. Taggart wants to be sure there's nothing more going on with that nagging cough."

Mr. Hambrick smiled. "Thank you, Eva. You always make my day better."

She gave him a wave as he shuffled off to the checkout area. Her duty here was bittersweet. Seeing all the elderly who had no one else at home or nearby to take care of them or the incredibly poor that had no other means of medical care tugged hard at her heartstrings. On the other hand, knowing that she made a difference in their lives was a soothing balm to her soul.

Certainly made her forget all about her own problems.

As if her mind wanted to remind her that her problems were close, she glanced over at Todd. He was bandaging Rhea Gleason's ankle. She'd managed to cut herself pretty deeply puttering in her flower garden. Eva had inspected Todd's repair work and been duly impressed. With a tetanus shot and an antibiotic just to be sure, Rhea, too, would be fine in a couple of days.

Todd offered his hand to assist Rhea to her feet and she smiled up at him as if he'd whispered a secret to her that only the two of them would ever know. Eva doubted a man as handsome and charming as Todd had ever provided the woman with medical care. Not that Dr. Taggart wasn't charming and quite handsome in his own way—he was. He was also more giving than any doctor she knew besides perhaps Dr. Pierce.

Rhea glanced at Eva and smiled. Todd did the same.

Pretending she hadn't noticed the latter, Eva turned her attention to the sign-in sheet. She called the next patient's name and chatted with the older man as if all were right in her world. Last night should never have happened. She wanted to be glad she'd broken the tension mounting between her and Todd...but she wasn't. The strategy she now recognized as fatally flawed was supposed to prove that Todd Christian wasn't as amazing as she remembered. That the lovemaking skill of the man couldn't possibly be as incredible as the memories. That he would never be able to make this more experienced and mature Eva feel as if her world had tilted on its axis.

You were so wrong, Eva. So, so very wrong.

She'd hoped that at barely nineteen and with no experience that what she remembered was nothing more than blind passion driven by the sweet innocence of first love. Not the case at all. She now fully and undeniably grasped the reason no other kiss, much less any other aspect of lovemaking, ever lived up to his. He was the master. A fantastic lover.

But great sex did not a real relationship make.

Relationship?

She wasn't looking for a relationship.

"Is the old ticker still beating?"

Eva blinked away the distraction, realizing she'd had the diaphragm of her stethoscope against her patient's chest for far longer than it should have taken for her to listen to his heart and lungs.

She smiled and listened a little longer to cover her slip-up, then she removed the tips from her ears. "Sounds as strong as ever, Mr. Fry. Lungs sound clear, too."

Lawrence Fry was seventy and he'd lived in Chicago his whole life. He'd spent most of those years playing a saxophone in various clubs downtown and eventually in the street for donations. He'd told her how the basement of this very church had once been used to hide booze during Prohibition—unbeknownst to the reverend at the time, of course, he always clarified. Fry was one of the most knowledgeable people Eva had ever met when it came to Chicago history, especially the more infamous history.

Like many of their patients he had no family. This free clinic was the only medical care he received. Yet the kind older man never complained. What he did was consistently promise Eva that he intended to play his sax at her wedding. She didn't spoil the moment by informing him there were no plans for a wedding in the foreseeable future.

"That's always good news."

Eva placed the BP cuff around his right arm. "What brings you in today? Are you experiencing any symptoms I need to know about?"

"Actually, I only came so I could see you." He glanced around and leaned forward. "I heard through the grapevine that you're in trouble."

Surprise followed by a trickle of fear made its way into her veins. "You don't need to worry about me, Mr. Fry. I'm doing great, I promise. Where did you hear this?" He kept quiet while she pumped the cuff and took the reading. "One fifteen over seventy. BP looks great."

He took her hand when she reached to undo the cuff. "Word is all over the street that Miguel Robles wants to find you. You aren't safe here or anywhere else, Eva. Don't stay around here so long today. I know this man. He's the worst of the worst. I got mixed up with him and his crew years ago—before he was the big cheese he is now. He's bad, bad news. Watch your back, my friend."

Eva removed the cuff and gave him a nod. "I will. I promise."

He stood and gave her a pat on the shoulder. "I won't take up any more of your time, then. I have a gig over on Harrison Street."

"You be careful, too," she said.

"Always." Mr. Fry winked and ambled on his way.

She watched him go, worry gnawing at her. Nothing he'd said should surprise her, and yet, somehow it did. She kept thinking if she just went on with her life the whole thing would go away.

Not going to be that simple.

Not only was the problem not going away, the news was spreading. Miguel Robles had no choice. He had to save face or risk a revolution against his reign of terror.

The cell strapped to her ankle vibrated. Eva decided to take a break and answer the call in the ladies' room. She moved to the next temporary cubicle to let Betty James know she was taking a break. The exam rooms, so to speak, were made up of all sorts of donated decorative screens from sleek black Asian-inspired wooden ones to metal and fabric shabby chic creations.

Betty gave her a thumbs-up. Eva weaved her way around the makeshift exam rooms and to the entryway of the sanctuary where the restrooms were located. The small entryway was flanked on the left by the women's restroom and on the right by the men's.

A double door front entrance was monitored by two uniforms from Chicago's finest. One of the officers, Kelly O'Reilly, waved at her. Every time she worked in this neighborhood he made it a point to stop by and ask her out. Rather than merely stop by today, he and his partner were hanging around. She decided that either Detective Marsh or Todd had warned him about Eva's situation. To avoid questions about her current dilemma or that inevitable awkward moment when she would have to come up with another excuse about not going out with him, she ducked into the restroom before he could catch her.

She'd had more than enough awkwardness today already.

Eva snagged the phone from her ankle and checked the screen. *Lena.* Her heart sped into a run. She hit the screen to return the call and tried to slow the pounding in her chest. When she heard her sister's voice, her knees almost buckled. Thank God. She should have called her already. They lived in the same city and still both of them were bad to let too much time pass between calls and visits.

"Why haven't I heard from you since you moved to this secret location?"

Eva smiled, relieved to hear her sister's snarkiest tone. "Because I've been busy." Flashes of sleek skin and flexing muscles flickered in her brain. Eva pushed them away.

"So, how's it going with Dick?"

Eva laughed. Her sister always did have a way with words. The ability to summarize a situation quickly and eloquently had made her one of Chicago's most beloved reporters. "Things are fine with *Todd.* He's an excellent bodyguard." More of those sensual images and sounds from last night whispered through her mind.

"There was never anything wrong with his body," Lena retorted. "It's his heart where the trouble lies."

"I'm not having this discussion. How's it going in DC?" Why she felt any need whatsoever to defend Todd she would never understand. The idea that her sister's words inspired a glimmer of anger made her want to scream in frustration. But she wouldn't do that either.

"Oh my God."

Those three words told Eva that she was in trouble.

"You slept with him already."

Humiliation and frustration roared through her in equal measures. "I did not sleep with him." It was true. They had sex. There was no sleep involved.

"You never have been a good liar, little sister. You had sex with the man which means that when I get back I have to kick his ass."

Eva burst into full-on laughter. "Kicking his ass will not be necessary. I ended a long dry spell. No big deal. It was just sex."

"Who do you think you're kidding? You ended your dry spell with the jerk who broke your heart when you were just a baby. We need to have a long talk when I get back, sweetie. You have got to start getting out more."

"I was not a baby. I was nineteen." She ignored Lena's other comments. They had been down that "fix her up with this one and then that one" road. Her sister was a great reporter but she totally sucked at matchmaking. "Everyone gets their heart broken, Lena. It's not the end of the world."

She made a rude sound. "It's different when it's your little sister."

"Are you being extra careful?" It was time to change the subject. Eva knew Lena would not let it go unless she ignored further attempts to discuss the matter. Maybe not even then. Persistence was another of her award-winning traits.

"I am. I'm so bored I could take a cooking class. I know this political stuff is super important right now but I'd much rather be back in Chicago doing something that feels more real."

"How about I give you an exclusive when this is over?"

"That's as real as it gets," Lena said softly. "You sure you're okay? You could come stay with me. I'm sure Dick knows what he's doing but I can't help but have reservations."

"He knows what he's doing and I'm being very careful." She stared at herself in the mirror. "I'm at the church clinic today so I really should get back out there."

"I'm doing a story on that soon," Lena warned. "You guys are doing great work. I want the city's uppity-ups to hear about it more often."

"We can always use more donations," Eva admitted.

"You got it. Love you."

"Love you." Eva ended the call and tucked her phone away.

Lena reminded her more of their mother every day. There was just one place where the two had differed immensely. Lena might never forgive Todd for walking away all those years ago when their mother, Stella Bowman, had loved Todd even after he was gone. When he left she had held Eva and promised her she would be fine. She'd also made a prediction or maybe it had been nothing more than wishful thinking. Either way, her mother had been adamant about her conclusion on the matter.

He'll be back one day. You'll see. Todd Christian loves you in a way that can't be ignored.

Tears burned Eva's eyes even now and she swiped them away. "Miss you, Mom."

Eva knew her mother had meant well. She never gave up on anyone she loved. Eva hoped she hadn't spent the last decade unconsciously pushing everyone else away because of what her mother had predicted.

Stella Bowman had been right about one thing. He was back.

But it wasn't for the reason her mother had meant. It was coincidence. And when the tragic events that had aligned to create the chance reunion were no longer a threat to her, he would be gone. Just like before.

Eva drew in a deep breath and pushed out the door. She jumped when her gaze collided with the blue eyes she feared would haunt her dreams for as long as she lived.

"You ready for lunch?" Todd rubbed his lean abdomen. "I'm starving." He hitched his head toward the cop who had a crush on her. "O'Reilly tells me there's a great taco stand next to the Mickey D's across the street. He's even offered to make the food run."

Eva smiled. "Sounds good." She turned to the cop

watching Todd like a hawk. "I would love to have lunch with you, Kelly."

He looked from Todd to her and his fierce expression softened. "Text me your order and I'll be back in a snap."

Eva asked Betty and Dr. Taggart if they would like something from the taco stand, and they both declined so she sent her order to Kelly. When he returned she made it a point to chat mostly with him as the three of them ate lunch together.

As she returned to seeing patients she felt Todd watching her. She knew it wasn't right but she was enjoying ignoring her bodyguard. The idea that he seemed jealous made her far happier than it should.

Sometimes being bad just felt so damned good.

Chapter Ten

6:15 p.m.

Officer O'Reilly and his partner descended the steps at the front of the church with the final two patients of the day. The fondness in Eva's smile as she told Todd how the elderly women who came each week to have their blood pressure checked stirred an unfamiliar longing inside him. The women were sisters, twins no less, and they had lived together since their husbands passed away twelve or so years ago. Both had flirted relentlessly with Todd until he'd escorted them to the door and then they'd turned their gregarious attention to the officers.

Todd hadn't minded. In fact, he hoped he was as healthy as those two when he reached his eighties. He'd been only too happy to take care of the ladies while Eva and the other nurse packed up for the day. While he'd attended to the twins, the screens and portable tables had been stored away in a large supply closet and the remaining medical supplies had been taken away by Dr. Taggart. Eva's team had the set up and the cleanup down to a well-practiced routine.

They would be out of here in the next fifteen minutes. As he surveyed the boulevard that ran in front of the church, he noted the car parked across the street, dark, heavily tinted windows and big, shiny wheels. His warm thoughts of family and all those lifelong connections he'd missed, and suddenly found himself wanting, faded with the reality of what was no doubt about to go down.

Trouble.

Easing back into the entryway, he waited until he was out of sight of anyone in the car and then he turned and moved from window to window, checking the streets from every available angle. Thankfully only four of the windows in the main sanctuary were stained glass—the rest were clear, allowing a view of the streets that ran along two sides of the church. Eva had said that donations were slowly but surely replacing all the windows with stained glass to look like what would have originally been in the church. Today, Todd was grateful the renovation was not complete. He spotted at least one other suspicious vehicle.

Damn.

"Christian."

He turned to Rob Gates, the officer working with O'Reilly. Gates hitched his head toward the front entry as O'Reilly joined him. Todd glanced over to Eva and her friend who were finishing the cleanup before joining the two uniforms.

"You saw them, too?"

O'Reilly nodded. "My captain told me to keep an eye out for potential gang members." He nodded toward Eva. "Gates and I have monitored the streets all day. Those lowlifes showed up about two minutes ago. I've already alerted my chain of command that we may have a problem."

Relief rushed through Todd so hard and fast he almost hugged the guy. "You have an ETA for backup?"

"Six, seven minutes." O'Reilly glanced back at the front entrance. "As long as they don't make a move between now and then, we should get out of here with no problems."

But nothing was ever that easy—not when the nastiest of thugs were on the trail of their target.

As if the enemy understood they'd been made and time was short, the first hail of gunfire shattered the glass in the double front doors and burrowed into the brick walls on either side of the entry.

As O'Reilly and Gates readied to return fire, Todd rushed to Eva and her friend. "Under the pews."

The pews weren't bulletproof by any means but the thick, dense older wood would provide some level of protection, and some was better than none.

Eva grabbed Betty's hand and hurried to do as Todd asked. He took a position at a window facing Warren Boulevard. A quick look verified his worst fears. The bastards were moving in.

"We've got movement," O'Reilly shouted.

Todd kept his head down as he moved back to where the women were hiding. To Eva he said, "They're coming in. We need to find someplace else to hide the two of you."

"The basement," Eva said, fear shining in her eyes.

He shook his head. "We don't want to get pinned down where we can't get out."

"There's a tunnel," Eva explained. "Mr. Fry told me about it."

Todd hesitated again. "What if he's wrong?"

Eva shook her head. "I don't think he is. It's a risk I'm willing to take."

She turned to her friend and the other nurse nodded. "I'm with you."

Eva led the way to the storeroom that had once been a coatroom. A single door on the far side of the room opened to a narrow staircase that plunged nearly straight down. Todd pulled her back. "I go first."

She stepped aside and allowed him to take the first step down. Since he didn't spot a light switch or pull string, he used his cell's flashlight app to see where the hell he was going. "Close the door," he said over his shoulder, "and stay close behind me."

The steps continued downward for about ten feet, ending abruptly at a brick floor. He felt along the wall next to the final step. No switch. Using the flashlight app, he surveyed the small basement and spotted a pull string that led up to an old single bare bulb fixture on a rafter overhead.

He gave the string a yank and a dim glow came to life. Boxes covered in dust lined the far wall. Rows of shelves with books and literature lined another. A couple of tables and several chairs were piled in yet another corner. No windows and no doors.

"Where is this tunnel supposed to be?" Todd looked to Eva.

She shook her head. "I don't know."

"I'll start looking where the books are stored," Betty offered.

Eva headed toward the stack of tables and chairs.

Todd surveyed the bare wall beneath the staircase. No sign of an opening there so he moved on to the boxes. Some of the boxes were fairly heavy, others were so light he wondered if there was anything inside. Then he found the reason for the lighter boxes. Behind them was a small door, maybe two feet by two feet. The door was wood and reminded him of an old-fashioned crawl space door. Both the houses where he'd lived as a curious ten-year-old had doors exactly like this one that led to the area under the house. He and another foster boy had explored the space too many times to recall.

He opened the door. Sure enough, it led to a tunnel that looked to be five or six feet tall, maybe three feet wide and disappeared into the darkness well beyond where his flashlight app would reach. If the exit was sealed off, the find wasn't going to help much. In fact, they could end up trapped like rats.

If there's no exit, you already are.

A deep whoosh resonated overhead. Todd stilled and evaluated the sound. Not gunfire. Not a bomb.

Fire.

"Here!" Todd called, keeping his voice low despite the worry pounding inside him.

Eva and Betty hurried over to his position. "The two of you go first." He pulled the string to extinguish the light. "I'll pull some of the boxes back to the opening to conceal it and then I'll be right behind you."

Footsteps pounded on the stairs. Todd shoved his cell in his back pocket and drew his weapon with one hand and ushered the women into the tunnel with the other. A flashlight beam roved over the room.

"Christian? Eva? You guys down here?"

O'Reilly.

Todd straightened, allowing the officer's flashlight's beam to land on him. "What's going on up there?"

"Molotov cocktails," Gates said. "The old wooden pews are burning like kindling."

"We have to get out of here," O'Reilly urged. "Where're Eva and Betty?"

"This way." Todd ducked into the tunnel. They might die from smoke inhalation if they were trapped in this tunnel, but, hopefully, if it was long enough they could stay away from the danger until help arrived and put out the fire.

Eva and Betty were already at the farthest end of the tunnel.

"There's a ladder," Eva said. She tilted her cell phone flashlight app toward the old wooden ladder. "I don't know if it'll hold us or if the door at the top will open."

Where the ladies stood, the tunnel did a ninety-degree turn, moving upward. The opening was still only three or four feet in circumference but soared upward maybe ten feet.

"Only one way to find out." Todd put his weapon away and grabbed onto the ladder.

He measured the soundness of each rung before putting his full weight onto it. When he reached the door it was much like the one in the basement that had accessed the tunnel, about two feet square. It took some doing to force it open. When he did musty air hit his nostrils. He moved up a couple of rungs and looked around with his cell. The stone piers, the plumbing and ventilation ductwork that snaked around told him it was a crawl space. He climbed out of the hole and looked around a little more. Definitely a crawl space.

"Come on up," he called down to the others.

Eva climbed up the ladder first. Todd helped her out of the tunnel. "Watch your head."

Betty came next, then the two officers.

"This must be the crawl space under the old parsonage," O'Reilly suggested.

"There should be a way out somewhere along the foundation," Todd said, already scanning the outer perimeter. He spotted the small door in the beam of one of the flashlights roving the darkness. "There." He pointed to the north end of the crawl space. "We just have to watch out for the plumbing and the ductwork as we move in that direction."

"And spiders," Betty said.

Eva groaned. "I hate spiders."

"Spiders don't bother me," O'Reilly said. "Snakes, that's what I hate."

Eva and Betty insisted on staying behind the men as they made their way across the cool, musty space. As they crawled toward the exit, the blare of sirens grew closer and closer. Two minutes later they were crawling out into a fenced backyard. What had once been the church parsonage had been turned into apartments. Todd was grateful for the six-foot wood privacy fence that ran between the yard and the church parking lot. The instant he stood he spotted the smoke from the fire at the church.

He swore and shook his head.

O'Reilly took a call as they dusted themselves off. When he put his phone away, he said, "My sergeant says it's all clear. We can head back to the church."

Todd hitched a thumb in the other direction. "I

think Eva and I will take another route, just in case they're watching my car."

O'Reilly nodded. "Good idea. They might be laying low, waiting to see if the two of you make it out and planning to follow you away from the commotion at the church if you did. I can have a cruiser pick you up."

Todd shook his head. "One of my colleagues is already en route." He thrust out his hand to the other man. "Thanks for your help."

O'Reilly gave his hand a shake as he glanced at Eva. "Keep her safe. We count on her around here."

Eva and Betty shared a quick hug. Both swiped their eyes. Those bastards had destroyed an important part of this neighborhood—a part all those people who came through the makeshift clinic today depended on. Todd hoped he got the chance to make Miguel Robles pay.

Gates followed his partner's lead and shook Todd's hand next. "Keep your head down, Christian."

"Count on it."

The two officers and Nurse Betty James slipped through the gate next to the house and disappeared. Todd took Eva's hand in his and gestured to the gate at the rear of the yard. "Let's go this way."

EVA WOULD HAVE preferred to go back to the church and assess the damage but she conceded to Todd's judgment. She would find out how badly the church was damaged later. Right now, staying out of sight of those thugs was top priority. Anger roiled inside her at the idea that they had damaged the church to get to her. Now they'd have to find a new place willing to allow them to treat patients from the neighborhood.

Every day it was as if her troubles swallowed up more innocent victims. She had to find a way to end this.

As if he sensed her tension, Todd tightened his grip on her hand and urged her forward a little faster. Apparently being lost in thought wasn't conducive to moving quickly. She wondered if he had contacted Ian Michaels again for a ride. She had to give him credit. He was smart not to go back to the car in which they had arrived. Those thugs would be watching. When they'd attacked the church they had known the people inside would have no choice but to find a way out. Made sense that they would eventually end up back at their cars.

But Todd was a step ahead of them.

His strong grip infused her with confidence and warmth, keeping the cold worry and fear at bay. Who would ever have imagined all those years ago when he'd left her brokenhearted that he would one day come back to save her life?

Fate really did have a twisted sense of humor.

They moved along the alleyway between the rows of duplexes and old buildings that reminded her that this part of Chicago represented a century or more of the city's history. The traffic sounds of evening commuters hummed in the air. In another hour it would be dark. Several blocks stood between them and the trouble they'd barely escaped. Eventually they rounded the corner and slowed, walking along Washington Boulevard. Eva recognized the old Fahrney & Sons building. She had an antique medicine bottle from the late nineteenth century with the company name stamped into the glass that had belonged to her grandmother. Her mother had used it as a bud vase. Eva did the same.

Judging by the signs and the scaffolding around the historic building, the piece of Chicago history was finally being renovated. Eva squinted, staring ahead. How much farther did he intend to go on foot? It wasn't that she minded the walk/run pace but she'd been on her feet all day and she was exhausted. Not to mention, she couldn't help but worry that Robles's people would find them somehow.

She tugged on his hand, drawing his determined forward advancement to a halt. "Is your friend coming to pick us up?"

"Yes. We need to keep moving until he gets here."

The sooner they were off the street the happier she would be. The adrenaline had started to recede, leaving her limbs weak. She worked hard not to tremble. No need to show him her fear even if they could have been killed back there.

Betty could have been killed. Their final patients… the two officers Eva had come to consider friends. Her neighbor was dead because of her. A young girl was fighting for her life in the hospital at this very moment because of her.

How foolish she'd been to think that putting herself out in the open and going on with her usual daily activities would somehow make a difference. All she had managed to do was bring the danger to the place she loved most—her work.

"I should go back." She shook her head. "They're never going to stop until they have what they want. Running is doing nothing more than putting off the inevitable."

Todd grabbed her by the shoulders and gently shook her. "So you think giving up is the answer?"

The thought of Mr. Fry or any of the other people she had come to care about being hurt because of her—the way Mrs. Cackowski had been—was more than she could bear. "This can't be fixed by doing nothing but protecting me. Miguel Robles has to be stopped."

"And you believe you can do that?"

The fury in his eyes and in his voice warned that he had lost patience with her on the subject. He'd acquiesced to her demand of going on with her life as usual in an attempt to draw out Robles so the police could catch him. In her defense, she had hoped by baiting him that she would lure him into a mistake. She should have known better. He would simply send more of his minions. He would never risk his own safety.

"I don't know." She closed her eyes and shook her head. "I have to do something."

"You don't let him win," Todd said, his voice softer now. "That's what you do."

Eva steadied herself. "How do I do that without putting everyone I care about in the line of fire?"

And there it was, the million-dollar question no one seemed able to answer.

"We'll talk about this back at the safe house. Our ride is almost here."

She relented, allowed him to usher her forward. He put off answering her question because he couldn't.

The roar of a car engine followed immediately by gunshots jerked Eva's attention to the street. A dark car rocketed toward them.

Todd yanked her toward an old building on their right. He shoved her behind the plywood barrier that blocked off the entrance. Bullets splintered the plywood.

"Keep your head down!" he ordered.

She hunkered down and raced after him. He slammed his body into the sheet of plywood that had been nailed up over the original entrance to the building. More bullets punctured the outer wall of plywood and bit into the brick of the building. She made herself as small as possible and scooted nearer to Todd.

Another slam into the wood and it burst inward. He grabbed her by the hand and ran, clambering over the downed plywood.

With a quick survey of the gutted space, he spotted the staircase and headed that way. The staircase actually looked as if it were standing from memory since not much else appeared to be supporting it. The building had been erected on this piece of property more than a century and a half ago. Hopefully it wouldn't go down so easy. The next staircase looked no better. They rushed up it so fast Eva wondered if their feet even touched the treads.

No sooner than they reached the second floor, the sound of running footfalls echoed from the first floor.

With no police around, the thugs had apparently decided to give chase beyond the protection of their cars.

Just her luck.

Todd stalled.

Eva plowed into his back. Rather than ask why he'd stopped moving she stared at the place where the next staircase should have been.

It was gone.

They were trapped.

Todd checked his cell. He surveyed their situation once more as he shoved the phone into his back pocket.

Then his hand tightened on hers once more and he said, “This way.”

Shouting downstairs warned that the men were closing in on the second staircase.

She and Todd reached the backside of the building. He moved toward a large hole that might have once been a couple of windows. It wasn’t until they skidded to a stop at that hole that she saw the slide-like setup going from this floor down to the huge construction Dumpster on the ground.

“I’m going down first,” he said as he slung one leg onto the slide. “Grab on to my waist and stay tight against me so I can cushion your landing.”

There was no time to question the proposed exit. She grabbed on to his lean waist and held on tight.

Her stomach shot into her throat as they whooshed downward. They landed on a pile of construction debris.

Todd grunted.

Before she could ask him if he was okay, he forced her up and over the side of the Dumpster. He was right behind her.

A dark sedan rolled toward them.

Eva stalled, her heart dropping to her feet in a sharp free-fall.

Todd pulled her against him and sprinted the last few yards—toward the car. He yanked the rear door open and they landed on the back seat with the car still rolling.

“Go! Go! Go!” Todd shouted.

The car spun forward. Todd jerked the door shut and ushered Eva onto the floorboard.

Bullets pinged against the metal exterior.

Todd was suddenly on top of her and they were speeding away.

Chapter Eleven

Colby Safe House, 9:30 p.m.

Eva set the hair dryer aside and reached for the hairbrush. She dragged it through her hair, her thoughts far from the task. The fire gutted the church. She felt sick at the news. Dr. Taggart had sent her a text assuring her he'd spoken to the reverend and there was insurance which would eventually do the repairs, but there was no way to know how long that would take.

At least no one else had died.

Ian Michaels had explained that two other Colby Agency investigators were working on the case. Their efforts were being coordinated with Chicago PD. Eva appreciated the lengths to which they were willing to go. She hoped they were more successful than the local police had been so far.

Not fair, Eva. The police couldn't stop Robles if they had no evidence against him.

She braced her hands on the counter and stared at her reflection in the mirror. Her resolve was faltering, her determination running on empty. The past two days had been some of the hardest of her life. As exhausted and keyed up as she was, she wouldn't be going anywhere near the wine tonight. Not after how she'd allowed herself to go completely over the edge last night.

She turned away from the sad, uncertain woman in the mirror and padded back into the bedroom. A single functional brain cell reminded her that she should eat, but food was the furthest thought from her mind. Her mood fluctuated between defeated and furious. In her whole life she had never felt more helpless...more uncertain of the future. To make matters worse, she had lost her cell phone in the fray of today's frantic escape. Tomorrow she'd have to pick up a new phone and deal with transferring her contacts and other content. Eva sighed. Sometimes it felt like more of her life was available as data rather than as a real life. When had her existence become so dependent on notifications and alerts coming from a tiny object scarcely larger than a credit card?

She wandered to the door. Todd had promised they would talk about her concerns later. It was later and he'd avoided a face-to-face with her since they'd agreed that showers would do them both a world of good. He'd headed to his room and she'd headed to hers. Scarcely five feet of carpeted hallway stood between the two doors. She should just go over there, knock on the door and demand to know if he was ready to talk, or simply tell him she was heading downstairs and would be waiting for him so they could have the promised discussion.

Dredging up her battered wherewithal, she opened her door and took the three strides to his door. She curled her fingers into a fist and reached up to knock and his door abruptly opened.

He blinked, stared at her and then his lips parted as if he intended to speak, but no words made it past the tip of his tongue.

She took a breath and prepared to launch the first question but her attention stalled on his bare chest. It wasn't like she hadn't seen his chest hundreds of times. Well, maybe not hundreds but at least one hundred. His skin was damp as if he'd hastily scrubbed the towel over that sleek terrain. A drop of water slipped down his lean, rippled abdomen. She jerked her gaze upward as his torso widened into the broad shoulders where she'd lain her head dozens of times, moving on to the strong, muscled arms that had held her close on so many occasions.

Her attention whipped back to his right shoulder. A wad of gauze stained with crimson was stuck there. "What happened?"

He grinned, the expression a little lopsided. "I guess a nail or something from the construction heap snagged me. I can't reach it with both hands to do the repair."

Eva frowned. She remembered his shirt being torn in a couple of places. Hers had been as well but she'd walked away with nothing but a few sore places that would likely turn into bruises. "Let me have a look."

He moved into the hall, stepping away from her as he did. "I'll get the first aid kit then you can take care of it. I'll be right back."

He hurried down the stairs before she could do the smart thing and suggest they take care of his wound in the kitchen—far away from sheets still perfumed with their lovemaking. Instead, Eva stared after him for a few moments, then she hugged her arms around herself and entered his room. She felt somehow cold and too warm at the same time. No one had been seriously injured or killed today, she was grateful. Still, the potential…the what-ifs throbbed in her skull. Betty or Dr. Taggart could have been hurt. Officers O'Reilly and Gates—Todd could have been killed trying to protect her and Betty. If not for the quick thinking of Todd and O'Reilly, the day may have ended far more tragically.

How in the world did she fix this and stay alive?

She needed some plan of action. Todd's military training and work with the Colby Agency made him the better choice at figuring out a doable plan of action. Her problem was getting him to go there. He would like nothing better than for her to stay in hiding until this was over. That route wasn't feasible. Deep down he had to know this. Dr. Pierce surely grasped that fact as well—which brought up a whole other issue. How could she expect Pierce to hold her position without a reasonable return-to-work date?

She couldn't.

Pushing the troubling thoughts aside she surveyed Todd's bedroom. She hadn't gotten much of a look at it last night. Flashes of bare skin and flexing muscles filtered through her weary mind along with whispered words and soft sounds. How had she ever believed for even a minute that any other man could make her feel the way he did? There had been others, a few. Not one had been able to touch that place inside her that only Todd Christian had reached.

Again she cleared her head and focused on the mundane details. The layout of his room was much like her own, a large space with elegant furnishings.

The closet door was open, as was the door to the en suite bath. He'd tossed a T-shirt on the bed.

Her throat tightened as her gaze moved over the rumpled bed.

Closet. Stick to the far less dangerous spaces. She shifted her gaze to the closet. His duffel bag had been delivered here which made her wonder again why she'd ended up with a new wardrobe. Maybe it was the privacy issue of going through her things. On the other hand, it might simply be the best way to ensure nothing of sentimental value that belonged to her was damaged in all this running for their lives.

She ran her fingers along the shirts and tees that hung in a neat row in the closet. Jeans and a pair of black trousers were efficiently folded and placed on a shelf. A pair of leather loafers sat on the floor beneath the hanging shirts. The military had made him a little neater than she recalled.

With a deep sigh that made her heart uncomfortable, she turned away from his clothes and wandered to the door of the bathroom. A bottle of aftershave sat on the counter alongside a comb and a razor. The aftershave was the same one he'd always worn. Subtle hints of leather and sandalwood with the tiniest trace of citrus. She didn't have to look in the shower to know there would be a matching bodywash. The gentle fragrance of the toiletries he chose was so understated that his own natural scent was by far the more distinct.

His clothes, his car, even the apartment where he'd lived before had been modest, understated. The man himself had always been what stood out. How was it that a man so unpretentious and kind could have stolen her heart and then walked away without looking back? So many times she had asked herself that question. Had he found someone new? Had he grown bored with her? Had she done or said something that pushed him away? Yet, deep down she somehow understood that his decision was not her fault. He'd left for reasons she did not comprehend. But she hadn't come to that conclusion overnight. It had taken months, perhaps even years to realize that she'd done nothing wrong. Todd Christian had decided to walk away.

End of story.

"Sorry. It took me a minute."

Eva turned to face him. She'd intended to tell him to have a seat so she could look at his shoulder. Instead, she blurted, "Why did you leave without so much as saying goodbye?"

His fingers tightened on the first aid case. Eva vaguely wondered if it would suddenly crack and fall to pieces as her heart had all those years ago.

"What?"

His apparent confusion frustrated her. "You just left one day and never came back." She shrugged. "You didn't say a word or leave a note. I never heard from you again. I'm asking you why. Why did you do something so callous?"

He gave a single, small nod of his head. "Fair question." He waved the first aid case toward the bathroom. "I'll give you the best answer I know how while you work."

Surprised that he'd caved to her demand so easily, she followed him into the bathroom where he closed the toilet lid and sat down. He placed the case on the counter and stared at the wall he faced.

Eva decided to give him a moment while she surveyed the available medical supplies. The case offered the usual home first aid kit supplies with a few extras. In addition to the usual items, bandages, gauze, antibacterial and antihistamine creams, and antiseptic wipes, there were suture kits and butterfly bandages, tweezers and even a small scalpel.

"There's no lidocaine." Not a good thing in her opinion. "You're going to feel this."

"Just do it. I've endured worse."

His words had her wondering about the small scar on his cheek and the others on his back, but she decided not to distract him from the question she'd already asked. She washed her hands and walked around one muscled leg to reach his shoulder. The position put her square in the *V* of his muscular thighs. Her body reacted with a familiar twinge between her own thighs. How would it be possible not to react to the half-naked, good-looking man who'd saved her life? Particularly one who still owned a considerable chunk of real estate in the vicinity of her heart?

He will never know that sad truth.

Putting those reactions on ignore, she slowly pulled the gauze free of his skin and then tossed it into the sink. The gash was not too deep, not so wide, but the sides were not going to stay together without some assistance. She considered the butterfly bandages but she doubted those would hold the next time they were in a desperate situation. A few stitches would do the trick.

"I cleaned it with bottled water and a little bleach since I didn't have any betadine handy. I didn't see any debris that shouldn't be there, like splinters."

"Good." Eva threaded the eye of the needle with the sutures. She pulled the wound together, getting it as close to pre-gash condition as possible. "You were going to answer my question." She located the spot where she wanted to begin and inserted the needle through the skin.

He grimaced, made a small sound, not quite a grunt.

"Sorry." She secured the first suture and began working back toward the edge. In, out, pull, repeat.

She'd almost reached the final suture when he finally spoke. "I shouldn't have left the way I did. I was a coward."

Of all the answers she'd expected him to give, that was not one of them. Rather than say so, she kept her lips in a tight line and finished sealing the wound with a precise knot to keep the sutures just snug enough to aid in healing without injuring the skin further.

"I spent most of the first eighteen years of my life being tossed from foster home to foster home." He exhaled a big breath. "You were the first person I ever really wanted to please—beyond physically, I mean."

Struggling to keep her hand steady, she set the suturing tools aside and reached for antibacterial ointment. She applied a thin layer and then prepared a proper bandage with gauze and tape. All the while her heart pounded at his confession.

"I'd never wanted to make anyone happy like that before. I wanted to give you everything...to be everything you wanted."

Anger sparked. "I never wanted everything."

He shook his head. "Even if you'd said so at the time, it wouldn't have changed what I wanted."

Her work complete, Eva closed her eyes and dropped her hands to her sides. When she could say the words without her voice trembling, she opened her eyes and asked, “What changed your mind?”

“One morning I woke up and you were still sleeping.” He turned his face up to hers, his blue eyes begging for forgiveness or understanding. “I stared at you for so long, wondering how I would ever be the kind of man you deserved. I had no pattern to follow. How could I be the kind of man you could depend on when I wasn’t sure I could depend on myself?”

On some level she wanted to understand his reasoning, but she couldn’t. How selfless of him to throw away all her hopes and dreams to ensure he didn’t hurt her. Ha! Outrage flamed deep in her soul, raging instantly out of control. “Wow. You really gave up everything to save me, didn’t you? And all this time I thought you were a selfish ass for leaving without a word.”

He looked away. “I needed to grow up. To learn to trust myself before I could let you put all your trust in me.”

Incredible. “What a shame your timing was about six months too late.” Eva moved away from him, threw the supplies back into the case. “I’m so glad we had this talk. I totally get why you left now.”

He pushed to his feet, moved in on her and stared at her in the mirror when she wouldn’t look at him. “It was the hardest thing I’ve ever done. Leaving you tore me apart.”

Eva glared back at him. It would be so easy to believe him. To fall back into loving him, just like before.

"So you went off to the military and let them make a man out of you, is that it?"

"Pretty much. That and time."

"Well, I'm glad I was a part of your learning curve." She scooted away from him and headed for the door.

She was halfway across his room before he caught up with her. His fingers curled around her arm and pulled her to a stop.

"What?" she demanded. The sooner she was out of here, the better. She should never have gone down that path with him. Now he knew that a part of her still pined after him. How pathetic was that?

TODD HAD MADE a mess of his explanation. Every damned word had come out wrong. Rather than explain himself, he'd excused himself. Not what he'd intended. "I was wrong. What I did was wrong. There is no excuse."

She glared up at him and the hurt in her beautiful green eyes made his chest ache. "Glad you've seen the error of your ways. Now, if you'll excuse me, I'd like to get some sleep."

He released her but he wasn't ready to let her go. "I thought you wanted to talk about a plan for getting Robles."

She hesitated at the door. "I already know what to do." She turned to face him. "I tell the police I'd like to help set a trap for him. The sooner the better. It works in the movies all the time."

He moved toward her, choosing his words carefully. "This isn't the movies. Real life rarely works that way."

"I've run out of ideas and I refuse to be a party to

another day like this one or like yesterday. I want to finish this thing I set in motion when I killed that son of a bitch."

When she would have turned to walk out the door, he reached over her and closed it. "I won't let you do that."

She turned and glared up at him. "You can't stop me."

He moved in a step nearer, trapping her against the door. "Watch me." He cupped her face in his hands and leaned in close. "I will not let you do this."

She tried to back away, but the door stopped her. "Is this your way of making up for the past? You'll keep me safe and assuage your guilt?" She shook her head. "Like you said, this isn't the movies, this is real life. You can't repair the heart you shattered all those years ago by being the hero today. I can't forgive you for what you did, Todd. If that's what you're expecting, you've overestimated your worthiness."

Her words were like daggers twisting in his chest. "You hate me, is that it?"

She blinked. "Maybe."

"You hate me so much—" he braced his forearms on the door and leaned into her, putting his face right up to hers "—that you came over and over in my arms last night."

She stared at his lips a moment and he longed to taste her. "That was sex," she argued. "Nothing more."

"Sex?" He traced her cheek with his nose. "Just sex?"

"Yes."

The feel of her lips moving against his jaw made him so damn hard he could barely breathe. "Then you won't mind if we do it again, just to be sure it was only physical." He brought his mouth around to hers. She gasped. "It doesn't mean anything." He nipped her bottom lip. "Just sex."

She stilled, lifted her eyes to his. "I've already experienced all your parlor tricks, Christian. I doubt you can show me anything new. I'd suggest you save your strength for helping me take down Miguel Robles."

Parlor tricks, eh? "Give me a minute to change your mind."

When she would have argued, he dropped to his knees. He reached for the waistband of her lounge pants and slid the soft fabric down her thighs, letting them fall to the floor. No panties. His body reacted with a rush of need that rocked him and had his cock pushing against his fly. He kissed her belly button, traced over her belly with his tongue. She pressed against the closed door as if to escape the exquisite torture, her hands braced on either side of it.

He lifted her right leg and settled the crook of her knee onto his left shoulder. Let her try to escape. He was only getting started. She gasped as he bent his head toward the tender flesh between her thighs. He kissed every part of her, slid his tongue along that delicious channel. She whimpered softly. Still she kept her hands plastered against the door. He delved deeper, using his mouth to draw on that place that caused her to cry out. He dipped a finger inside her, savored the moist, sweet heat and then tested her with another.

Her fingers suddenly dove into his hair as if to hold him back. He stilled and then she gasped, surrendering as her body started an instinctive, rhythmic undulating. He used his fingers, his tongue, his lips to explore all of her most intimate places, to bring her to orgasm. She cried out with the pleasure. He kissed her belly, moved up her torso, letting her leg slip down, her foot land on the floor, as he tasted his way to her breasts. He wanted to memorize every inch of her. He savored her breasts with his mouth while he used his fingers to draw her toward climax again. Hot, firm nipples peaked for his attention while those sweet feminine muscles tightened around him. He pressed the pad of his thumb harder against her clitoris. She fought to restrain her cries, but he could feel how hard and fast she was coming undone all over again. Her fingers found his fly and struggled to unfasten his pants. She managed to push his jeans down, releasing his aching cock, but he refused to give her what she wanted just yet. She whimpered with need, rubbed him wantonly with her hands.

When she reached that edge…so very close to exploding with pleasure yet again, he turned her around so fast she lost her breath. He pushed between her thighs, reached around her small waist with one hand and down to that wet, pulsing place to guide himself into her. She screamed with pleasure as he pushed deep inside her. He kept one hand focused on that hot, pulsing nub and the other on her breasts, kneading each one in turn, tweaking those perfect hard nipples. He pressed her against the door as he thrust in and out. This position took him so deep, stretching her to the very limits and she cried out for more.

One more hard, deep thrust and they came together.

With her back pressed against his chest and his

cock deep inside her, he carried her to the bed. When he would have pulled out of her, she arched her bottom, keeping him deep inside that hot, wet place as they started that sweet, slow rocking motion all over again.

Chapter Twelve

Saturday, May 12, 8:00 a.m.

Eva couldn't blame the wine this time.

Todd had broken through all her defenses, lowered every wall she had so carefully erected over the past ten years to protect her battered heart. Bared her every vulnerability, revealed her rawest emotions. By the time they'd both collapsed, utterly exhausted, she couldn't have argued about the best course of action to take against Robles any more than she could have crossed the hall to her own bed.

When she'd awakened, he'd already been downstairs. She was glad. She'd needed the past forty minutes to gather her scattered composure. This morning she intended to get straight down to business. She had a life she wanted to get back to. She wanted this ugly situation cleared up before her sister returned to Chicago. She needed distance from Todd before she lost her heart and soul to him all over again.

A quick shower had washed his scent from her skin but nothing could scrub those hours from her memory or the sweet ache from her muscles. The way he touched her, as if he knew every part of her and understood how to reach her deepest desires. He had explored every inch of her and she had done the same, relearning his lean, muscled body. Tasting him, touching places that had haunted her dreams for so very long.

She wasn't the only one who had been pushed beyond all carefully lain boundaries—she had given as good as she got. She had made him groan with need, watched his fingers clench in the sheets, made him beg for more. He'd whispered her name over and over. They'd climaxed together so many times, she felt weak with pleasure even now, overwhelmed with the need to touch him again and again.

Todd Christian was a drug she would never be able to resist.

With that undeniable knowledge tucked away for later contemplation, she left her room and headed for the stairs. The smell of bacon lingered in the air as she descended the staircase. Her stomach rumbled and she suddenly realized she was starving. More often than not she grabbed a cup of yogurt and a piece of fruit for breakfast. After what she'd been through the past few days, she had every right to splurge with a self-indulgent breakfast.

Todd looked up from the stove as she walked into the room. His grin was sexy as hell and made her heart skip a beat. "Good morning."

"Good morning." She headed straight for the coffee pot and poured a cup. The rich aroma had her immediately lifting the cup to her lips. Bold flavor burst on her taste buds and she made a satisfied sound. "So good."

"I hope you still like pancakes."

She turned to him, the warm cup cradled in both hands. "The ones with nuts and whole wheat flour?"

"That's the ones." He paddled three pancakes onto a plate and slathered a pat of butter on top, then piled on the bacon. "Since we discovered this recipe, I've never made pancakes any other way."

She wondered how many other women he'd made them for after a long night of hot sex. *None of your business, Eva.*

She claimed a stool while he prepared his own plate and poured them both a glass of orange juice. This could be her last breakfast. After what happened yesterday, it was clear Robles didn't intend to back off. She should claim whatever pleasure available. She blocked more images from last night and focused on the aromas making her mouth water this morning.

"Wow." She dismissed the foolish and wholly unfounded worry about other women. "I can't believe you remembered how I like my pancakes."

He reached around her and poured on the syrup. "You're the only person I've ever made pancakes for."

She smiled, ridiculously pleased by his comment as she lifted a forkful of deliciousness to her mouth. Another of those happy moans vibrated inside her. The pancakes were so good. She grabbed a slice of crisp bacon and devoured it before reaching for her juice. "I might just die right here."

He laughed. "Then I'd have to face the wrath of Lena."

Eva put her hand over her mouth to prevent spewing orange juice. "True."

He fell silent for a minute but she sensed he had more to say. Had he learned something new about her case?

She set her fork aside and turned to him. "Did

something else happen?" *Please, don't let anyone else be dead because of her.*

Realization dawned in his eyes. "No. No, nothing else has happened." He dropped his fork onto the counter. "I was thinking about your mom and how sorry I am that I didn't get a chance to apologize to her for what happened. She must have hated me after... after I left."

Eva picked at her pancakes. "No. She didn't hate you. She adored you."

Surprise replaced the sadness she'd seen in his expression only moments ago. "Are you sure about that? I mean, Lena made it pretty clear how she felt."

She would not—could not—tell him all her mother said. "Lena is Lena, but trust me when I say my mother adored you until the day she died."

"Thank you." He reached out and gave her hand a squeeze. "I appreciate you telling me."

Eva blinked, then looked again. The shine of emotion was heavy in his eyes. She turned away. Maybe slaving over a hot stove had made him teary-eyed. "It's true. She loved you." She clamped her teeth together, could have bitten off her tongue. She hadn't meant to use the *L* word, though her mother made her feelings about Todd clear on numerous occasions. He was the son she never had.

He drew his hand from hers as if her blurted words had stung him almost as badly as they had her. It was definitely time for a change of subject.

"So you joined the army." Her voice sounded too high-pitched and she cursed herself for even speaking again.

He shifted his attention back to his plate. "I did. My

specialty was communications at first." He shrugged. "Apparently there was a shortage in the field since I expected to be an eleven bang-bang—an infantry soldier."

"You were an officer?" He'd just graduated with his degree in science. For hours on end he would talk about how he wanted to be a teacher. A few teachers were the only people who had ever made him feel as if he could be more than what he'd come from.

"No." He shook his head. "They offered me the opportunity but I didn't want to be an officer. I wanted to do what all the other enlisted soldiers had to do."

"Really?" Surprised, she munched on another slice of bacon. "Did you travel the world?"

"Not so much at first." He reached for his coffee. "A couple years after my enlistment, I was recruited by Special Forces. Everything changed then."

She laughed in hopes of lightening the moment. "I suppose you went on all sorts of exciting top secret assignments in Special Forces."

"Now and then." He poked at the pile of pancakes on his plate.

"Is that where you got the scars?" She touched her cheek in the same spot where the scar was on his. It was such a small one, but there were several larger ones on his back. Not a single one detracted from his good looks. She bit her lips together for fear she'd throw in that part, too.

"Shrapnel. I was one of the lucky ones."

Shrapnel meant a blast…a bomb. He could have been killed—probably numerous times. The realization made her angry. Why had he worked so hard in college to achieve his degree—not to mention he'd been accepted into a master's program—just to throw it all away? "What happened to the teaching career you talked about?"

He stared at his plate once more and lifted one shoulder in a halfhearted shrug. "I guess that was another one of those things I figured I didn't deserve."

Why had she never once noticed that deep-seated worry about his self-worth when they were together? Had she loved him so much that she couldn't see the pain? The idea made her sad. But she'd been so young…

"What about Kevin? Have the two of you kept in touch?"

He smiled, and the beauty of it took her breath away. "He graduated law school last year. He just got married. I was his best man."

"That's great." How many times had she planned *their* wedding before he ran away?

The rest of the meal was eaten in silence. Eva had said more than enough. So had he. She couldn't decide which was worse: all the things she'd told him, or the things she allowed herself to do with him.

Or maybe it was all that he hadn't told her when it mattered most.

With every fiber of her being she understood one thing with complete certainty: when this was over—assuming she survived—she would be heartbroken once more because he would leave again.

Some people just never learned.

EVA INSISTED ON cleaning up. Todd tried to help but she shooed him away. "You cooked. I'll clean."

He held up his hands and backed away from the sink. "Have it your way."

A break would do him good. He'd been on edge all morning. Well, no, maybe it started last night after hours of incredible lovemaking. He'd lain awake for hours just watching her sleep. No one had ever made him feel as important and as helpless at the same time as Eva did. She made him yearn to be more…to give her more.

"I'll be in the office." He hitched a thumb toward the hall. "We can have that talk about Robles and where we go from here when you're done."

Her eyebrows reared upward. "Seriously? You're not going to find a way to put me off again or to change the subject?"

His last attempt to distract her had taken an unexpected turn and he'd ended up on his knees. Who was he kidding? He'd dreamed of savoring all of Eva from the moment he saw her again. For years he'd kept thoughts of her—the memories—locked away in a place in his heart that refused to let go of her. He'd ignored those memories for years, unable to touch them. Then he'd returned to Chicago and he'd seen her by complete accident for the first time in more than eight years. She hadn't seen him so he'd followed her and his entire being had ached with the need to touch her…to know her again. If he was honest with himself, he would admit that he'd been trying hard to work up the nerve to talk to her for more than a year. He'd followed her enough times that he felt like a stalker.

Gotta get your head straight, man.

Right now he had a job to do. One of the most important of his life; he had to keep Eva safe. As he walked toward the office he called Michaels to see if there was any news on the agency's investigation into Robles.

Michaels said, "I was about to call you."

Not a good sign. "I take it you've found someone willing to talk."

The agency had concentrated on finding evidence of the gang leader's crimes while Todd focused on protecting Eva. Victoria wanted to do what the police had not been able to—find someone willing to testify against Robles.

"We have and that source warned that Robles is about to make a direct move against Eva. Since her sister is her only family, I've contacted a colleague in DC to put eyes on her. That's a considerable reach for Robles, but at this point he's likely feeling desperate to avenge his brother. More than a week has passed and he hasn't managed to follow through with his declaration of vengeance."

"Never a good thing for the minions to see." Todd agreed completely. Robles was no doubt damned desperate by now. He'd probably exterminated every member of his gang who'd failed to bring Eva to him.

"If our source will testify against Robles, we may have a starting place for Gang Intelligence to build a real, prosecutable case. Until now, they haven't had a source willing to speak out against Robles. But his credibility is in question now. Every day he fails to honor his brother, his followers grow more restless."

"Maybe the world will get lucky and they'll start killing each other." As crazy as it sounded, it happened. Someone inside could decide Robles was too weak to continue to be their leader. It was a long shot but a guy could hope.

"Until then we keep Eva and her sister safe and we continue pursuing potential sources."

They discussed the various avenues for further infiltrating the True Disciples as well as Victoria's urgent requests to her higher-level resources. If anyone could find a way to Robles, it was Victoria.

"Thanks for the update." Todd was grateful for every step that brought them closer to ending the danger to Eva. "Keep us posted."

He ended the call and put his cell away. Now if he could convince Eva to be patient a little longer—

"What update?"

He did an about-face and produced a smile. Eva was the only person who had ever been able to sneak up on him. He'd decided back when they were together that it was because she was such a part of him. They were one. His senses wouldn't alert him to her presence any more than they would warn his right arm that his left was nearby. They began and ended together.

Evidently his instincts hadn't realized that wasn't the case anymore.

Whispers and glimpses of last night's urgent lovemaking echoed through him. Maybe in some ways it was still the same, which was a blessing and a curse at the same time.

"We have a source who may be willing to testify against Robles."

Her eyes widened with anticipation. "Would that be enough to get him off the streets?"

"Depending on what information he has and how much of it he can back up, it's possible. If we're really lucky charges could be brought and the judge would deny bail." He resisted the urge to reach out and touch her in reassurance. "It's a starting place."

He decided not to tell her about Michaels's other concerns. Michaels was on it. Lena would have protection ASAP if it wasn't in place already.

Eva moved into the room, her arms folded over her breasts in a protective manner. "Do you believe he can be stopped this way? I don't understand why that hasn't happened already if it's so simple."

His hands twitched with the need to pull her close and hold her as he explained what Michaels had told him. "He's swiftly losing credibility. Power and fear are the two main ingredients of a dictator's reign and that's what gang leaders like Robles are. He has hundreds of followers and they do as he tells them for various reasons. Some idolize him. Others are too afraid to do otherwise. The life—meaning their membership in the gang—is all they've ever known."

"Afraid?" She frowned. "Why would coldhearted killers be afraid of anything?"

"Those who have second-guessed the life are in too deep to turn back now. Leaving isn't an option. They'd be hunted and killed as would the people they care about. For others, they might be fearless when it comes to fighting, maiming and murdering, but they're terrified of not having the unity they find in the gang. In some cases, it's the only family they've ever known. If their leader fails, someone worse or someone who might not want them could take over. For those guys, protecting the life is all that matters."

"Either way it seems like the empire Robles has

built might be on shaky ground." Hope glimmered in her eyes.

Todd was grateful the news had given her something to hang on to. Maybe it would be enough to keep her smart about how to proceed. "Every day that you're breathing, his credibility weakens. Someone else could step up and go for a takeover."

"How can I help make it happen faster?" She turned her palms up in question. "I could go on the news. Speak out about what a coward he is."

Todd managed a stiff laugh that came out more like a cough. "I think we'll hold off on that avenue for a bit."

"This is good news, though." She hugged herself again, rubbed her hands up and down her arms as if she were chilled. "I should call Lena. Let her know I'm okay. We haven't spoken since early yesterday." A frown furrowed her brow. "She hasn't answered that text I sent from your phone last night letting her know I was okay after what happened at the church."

He dug his phone from his back pocket and offered it to her. "She hasn't. Why don't you give her a call? I'll have a new phone brought to you, if you'd like."

She accepted the phone. "I'm guessing that means we're staying in today."

Before he could answer, his cell rang. Eva jumped and almost dropped it.

She passed it to him. "Geez, that scared the hell out of me."

Todd didn't recognize the local number. "Christian."

"Christian, this is Detective Marsh. We have a problem."

"I'm listening." Todd moved to a desk and awakened a computer monitor just to put some distance between him and Eva without being too obvious about it.

"Someone broke into Lena Bowman's townhouse last night. They tore the place apart and left a vic in the bedroom. We're going to need Eva to come over here and make an identification."

Todd's heart stumbled. "Can you give me a few more specific details?"

"The vic is female. We can't be sure whether or not it's her sister. The general height and weight, hair color are right, but there's too much facial damage to be certain."

Fear snaked around his chest and tightened like a vise. Lena was out of town. Couldn't be her. Still, his gut churned with worry. "We'll be right there."

With great effort he slid the phone back into his pocket without allowing his hand to shake. The worry and no small amount of fear crushed against him. "We have to go to Lena's apartment." He started for the door, taking Eva by the arm and pulling her along as he went.

"Why?"

He kept his gaze forward. Making eye contact right now he feared would show her what he didn't want her to see—not yet anyway. "Someone broke in and ransacked the place."

"Okay," she said, the word thin.

He wouldn't mention the rest until they were there. Having her get hysterical while he needed to watch for a tail could get them both in trouble.

As if she sensed there was something more he wasn't saying, she didn't ask anything else as they loaded into the black Camaro. The next forty-five minutes were some of the longest in his life. Eva tried four times to call her sister. Each time the call went to voice mail. His tension rocketed higher. Thankfully, Eva didn't start asking questions.

By the time they reached Lena's townhouse on East Elm Street, Eva was quietly falling apart piece by piece. Her hands were trembling and she stared out the window. He roared right up to the police perimeter and two uniforms shouted orders for him to move and that this was a crime scene. Like the strands of yellow tape weren't sufficient evidence it was a crime scene. Pedestrians and neighbors stood on the sidewalk across the street and behind the tape. A couple of news vans were already on the scene but they had been held back a full block.

"Detective Marsh is expecting us," Todd said to the officer who marched up to him.

A sharp whistle sounded from the townhouse steps. Marsh motioned at the officer. "Let 'em through."

Todd put his hand to Eva's back and guided her to the steps. Her shoulders were square and her stride was firm, but he felt her body trembling. Marsh waited on the sidewalk to walk up with them. Lena's place was the upper of the two units.

"I'm sorry I had to call you over here, Ms. Bowman," Marsh said as they walked through the front door.

"Can you give us a minute?" Todd asked when they stood in the entry hall with the front door closed, blocking out the prying eyes on the street.

Marsh gave a knowing nod. "Sure. I'll wait in the living room."

Todd turned to Eva and he would give anything in the world not to have to tell her the part he'd been holding back.

As if she suddenly understood what he was about to say, Eva shook her head. "She isn't here. Lena's in DC. You know that."

"I know." He wished his heart would stop pounding so hard and that his hands would stop their damned shaking. "There's a woman, Eva. She was murdered in the bedroom."

Eva fought to keep her expression clean of emotion but her lips trembled and she made this hiccupping sound that ripped his thundering heart right out of his chest even as she shook her head adamantly once more. "She's not here."

He tried to take her hand but she dodged the move. "You're right," he said, the two words uttered out of sheer desperation. "Marsh thought maybe it was one of her neighbors. He hoped you might be able to help them with the identification."

More of those painful sounds wrenched from her throat. "Liar."

"Come on." He closed his hand around hers before she could snatch it away from him this time. "Let's do what we can to help Marsh and then we can get out of here."

She nodded, the movement jerky.

He held on to her small, trembling hand and prayed like he had never prayed before as they went into the living room to catch up with Marsh. The furniture had been turned upside down. Drawers and their contents were strewn over the room. The kitchen and dining room were the same. Broken china and silverware flung across every surface. Chairs were overturned.

They passed the first of two bedrooms, which was Lena's office. Like the other rooms, it had been ransacked, furniture overturned. Files and papers were scattered across the hardwood as if a hurricane had blown through the space.

In the final bedroom—Lena's room—the dresser drawers were tossed in every direction. Framed photographs of the sisters that once sat on the dresser had been crushed on the floor. Lingerie was tossed from one side of the room to the other. The bed covers were torn from the mattress.

Bare feet were visible beyond the end of the bed.

Eva yanked free of his hold and ran to where the victim lay on the floor. She dropped to her knees. His entire body vibrating with fear and tension, Todd crossed the room and crouched beside her. The woman had long brown hair...like Lena. The height and weight were right, as Marsh had said. She wore yoga pants and a bra-like top. Her face was beaten beyond recognition.

Damn these bastards.

For ten full seconds Eva stared at the woman, tears flooding down her cheeks. Todd held his breath and prayed some more.

"It's not her."

Relief rushed through his veins even as regret that someone else's sister or daughter or wife had been murdered tugged at his gut. "You're sure?"

"Look closely," Marsh urged.

"Her hair is too long. Her fingers are thicker than Lena's and her fingernails are too short." Eva drew in a shaky breath. “Lena gets her nails done every week.” She gestured to the woman’s bare midriff. “Lena has a birthmark on her right side. It looks like a little white cloud.” She looked up at Marsh, a shaky smile on her lips even as the tears continued to flow. “She always hated it.”

“Okay.” Marsh nodded. “Does your sister have a friend or a neighbor with long brown hair?” He looked to the victim. “One who fits what you see here.” He shook his head then and looked away.

Eva moved her head side to side. “Lena has so many friends. I’m sorry. I don’t know.”

Todd helped her to her feet and asked the detective, “We done here?” She’d been through enough. Whatever else Marsh wanted to know he would need to ask Lena.

He nodded. “For now.” To Eva he said, “I really am sorry we had to put you through this, Ms. Bowman, but we didn’t have a lot of choice. Every minute we waste with red tape is a minute we can’t get back. Waiting for the medical examiner to come and remove the body before we let you have a look down at the morgue would have eaten up hours.”

Eva took a deep breath. “I understand. I’ll let my sister know what’s happened.”

Marsh had one of his officers bring the Camaro right up in front of the townhouse. Todd ushered Eva into the car as quickly as possible.

Somewhere amid the crowd, Robles’s men would be watching.

Chapter Thirteen

Colby Safe House, Noon

Eva paced the living room. Ian Michaels had delivered her new phone. She had finally reached Lena's boss who called a point of contact in DC that confirmed Lena had an early morning interview. According to the contact in DC, she should be finishing up soon and be available to return Eva's call. Lena's boss assured Eva that it was common for a reporter to shut off his or her cell phone during an important interview. She understood that part—Lena had told her as much on numerous occasions—but the knowledge did nothing to alleviate Eva's mounting concern. She couldn't possibly relax until she heard her sister's voice.

Another woman was dead. Eva couldn't pretend that the woman's life or Mrs. Cackowski's mattered less than her own. She possessed the ability to stop the bloodshed, and putting off that necessary step was unequivocally wrong.

She summoned her courage, folded her arms across her chest and said as much. "I want to meet the person the Colby Agency found who might be willing to speak out against Miguel Robles." She met Todd's startled gaze with lead in her own. "He might be able to help us end this now."

"First," he countered, "leaving this house is growing increasingly dangerous. It's my job to protect you and I take that job very seriously."

When she would have argued, he held up a hand and continued, "Second, allowing you to even know the name of the man who's talking to the agency much less speak with him could shut him down. Even if for some strange reason he agreed to meet with you, some small thing you say or do might change his mind. We can't risk rocking that particular boat right now. He's far too potentially valuable to the investigation."

"You promised we'd talk about what I *can* do." She checked her new cell phone, willing it to ring and growing all the more frustrated when it didn't. "I can't stay hidden forever. I thought you understood my feelings on the matter. So let's stop going over what I can't do and discuss something I can."

Maybe it was wrong to lay a guilt trip on him but she was desperate. If she didn't hear from Lena soon she might just lose it. It was either that or fall apart and she'd done that once already today. Going there again wasn't an option. She needed to be strong and focused. Two people were dead and another was in the hospital because of her. Eva had to do something besides hide and wait.

He opened his mouth to answer and her cell rang. The number for the television station where Lena worked flashed on the screen. A new stab of worry sliced deep into Eva's heart as she accepted the call. "Hello."

"Eva, this is Scott Mason from Channel 7."

Lena's boss. Eva's fingers tightened on the phone. "Did you hear from Lena?"

"Not exactly." He hesitated and Eva's heart fractured. "I spoke to the cameraman who was supposed to be at the interview with her this morning. He said Lena cancelled the interview because she got word that her sister had been in an accident. She left DC around eight this morning. No one has heard from her since."

Eva's world tilted and the crack in her heart widened. "Thank you, Mr. Mason." He was still speaking when Eva ended the call. She couldn't listen to more of his regrets and offers of comfort. She turned to Todd. "Lena came back to Chicago." Outrage roared through her. "I have to find her. Now."

"Give me five minutes. Let me make some calls."

Rather than debate him, Eva sank into the nearest chair. She wanted to believe that this was some sort of misunderstanding. Maybe a friend who'd heard about the explosion at the church had gotten her wires crossed. Maybe the cameraman misunderstood what Lena said when she cancelled the interview. Even as she turned over all the possibilities, every instinct warned that it wasn't a mistake. Lena had been lured back here by that monster Miguel Robles and now she was in trouble. A new surge of fear and pain extinguished the outrage. Her sister could die…she could be dead already.

Todd ended his call and slid the phone back into his pocket. "I've got the agency verifying that Lena boarded a plane headed for Chicago. It'll take a bit of time, but we'll know one way or the other soon enough. Until then, let's keep in mind that Lena is a very savvy investigative journalist. She wouldn't be fooled easily."

Eva dredged up her fleeing courage. She agreed with his statement; it was a valid point, to a degree. "If that's true, then why hasn't she answered my calls or called me back?"

"Her cell battery may need to be charged. She might be on her way to the agency offices as we speak." He crouched in front of her and searched her eyes a moment, his so certain of his words. "Lena is a fighter. If Robles lured her into a trap, he's in for a hell of a surprise."

Eva managed a faint smile. She would love nothing better than to cling to that scenario, but deep in her heart she knew there was only one explanation for why they hadn't heard from Lena. Every ounce of warmth leeched out of her body. "She hasn't called me because she can't call me. And you're right, she is a fighter, but there are some battles even the strongest person can't win. I'm not going to pretend the situation isn't exactly what it is."

He dropped his head for a moment before meeting her eyes once more. "Until we know for certain she's with Robles, we should stay calm and hope for the best."

Eva wanted to laugh at the suggestion but she couldn't form the sound.

Her cell rang.

Eva stared at the device clenched in her right hand. Lena's face and name flashed on the screen. Her heart thumped hard against her ribs. "Lena."

"Eva."

Lena's voice sounded raw and edged with uncertainty. Eva went numb. "Where are you?"

"They want me to tell you where I am so you can come to me."

The undeniable nuance of fear in her sister's voice stole Eva's breath.

"Put it on Speaker," Todd whispered.

Her hand trembling, Eva touched the speaker image on the screen with one icy finger and said, "I can come right now. Just tell me where."

"He told me to tell you that you can't tell anyone, Eva, and no matter what else happens," she said, her words stilted as if she were taking great care with each one, "don't come!" Lena shouted the final two words.

More shouting and scuffling echoed from the speaker. Eva's heart flailed in her chest. "Lena!"

Todd reached for the phone but Eva twisted away from him. "Lena!"

"Your sister is not a very smart woman," a male voice said.

Eva instantly recognized the voice. *Miguel Robles.* Had to be. This was the same voice that had taunted her about the Chavez woman's shooting. "Tell me where she is. I'll come right now."

"I will send you instructions at six thirty this evening," Robles said. "Keep your phone close. If you deviate from my precise instructions, your sister will die."

"I can come now!"

The connection severed.

Eva pushed to her feet, brushed past Todd and stood in the center of the room. She had to think. She turned all the way around. Where was her charger?

She needed to make sure her phone battery stayed fully charged. The bastard told her to keep her phone close.

Todd was on his cell, his voice low and quiet. Eva ignored him. It didn't matter to whom he was speaking or what he thought she should do; she was doing exactly what Robles told her to do. She would not risk Lena's life under any circumstance. Whatever Robles asked her to do, she would do it. Defeat and certainty settled deep into her bones.

This moment had been coming all week. Fighting it any longer was futile.

"Michaels has a friend at NSA."

Eva dragged her thoughts from the haze of worry and struggled to focus on the man staring at her with such immense concern. "How will that help us?" A numbness had taken over. She felt as though she were under water. She could see and hear but it was all distorted and so far away. The moment felt surreal…as if it were happening to someone else and Eva was only watching.

"NSA can track any cell phone. They can determine in minutes what it takes others days to figure out. That call from Lena's phone will give us what we need. We find the phone and we'll find her. The way I see it, we have a little better than five hours to find her before Robles makes a move."

"I will not take any chances with my sister's life." Eva lifted her chin in defiance of whatever he might have in mind. "I hired you. I can fire you. Unless we do this my way."

"I agree completely." He reached for Eva's free hand. "But for the next five hours I need you to trust me. I've carried out a lot of high-risk rescues. I know what I'm doing."

Eva searched for calm. He had been in Special Forces and the Colby Agency was the best in the business of private investigations and security. "What's your plan?"

He visibly relaxed. "First we find the location the call was made from. Robles was careful. He kept the call short. He feels confident we won't be able to trace him. And he's right, we can't. But there are people who can."

Eva had heard about the NSA's ability to track the cell phones of suspected terrorists but that was the extent of her knowledge on the subject. "How can we be certain the location is accurate?"

"Lena uses a smartphone. At this very minute her phone is attempting to locate cell towers and Wi-Fi hot spots. NSA can narrow her location down to a city block or less within the hour. We will find her and then we'll get her out—safe."

For a moment Eva wanted to argue with him. This was her sister—the only family she had in this world. Eva would do anything to make sure she stayed safe just as Lena would do anything for her. She'd told Eva not to come. Her sister would without hesitation willingly die for her.

But this wasn't about Lena. This was about Eva and if anyone else was going to die today, it would be her.

West 47th Street, 5:40 p.m.

ROBLES CHOSE THE home field advantage. The Back of the Yards neighborhood was one of Chicago's most notorious where more residents than not felt the city had abandoned them, leaving gangs to take over. Century-old houses and aging apartment buildings butted up to derelict warehouses and industrial buildings that once infused life into the economy that was now dying. The handful of determined business owners hanging on to their small shops and slivers of new development and refurbishment continued to provide a glimmer of hope for change, but little actually changed.

Robles wasn't the only one at home along the most dangerous streets of the Windy City. Todd had done some time here. From age fifteen to sixteen he'd lived with a foster family on the fringes of this neglected, gang-infested territory. The mom-and-pop shops had been his favorite haunts, the rail tracks and the box-cars his playground.

The commercial equipment rental company that Robles and his men had taken over for the evening's event extended a full city block. Compressors, back-hoes and excavators lined the parking lot behind the security fence. Warehouses and the main office formed a boundary on three sides, leaving only the front with its ten-foot-high fence to afford a visual onto the property. Directly across the street was the rail yard, and behind the rental compound was a street lined with trees and more of those early twentieth-century bungalows built by immigrants and stock-yard workers.

Way too many people lived around the target to go in without backup from Chicago PD. Eva hadn't taken the news well. He'd had a hell of a time talking her out of walking away from his protection. Her concerns about involving the police were understandable but hardly reasonable. Ultimately, they'd reached a standoff and he'd called Marsh. Eva had told Todd in no uncertain terms how she felt about his decision.

If this operation went to hell and her sister was hurt or worse, it was on him.

"We have eyes all around the property," Sergeant Carter assured them now. "We've quietly evacuated residents for two blocks in either direction."

"We're making sure none of the evacuees uses a cell phone until this is over in an effort to ensure no one alerts Robles's people," Marsh added. "We're keeping the folks entertained over at St. Joseph's on Hermitage."

Eva shook her head, her doubts about how this would go down clear. "If any of his men spot a cop—"

"Don't worry, Ms. Bowman," Carter said, "we've got this. We've even got unmarked units monitoring traffic all around our position."

To Todd's surprise Eva didn't say another word. Instead, she walked around the corner of the double boxcar and stared through the bushes and trees separating the rail yard from the street. If her sister was with her cell phone as they believed, she was likely no more than twenty, twenty-five yards in front of where Eva stood. Todd tried to think of something reassuring to say as he followed that same path.

"He's going to call or text me with instructions and they'll go in." She shook her head and hugged her arms more tightly around herself. "This plan is too risky. I'm not willing to risk Lena's life this way."

"Do you really believe Robles will let Lena go if you surrender yourself?" They'd been over this same territory twice already and her answer was always the same.

"It's a risk I have to take."

Todd glanced back toward the huddle of cops. He hadn't planned to share the other op already in motion with her until they had eyes on Lena. At this point he would do just about anything to give Eva some sense of relief.

"Marsh and the others don't know that we have a two-man team working their way inside." Her shoulders stiffened as he spoke, but she kept her attention straight ahead. "They were already here," he went on, "and in place before Chicago PD developed their game plan and moved in."

For the first time since he told Eva the Colby Agency had coordinated with Chicago PD after Robles's call, she looked him in the eye. A faint glimmer of hope stirred in hers. "Can they see what's happening inside?"

"They have eyes in the main office. So far they haven't seen Lena but they've watched two men going in and out of an inner office. We believe Lena and Robles are in that office. His disciples are scattered all over the property. All heavily armed."

"I don't understand why he would put himself in this position." Her gaze shifted back across the street. "He must have known there was a chance I would go to the police. How does he expect to escape when all hell breaks loose?" She shook her head. "It feels like a setup. Her phone might very well be here, but Robles and Lena could be anywhere."

Todd glanced at Marsh and Carter who had separated from the main huddle and appeared to be in deep conversation. "We're prepared for that move as well. Michaels is standing by to take us wherever we need to go."

His phone vibrated. Todd pulled it from his hip pocket. The name *Jim Colby*, Victoria's son and head of field operations at the agency, appeared on the screen. Todd's gut clenched as he answered the phone. This couldn't be good news. "What's happening inside?"

"Robles's troops are leaving."

As if on cue the large gate across the street slid open and a line of pimped-out automobiles rolled onto the street. Dread congealed in Todd's gut. "All of them?"

"Every damned one our scouts can see from their vantage points have picked up their weapons and walked out."

"What about the ones you can't see?" Todd resisted the urge to race across the street and yank one of the bastards out of a car and beat the truth out of him. The whole damned parade moved nice and slow as if they wanted those watching to get a good look at the show.

"We're working on getting eyes into that room from a ceiling vent."

"Hello."

Todd turned at the sound of Eva's voice. Her eyes were wide with fear as she listened to the caller. Todd checked the time. Robles was early by fifteen minutes.

"Hold on," he said to Jim.

Eva drew the phone from her ear and stared at the screen, her hand shaking.

"What did he say?"

"He said further instructions are coming by text and that he's sending me a photo of Lena."

The call to Eva's cell had drawn Marsh and Carter. They both looked to Todd. "I'm putting you on speaker, Jim." He set his phone to Speaker and moved closer to Eva to watch for the message from Robles.

The text appeared on her screen.

Your sister is waiting across the street from where you are standing. You have five minutes before she dies.

A photo appeared on the screen.

Lena was gagged, blindfolded and tied to an office chair with a package strapped around her chest. On the package was a clock counting down the seconds.

Bomb.

Chapter Fourteen

"We need the bomb squad! Now! Do not let her move!"

Eva heard Todd's words but her brain refused to assimilate the meaning behind them. She stared at the photo of Lena. Tears had dragged streaks of mascara past the blindfold and down her cheeks to melt into the gag tied around her mouth.

Bomb.

A bomb was strapped to her sister's body.

Todd, Sergeant Carter and several police officers rushed across the street. Detective Marsh gripped Eva by the arm. "Let's move back behind the rail cars."

Eva stared at him for two or three seconds and then she looked back across the street to the men now disappearing into the center building of the equipment rental company.

Lena was in there.

Bomb.

Eva jerked out of the detective's grip and ran. She sprinted across the street.

A horn blared. She lunged forward and the car whipped left, barely avoiding hitting her. Adrenaline fired through her veins. Her heart soared into her throat but she didn't slow. She had to get to her sister.

She reached the building the others had gone into before Marsh caught up with her. She wrenched open the door and rushed inside with him shouting for her to stop.

Can't stop. Gotta get to Lena!

Cops stood seemingly frozen all around the room on this side of a long service counter. Behind the counter, a door stood open. All eyes were on that door.

Sergeant Carter suddenly appeared in the doorway. "Everyone out of the building! Now!"

While the others hurried to obey the sergeant's order, Eva sprinted for the counter. She dodged Marsh as he reached for her again. She rounded the end of the counter and reached the door to find Carter blocking her path to the office and to Lena.

"You need to go with the others," he ordered.

"Get out of my way," she demanded, fear and anger making her shake so hard her teeth nearly chattered.

For one long moment the man stared at her. Whether he sympathized with her plight or simply didn't want to waste time arguing, he stepped aside.

Eva moved around him and into the office. Her heart sank to her feet as she watched a man clad completely in black and whom she didn't recognize remove the gag from her sister's mouth. The blindfold was already gone.

Lena's fear-filled gaze collided with hers. "Get out of here, Eva!" she cried.

Eva moved forward but the man attending to Lena stopped her with an upraised hand. "Don't touch her. We don't know what might trigger the detonator."

Todd was on the phone explaining what the bomb

looked like, she assumed to someone from the bomb squad.

She swallowed hard. Help couldn't possibly make it in time.

Eva eased as close as she dared to her sister. "I'm so sorry." Hot tears spilled down her cheeks as she watched the readout on the clock go from 2:00 to 1:59.

Please don't let his happen.

Another man dressed in black burst into the room. "Wire snips!" He handed the tool to Todd. She realized then that the two men in black were probably the two from the Colby Agency who had infiltrated the building.

Lena smiled up at Eva, her lips trembling with the effort. "I love you, little sister, and I appreciate that you're sorry but you need to go. If we both die, he wins."

Eva dropped to her knees next to Lena and dared to take her hand. "Then let him win."

Todd glanced at her for one second before reaching into the mass of colored wires and snipping one.

1:29

He moved to another as the voice on the phone instructed, she presumed. "Please leave, Eva," he murmured as he reached for the tangle of wires again.

"Sorry." She drew in a shaky breath. "Can't do it." Nothing could make her leave the two people she loved most in the world.

Todd swore and snipped the second wire.

1:18...1:17

"This is not working," he muttered.

Eva thought of all the wonderful times she and her sister had shared. Of how much she loved and missed their parents…and she thought of Todd and how she had missed him…how she loved him so much her heart wanted to burst even now—particularly now. He was prepared to give his life for Lena. He was a hero. He'd always been one, she'd just been too hurt to see it.

In that terrifying moment one truth crystalized for Eva. She should have gone after him. All this time she had been angry and crushed because he'd left and not once had she considered going after him. She had been well aware of how difficult his childhood was. She should have recognized that he might have trouble committing and tracked him down and demanded answers. Pride had kept her from taking that step.

"If my cameraman was here," Lena said as more tears slipped down her blackened cheeks, "this would make a hell of a breaking news story." Lena laughed but the sound held no humor.

Eva nodded. "You can tell Channel 7 viewers the whole story on the late news tonight."

Lena gifted her with another of those shaky smiles. "Absolutely."

Carter rushed back into the room with a larger tool. Using what appeared to be large pruning shears or maybe bolt cutters, he and the man standing next to Lena attempted to cut through the thick nylon straps holding her and the bomb bound to the chair.

0:59

Fear tightened its ruthless grip on Eva. *Hurry!*

Lena squeezed her hand and whispered, "Please go."

Eva shook her head and held her sister's hand even tighter. "No way."

"Hold on a minute," Todd said to the man on the phone. "Something isn't right."

The bottom dropped out of Eva's stomach. *Oh no.* What now?

0:42

Carter and the other man Eva believed to be from the Colby Agency carefully cut through another of the straps as Todd explained something about the bomb that Eva couldn't hope to comprehend.

Her heart fluttered so wildly she felt light-headed as the men cut away a third strap. *Please, please hurry.*

Todd suddenly tossed his phone aside. It slid across the tile floor as he grabbed the remainder of the wires and yanked them free of the box.

0:19

Eva held her breath.

Lena's face paled to a ghostly white.

Todd gripped the box and pulled. The face of the box as well as the clock came loose in his hands.

Inside the black box strapped to Lena's chest there was nothing.

It was empty.

"Son of a bitch," Todd muttered.

The last strap fell away from Lena. Eva scrambled to her feet as the man in black whose name she didn't know helped Lena out of the chair. Lena's knees gave way and he scooped her into his arms.

"Get everyone out!" Todd commanded.

Before Eva could ask what was happening now, the double doors of a large cabinet on the other side of the room burst open. What the hell?

Eva saw the weapon first, then the man. The scream

that filled the air was hers; she couldn't seem to stop the sound.

He leveled the barrel of the weapon on her. "Die, bitch!"

The blast exploded, shaking the air in the room.

Todd's body slammed into her where she stood frozen to the spot.

They crashed onto the floor. Eva grunted as the breath burst from her lungs.

Lena's mouth opened in a scream.

Time lapsed into slow motion…drawing out the sound of her sister's scream. Other voices shouted but Eva couldn't make out the seemingly distorted words.

The man with the gun charged forward, his face contorted with hatred, his weapon still in his hand.

The eerie quiet was ruptured by one, two, three more gunshots.

Then there was silence again.

Eva dragged in a breath, the sound shattering the dreamlike slow motion.

Todd moved off her. "You okay?"

His voice sounded strangely far away.

Eva tried to nod but her head bobbled. She felt disconnected and tattered.

The muffled sound of Lena crying came from somewhere.

There was blood…so much blood.

"He's down," Sergeant Carter said.

"We need an ambulance," someone else said, one of the men wearing black maybe.

Eva looked first at Lena. No blood. She was okay. The man who'd been holding her had stood her on her feet and was now providing directions for the ambulance.

Eva stared at her bloody T-shirt. Where was all the blood coming from? Had she been shot? She was reasonably sure not, but considering the sluggish way her senses were reacting she wasn't certain of anything.

The man who'd come out of that cabinet intending to shoot her lay on the floor a few feet away, his eyes open, a bullet hole in the center of his forehead.

Todd reached down to her.

She stared at the wide hand and fingers that had touched her body and soul. The blood smeared on his palm showed her what she hadn't wanted to see.

She hadn't been shot…it was Todd. Blood had soaked into his shirt. The bullet appeared to have hit his left upper arm in the area of the deltoid muscle.

Hers shaking, she took his hand and got to her feet. "Oh my God. You're…"

He grinned. "It's nothing. Besides, I know an excellent nurse."

The Edge, 9:00 p.m.

TODD FLINCHED.

Dr. Marissa Frasier smiled. "Good thing that was the last one." She finished the final suture and stepped back from the exam table.

"Thanks, Doc." Todd moved his arm, wincing at the pain.

Frasier peeled off her gloves and tossed them into the trash receptacle. "The nurse will be in shortly and she'll bandage that for you. Thank you, Mr. Christian, for keeping Eva safe. She means a great deal to all of us."

Todd gave the lady a nod. When she'd left the room he exhaled a big breath. He'd never felt more tired in his life. He closed his eyes. Those few minutes with that clock ticking down had been the longest and most terrifying of his life. If Eva or Lena had…

No. He couldn't think about that. It was over. They were both fine. He was fine. The nightmare was over.

The door opened and he looked up, his heart lifting in expectation.

"Looks like you're good to go," Lena said.

"No worse for the wear," he returned, tension rifling through him. He'd expected Eva to walk through that door or maybe one of the other nurses. Lena was about the last person he'd figured he would see again tonight. Didn't she have a hot breaking story to report?

She folded her arms over her chest and stared at him for a long moment. He braced for all hell to break loose.

"You broke my sister's heart when you left."

He couldn't deny the charge. "I won't offer you an excuse because I don't have one. I was a coward who didn't deserve her."

She looked surprised at his confession "A coward for sure. And a jerk as well as a—"

He held up a hand. "I was all those things, yes. I've apologized to Eva."

Lena threw her head back and laughed. When she finally regained her composure, she said, "I love my sister more than anything else in this world. You hurt her again and I will make you wish you had never come back to Chicago."

He nodded. "Got it."

She turned and stepped toward the door. Her hand on the handle, she hesitated a second or two before turning back to him. "Thank you." She stared at the floor before meeting his gaze once more. "It's a rare man who would willingly give his life while trying to save another. Whatever you were ten years ago, you're a good man now. I saw that today."

A smile spread across his lips. "Thank you. Hearing you say that means a lot."

She pointed a finger at him. "But I'll still kick your ass if you hurt her."

With that she left the room. Kim came in next and bandaged his freshly sutured wound while going over the care instructions the doctor had left.

"There you go, Mr. Christian." She handed him his discharge papers. "You're all done." She sighed. "It's a little crazy tonight so we had to put Eva to work. She told me to tell you that if you didn't want to wait she would understand."

Todd hopped off the table. "I'll wait."

Kim flashed him a grin and said, "I thought you might." With that, she hurried out the door to move on to the next patient.

He'd waited a long time to have Eva back in his life. What was a few more hours?

West Grace Street Apartments, Midnight

EVA CHECKED HER door one last time. Locked. She pressed her forehead to the cool surface and thought of Mrs. Cackowski's door across the hall. However longer Eva lived in this building, on this floor, she would never be able to pass that door without thinking of the sweet lady. Eva hoped Miguel Robles died screaming for what he'd done. With Lena's help the police had identified the murdered woman found in her town house. She had worked at a coffee shop down the street from where Lena lived. Robles's people had likely chosen her because she and Lena had similar features. *Bastards.*

Another innocent victim slain for no other reason except to terrify Eva.

But Miguel Robles wasn't getting away with his heinous deeds anymore. The police had found him with the help of their new informant, thanks to the Colby Agency. Robles had been so certain that his chosen assassin would kill both Eva and Lena, he had personally and boldly tortured Lena with promises that both she and Eva would die today—all as he held her hostage. With the informant's testimony as well as Lena's, Robles was done. He would spend the rest of his life in prison.

"I'm starving."

Eva turned away from the door and smiled at her hero. "If you'll give me a moment to change, I'll prepare you the most amazing meal you've ever eaten."

It was the least she could do after he'd saved her life. Her heart squeezed. He'd taken the bullet meant for her. He'd kept her safe and protected her through this entire nightmare. Now he had matching bandages, one on his right shoulder, the other on his left upper arm. Poor guy.

At his skeptical look, she said, "I've become quite the chef since college."

Propped against her kitchen counter, his gorgeous

chest bare, he grinned. "Been keeping secrets, have you?"

He'd tossed his shirt at the hospital. She'd been so damn glad the bullet hadn't caused any real damage she wouldn't have cared if he'd walked out of there naked. Every female in the vicinity had swooned as he walked by as it was. She'd had to help out with the Saturday night rush for a couple of hours and Todd had stationed himself where he could watch. Every time she glanced at him she saw the hunger in his eyes, but she was pretty sure it had nothing to do with food. Her entire being tingled with anticipation.

"I have," she confessed. "A woman should always have at least a few secrets." She headed for the bathroom. "Relax. I'll only be a minute."

Shutting herself away in the room that now felt like a closet compared to the bathroom she'd had at the Colby safe house, she stared at herself in the mirror for a long moment. "What're you doing, Eva?"

She'd insisted on bringing Todd home with her. He shouldn't be alone. He had been shot after all. But that had been an excuse. This wasn't about taking care of him for the night or even showing her gratitude for his protection. This was far more.

She wasn't ready to let him go. When Kim had told her that he intended to wait while Eva helped out, her heart had started to beat so fast she could hardly stay focused on her work. He was here and there were things she needed to say. Before Lena left the hospital tonight she had made Eva promise that she would tell Todd the truth. Apparently her big sister had recognized that truth just watching the two of them together.

You're still in love with him.

Eva had denied Lena's accusation. She'd spent the better part of the past decade pretending she hated him. She peeled off her scrub top and shimmied out of the bottom and tossed both aside. She'd changed out of her bloody clothes at the hospital to help out. Sometimes sudden bursts of incoming patients happened like that, especially on the weekends.

Eva drew in a reaffirming breath. Lena was right. Eva did love Todd. She hoped her sister was right about the other as well. Lena was convinced that Todd still loved Eva. Eva wasn't so sure. Yes, Todd had stepped in front of a bullet for her, but that had been his job.

She thought of the way he touched her. The way he had apologized for leaving, admitting that he'd been afraid he didn't deserve her.

Maybe he did still care for her. Her mother had sworn he would be back.

"Stop." Eva shook her head. She was setting herself up for major heartbreak. Time to give it a rest. She would know soon enough how he felt. Frankly she was surprised Lena hadn't scared him off with her warning. If Eva hadn't been so busy with patients, she would have headed off that awkward scene.

He'd taken Lena's scolding and still waited for Eva. That was something. She ran a brush through her hair before going to her closet where she shuffled through the offerings until she found another tee and a pair of lounge pants. What she really needed was a shower, but Todd was hungry and she didn't want to make him wait.

A knock at her door was followed by, "Hey, I found what I really wanted."

"Oh yeah?" she asked as he opened the door. Holding the tee and pants to her body as if she needed to hide the fact that she was standing there in panties and a bra, she beamed a smile she hoped covered for the worrisome thoughts nagging at her. "Can't wait for a decent meal, eh?"

He held up the chocolate frosting as he took a step toward her. "I decided I wanted to go straight to dessert."

Her skin felt on fire. "You're an injured man." She tossed the clothes aside. This was one aspect of their relationship where she had nothing to hide from him. "I'm not sure you're up for dessert."

He licked his lips and her nipples stung. "I think I can hold my own."

She reached behind her and unfastened her bra, letting it fall forward, revealing her breasts before falling into a wisp of lace on the floor. "There are things we need to talk about."

Another step disappeared between them. Her breath caught. No other man had ever made her wet by just walking toward her. How could she possibly ever deny how much she loved this man? She loved every perfectly sculpted inch of him. His gorgeous body, scars and all. That handsome face. Blue, blue eyes and lips so kissable her mouth ached to taste them. That thick hair she loved running her fingers through.

"What kind of things?" he asked.

And that voice. So deep, it wrapped around her and made her want to close her eyes and fall into the sound.

He stood right in front of her now, waiting for her

answer to his question. "Like," she stammered, "what *this* is?"

The way he looked at her—as if he intended to devour her rather than the chocolate—she knew she was in trouble.

"This," he murmured in that steamy, sexy voice as he moved closer and closer, forcing her to step back until he'd backed her all the way to the bed, "is me wanting you so badly I can barely breathe."

He moved in another step and she dropped onto the bed, scooted out of his reach. He tossed the chocolate onto the covers and climbed onto the bed on all fours, crawling slowly toward her.

"This is us taking back what I let slip away before." He moved over her, lowered his mouth to hers and kissed her so softly she whimpered with the sweetness of it. "I ran away before because I was afraid." His lips hovered just centimeters above hers. "I swear to you I'm not afraid anymore. I'm here to stay, if you'll have me."

She reached up and nipped at his lips. "I might need a little more convincing."

He grinned, his lips brushing hers. "Happy to oblige."

He sat back on his heels and reached for the frosting. He tore open the package and dipped his finger into the luscious chocolate. Slowly, he traced a path down her throat and around her breasts, tipping each nipple with the sweet stuff before dipping down to her belly button. He leaned down and traced that path with his tongue. It was all she could do to bear the exquisite torture. She shivered and moaned, reminding herself to breathe as her fingers fisted in the covers.

He moved slowly, savoring the chocolate as he went. Then he made a new path, this one right down to the waistband of her lacy panties. He dragged the strappy lace down her legs and off before crawling back up her body until he reached her belly button. As he teased her belly button with his mouth, he stroked her inner thighs with his fingers, tortured her clitoris, pushing her beyond her limits.

By the time he reached for his fly she was writhing with need. "Hurry," she whispered.

She helped him push his jeans down his lean hips and then guide himself into her. With her legs locked around his, she closed her eyes and melted with the feel of him filling her body so completely.

He kissed her cheek, tracing a path to her ear as he held his body too damn still. "I love you, Eva," he whispered.

She stared into his eyes, trailing her fingers down his sinewy torso and wrapped her arms around his waist. "I love you, Todd."

The rest of what they had to say, they said with their bodies.

Chapter Fifteen

Sunday, May 13, 9:00 a.m.

Victoria sipped her hot tea and smiled. Her husband was doing what he always did on Sunday morning: reading the newspaper while his second cup of coffee cooled. She and Lucas Camp had been friends for most of their lives, husband and wife for a good number of years now.

When she studied him like this, she wondered how it was possible to love him more each day, but she did. Ten or so years ago they had decided to retire. They'd even moved to the warmer climate of Texas and pretended to relax for a while. But that hadn't worked out so well. The Colby Agency was too much a part of the fabric of their lives. Cold, windy Chicago was as well. Their children and grandchildren were here. The worst tragedies of their lives as well as the happiest days of their lives had all played out right here. After only a few months away they had made a mutual decision to return and to never again leave their beloved home.

The two of them would go into the office Monday through Friday until they drew their last breaths.

Lucas still consulted on cases with his old team at the CIA. He and Thomas Casey, the former director of Lucas's shadow unit, still had lunch once a month. It was hard to let go of a life's work, and the powers that be still needed old-school spies like Lucas and Thomas.

Victoria felt immensely grateful that she and Lucas spent most of their time helping others. Life could be so difficult sometimes. They were both committed to seeing that her son Jim and Lucas's son Slade followed in their footsteps. The Colby Agency had become a cornerstone of Chicago; that legacy must be carried on.

Victoria smiled. "I'm very pleased with Jamie's ability to work without supervision. She's learning quickly to anticipate the necessary steps in a case."

Lucas folded the newspaper and set it aside. "It's refreshing to see such ambition in a young lady her age."

Victoria set her teacup aside. "I hope Luke is as excited about following in his father's and his grandparents' shoes as his older sister."

Lucas laughed. "Give the boy time. Girls mature much faster than boys."

Victoria had to laugh. "This is very true."

The sparkle of mischief in her husband's gray eyes made her smile. "But our women love us anyway."

"We do, indeed." She could not imagine her life without this man. They were two of a kind. "Tell me, did you discover anything useful in your search into Dr. Pierce's past?"

Dr. Devon Pierce, former renowned surgeon and the genius behind the Edge facility, had a ghost from his past haunting his newly found success. He'd ignored it for some time but when he and Victoria had been discussing Eva Bowman's troubles, Pierce had confessed to having a problem of his own.

Lucas raised his cup to his lips, savoring the bold flavor of his favorite blend. When he'd placed the cup in its saucer once more, he considered her question a moment longer. "Pierce's background is littered with tragedy."

Victoria was aware of his personal tragedy. He and his wife had been visiting her family in Binghamton, New York, for the holidays when an awful car accident left her gravely injured. Pierce had been severely injured himself and the local hospital simply wasn't equipped to handle their needs. With no time to wait for his wife to be airlifted to another hospital and no surgeon available to help her, Pierce had tried to save her himself. She died on the operating table.

Eventually he had returned to work as the head of surgery at Chicago's prestigious Rush University Medical Center. Within a year he had resigned to focus solely on reinventing the Emergency Department. Six years later his creation, the Edge, was the prototype for new facilities all over the country.

As much as Victoria respected Devon Pierce, she felt sympathy for him as well. He had not allowed himself to have a real life since his wife died. Work was his only companion. He continued to live alone in the massive mansion in Lake Bluff he'd built for her. Victoria and Lucas had been to his home once, before he lost his wife. They'd hosted a fund-raiser for a new wing at Rush. The Georgian-style mansion had been more like a castle than a home.

How sad that such a brilliant and caring man refused to open his heart again.

"You didn't find anything th
trouble in his career since develop

Lucas propped his elbows on the ta
his hands in front of him. "Not yet, but, m
know as well as I do that you don't rise to
in anything without leaving a few skeletons in
closet."

Her husband was full of sage proverbs this morning. "Then we must find the one doing the rattling."

Lucas gave her a nod. "You have the perfect investigator for the job."

"Isabella Lytle," Victoria agreed.

"Shall we schedule breakfast with Bella in the morning to discuss the case?"

Victoria reached across the table for her cell phone. "I'll send her a text now."

Once Dr. Pierce's troubles were resolved, perhaps he would finally let go of the past and live the life he continued to ignore in the present.

As if he'd sensed her thought, Lucas laid his hand on hers. "Don't worry, my dear, the Colby Agency never fails a client."

That was one truth she intended to spend the rest of her life backing up.

* * * * *